# *Always*
# & NEVER

by
## Donn Fleming

*Always &* NEVER
Copyright © 2017 by Donn Fleming

FIRST EDITION

Published by:
**PALMWIND PRESS**
1674 University Pkwy
Sarasota, Florida 34243

Printed in the United States of America

Cover Concept: JBF
Author photo: Matthew Isaac
Cover Design and Book Layout: Eli Blyden

ISBN: 978-0-9909054-1-7

# BOOKS BY DONN FLEMING

*Sarasota Sunrise*

*Mangrove Murders*

www.DONNFLEMING.com
Author correspondence: FLEMWRIGHT@AOL.com

iii

For:
*Jennifer and Jillene*

~

# *Always*
# & NEVER

# PROLOGUE

*She is so beautiful, he thinks, the thought bringing a warm smile to him. She lays quietly, her head making a soft indentation on the flowered pillowcase. He stands at the side of their bed, her husband in his Sunday suit, silently watching the morning sun illuminate her delicate countenance. Her repose touches him. He bends cautiously, not wishing to disturb her, and gently kisses her cheek. His muted footsteps leave the room.*

*Outside, the sun watches the old man exit by the back door and walk in a slow gait across the gravel way to the pickup truck sitting over by the wooden fence. He opens the driver's door and leans the back of the bench seat forward, retrieving a long rope. It is new and strong, curled in a circle, and the thick twine of it is stiff in his hands. He begins to loosen it by twisting the rope first one way and then the opposite, his hands on either end of the rolled rope. He is walking towards the barn along the weathered fencing, twisting the rope and looking out into the boundless fields, bright in the rising sunlight. At the barn door he stops and turns, dropping his hands to his sides and looks back to the house they have shared throughout the six decades of their marriage. He spends a moment doing this, then slaps the rope against his thigh and enters the barn.*

*The old man climbs the wooden stairway against the wall and enters the hayloft. He begins unrolling the rope, dropping it into a loose pile at his feet until he gets to the end. Carefully he pulls a length of it and begins forming an ominous knot. He is prudent working up the knot so as to prevent the twine from kinking which will weaken the rope.*

*There is a difference between a gallows knot and a hangman's knot. The gallows knot has a dark history to it. Made for the gallows tree, it was crude and most times quickly made from any readily available rope or cord. It did its job by being cinched tight and killing slowly by strangulation. The hangman's noose is made with a better grade of rope and the force to close it is adjusted differently - bigger in the neck. It breaks the neck more easily, thus making the death more merciful.*

He finishes with the initial knot, called the simple noose, which is used as a base for the further work. Then he loops the rope up and over applying the force from the inside as he builds the rope into a hangman's noose. A firm running-knot prevents opening the loop. He wraps the remaining end of the rope tightly around the top of the noose eight times, producing the familiar looking finished product, then secures it with a simple overhand knot at the end. He tests it to make sure it is tight and the pull is easily adjustable.

The old man stands on the edge of the hayloft and throws the heavy noose up and over the strong center beam high above him. Using a long piece of furring that he has attached a hook to the end of, he pulls the swaying rope close to him and throws it over again. He does this three more times and then secures the remaining length of rope to a block pulley anchored at the farther end of the loft. He pulls the rope through the pulley until it is tight, and then flips the metal bar at the bottom that locks the pulley. He tests the tautness. Satisfied, he walks back to the edge of the loft.

He loosens the knot of his tie and unbuttons the first button on his shirt, although he's not sure why he does this. Using the long pole again, he retrieves the swaying noose and slips it over his head. He tugs it tight to his neck, making sure it is uncomfortable. He thinks of her, and then, without hesitation, steps off the loft.

# 1

## *PARIS*

Fashion was alive and well in Paris. On the grounds of Castle Frontenac, plush with colorful Impressionistic gardens, meticulously manicured shrubbery and velvet landscaping, stood an expansive catwalk, snaking and curling its way throughout the thousand fashion aficionados gathered on this hot summer evening to lend acclaim to haute couture's premiere line – *Lady Maddison*.

The private mansion, originally home to France's elite aristocracy, sat in her venerable grandeur like a queen on her throne, high atop the Left Bank, wearing her elegant landscaping like a hooped gown ringing her wide and far to the river's edge, to the white docks perched in the September waters of the Seine. Tonight a treasure trove of high-priced yachts sat moored in the pastel colors of the French twilight. At the front of the estate, the wide cobblestone drive was crowded with an assemblage of stretch limos and expensive European sports cars.

On the catwalk a myriad of fabrication flowed from the tall lithesome bodies of the worlds' most glamorous and renowned fashion models; strutting their wares for the international mix of couturiers, movie stars, globe-trotting socialites, boutique owners, the press, and any number of opulent fashion groupies. They, the tableau vivant of the fashion world, swarmed and pulsated in rhythmic waves to the pounding orchestrations of an energized twelve-piece band. Anxiously, they mingled and pressed against one another, sipping champagne from long-stemmed flutes, awaiting the appearance of couture's hottest designer - fashion's preeminent Dodge Maddison.

Wrapped in the excitement of the premiere, the models hurry off the runway and gather inside the mansion. They are ablaze with the bursting

1

pride and effervescence of their profession - swooning in the accolades of their peers. Their performance has been spectacular, titillating and provocative, fired by the sensational designs and fabrications of the innovative and talented Dodge Maddison. But their work is not yet over; they have one more walk to do. Hastily the dressers and make-up artists descend on them; fluffing and pruning, dabbing and brushing, sustaining their doll-like perfection and stroking their delicate egos. Standing regally in the midst of them all, is the world's reigning super-model, Dana. She is tall, reed thin and posture perfect, her cropped golden-blonde hair shines like a polished crown and her azure eyes are sparkling jewels. Her lips are full and her teeth as bright as polished ivory. Her smile is charming and impetuous, devilish and captivating. She is ravishing and stunning, elegant and ethereal. Dana was not born of earthly parents. She is a goddess, sculpted by the hands of an angel who made her in her own breathtaking image. Looking at her is looking at perfection. Her beauty is so stunning, so striking and so innocently pure that one could actually visualize angelic wings spread wide across her back.

With their touch-ups completed the models line up one by one behind Dana. She leads the extravagant parade in a grand finale out from the ballroom, along the elegant veranda and down into the cheers of the captivated glitterati. The tanned nimble entourage dances to the beat of the band, their bodies glistening in the heat of the night beneath their thin veils of fashion. The ecstatic crowd cheering and whistling and shouting … *Bravo!*… *Bravo!*

Music is pounding, strobe lights are flashing and fabrics so sheer and tantalizing come alive with color, and cling to the models' moist gyrating bodies one moment, then lash out at the audience the next – propelled by the winds of giant fans positioned on scaffolding above the runway - the electrifying air all around them, deliciously exciting and devilishly overpowering. One could not help but be submissively caught up in the dizzying excitement. It is wild, like viewing a magnificent Las Vegas extravaganza through a fast turning kaleidoscope.

Then suddenly, as if by sleight-of-hand, the models disappear, the music stops, the grounds go dark and for an instant the perplexed crowd is hushed. A long minute lapses. Then, with brilliant timing and a magician's choreography, there is a huge pyrotechnic explosion of fireworks and multi-colored lights. The air is filled with smoke and confetti and balloons everywhere - simultaneously skyrocketing upward from the grounds, and then downward, cascading from the tall towers of the mansion. In the midst of it all, from a huge plume of pink smoke magically emerges the entire ensemble wrapped in long flowing silk fuchsia - *Lady Maddison's* signature color. The catwalk becomes a stage. The models, holding long pieces of the flashy fabric in their outstretched arms, walk in a fast circle, round and round Dodge Maddison, the silk fuchsia encircling him like streamers around a Maypole. The spotlight narrows and focuses solely on him. He stands tall, fit, and Hollywood handsome with his sun-streaked blonde hair, thick and disheveled in a way that intensifies his strong sexuality as his trademark deep blue eyes lure you to his chiseled countenance - his smile pleasing you and weakening you at the same time. He is mystifying. Women love him. Even more so because he is a bachelor and the knowledge of this strikes a furtive, lusty chord, in the women who meet him – even the married ones.

The crowd is ecstatic. The applause as deafening as the pounding music. Dodge Maddison stands in the midst of the cheering crescendos, waving to his fans, accepting their praise and gathering the long-stemmed pink roses littering the stage. Quickly, on cue, the entourage turns and saunters single file back along the runway into the grand ballroom; Maddison, at the rear, stopping at the door. He bows at the waist and then straightens, standing tall and clasping his hands together in front of him in a show of gratitude.

He disappears into the room and joins his models; clapping and jumping with praise, living the thrill of the moment. He is showered with flowers and kisses. The evening has been a huge success and the designer makes it a point to hug and thank each of them personally. It was a wonderful premiere.

"Dodge ... Dodge ..." it was Harlow, Dodge's personal assistant, trying to break through the crowd and get his attention. She was calling his name and pointing to a cell phone in her hand. He caught a glimpse of her and shook his head as if to say, "Not now."

Outside, the guests were relentless in their chant, "Dodge, Dodge, Dodge, Dodge ..." and wanted more of him.

He needed to do a final solo along the runway, and was breaking away from his well-wishers when Harlow caught his arm.

"Dodge, this phone call," she yelled above the deafening chants, "I don't know who it is, but he insists it's extremely important."

Dodge, wrapping an arm around Harlow and pulling her closer, spoke loudly into her ear, "Who the hell is it?!"

"I don't know, but he's awfully ornery." They were locked head to head trying to hear each other above the din.

"Tell him to hang on a minute."

"I've been telling him that for ten minutes, but he's a real pain in the ass! Says he needs to talk with you now, and won't take no for an answer."

"Well tell him..." suddenly Dodge was whisked away by the pressing entourage of models pushing him through the huge arched doorway and out onto the runway.

He made a slow sprint to the end of the platform, bowing in every direction saying thank you and blowing kisses to the thousand-plus guests, most of whom he knew personally and counted amongst his friends.

As he returned to the ballroom, shaking hands along the way, he had already forgotten the phone call.

"Dodge, it was fabbbulous!" screeched Dana, as she placed a huge lipstick kiss on his cheek.

"Thanks, Dana," he kissed her back, "but it wouldn't be anything without you and the gang."

Dana and Dodge walked arm in arm comfortably mingling with the crowd, further fueling the lurid rumors of their romance. The champagne was flowing and the "premiere pressure" was subsiding.

"Dodge!" it was Harlow again. "You've got to take this call. This guy won't give up."

Dana rolled her eyes.

"Who is it?" he asked.

"I don't know. I can hardly understand him. The connection's terrible. Sounds like an old man. Real pain in the ass." She took the champagne glass from his hand and replaced it with the cell phone. "He's all yours," and with a short glance at Dana, still clinging to Dodge's other arm, Harlow turned on her heels and disappeared into the revelry.

"Hello ..." Dodge said. Silence. "Hello, hello," louder. "Dodge?   ... that you, boy?" an almost inaudible crackling voice came from the other end of the phone. The designer immediately recognized Percy's voice. "Percy. Old Percy. Is that you?" he asked as he unwrapped himself from Dana and moved into an adjacent, quieter room.

"Goddamn it boy." The connection sounded better now. "I've been standin' out here in the yard trying to get decent reception on this goddamn cell phone you got me and it's been drizzlin', suntabitch. I told Cora we shudda kept the house phone."

"Well, you cranky old bastard, I should have known it was you when Harlow said there was an old pain in the ass on the phone."

"What? ... What?" Percy pushed the phone into his inner ear trying to hear better, halfway around the world.

Dodge laughed, "God, it's good to hear your voice again, Perce."

"Wind's blowin' like a bastard. Big black cloud over ta Northwest," Dodge heard Percy saying to himself. He could picture him twisting and turning his head skyward, checking out the clouds as he always did. "Gonna rain like a sunta bitch."

"Old Percy, come on back down to Earth. You calling me in Paris just to give me a weather report from New England?" Dodge chuckled.

There was a silence, and Dodge thought for a moment the connection had been lost, but then he heard Percy clear his throat. "Dodge, I got hard news for ya, boy," he paused, "and I sure as hell hate to give it to ya this way."

"What's the matter Perce, you alright?"

There was an even longer pause. "Perce?"

"It's Emma, Dodge ... she's gone."

Everything stood still for Dodge; his heart, his breath, his world. There was only one thing those two words could mean, and that cold recognition seeped into him like a dark, black oil spill into pristine ocean waters, seeping, crude and cold into his insides and chilling him to the bone. His knees got weak and he turned looking for a chair. And then it got worse. "And Dodge," Percy said quietly, swallowing the lump in his throat, "Jed, too."...

# 2

# *MADDISON DESIGNS*

M*addison Designs* was located in SoHo, New York City, South of Houston. It occupied a six-story loft building on an attractive corner. The street level frontage was all glass and polished brass. Elegant window displays enticed, not only the rich and famous who pulled up in long shiny limos, but more importantly, the working girls. The ones who had discovered Maddison's tiny shop early on, and had gone back to their offices and out to their clubs adorned in his hand-made fashions. The ones he thought of each time he sketched a new design; the ones he held closest to his heart - the women in love with fashion.

The building rested on a turn-of-the-century foundation, which provided a small parking garage for Dodge and the few employees, like Harlow, who commuted by car. The spacious first floor was dedicated to retail where you could shop comfortably on the polished flooring in a wide open atmosphere emanating a blend of antiques and grand, ornate-framed cheval mirrors poised amidst the wide, modern counters and the clean, colorful, well-merchandised racks. The room was complimented with large refurbished factory windows set along the length of the old exposed brick walls.

A beautiful wooden spiral staircase took you curiously to the second floor loft where you could sit and chat and dine in *Café Mad*. Or peruse the walls and easels, upon which Dodge placed fresh sketches of his fashions intermingled with framed "ideas" from the early years that had made him famous. It was a very relaxed and soothing atmosphere. There was even a salon and spa complete with masseuse if you felt so inclined – *Lady Maddison* was born to be pampered.

The third and fourth floors housed the manufacturing facilities, or as Dodge put it, "the guts of it all". These two floors belonged to a hundred proud and diligent employees, well respected for their craft. Dodge was often seen sitting at the machines, working side by side with the seamstresses, the fabricators, and the pattern makers. He felt comfortable in the din of the machinery and the banter of the workers. Here was where the design ideas created in the Studio on Level 5 made their metamorphosis from paper to fabric.

Above the studio was Dodge's apartment with another staircase spiraling to the roof, replete with lush garden foliage to keep him in touch with his New England roots. For Dodge the roof was a private place to stir the creative crock-pot. It also offered superb star gazing on clear nights, a habit he picked up early on from Old Percy.

This morning he was standing on his roof, tired and jet-lagged from the hasty, long flight home from Paris. He stood, melancholy and introspective, peering into the dark early sky looking for faint stars, searching for a celestial reason, a meaning for life, and for its necessary death. How many times had he stood here on top of his building looking at the stars? His building ....

\* \* \*

Twenty years ago, a dreamer with a well-worn leather portfolio had walked into this building. Back then the windows were empty and soaped up. There was only a small weathered sign hanging above an indistinct doorway reading, *"Silverman & Sons, Mfg. Co.".* The door entered Dodge into a large, dusty, noisy area loaded with boxes and large worktables with more boxes atop them. There was a lot of hustling and bustling going on. Failing to get anyone's attention, Dodge took it upon himself to venture up the cluttered stairway in the direction of an arrow painted on the wall saying nothing, but at least pointing up. He reached the second floor landing facing a door with smoked glass and black lettering identifying "Office". Bravely he turned the knob and entered.

The room was just as cavernous as the first floor, and didn't really look much different, except for a rather large man sitting at a rather large desk directly in front of him. The man was chewing on the stub of an unlit cigar and talking loudly into his telephone. The conversation was taking a rather long time and Dodge stood there feeling invisible to everyone in this building. It was either, turn and go, or stay and wait. His feet, tired from pounding the pavement incessantly for the past two weeks, made his decision for him. Dodge took a seat in the dusty chair on the side of the desk. This caught the attention of the big man who interjected into his conversation, "Sit down, sit down," and kept rambling on.

A few moments later at the end of several loud cuss words the man hung up saying, "Goddamn Europeans They're worse than the South Americans." Remaining seated, he stretched out his hand, "Stanley Silverman."

"Dodge Maddison," Dodge said rising to his feet.

"Sit down, sit down." Stanley pushed a button on a box on his desk, "Edith, where the hell are those purchase orders from Macy's?" Without waiting for a response he bellowed, "Get them and get them up to Les and tell him to get those goods boxed up and out tonight. Tell him to make sure it's something new." He released the button and looked over at his guest and said in a mocking tone, "Something new. Everyone wants something new."

The phone rang and he picked it up saying, "Hang on!" into it. Pounding the hold button, Stanley turned a warm smile towards Dodge, stretched back into his vast chair, and said, "What can I do for you, young Mr. Maddison?"

"Well, Mr. Silverman," Dodge sprang eagerly to his feet and unzipped his portfolio. "I'm here answering your ad in the *Village Voice* for a designer and I've got here a sampling of my designs that I hope you can take a moment to take a look at and see if any of these are what you're …."

"Sure, sure," Stanley interrupted him, "sit down, sit down." Stanley picked up the portfolio, placed it atop the pile of paperwork on his desk and punched the release button on his phone. For the next ten minutes (which seemed like ten hours to the unemployed young designer) Stanley Silverman hollered into his telephone while casually flipping through the large laminated pages of women's dresses and gowns and blouses and skirts and lingerie.

Finally the telephone conversation ended. The big man closed the portfolio, took out a fresh cigar from his top drawer, sniffed the length of it, then placed it into his mouth and began chewing. Dodge waited on pins and needles while Mr. Silverman got his cigar chewed to just the right taste.

"Good stuff, good stuff," he chewed. "But can you design hats?"

"What?"

"Hats. You know, hats. Straw hats, felt hats, high hats, low hats, wide brims, short brims, come with varieties of hatbands…fedoras…hats…lots of people wear them," he grinned, "especially the ladies."

Dodge knew there wasn't one sketch of a hat anywhere in his portfolio. In fact, he hadn't even thought about hats. "Well I ahh … I'm not sure I …" he stuttered.

The big man rose motioning to Dodge, "Follow me."

Stanley Silverman was a sixth generation hat manufacturer whose ancestors had made hats for the czar of Russia. You could tell he was proud of what he was doing as he lead Dodge on a tour of his facilities, pointing out each and every aspect of his manufacturing business, and introducing him to various employees as they went along.

Dodge didn't quite know what he was feeling. He was confused and disillusioned, struggling with feelings of inadequacy. Maybe he had chosen too tough a career. His hard work and schooling at the Royal Academy of Fashion Design in London was all for naught. He had exhausted all the major design studios in the city, and now he was down in SoHo, far from Fashion Avenue, trying to keep pace with this big cigar chewing man who was almost jogging through this noisy, dusty, old building. "Hats .... *Hey Dodge, did you get that job in New York City? Who ya working for? Calvin Klein? Ralph Lauren? ....* Arrrgh!"

"And this is my son, Bruce, number seven." Stanley was introducing a young man about Dodge's age. "Bruce, meet Mr. Maddison. Fresh from R.A.F.D."

Dodge shook hands, "Nice to meet you, I'm Dodge."

"Nice to meet you too," Bruce replied and turned to Stanley, "Pop, Les says you want to pack up something new for Macy's? We don't have anything new."

Stanley stood still for a moment and shuffled his cigar from one side of his mouth to the other, "Well, I'm working on that. For now send 'em whatever we've got in-house that they haven't received for awhile. Put it in a different pre-pack. Maybe they'll think it's new. Come along, Mr. Maddison."

"Nice to meet you, Bruce."

"Yeah, take it easy, Dodge."

An hour later they were sitting back in Stanley's office. Stanley was quietly going through his new-cigar ritual, and, feeling uncomfortable with the silence, Dodge offered, "Do you have a big family?"

"Huh?"

"Number seven. You introduced Bruce as number seven. You have other sons and daughters?"

"Oh," he replied, "no, no. Just Brucie, he's the seventh generation. Someday this'll all be his, and Gertie and I, that's Mrs. Silverman, will be retired to our condo in Southern Florida. Soon I hope."

Again there was a silence, and Dodge could hear the bustling of the manufacturing business as a backdrop behind them. Stanley was slowly getting his cigar to the right taste, and Dodge was sitting with one leg over the other and his chin in his hand thinking about bartending.

Finally, "You know, Mr. Maddison, I'm not an educated man. I grew up on these floors. I was stuffing hats into boxes before I learned how to read," Stanley's gaze was steady on his young interviewee, "but there's two things I do know. I know hats, and I know people." He paused a moment, and continued, "Now, you've got great stuff in that portfolio of yours, and hell, someday you'll probably be a famous fashion designer, and I know you've got your heart set on joining some fancy design studio uptown. But I also know from looking at the bags under your eyes and the wear on your suit, that you've pretty much covered that territory, and now you're down here in SoHo on a wing and a prayer."

Dodge raised his chin off his hand and swapped his other leg to the other knee. He had sensed that Stanley Silverman was a proud man, but was surprised that Stanley was such a perceptive man.

"…And I like you. I think you've got talent, and I think you've got stamina. I'm not going to beat around the bush. I know this isn't what you're looking for, and I sure as hell can't offer you what they can uptown, but I *can* offer you two things. I can offer you an honest day's pay for an honest day's work, and I can offer you one helluva start in the *real* world of design and manufacturing. Now," he leaned back and continued, "we're busy. Hell, I've got more work lined up than I can shake a stick at. I haven't even had time to take a piss for two months. And we need new ideas." He paused for a moment, keeping his eyes steadied on Dodge. "If you can take some of those designs in that binder of yours and translate them into headwear, I think we can freshen up our line and stay on top of this industry." Stanley Silverman leaned forward, clasping his big hands together on his big desk. He let his comments sink into the weary, but eager mind of the young designer sitting before him. He winked at Dodge Maddison and said, "And you could feel proud."

With his hands still folded in front of him, Stanley shuffled his unlit cigar from one side of his mouth to the other. "What d'ya say, young Mr. Maddison?" he grinned, "...you could start tomorrow."

And he did.

\* \* \*

For the next three years Dodge's portfolio sat unopened beside his desk collecting dust. He had a makeshift office consisting of a small desk and a large drawing table surrounded by freestanding, neatly cluttered corkboards not too far from Stanley's office on the busy second floor.

The relationship between the two men prospered. Stanley took Dodge under his wing, treating him like a second son. Dodge and Bruce had bonded immediately and fell comfortably into their respective rolls of Dodge the Designer and Bruce the Businessman.

The new designer found himself immersed in the trenches of design and manufacturing, an invaluable education no schooling could possibly provide. He grew quickly, not only in a business way, but also in a people way. *The success to any business lies in your people skills*, Stanley had said, and Dodge was blessed with a warm, sincere, friendly personality that immediately won the friendship and hearts of those he met. He didn't know it then, but he was establishing contacts that would help build his future.

Everything was going well, and with the new *Maddison* line of ladies headwear, business was exceptional. *Silverman & Sons* became America's leading hat manufacturer.

One Friday morning, as Dodge stood sketching at his drawing board, there was a terrible thud that seemed to rock the second floor. Startled, he turned to see Stanley crumpled into a ball lying next to his overturned chair. Dodge jumped over his desk and a second later was at Stanley's side.

The phone was dangling off his desk, and the big man was sobbing uncontrollably, screaming, "No! No! Please God, No!" Bruce had been killed in a car accident on the Long Island Expressway.

In the following months, a helpless Dodge watched sadly as his friend and mentor, this big, kind, and passionate man so full of life and exuberance, shriveled into a hollow shell of himself.

Eventually, unable to rise above their grief, the Silvermans would withdraw to South Florida, leaving behind forever their world in New York City.

Silverman & Sons, Mfg Co. was sold to Stetson Headwear of Texas. Stanley knew that the NYC facilities would be of no interest to the new owners, and in the spirit of an old saying he remembered from his ancestors, *"From tragedy doth life flourish"*, he signed over the remaining two years of his lease (paid in full), to a newly created company, (which he had established unbeknownst to Dodge), called *Maddison Designs*.

Dodge was deeply touched by the gesture, and with Stanley's parting words, *"Dust off that portfolio and make something of yourself,"* still ringing in his ears, he sat quietly at his desk on the evening of their departure; in the dark, alone, and afraid.

The first year hurried by. Much happened. Conversations with key contacts not only boosted Dodge's confidence, but also set into motion his plan to sell off the machinery Stanley had left behind and convert the operation from headwear to fabric.

He kept on the best of the workers to cut and sew his designs that were flowing out of him at such a fast pace that he lost concept of time. He cordoned off part of the top floor for an apartment. The street-level windows were cleaned up, lit, and filled with mannequins displaying the new *Lady Maddison* line.

Almost immediately Dodge's tiny windows were discovered, and, with the typical fervor of New Yorkers, word spread like wildfire. Just everybody had to have one of those hot new dresses by this mysterious new designer down in SoHo.

In the second year the first floor was remodeled into a retail boutique, the staff had doubled, business was tough to keep up with, and Dodge Maddison signed a ten-year lease with option to buy. Which he did.

# 3

## *BREAKFASTS*

Morning twilight was widening in soft white colors before him, bringing Dodge back to reality. He headed downstairs, showered, dressed, and took the spiral staircase down to the studio. Harlow was already there.

"Well, you're in early." He greeted her and sat on one of the stools surrounding a large flattop drawing table used to spread out large designs.

Harlow, stubbornly steadfast and faithful as always, had accompanied Dodge home on the flight from Paris to New York. Dana wanted to return with him, but thankfully had an engagement in Milan to keep. As much as he liked her, Dodge was relieved that she had gone on. He could handle her twenty-year-old body, but at times, not her twenty-year-old mind. This was one of those times. He needed to be alone. And he was grateful to have Harlow by his side. She was more than his assistant, she was a close friend and confidante, and had been since he stole her away from a competitor's showroom a decade ago. She had become the supportive sister he never had, the understanding wife he had no time for, and a surrogate beer-drinking buddy he had all but forgotten. Theirs was a relationship that had matured beyond a business one, one of trust and understanding as only two people who worked so closely together for so long a time could relate to. And although sex had come close to them, they had never consummated the relationship, preferring to keep the purity of their friendship beyond the confusion that sexual commitments usually brought along. It wasn't always easy.

"Couldn't sleep. Too much jet lag or time zone change or something." She poured him a cup of fresh coffee. "I've called down for Roberto to get your car ready."

"No, that's not necessary," he sipped the hot coffee carefully. "I'm going to take the shuttle into Boston and rent a car at the airport."

"I think you'd feel better if you drove the old Ford up to New England," she placed a warm hand on his shoulder as she maneuvered around to take up a stool next to him. "The driving would help keep your mind off things, and besides, that old jalopy's been in storage too long."

He grunted, "I don't know," dropping his head and staring into the black coffee.

Harlow placed her hand under his chin and lifted his gaze to hers, "I think Jed would like it."

She raised her eyebrows as if to say, "You know I'm right, don't you."

Some toast popped up, and, rising from her stool, Harlow gave Dodge a kiss on his forehead and went into the kitchenette.

Dodge sat looking out at the white skyline lazily bringing the bright colors of the day into focus in front of the morning sun.

*  *  *

*"So, you want a car, do ya?"*

*"Oh, you bet I do! Four speed off the floor! There's a beauty down at McIntyre's, a Mustang! 289 V-8. Convertible. Fire engine red with a black interior. It's right on the front line. The salesman says it's a one-owner with very little mileage."*

*"Ya don't say," Jed said.*

*"And it's got mag wheels and bucket seats and everything!" Dodge was almost jumping up and down in his seat at the breakfast table. "And I'll be sixteen in a couple of months. It'd be so cool to have it ready for my birthday. I could pick up all my friends and take 'em for a ride."*

*"Cool, huh?" Jed muttered as he munched on his eggs.*

*"And I already know how to drive. You know that. I've been drivin' the tractors on the farm since I was eight, and Gramma has let me drive on the highway the past two times we've gone up to Vermont."*

*"That so?" Jed looked over at his wife.*

*"Yes 'tis, and he governs a car real well on the road," replied Emma with a little pride in her voice.*

*"Can we go down and take a look at it? Can we, Gramp, please?"*

*"Well, tell you what, Dodger, you go on up and get that room a yours cleaned up, and we might just go lookin' for a nice starter car for ya."*

14

*"Oh WOW!" Dodge was up and racing for the stairs.*

*"Hmmph. Mustang. Used ta be a horse," Jed said.*

*"You taking him down to McIntyre's?" Emma asked.*

*"Never said I was."*

*"Jedediah, what are you up to?"*

*"Nothin' Emma. Just think it might be as good a time's any for the boy to learn about cars. Car ain't no tractor y'know."*

*"Don't you "nothin' Emma" me, Jedediah Maddison. I know that look you're wearin', and when you're wearin' it, you've got something up your sleeve."*

*Jed got up and ambled his way to the kitchen door.*

*"Don't you be too hard on the boy," Emma said. "It hasn't been easy for him growing up without his Mom and Dad."*

*Jed stopped at the screen door and stood a moment. "It hasn't been easy for us growin' up without a son and daughter-in-law either Emma."*

*She came up slowly behind him, placed her hands lightly on his hips and lowered her forehead into the small of his back. Softly she said, "I know Jed ... I know. We miss them terribly."*

*Not wanting his wife to see the gloss on his eyes, Jed reached his arm behind him and stroked Emma's silk-fine hair.*

*"Tell him to meet me outside," he said, and walked out the door toward the barn.*

*A minute later, Dodge slid into the kitchen, embraced his grandmother and planted a big kiss on her cheek, "Oh Gramma, this is grrreat!"*

*"Well, knowin' your grandfather, I wouldn't count my chickens 'for the eggs was hatched if I was you." Her grandson didn't hear her. He was already out the door and climbing into the pick-up truck, saying to himself, "Come on Gramp, where are you?"*

*He waited a few minutes getting antsy before he saw Jed driving the big tractor out of the barn. Jed motioned to his grandson, and Dodge got out of the truck and walked over. "What are you doing, Gramp?"*

*"Hop on."*

*"But I thought we were gonna go look at the Mustang, can't we do this later?"*

*"Hop on."*

*Bewildered, Dodge jumped up and stood next to Jed as he drove down into the fields. They were silent as the tractor took them way out past the new corn and into the woods out along the stream that ran through the property.*

15

*They came upon an old faded black car covered with brambles. Dodge remembered it as a hiding place where he and his best friend Ben used to go when they were kids; but he hadn't been out here for years. Jed pulled around and backed down into the brush as close as he could get to the relic. He put the brake on and got down.*

*"Give me a hand with this chain, Dodger," Jed was at the back of the tractor.*

*The boy got down to help. "What are you doing, Gramp?" Dodge didn't know what was going on, but he wasn't having a good feeling.*

*"You said you wanted a car, didn't ya? Get under there and hook this chain around the front end and back out to the hitch here."*

*"But Gramp, I thought we were gonna go down to McIntyre's lot."*

*Jed was shooin' his hand for the boy to get under the car. Dodge did as he was told. A sick kind of feeling was coming over him; he could see his beautiful red Mustang slipping away.*

*They worked in silence pulling the car out, filling the tires with air from a portable air tank, and finally dragging it back through the fields towards the house.*

*Dodge was devastated. He didn't know what to say. They rode along quietly until Gramp said, "This is a great car ya know. 1940 Ford coupe. Flat head V-8. They don't make motors like that anymore," he glanced over at his dejected grandson, "strong motor."*

*Dodge, who was sitting on the tractor fender as they went along and looking away to hide the tears swelling in his eyes said, almost inaudibly, "But it don't even run," and swallowed hard to keep from all out bursting into tears.*

*"Oh hell, I know it don't run," Jed chuckled. "Hasn't run since I blew the engine racin' Ole Percy 'round the town common backwards when we was kids. Damn Chevy a his!" Jed reflected a moment, "But he beat me fair and square." He looked over at his grandson and decided to keep on talking. "Towed it back that night, and it's been here ever since. Never did get around ta fixin' it. Must a been fate. Don't worry, it'll fix up real nice. Helluva motor. Easy ta work on."*

*They reached the barn and pulled in.*

*"Come on Dodger, jump on down and unhitch her." He did.*

*"Now help me push it back into this space." He did.*

*When they got it positioned to Jed's liking, he popped the hood open, and, looking at the engine said to his young grandson, "You wanted a car," pause, "now make it run," and ambled out of the barn.*

*Jed went into the kitchen to pour a cup of coffee. Emma was looking out the sink window. She turned to him, "Jedediah, what the hell are you doin' with that old thing? And where's my grandson?"*

*Gramp, standing at the screen door, took a sip and replied, "Oh, I 'spect he's in the barn ballin' his eyes out and cussin' his old grandfather."*

*And he was.*

\* \* \*

"Sly old devil!" Harlow heard Dodge say.

"Huh?" she asked.

He smiled to himself, *"And I got that son of a bitch runnin', didn't I, Gramp. Took me all summer. Had no idea what the hell I was doing; but I guess you did."*

A tear came to his eye, "You old bastard," he said aloud with a smirk.

"What?" asked Harlow, sitting down beside him.

"He didn't even help me, just gave me a mechanic's book he borrowed from Wright's Garage, and sat there under the maple tree drinking his beer and chuckling at his pissed off greasy grandson determined to show him up."

"What the hell are you talking about?" Harlow was confused.

*"Best lesson I ever learned."* Dodge sat still as the memories and the tears came over him, *"I'm gonna miss you, Gramp."*

Harlow saw his eyes glossing up and put her arms around him, "I know how much they mean …. meant to you, Babe. You go home and do what you've got to do. I'll take care of things here. Don't worry, everything'll be alright."

He embraced her for a long time and hoped it would be.

# 4

## *DRIVING BACK*

Once out of the city, beyond FDR Drive, the Bruckner Expressway, and through the Bronx, you find Rt. 95 north, hugging the Connecticut coastline. Leaving the overwhelming presence of concrete and asphalt behind, the road broadens into a scenic ribbon, curving and stretching through fresh green foliage to its left, and the Atlantic Ocean, rolling and crashing onto the silvery shoreline, to the right.

Dodge was glad Harlow had talked him into driving the old Ford up. He always got a tremendous feeling of freedom and calm whenever he drove it. It was a great feeling to be on the road again. *Why didn't he have time to do this more often?*

The Coupe was purring like a kitten as Dodge maneuvered off the shoreline, inland up 91 north, onto 84 east, and over the mythical Podunk Pike. Over the years he had personally restored his first car to mint condition. It gave him great satisfaction, and reminded him of the values and rewards of hard work and determination. Whenever he escaped in the Coupe, he preferred to travel without the weight of his profession upon him. No cell phone, no tablet, no briefcase open on the seat next him, no pressure; just the feel of the wheel and the tone of dual glass-packs resonating in his ears. This trip would be no different. If anything, he needed the solitude more so. He trusted Harlow with the day-to-day running of the business, and had told her he'd be back in about a week.

The first hues of autumn greeted him as he entered deeper into New England. There were pleasant glimpses of color, early shades of red and orange and bright yellow, peaking through the vernal greens of the low lying hills and mountains from which Massachusetts gleaned its name.

This was the first time he had been alone since, when? He used to take time to be alone to re-charge on a regular basis. What had happened? *Too damn busy. Too wrapped up in it all.* Had he forgotten how he got here? When was the last time he saw Gramma Emma and Grampa Jed? They'd always been so supportive and understanding, and so proud. *How could I have let them down? Why hadn't I been there?*

He was on the road and his hands were on the wheel, but a mixture of sorrow and guilt was steering his mind in other directions, twisting and turning his thoughts in retrospection.

Dodge's parents were killed in the crash of the airliner bringing them home from an anniversary getaway to the Caribbean when he was five. He had a treasured picture of the three of them sitting on a fence out in the fields behind Grampa Jed's farm. He was in the middle of them. They looked so happy, and whenever he looked at it, he smiled and took some consolation in the fact that they had at least shared a wonderful week together before it happened. He missed them all the time.

He grew up on the farm with his grandparents, Gramma Emma and Grampa Jed. Across the street lived Old Percy and his wife Cora. She made great chocolate chip cookies, and Dodge and his best friend Ben, their eldest grandson, were very happy growing up with unlimited access to Cora's cookie jar.

Dodge grew up in the love and warmth of his Grandmother's house. Emma was a very fashionable lady. She made her own dresses, and many a lady could be found dancing in one of her designs on Saturday nights in the town hall ballroom. He figured he got his fashion sense from her and his strong work ethic from Jed.

His grandfather was a farmer. Long hours, hard work. Dodge was a part of that. He earned his keep, as Jed said, since early on. Weekends and other non-school days, he was up early and working the farm just as hard as any of the hands. Evenings were study time and TV. His favorites to watch with Jed were Bonanza, Hopalong Cassidy, and Zorro. Gramma Emma was into the old movies with Betty Davis, Clark Gable, Tracey & Hepburn, Bogie & Bacall, and other obscure black and whites, anything with romance and fashion.

This is when Dodge first started sketching. Sitting on the couch with a memo pad and a #2 pencil, he would mimic the lines and curves of the early Hollywood fashion designers. Emma watched him. He got quite good at it and when she realized his interest wasn't waning, that he actually enjoyed the sketching, she got him a real sketchpad with the proper graphite pencils. His talent grew onto pastels and inks, and before he knew it he was comfortable with oils and acrylics on canvas.

Throughout high school Dodge had excelled in all his art courses, but his flare was for fashion, and his thrill was helping Emma pick out and piece together the fabrics which brought his sketches to life. She was experiencing a nice little renown for her dresses in the local community, and Dodge was quite content working the farm, designing dresses for Emma, carousing with his teen-age buddies, and learning about girls. Life was good. He wasn't giving any thought at all to his life after high school. Luckily, his grandparents were.

They knew he had a talent beyond his hometown of Bryce Corner, Massachusetts, and wanted to give him everything they could. A chance to get beyond the death of his parents and growing up alone without any siblings, to get out into the world, to make something of himself, and, above all, to find happiness.

The Royal Academy of Fashion Design in London was touted as the best school in the world for talented, artistic, young designers. It was expensive, but Jed & Emma felt justified in sacrificing a few acres of their prime farmland to finance the education for their beloved grandson.

They knew they'd miss him, and Dodge wasn't too keen on traveling off so far from his home, but once in England he settled in and began taking control of his life and shaping his career. He wanted to make his grandparents proud. They were all he had.

*Where did I go wrong?*
*How did I lose touch?*
*When did I become so callous!?*

Alone on the two-lane highway, desolate and quiet as it passed through the natural preserve section, the road took on a surreal feel. Dodge felt like he wasn't even driving, like he was a passenger floating along the highway in a capsule, a time capsule ... *follow the yellow brick road, Dorothy.*

He pulled the Coupe over to the side of the highway, killed the engine, and got out.

*I must be over-tired.*

He walked down the embankment and into the tree line a ways to shake off the cobwebs and get a breath of fresh air. Coming to the edge of a marsh, he stopped and took in a deep breath. Goldenrod and cattails stretched out before him. It was quiet. The air was clean and fresh. He could hear crows cawing, and then saw them high in the pines beyond the marsh.

*What a different world this is.*

The whole area was calm. The sky a perfect blue with few white clouds skimming the skyline just above the mountain ridges beyond the marsh. Like a painting, the tips of the wetland brush were dabbed with the early colors of fall and stood motionless in the quietude. Dodge walked further into the scene. A dry twig snapped beneath his feet, and the sound startled a flock of Mallards. They'd been napping in the hidden solitude but were now awake and alert. Hastily they climbed to a safe and comfortable height, grouped into their familiar vee formation, and then headed south; their annual journey.

*I wonder where they go.*

# 5

## BRYCE CORNER

If Norman Rockwell had discovered Bryce Corner before Stockbridge, Massachusetts, he would have settled there to paint. His favorite subjects, made famous upon the numerous *Look* magazine covers, would have looked the same. "Main Street" would have been sketched while Norman sat on one of the benches on the vast town common, honored by *Yankee Magazine* as one of the most beautiful commons in New England. He would have then gone across the street to his studio to paint it. At any rate, the finished piece would have looked remarkably the same.

Nestled comfortably in the center of New England, Bryce Corner, named after its legendary settler Colonel Ebenezer Bryce, justly characterizes early Americana: white Victorian houses with slate roofs and gables, tall windows trimmed with lace curtains and functional wooden shutters, long, open verandas with gingerbread trim, wicker furniture and lazy dogs. The houses along the cobbled brick sidewalks are enhanced with deep green landscaping and granite hitching posts with black wrought-iron rings, all shaded by thick grand oaks and maples.

Neighbors say hello to each other each day as they pass by on their way to the country post office or the general store and gather together on the common for the fourth of July bonfire and summer concerts. In the center of town, next to the brick fire department with the oversized doors, the large and impressive town hall with the copper cupola and the loud steel bell houses the various departments of local government. Upstairs is the huge dance hall, which doubles as the town meeting place twice a year. And on the first floor just above the wide stone steps climbing to the tall double doors at the front of the building, is the police station looking out upon Main Street and keeping a peaceful eye on the goings-on of its quiet little town. Bryce Corner, Massachusetts has one general store, one gas station, one stoplight (on yellow most the time); one doctor, two lawyers, three antique dealers, and four preachers praisin' the Lord on Sundays.

There are no corporate logos or fast-food chains or cookie-cutter stores here, adamant town bylaws took care of that. But there is *Dot's Diner*, the popular gathering place for coffee and gossip, and of course The Tavern Pub, the other popular gathering place.

As you enter town eastward via route 9, you'll find another of Bryce Corner's amenities, Lake Wickaboag, spreading out to the north, covering over 500 acres. The lake is a year-round source of fun and recreation; especially active in summer, with boating, skiing, fishing, canoeing, and the like. Post Labor Day, with the summer people gone, the majority of the cottages dotting the shoreline amidst the changing foliage lay vacant, and the lake returns to a more tranquil pace.

Slowing down and looking out his car window, Dodge could just barely make out the Maddison's cottage across the lake, sitting tiny below a tall stand of pine trees on the eastern point.

His parents were in the process of converting the small fisherman's cabin into a year round residence when the accident happened. It hasn't been used much since. His grandparents rarely went there, and save for a few romps during his teen-age years, neither had Dodge.

A half-mile later, an approaching car coming around the bend flashing its headlights alerted Dodge to an eighteen-wheeler straddling the road. A short line of traffic was stopped, waiting as the large truck from *Atlas Moving Lines* maneuvered backwards into the driveway directly across the street from Jed and Emma's. The new owners were moving into Old Percy's house.

As the truck moved slowly off the road, the flashing blue lights of the town police cruiser came into view. Dodge could see his life-long best friend, Chief Ben Benson, standing in uniform in the middle of a small group of people on the porch. Directly in front of the chief, a man stood, flailing his arms in the air, over-empathizing a conversation. He looked like an ad for Ralph Lauren's Polo line. He was dressed in khakis, chambray shirt, cotton cardigan, and Docksiders. He sported a west-coast tan. An attractive woman in well-fitting jeans and a lightweight crop-top sweater leaned against the railing with her arms folded, looking disgusted. Next to her were two men in tee shirts with the moving company's logo, one held a clipboard. At the other end of the porch, in one of two rocking chairs, was Old Percy, sitting oblivious to all the commotion.

With the big truck finally perched on the front lawn, the line of traffic moved along, and Dodge pulled into his grandparent's driveway and parked his car.

He got out and walked across the street.

By now the chief and the woman had swapped places and she was speaking to Mr. Polo.

"Honey, calm down, he's not harming anyone."

"I don't care if he's harming anyone or not," he shouted back, "I just want him off my porch."

Then, to the chief, "These men are being paid by the hour," he ranted, "and this old coot is in the way. He needs to move on, and I need to get this underway and get to my office."

Mr. Polo was Alec Van Ness III, Chief Financial Officer for a California based Fortune 500 company. He was very used to being in charge and getting his way. He had no time for these small town shenanigans, and was absolutely fuming.

He had a lot on his mind; a challenging new position in a new area of the country, a new house in a new town, and a plush new office awaiting him atop the Prudential Tower in downtown Boston.

He had wanted to live in the city, in Back Bay, but reluctantly gave in to his wife's wishes. She was looking forward to the quaint charm of New England where she could return to her dance roots and open a small studio for ballet and tap.

Mrs. Van Ness turned to Ben saying, "I'm sorry Chief Benson, my husband's been under a lot of stress lately, and ... oh, my God," she recognized the designer walking up the brick pathway.

Ben pushed himself from the railing and stuck out his hand to greet Dodge as he climbed the steps. The two friends embraced.

"Good to see you again, ole buddy," the chief said.

"You too, Bennie."

The designer looked over at Mrs. Van Ness and said, "Hi."

"Hi, I ... I'm Katelyn. Katelyn Van Ness," she took his offered hand, "and this is my husband ..." she turned to find Mr. Polo abruptly walking into the house with his cell phone stuck to his ear.

"Nice to meet you, Katelyn," Dodge said with his natural charm. "Welcome to Bryce Corner."

"Thank you," she responded with a sly blush. "I didn't know you?... you?"

"Lived here?" concluded the chief. "Maddison's a born and breed Corner boy." he slapped him on the shoulder. "Not many know that little fact. They think he's from New York City."

"And just as well," Dodge looked around affectionately, "I kind of like keeping this little secret to myself. It's nice to have a place where you can just be yourself, away from the madness, and the paparazzi and all."

"Yeah, no paparazzi here." Ben winked at Katelyn Van Ness. "If they show up in my town, I just shoot 'em."

"Well, your secret is safe with me, Mr. Maddison. I'm a fan of yours from way back," she smiled. "I absolutely adore your work. I've got several pieces hanging in my closet right now."

"Actually, hanging in the van, ma'am," the mover interjected. "Could we please get the porch cleared so my men can start unpacking?" The movers disappeared into the house.

"Oh, yes, I'm sorry." Mrs. Van Ness looked down to the end of the porch where Old Percy was rocking, and then back to the chief of police."

"What's the problem?" asked Dodge.

With his eyes on Percy, the chief gave a heavy sigh. "He's an old-timer now, and he gets forgetful. Still thinks this is his house, his porch," he looked at Dodge, "maybe he's waitin' for Jed."

Then to Mrs. Van Ness, "Old Percy and Jed, Dodge's granddad from across the street, used to meet here on the porch every morning, for more years than I can remember."

He looked at his designer friend and continued, "And even though he's been in the nursing home for over a year, he still walks all the way down here every morning."

Glancing back to the rocking chair, Ben went on, "Causes hell with the nurses, and now, with what happened yesterday, I think he's slipped into one of his black holes or something. Doesn't seem to hear a word I'm sayin'."

Dodge moved away from Mrs. Van Ness and the chief and slowly walked the length of the veranda.

"Percy?" No response. "Old Percy?" Still no response. His eyes were fixed across the street at Jed's house.

Dodge sat in the vacant rocker. Slowly he began rocking, until he got up to the same slow speed as the other rocker.

Van Ness barged through the front door bellowing, "What the hell's ..."

Chief Ben stretched his big palm into the man's face, "Shhhh."

Quietly they watched as the two rockers began creaking together, reaching an actual rhythmic harmony, on the other end of the porch.

After a few moments, they saw Percy look over and put his hand on Dodge's arm. The two men passed several words between them.

Dodge rose, taking Percy's tired old hand in his, and the two companions stood to embrace.

"Jesus Christ!" Van Ness harumphed. "Kate, would you come in here and show the movers where you want this stuff set up?" He stormed back inside.

"I'll be right in." She placed her hand on Ben's shoulder. "I really appreciate your help, Chief. Please don't mind my husband. He's really a nice person. I think this whole move has been hard on him. We're really looking forward to living in your town."

She glanced over to the end of the porch, "And please extend my condolences to Mr. Maddison."

Reaching for the door handle, she added, "Oh, and please tell Mr. Percy that he can come sit on his old porch anytime," she smiled, "those rockers aren't going anywhere. No matter what my husband says."

"Well, what the hell you standin' there fur?" Percy barked as he approached his grandson the chief, "give me a ride back to that goddamn hell-hole you stuck me inta." He made his way down the stairs and slow-stepped to the police cruiser and got in.

Ben and Dodge stood alone on the porch with their hands on the railing.

"Hasn't changed much has he," the designer chuckled.

"Hell no. If anything, he's gotten worse, more cranky." Ben's parents had divorced years ago, splitting off to separate parts of the globe with new spouses and charging him with the caretaking of his maternal grandfather. "Hasn't taken well to the nursing home idea, but we had to do it. Wasn't an easy decision for the family, but with his medicines and all, it was the best we could do. This house got to be too much for him. Too big."

He looked over to Dodge, "He'll keep comin' back here, ya know. Doesn't know any better."

The designer glanced down the porch to the two rockers. "Oh, I expect Katelyn Van Ness will take good care of him," he smiled.

Dodge stood quiet, looking over at his grandparent's house.

"I need to know what happened, Bennie."

The movers were setting up their ramp onto the porch, and the two men had to step out of the way.

Ben said, "Listen, I've gotta get the old man back to the nursing home, and then do a couple things at the station. How 'bout we meet in an hour at The Tavern?"

"Make it two. I want to go over to the house for a bit, then I need to stop by the funeral parlor and make arrangements."

"I'm sorry about Emma and Jed, Dodge," the chief squeezed his buddy's arm.

Dodge nodded, his gaze fixed still across the street.

"See you in a couple hours," Ben adjusted his cap and headed down the stairs.

# 6

# *THE TAVERN*

B y the time Dodge got to The Tavern and moseyed up to the bar, Ben was already holding up his end of it with a cold draft in front of him, carrying on with Lindsey, the bartender.

"Hey, Dodge," she greeted him.

"Hi Linz, how you been?"

"Real sorry to hear about Jed and Emma, we're going to miss them around here."

"Thanks, Lindsey," Dodge paused, as if to say something, but didn't.

Lindsey offered, "Can I get you a drink?"

"Yeah, sure. I'll have a cosmopolitan, with Absolute Citron, please."

"A what?" Chief Ben bellowed, "Cosmopolitan? That's a magazine isn't it?" He was looking at Lindsey, "Get him one of these drafts, darlin'." Then looking back over at his buddy, "You're back home now, have a beer for chrissake."

"Okay with you, Dodge?" Lindsey chuckled.

"What is that?"

"Fleming's Pale Ale," the chief answered, "brewed local over in West Brookfield. Good shit."

"Yeah, what the hell, I'll try one."

Lindsey turned and headed for the taps on the other side of the bar.

"Cosmopolitan," Ben smirked. "What the hell's the matter with you? I gotta live in this town."

"Well," Dodge smiled back at him, "it's nice to have a chief of police that doesn't bully people around."

"Bully?" Lindsey said as she placed the beer in front of Dodge. "Are you kidding me? That's the only reason Big Bad Ben got a badge, so he could bully people around. You don't really think he's changed a bit since kindergarten, do you?"

"Kiss my ass, Lindsey."

"Anything you say, Chief." She puckered a kiss at him, and then, squeezing Dodge's arm, said, "This one's on me. Good to see you, Dodge," and walked back to her business.

Chief Big Ben Benson was indeed a big man. Two inches over six feet, two hundred-seventy-five pounds and still able to carry his weight around as well as he had on the high school football field. That's where he got his moniker Big Ben, because he was big and because he was as steadfast and sure as the clock in the bell tower in London.

He was your typical staunch, no-nonsense New Englander, not afraid to tell you what you should be doing or what you were doing wrong, and as a cop, not afraid to take a step or two outside the law to enforce the law and keep his town safe and in order. Big Ben was well-liked and respected.

He raised his glass to his best friend, "Sorry about the circumstances … but it is good having you back, buddy."

They clinked glasses and took a long swig.

Ben wiped his mouth on his uniform sleeve. "You still cavortin' with that sex-kitten? What's her name? One of those catchy solo names like Cher or Madonna – only starts with a D, right? … Diane … no … Danielle … nope … Diana, yeah that's it, Diana."

"Dana," the designer offered.

"Yeah … Dana … that's it. How old is she now? Twelve? Thirteen?"

"Twenty."

"Holy shit, she's past puberty!"

Dodge chuckled, "You are one fucked-up cop, you know that?"

"Aw shit, pal. Just tryin' to lift your spirits."

Dodge smiled at his lifelong friend, and raised his glass. "Thanks, Bennie."

Lindsey was across the bar bending over and reaching into the beer cooler. Her goldilocks' curls were cascading across her back and flowing long over each shoulder.

"I swear she must paint those jeans on," Ben was saying, "look at that. Great ass."

She spun around with two Buds in one hand and flipped her hair back with the other. She saw the two men gawking at her and gave Dodge a wink.

"And she knows it too," Ben added.

"Hey, if you've got it, flaunt it," his buddy said.

"Well, she's definitely got it, and she may as well start flauntin' it again."

"What do you mean?"

"She and the Dirt Bag finally split up."

"Yeah? But they've done that before, haven't they?"

"A few times, but this time's for good."

"Why do you say that?"

"'Cuz I took a personal interest," the chief looked over at Lindsey and then back to his companion, "I sorta stepped outside of my official boundaries."

"How so?"

"Well, I had warned the bastard before, a couple times actually. But he just couldn't keep his fists off her. I'd arrested him a few times over the years, but he never took it serious, never learned his lesson," he took a draw on his pint glass.

"Then one night Joe called me and said Lindsey hadn't shown up for work. Joe was here bartending for her and the Dirt Bag was sittin' right here at the damn bar drinkin'. He'd told Joe he had no idea where his wife was. So, I drove over to their house and found her cryin' her eyes out on the couch. She was beat up pretty bad and had a cut over her left eye. I took her down to Doc Keenan's and headed over here."

Dodge was listening and watching Lindsey, wondering how anyone could be so cruel to her.

"I tell ya, buddy, I was near out of my mind. He was sittin' there calm as could be, drunker than a skunk. So, I yanked him outside, tellin' Joe to keep everybody's nose to the bar."

Ben stopped for a minute thinking about it, and then continued, "I took him out back, and I told the sonofabitch that I was going to beat the living shit outta him and dump him into his car. And that *if* and *when* he became conscious again, he'd better get the hell outta town and stay out. Told him that if he pressed charges, or if I ever saw him again, I was going to kill him."

"Then what?"

"Did what I said. Haven't seen him since ... and don't expect to."

"Hey Lindsey," he hollered and held up two fingers for another round.

"She's a good kid, Dodge. Why don't you take her out to dinner or something while you're in town?"

Lindsey delivered the two beers and disappeared into the kitchen.

"What? You got 'match-maker' stamped on that badge too?" Dodge said kiddingly.

"Hey, you never know. She'd make a great catch, and you could stop playin' Hugh Hefner with those teenie-boppers of yours," Ben teased, "it can't be *all* that interesting."

Dodge gave him a look, and Ben said, "Well, except for the sex I mean, ole buddie," and poked him in the ribs.

"Speaking of sex-kittens," the designer asked, "how's Carlene?"

"Oh, she's great, just doin' great."

"Can't believe she's still putting up with you."

"Twenty years and counting." Ben grinned. "She's expecting you for dinner, and told me not to take no for an answer."

"You know, that'd be great. I'd really like to see her, and I honestly can't remember the last time I had a real home-cooked meal."

"Hey," the chief smirked, "I hear Lindsey's a great cook." and they both broke out laughing.

\* \* \*

It was late afternoon and the local carpenters and contractors were drifting in for a cold one. They all said hi to Big Ben, and those that knew him, said hey to Dodge and expressed their condolences.

Ben got up and headed into the men's room. When he returned and took his seat, he heard his old friend saying, as if to himself, "You know, it feels good to be back here," he paused, looking around, "guess I haven't had much time lately to relax and just ..." his thoughts drifted off. A quiet settled upon the two men.

The chief thought about his friend for a moment, and imagined how hectic and stressful his life-style must be. He was sure that, beyond all the glitter and the glamour of the fashion world, Dodge worked like a dog, and probably hadn't taken any real time for himself in years. And now, with his grandparents gone, there was a tremendous hole in his life. He knew how important Gramma Emma and Jed had been to him. They were basically all he had.

"Whatdaya say we round up some of the guys and go hunting? We'll go up to the shack ... after the funeral of course."

This broke the quiet, and Dodge laughed, "Hunting? Are you nuts? We never hunted a damn thing up there."

'The shack' was just that. An old slapped-together wooden shack, way up on the top of Crow Hill. Nobody seemed to know who had built it, but Jed and Old Percy used to go up there for a couple days at a time roughing it with a few bottles of booze, sandwiches, and some great old stories. When the boys had gotten old enough, they'd taken their grandsons along with them, 'hunting'.

They sat silent with the discord of The Tavern surrounding them. Finally, in a solemn tone, Dodge said, "Tell me about it Bennie."

The chief, regretting the upcoming conversation, took a long swig from his pint glass and lowered it slowly to the bar top. "I was coming out of my office on my way home for lunch and Old Percy was sitting there on the town hall steps. At first I thought he wanted a ride or something, but he didn't say anything, just sat there staring at the steps. Now, considering his state of mind, with the old age or Alzheimer's or whatever, that's not an uncommon thing for him. I asked him if he wanted to come home with me for a sandwich, and again, he just stared. So, I was going to just leave him be. It was a decent enough day, and he seemed okay, in an Old Percy sorta way, so I headed for my cruiser." He took another draw on his beer.

"I got my hand onto the door handle when I heard him mumble something, so I go back over to him and he says, "You better go down to Jed & Emma's.

"I asked, 'what's up'? But he just got up and walked away. I hollered after him, but he kept on walking."

He looked over at Dodge listening with both hands on his pint glass, and continued; "When I got to the house, I knocked on the door - probably the first goddamn time I ever knocked on that door - but I'll tell ya Buddie, I was nervous. Didn't have a good feeling.

"Anyways," he leaned back folding his arms across his chest, "I walked in calling out, but got no response, so I checked out the kitchen and the living room, and finally went upstairs to the bedroom, and that's where I found Emma. She was lying on top of the bed all dressed-up."

"What do you mean all dressed-up?"

"She had on a dress and shoes and her hair was all done up, like she was goin' to church or something."

Dodge pondered this for a moment.

"I went over to her and checked her pulse. She looked so peaceful. It was eerie." Ben came forward to his beer glass. Turning it slowly in his big hands he spoke with a soft coarseness in his voice. "I headed back downstairs to find Jed.

"I hollered a couple more times but figured he wasn't in the house, so I went outside. His truck was parked out back by the barn, and I noticed the barn door was open."

The chief's eyes were reliving the scene deep within the frosty head on his pint glass and it took him a moment. "He was hanging from the hayloft."

In one long gulp Ben finished off his beer and motioned to Lindsey. Dodge hadn't touched his, and sat silent in his remorse.

They spent awhile lost in their respective thoughts. The chief could sense the questions running through his friend's head. He decided to give him a moment and walked over to the jukebox. He stood there staring at the revolving selections.

"Any note?" Dodge came up behind him.

"Just this," he took a card out of his breast pocket and handed it to Dodge. "Found it in Jed's coat pocket."

It was a well-worn card. A Hallmark card. One of those candid photographs of two little kids taken in black and white then later colored for effect. It was a cute shot of a little boy in a straw hat plucking away on a guitar with a cute little girl sitting next to him all dressed up in a lacey dress and holding a bouquet of flowers. Inside, in Gramma Emma's hand was written simply, *You are my favorite song.*

"What's it mean?" Ben asked.

"Emma had this saying about her and Gramp … she always said *there's a certain poetry about growing old together*," Dodge held the card reverently in both hands, "*it's like your favorite song, taking on a sweeter harmony.*"

He put the card inside his shirt and leaned against the jukebox. He ran his hands through his hair, clasped his fingers behind his head, and stared up at the ceiling fan.

"This whole thing doesn't make sense to me, Bennie. I mean, I knew Gram had her heart condition, but I just spoke with her a couple weeks ago," he threw his arms down loudly to his side, "and why the hell would Jed hang himself? Dammit!" he paced, "I should have been here more often instead of touring the fucking world!"

"Listen buddy," Ben stopped him, grabbing his shoulders straight on, "it's done. Don't beat yourself up over this. Her heart gave out and Jed couldn't face goin' on without her. It's as simple as that. There wasn't a damn thing you could have done."

Dodge shook off Ben's grasp and returned to the bar. *I could have been there.*

One of the town's selectman found the chief's ear, and they stood off to the side in conversation. Dodge sat quietly with his beer looking at the faces surrounding him.

The Tavern happy hour was in full swing. The girls from the bank were dropping quarters into the jukebox, keeping the atmosphere lively. The same old group of locals sat at the same old corner table for their afternoon meeting of beers and bullshit. Dodge recognized them all, had grown up and gone to school with them; Tony the attorney, Jimmy and Glenn of J&G Masonry, Clay the arborist, the Daley brothers, Jim and Wilbur who owned the marina on the lake, Mikey The Carpet Guy, PT the truck mechanic, Johnny the dry-waller, J. Roper the painter. And then off to the side he spotted MJ, the architect, chatting with Dick from the Sportsmen's Club and some former neighbors Brian and Richie. The librarian Holly was chatting with some longhair guy about setting up a book signing. And the elementary teacher Peggy was on a good run at the pool table much to the chagrin of her "pool shark" husband Gary.

Behind him Dodge became privy to a conversation.

"But I thought because of your nickname you would have knowledge of chickens," the yuppie newcomer to town said.

"Nope, can't say that I do," Eggman responded.

"But someone said you had a chicken farm with over ten thousand chickens."

"Used to. Doing landscaping and carpentry now, don't know nothing about chickens anymore."

The yuppie scratched his head as Eggman took a sip of his pint and smirked at Dodge, making him laugh.

"Listen, my wife has got this chicken coop being delivered tomorrow and I've got to get a few chickens. Can you at least tell me where I might get some?"

"Chicken store, I guess."

The yuppie gave up and walked away. Dodge was shaking his head and snickering. Eggman was a good friend of his renown for pulling legs.

"How you doing, Dodge?"

"Good, Eggman. You?"

"Fair ta middlin'. Sorry to hear about your grand folks." "Thanks."

They spent a beer catching up on things and then Eggman said, "Well, I got to go tend to my chicks. Stop up to the farm before you head back to New York. Always got beer in the fridge."

As he sat on his stool turned to the room, Dodge could feel a simple warmth here, a closeness. Hometown camaraderie. He wondered if he'd ever appreciated it before, or if he'd been running from it all his life.

* * *

*"Why New York City? It's so far away."*

*"It's only a few hours, Gram, and if I'm going to be a fashion designer, that's where I've got to be."*

*"What's wrong with Boston? That's a lot closer. You could come home on the weekends."*

*Dodge gave his grandmother a hug. He loved her very much. They had forged his career together. She and Grampa Jed had even flown over to England for his graduation last month. He'd seen them sitting in the audience together, Jed holding onto Emma's hand. They were so proud of him and he held the rolled parchment high in his hands in a rejoiceful salute to them as he descended the stage. He saw the tears of joy in her eyes and the proud smile on her lips. Her dream was coming true. Mentally he pictured his parents there, sitting next to them. His father clapping and his mother wiping her eyes with the white pocket hanky he'd handed to her.*

*"Don't worry, Gram, you'll see so much of me that you'll get sick of me," Dodge said into her ever-bright eyes, holding her shoulders in front of him. In the kitchen of the farmhouse he was taller than her now.*

* * *

"You okay?" Ben climbed onto his stool.

"Yeah," Dodge replied, his thoughts coming back to the events of the past two days. "It's all just starting to sink in. I guess I thought this would never happen, especially in this way," he rubbed his eyes, "I'm just tired and confused."

Lindsey approached the two men with a cordless cradled on her shoulder. She was chuckling, "Nope, ain't seen hide nor hair of them, Carlene."

"Uh oh." Ben said.

"But," Lindsey continued into the phone, "There is a real cute one sitting next to a big ole ugly cop. That be them?" she laughed and handed the phone to Ben.

"Yes Boss? ... un huh ... only a couple, honey ...I know, I know, I've been tryin' to tell him that, but that damn Dodge just keeps buyin' rounds and ... we will ... we're on our way now darlin' ... nope ... yup, ... sure, red or white? ... okey-dokey, we're on our way Sugarplum." He hung up and drawled, "What a sweet thang she is."

"She certainly is Benjamin," Lindsey chided, "and you'd best not forget it. Here's your check."

"Put it on my tab, darlin'."

"You don't have a tab."

"I know, I know, put it on it anyways." It was a familiar game they played.

"We'll see you at the funeral," she said to Dodge, then asked, "You going to be in town awhile afterwards?"

"I'm not really sure, depends on how much there is to take care of."

"Well, if you get antsy, come on down and I'll whip your ass on the pool table."

"Darlin'," Ben interjected, "you can whip my ass on any table anytime."

"In your dreams, cop'er." She threw a bar rag at the chief.

"Take care, Dodge."

"Yeah, nice seeing you again, Lindsey. I'm sure I'll be back in before I go."

They said a few parting words to some of the patrons and made their way out the door.

\* \* \*

Outside, the wind was blowing strong in the evening twilight. Bryce Corner's typography, with the lake, the river valley, and the surrounding hills, was fodder for impromptu storms - and late summer September could spawn ferocious ones with no notice. Tonight was evidence.

"Holy shit. Where'd this come from?" Ben yelled above the howling winds. "I've gotta stop by the package store and get some wine, gimme your keys."

"What?"

"Gimme your keys."

Dodge handed his car keys to the chief, who immediately jogged off, shouting over his shoulder, "mine are in the ignition, see you at the house," he laughed.

"Bennie!" it was too late, he was already firing up the Coupe. Dodge jumped back as his childhood pal screeched the car almost into his kneecaps, "I love this thing!" and tore off over the curb burning rubber as he shifted fast through the gears.

"You asshole," the owner yelled into the blue smoke wafting back at him.

Walking over to the police cruiser, parked off to the side of the small parking lot, Dodge was smiling to himself thinking of how fortunate he was to have a crazy old friend like Bennie in his life. He missed him. It was good to be back.

Looking up into the night sky, he could feel the first large drops of rain spitting down, loud like hail, but not hard. They were intermittent and sporadic, in short spurts, precursors to the impending storm. Heavy rain was going to fall.

# 7

## DINNER AT CARLENE'S

Carlene Jean Benson was a proud woman. She evoked a typical
Vermonter's no-nonsense attitude. You never had to worry where
she stood on any issue, she spoke her mind – whether you wanted to hear
it or not. Her family had moved from Vermont to Bryce Corner during
her second year of high school. Her dad had merged his custom
woodworking company with a larger manufacturer just outside Boston.
She met Benjamin J. Benson in the high school band. He carried the bass
drum. Couldn't play it well, but liked the prestige of carrying around the
big drum with the Tigers logo on it, especially at the football games. She
dated him through graduation and on into the years she spent at
community college, and he at the police academy. They were married
two weeks after her E.P.T. tape turned pink. Yup, she was pregnant at the
altar and didn't give a shit who knew it. She wasn't about to have her
baby out of wedlock. Bennie was thrilled. He'd of married her the first
day he laid eyes on her.

She was a good woman, perfect for Ben, a big lovable man who had
never really grown up. A loving mother to her two teenagers, a caring
veterinarian's assistant, a great ear to her steadfast friends, and an avid
country music fan not afraid to pick up her guitar and play a lick or two
with The Country Cousins at the summer Concerts-on-the-Common.
Carlene was also one helluva cook.

Keeping warm in the oven was a pasta dish she had prepared earlier,
a combination of chicken and farfalle in a thick white Parmesan sauce.
Pressed for time, she had collaborated with Paul Newman on an Italian
dressing and had dumped a pre-made bag of salad into a large stoneware-
serving bowl. They'd never know. Sitting at her large scrubbed-pine
table Carlene stared into a jug of wildflowers from her backyard garden

wondering if she could talk her husband into one of the Cocker Spaniel puppies she had helped deliver that afternoon.

Dodge pulled up to the stately white colonial the Benson family called home. Ben and Carlene had purchased it when Carlene was pregnant with their second child, Penny. Attorney Lyman Wheelock and his family had owned the light-filled eighteenth century farmhouse until it got to be too much for Mrs. Wheelock to handle after the death of her husband. It had plenty of rooms for them, nine in all. Carlene had immediately fallen in love with the big country kitchen and couldn't wait to fill it with her colorful collection of vintage cookware to compliment the period-style woodwork, raised panel antique cupboards, soapstone counters and the random-width pine floors. She outfitted the large living room with the exposed beams with comfortable country furniture; the plump couches sitting on the warm Oriental rug, piled high with fluffy pillows and colorful quilts. It had a dining room that came with a two-board pine table and a large open- door cupboard; a grand family room which they painted in pale hues to maintain the open feeling; and a generous bath with claw-foot tub, pedestal sink, and a bold old fashioned checkerboard patterned floor. Off the foyer with the wide staircase, Ben had converted Attorney Wheelock's office into a den. "Ben's Den" his wife called it, a mini police station and museum for his cop memorabilia. Upstairs was the master bedroom with a full bathroom; the kid's rooms, one for Brent and one for Penny; another smaller bathroom and the spare room Carlene used for her music room. Here she could retreat and spend hours strumming away on her guitar and listening to her favorite CD's. She had been pleased by Brent's early interest in music and had taught him to play in this room.

Over the years, as time and money permitted, Ben and Carlene toiled on the renovations of their old home by fits, lived their lives, raised their family, and went back to the project in spurts. The refurbished aesthetics of a new roof, new windows and shutters and fresh paint had brought the exterior back to its distinctive nineteenth century grace and refinement. All the rooms and woodwork in the interior were also tastefully redone with period wallpaper and radiant paint schemes embodying the classic décor - except for Brent's room which looked like the inside of a rock group's tour bus, and Penny's room, which couldn't possibly contain one more Panda bear. The Benson home was comforting, warm, and filled with things they loved. It had actually been on the cover of Country Home last year and Dodge passed the framed cover with accompanying article hanging in the foyer as he made his way into the house.

With the music cranked-up, she hadn't heard her guest come in and was startled when he wrapped his arms around her waist from behind.

"You scared the daylights outta me!" She spun around and hugged him tight.

"Nothing can scare a pretty woman like you, Carlene."

"Ahh, still got your charms, eh," she stretched up on her toes and gave him a kiss on the cheek. "Sorry 'bout Emma and Jed." She placed her head into his shoulder.

"Thanks Carlene. You know they thought the world of you and Bennie and the kids."

"Yes, they did, and we all loved them very much."

They stood embraced in the middle of the kitchen.

Ben came in through the back door carrying a grocery bag, "Whew, that wind is really blowin' out there." Seeing them he added, "Hey, what's going on in here?"

"Just huggin' and kissin' with your wife," Dodge replied.

"Oh," the chief placed two bottles of wine on the counter, "well as longs it doesn't go any further."

"Too late," Carlene teased, giving her husband's best friend another kiss, "we just finished." She went over to the kitchen island, opened a drawer, got a cork screw and handed it to Ben, "You pop the wine and I'll go call Penny."

"Hey, I'll get her," Dodge said, "I've got to hit the bathroom anyways, too many of those frosties."

"Just don't scare her like you did me!" Carlene warned.

\* \* \*

Dodge made his way through the dining room, already set for dinner, and back into the foyer. Ascending the steep narrow staircase he passed several pictures hanging on the wall. Baby pictures of the kids next to a more recent one of them together in front of the fireplace, it looked like a blow-up of the one they sent out as a Christmas card last year. Ben & Carlene's wedding; Percy & Cora's fiftieth anniversary; Ben in front of his police car the day he made Captain; the family atop the dunes on Cape Cod; and at the top of the stairs, a teen-aged Ben and Dodge standing between Old Percy and Jed up at the shack. They were all holding hunting guns, and had done a poor job of hiding the beer bottles and the shine in their eyes. The memory got a laugh out of Dodge.

He rounded the landing, heading along the hallway, passed Brent's bedroom door, where a collage of stickers exhibiting his admiration of the first amendment surrounded a large KEEP-OUT sign. Down the hall he stopped to peer into Penny's room. She was lost in a sea of black and white panda fur, clicking away on her laptop.

"Hey Panda Girl." he whispered.

With the spontaneous exuberance of a thirteen-year-old, Penny was up from her keyboard jumping onto Dodge feet first, wrapping her heels around his waist, and almost knocking him over.

"Uncle Dodge!"

"Whoa!" he fell back a couple steps to keep his balance, "you're frisky as ever."

"I'm just glad to see my favorite uncle," she slid back down onto the floor. He wasn't really her uncle, but as far as they were concerned he was. Dodge was proud of his niece and nephew, and had been close to them since they were born. With her arms still wrapped around him, she asked, "Are you gonna stay with us? You can have Brent's room. He can stay at one of his friends."

"Well I'm not sure yet, I just got here," he looked at her in her jeans and tee shirt thinking of how fast she was growing up. "Time's flying, Penny Lane," using his pet name for her.

"Thank God you're the only one who calls me that."

He laughed. "Where's the rock star?"

"Down at the freight house, practicing," she gestured with an air guitar.

"What freight house?"

"The empty brick building down by the tracks, you know."

"Oh, yeah."

"Mr. Peterson lets them use it. Keeps that awful noise they make away from civilization," she sneered.

"You never know, you might see your brother on TV someday."

"Yeah, right!"

"Anyways, your mom wants you to come down to dinner."

"Okay," she spun around, "I'll be down two minutes, I'm in a chat room with some friends from Australia," and jumped back onto her laptop.

Uncle Dodge went along to the bathroom. It was as neat as a pin. With a full time job, two teenagers, a big house and Ben to contend with, he wondered how Carlene had time to keep up with everything. You could walk into her house unannounced anytime and it'd be picture perfect. "How does she do that?" he asked a Panda bear sitting on the window ledge.

\* \* \*

Carlene dimmed the lights of the overhead chandelier, lit two candle tapers, and joined her husband at the dining table. "How's he doing?"

"Well …" Ben poured his wife some Pinot Grigio, "fair, I guess." He placed the bottle in a chilled marble wine cooler, "I think he's feeling guilty."

"Guilty? Why?"

"Thinks he should have been here."

"There wasn't anything he could have done," she paused a moment, "except for Jed?" she leaned closer to her husband, "Is that it? Does he think if he had been there he could have stopped Jed?"

"I dunno."

Carlene sipped at her wine, thinking.

"Well, actually he hasn't been around much lately, hardly at all during the past year, except for Christmas."

"Guess he's been busy."

"No, that's not it, he's always been busy."

She rested the rim of her wineglass on her lower lip and held it there in her fingertips. "I think he knew," she said matter-of-factly.

"Knew what?…That his grandmother was gonna have a heart attack in her sleep and his grandfather was gonna freak-out and hang himself in the morning?"

"No, not that, I just think he knew somehow."

"Aw Carlene."

"Like he was afraid it would happen to him again, like when he was a little boy."

The chief was shaking his head from side to side, pouring himself another glass as she continued, "I think he's had an inherent fear of losing those close to him."

"Who doesn't?"

"Everyone does, Ben, but I think his has been heightened with his background and all, he's naturally more sensitive, and he had a premonition of sorts and didn't want to face it. That's why he's been so distant lately."

"You been on that psychic hotline?"

"I just think it's possible, that's all."

"'Lene," Ben reached over and placed his big hand onto her smaller one, "I think you're way off. It's a tragedy. That's all. They were both in their eighties; you can't go on forever, Babe."

Footsteps on the stairs alerted them to their friend's approach. Ben lifted the Pinot to fill a glass for their guest.

"Wow, I can't believe that daughter of yours, she's really growing up," Dodge said, entering the room and taking a seat.

"Yeah, she's wearin' bras now and everything," Ben snickered, "pretty soon she'll be into her mom's bras."

Pushing out her chest his wife said, "She's got a long way to go to catch up to these babies." They laughed.

"I swear darlin'," Ben kidded, "I think you're more proud of your tits than Dolly Parton is of hers."

"Hey, at least mine are real."

Penny Lane scrambled down the stairs and into the room, "Mom, can I go over Joanne's? I already did my homework, but she needs some help with hers."

"We're having dinner, Penny."

"I know, but I made a plate for myself earlier and I'm not hungry." She put her arms around her uncle's neck and added, "besides, you've got a special guest to entertain and you don't really want a silly teenager hanging around do you?"

Her father poked some fun at her, "You sure she needs help with her homework? Or you gonna talk about boys?"

"Wellll …"

"Okay Lady," Mom said, "but you be back in this house by nine o'clock sharp."

"Thanks Mom." She smacked a kiss on top of her uncle's head and ran off.

"Put a coat on," Ben said, "it's gonna storm hard out there."

"It's only next door, Daaad," she called back in typical teenager tone as she exited by the back door.

\* \* \*

They passed the next few hours in the warm conversation that good cuisine and rekindled friendship inspires.

Carlene had all the questions. "When's the funeral?" *Friday.* "Are you going to have calling hours?" *No, I thought just the memorial service would be nice. Get everyone together once, at the same time.* "Yes, that seems appropriate. Who's going to do the service?" *Reverend Blackmer.* "That's nice, he'll do a good job. Is Harlow coming up?" *Yes, I believe so.* She glanced over to her husband, then back to her guest, "Where's she going to stay?" *I'm not sure, probably get a room, I guess,* his brow furrowed realizing he hadn't given it any thought. "Nonsense, she can stay here. I'd love to see her again, she's such a wonderful lady." Ben gave her a look of caution. He knew Carlene and Harlow were close, and that his wife held a soft spot for a Harlow/Dodge union, but didn't want her to go there. She caught the warning and changed subject. "How was Paris?" *Fine, well a little hectic actually, but the premiere came off very well.* "Is it going to be on the E! channel? I'd love to see it." *Umm, I think so, they were there, so I imagine they'll air it.*

Ben left the two of them to their conversation and busied himself with clearing the table, putting the dishes into the dishwasher, and preparing three Remy Martin's. A few minutes later he re-entered the room, placed the brandy snifters onto the table, and then went to check the front door. It wasn't raining through the kitchen door, but that was on the eastern side. The storm was coming out of the southwest. It was a Mexican storm, originating in the heat of the Yucatan, gathering warm tropical moisture as it traveled across the Gulf, then inland, through the Florida Panhandle and up the eastern coast along the valleys of the Appalachian Mountains. When it got to New England and began its futile battle with the stronger, cooler high-pressure system pressing down from Canada, (before it would eventually give in and fizzle out over the waters of the North Atlantic), the storm lashed out with a final ferocity. It was fluctuating between heavy downpours, distant thunder, and sporadic lightning flashes, then lapsing calm. In the flash of a lightning strike he saw thousands of raindrops glistening on the door screen like huge bright diamonds. He decided the moisture lying on the slate foyer floor wasn't enough to warrant closing the door. Besides, the storm had cut the humidity and the cool felt good. But he'd better check the upstairs windows to be safe.

"Have you given any thought as to what you're going to do with the house?" Carlene was steering the conversation.

"No, it's all just starting to hit me now."

"What about Harlow?"

"What do you mean?"

"You know what I mean, what about *you* and Harlow?"

The designer had both elbows on the table and held the snifter in both his hands, swirling it slowly, watching the rich copper hues of the brandy rolling from side to side. "She is a great lady, and a good friend," he paused, "and one helluva businesswoman. My business certainly wouldn't be where it is today without her. But I don't know."

"Dodge, you can't be happy jumping from one model to the other." She was getting serious now.

"Well, I don't know if you'd call it jumping or not, a lot of that is just tabloid rumor."

"Maybe it's time in your life to get serious," she put her hand on his forearm, "settle down, think about kids and a family. Hell, you don't need the money, but if you needed to, you could run the business from here." She was on a roll. "You should cut back, Dodge. You're running yourself into the ground, there's more to life than fame and fortune."

Ben re-joined them. He had caught part of the conversation on his way in. Retaking his seat, he gave Carlene a *I love you baby, but you've got a big mouth!* look. To which her returned glance said, *What?!*

Dodge stopped playing with his brandy glass and put her hand between his and gave her a warm smile. "'Lene, I love you for your big heart and your genuine concern, but, just twenty-four hours ago, I was standing on a platform on the grounds of a beautiful mansion in Paris, feeling like I was standing on top of the world. Now I feel as if my whole world has collapsed, crumbled beneath me, and I'm not sure what I'm standing on anymore."

She placed her free hand on top of his, still holding hers, and, holding back an emotional tear or two, looked into the eyes of this gentle man. This good friend, her husband's best friend, caring uncle to her children, this grieving man, lost, but at least home, with perhaps now the two closest people in his life.

"Dodge, you're tired. You haven't had any real sleep in probably the past thirty-six hours or more. Add to that the travel, the melancholy, and the stress you're under, and it's a wonder you're coherent at all. Why don't you stay with us tonight and get some rest. Things'll look better in the morning."

Carlene had said this as a statement, with her comforting but inexorable mother's voice. Getting up, she gave him a kiss on the cheek and whispered into his ear, "Things'll work out."

She left the two old friends and headed into her kitchen to double-check her husband's handiwork. She figured she'd find a few things out of place.

Working up a wide grin, Dodge said, "You've got yourself a good woman there, chief."

"Yaa-up." he replied with an even wider grin, "she's one of a kind, ain't she?"

They sat quietly for a few minutes until the designer broke the silence, "It was weird going into the house, Bennie ..."

Ben let him go on.

"Everything was just as usual. Like it always is. It was like they had just gone down to the supermarket or something. I just walked around and then sat in the kitchen waiting for them to come into the driveway. Like I had driven up to surprise them or something."

Ben gave him time.

"I just sat there, listening to the grandfather clock ticking away." Dodge sat back in his chair and blew out a heavy sigh. "Then I went into the barn. And that was just the same as always. I don't know what I expected. I called out for Jed. I actually hollered out 'Jed, Grampa Jed!' But it was just me. I paced around awhile trying to figure out a reason, but it was just me."

Ben didn't know what to say, so he didn't.

"You know, I can't figure out why Gramma Emma was all dressed up and lying on top of the bed."

"I can," Carlene said. They hadn't seen her leaning against the doorway. "We all know what a proud lady Emma was. She wouldn't have had it any other way. I don't think she'd want anybody to see her not at her best. Jed knew this too. I think he dressed her as she would have wanted to be found."

Dodge took this in. "And Jed?" he asked her.

Carlene turned her head to her husband, and Ben answered, "I guess he was devastated. 'Lene's probably right about him dressing her. I think he wanted her to feel as if she had gone on with everything in order. You know, herself, the house, you know ..."

"But why Jed?" There was anger in his voice. "Why would he do that to himself?.. To her?.. To me?.. I don't get it, Bennie." He was clearly upset. "Why no note?!... No goddamn reason!" Dodge slammed his fist hard onto the table, the brandy glasses jumped and the candlesticks wobbled. "Nothing to help me understand any of this."

The air got thick and heavy. They all sat quiet. The candle flames rocked back and forth in the thick air, seeking their former, more peaceful stance.

Penny came bounding into the room, breaking the somber mood. Her hair was flat and stuck to her head and her clothes were soaking wet.

"Look at you." her mother reacted, "what have you been doing?"

"Joanne and I were standing in the rain soaking it all in," she laughed, not seeing anything at all wrong with her appearance. "It's beautiful outside. The rain's so warm. It's like taking a shower."

"Which is exactly what you're going to do this instant, Penelope." Carlene took her resisting daughter by the elbow and headed upstairs.

Alone at the table, the two friends sitting opposite each other, both tired and speechless from a long day, made eye contact.

"Did you have to pound the shit outta my table?" Ben asked.

"Nope," Dodge replied, "but it sure made me feel better."

# 8

## DOWN TO THE LAKE

Carlene was right; he could use some rest. He was emotionally worn out and physically exhausted. Dodge had graciously declined their offer to stay with them, and when asked if he was going to stay at his grandparents' house, had told Ben and his wife that he didn't think he'd feel comfortable there, and would rather head down to the lake and stay at the cottage. *"Maybe open it up and collect my thoughts from there."* He had given them a hug and promised Carlene he'd let Harlow know she had the guestroom awaiting her.

Getting in the car, he remembered the two bottles of wine, one white, one red, that he had taken from Gramma Emma's kitchen and placed on the passenger seat. He checked their position to make sure they wouldn't roll off the seat as he backed out of the Benson driveway.

The short ride back through the center of town, took him out along Wickaboag Valley Road for two miles, then left, down onto an almost invisible dirt road with a half dozen secluded cottages. The Maddison cottage sat at the end. Dodge crawled along the narrow bumpy pathway, the Coupe creaking and swaying, reminding him that it's suspension was old and fragile. Slowly they lumbered together at a five-mph pace. In the headlights he could see fallen pinecones and small tree branches, remnants of the passing storm, scattered as they had fallen, moist and black on the brown muddied road. Coming up to the short rickety bridge, spanning the tiny brook that ran through the marsh and emptied into the lake, he startled a huge beaver. The nocturnal worker glared at his intruder for a frightened instant with bright laser-like eyes, before it dropped the large chunk of tree it was pulling along, and dove quickly into the water. Dodge had to get out and remove the log lying across the road. He picked it up at the gnawed end and dragged it into the brush. *Damn, this is a tree trunk!* The beaver, not far away, angrily slapped his tail on top of the midnight-black water. The noise echoed across the dark water.

He pulled onto the property and sat with the headlights washing onto the small cottage nestled amongst a grove of tall pines on the water's edge. It was his, passed on with the death of his parents. He held few, but cherished memories of living here as a young boy. Sentiment kept the deed in his name, although he rarely came here. With Dodge's best wishes, Ben and Carlene had utilized it during the summers when the kids were young. Of late though, with busy teenage things to do, they had lost interest, and it had been vacant the past couple seasons. The chief checked on it from time to time, making sure no one was up to mischief in it. Dodge could see that the outside was worn and could use some fresh paint. He wasn't sure why he was here and almost backed away, but something told him to stay.

Walking up the stone pathway in the dark, Dodge could see Jupiter shining brightly in the clearing night sky as it dropped slowly into the western horizon. Its neighbor Saturn accompanied it to the right, and the star Aldebaran was along for the ride off to the left, just ahead of Orion.

On the porch he found the key still in its place over the back door, and as he dropped his garment bag and fumbled for the keyhole in the dark, he stopped and realized he'd forgotten how quiet it was here. He stood a moment and listened. The howling winds of earlier had subsided. A bullfrog bellowed, occasionally as they always do. That was it. A bullfrog in the quiet night. No city noises, no traffic, no airplanes roaring in and out of international airports, just the quiet solitude of the lake on an average country night.

The door opened into the kitchen. It was a small, but well laid-out component of the open floor plan. Flipping a switch on the wall produced a soft glow from recessed overhead lighting that fell warmly from thick wooden beams crisscrossing the cathedral ceiling. The soft lighting pulled out the rich grainy colors of the pumpkin pine flooring and fell luminously on the knotty pine walls and maple cupboards. Four tall stools set in front of the high counter facing the lake. The countertop held a layer of dust.

The cottage, which the family had named Camp Nyla after the first Scottish ancestor to set foot on American soil, was originally built as a fishing camp in the early fifties. It was essentially one big open room with a mix of new and antique furniture in striped fabrics. It was filled with vintage model boats, weathered oars, decoy ducks, antique fishing baskets, and lots of stars, essential for every sailor to steer by. Twin ceiling fans were suspended from the center beam, which ran the length of the room over to the opposite wall to a fieldstone fireplace. A pile of wood was stacked against it. Adjacent to this, fronting the lakeside, stood two sets of sliding French doors which brought you out onto the deck hovering just a few feet above the shoreline. You could actually fish from the deck - the water was that close. On the opposite side, below the sleeping loft, were two small bedrooms with iron beds painted in pastel tones to keep the rooms light and airy. There was a tiny bathroom between. A tall blue apothecary chest with red doors anchored the wall of the living area. Dodge had bought it in New York and had managed somehow to transport it to the lake in the Coupe. Over the years he had fleeting illusions of furnishing the cottage to his liking. Fleeting because he was hindered by the demands of his business, and fleeting because the passion for it never quite outweighed the feeling of loneliness harbored there. He never had anyone to share it with. He periodically brought pieces of furniture and fabrics to the lakehouse, blending them with the legacy his parents had left him and perhaps subconsciously attempting to weave some fortitude, some reason into the ragged fabric of his past.

Dodge threw his bag onto the couch in front of the fireplace and turned into the kitchen area and put the white wine into the fridge. Reaching up and opening the cupboard, he was greeted by a furry brown mouse munching on its midnight snack of hoarded acorns. The mouse wasn't startled, nor about to move. He'd been living here quite comfortably for a while now, and decided if he outstared this intruder, that he'd shut the door and go away and leave him be. *I thought acorns were for squirrels,* Dodge observed. Getting no response he placed the bottle on the countertop and said to his tenant, *Okay, look, I'm way too tired to mess with you now, but in the morning, I want you packed up and outta here!* Still no response, just a blank stare with beady little black eyes. *Got it?* He shut the door.

In the bathroom, he reached for the faucet and then remembered that Ben had reminded him the water wasn't on, shut off last fall so the pipes wouldn't freeze during the winter. Dodge made a mental note to drive down to the town maintenance barn in the morning and have the water department come out and turn it on. Wanting to wake up early with a view of the lake, he pulled back the curtains in front of the wide glass doors before climbing into the loft and falling onto the bed exhausted.

# 9

## DANCIN' TO THE MUSIC

*E*ight days a week, I la la la la love you ... eight days a week is not enough to show I carrrrre!*

She had an oldies station cranked up on the radio. She was dancing on the braided rug in front of the fireplace, 'round and 'round the colored lanes, singing along at the top of her lungs. The music drowning out the wind outside, howling in the tall trees high above the tiny log cabin. The rain storming fiercely across the lake and pounding against the closed windows, trying to get inside and join in the fun.

*Ou I need your love, babe, can't you see it's true ....*

She was letting go, unwinding, really unwinding for the first time in years. She had already popped the cork from a bottle of her favorite champagne, and now the bottle of Moet was empty and on its side in front of the fire. A champagne glass, full and perched atop the mantel, watched her gyrate and spin around the small rustic room, wondering when she was going to collapse. Hundreds of feisty bubbles streaking upward through the golden liquid were popping unheard in the loudness of the frivolity.

She was celebrating. Celebrating being alone and by herself. No business to run, no children to fuss over, no husband to feel lonely with; clandestinely away from a marriage with a big hole in it. For the first time in years she felt like a kid again; carefree, uninhibited, playful and free. She reached for the long stemmed glass, placed it to her lips and took a tiny sip. The effervescence rushed into her nostrils and exploded into her senses ... she felt great! She placed the glass back upon the mantel and steadied it there with her hand, the golden champagne sparkling in the fire-glow. She stared at the well-worn gold band still shiny on her ring finger, even after twenty-two years. It felt heavy, its

51

weight sitting like a heavy quarry stone cemented around her slender finger. Bravely, in a long overdue instant, she slid her wedding band off her hand and tossed it onto the mantel. It rolled across the polished wood and careened into the wall, sliding along it, tottering back into the center of the mantel, then flopping into an unsteady gyration, spinning slowly on the flat surface and settling quietly by itself at the further end. It hadn't been as hard to do as she had thought.

*Can't you see it's true? Hold me ... love me ...* she was dancing again *... hold me ... love me, I ain't got nothin' but love babe, eight days a week ...* spinning 'round and 'round *... eight days a week ... eight days a week ... dah dah dah dum ... dah dah dah dum ... dah dah dah dah dahhhh!*

On the last note she pirouetted and fell into the over-stuffed wingback chair. It's hot, she said as she sat up and slipped off her top, freeing her breasts, bare and glistening with the sweat of her dancing. She stood and stepped to the mantel to the champagne glass and saw her ring lying there. She touched her finger where it had been and flexed her hand with a newborn freedom. It felt good, symbolic perhaps, but still good. She had no intention of putting it on again. She was here for herself. Alone, hiding away and doing something for herself for once. Turning, she saw her reflection in a long mirror surrounded by an ornate frame at the end of the small room. She saw her naked breasts rising and falling as her pulse rate calmed from her impromptu aerobic performance. She felt good. She looked good. She had managed to keep herself in shape even after the two kids. Her hectic workweek had helped, always on her feet, always running around. The stress and worry over her dying marriage had stolen a few pounds too. She watched the woman in the mirror, slipping off her drawstring sweatpants and kicking them to the corner. She looped her thumbs into the waistband of her panties and slowly lifted her left leg up and through them. She stood with her legs apart watching the silk panties fall the length of her right leg. She caught them on her foot and slid them off her painted toes into the colors of the braided rug. The mirror framed her as the blaze from the log fire swathed her naked body with a soft golden sheen.

She had trimmed herself earlier when she was pampering with champagne and a bubble bath. It was an exciting new feeling. She had never done that before. But she liked it, it looked good, a dark trimmed triangle below her flat tummy, narrowing down between her legs, catching fire as the embers pulsated their hot colors into the glistening mirror. Her hands swirled over her breasts. Slowly one hand slid from her breast and onto her stomach, reaching its slender fingers toward the dark triangle. Nails, freshly polished, inched their way into the short coarse hairs. Her hips began to sway. She widened her stance, spreading her legs for better balance against the dizzying emotions swelling inside her in the vortex of her new triangle. A finger slid into the wetness and she gasped, catching her breath, hot and rising from her belly. Unable to take her eyes from the mirror she watched as another finger disappeared. Her breathing became heavy and punctuated with short gasps. Her knees weakened with a sense of vertigo and she took her hand off her breast and steadied it on the arm of the wing back chair. Her head was getting lighter, she watched as a dizzying white mist formed in the mirror before her. She slid onto the floor. She closed her eyes and turned her cheek to the floor, her hips rolling in a back and forth motion on the carpet - first in a slow controlled movement and then more wildly. Her body writhed unrestrained in a new sense of freedom, rising higher and higher into the burning heat of the moment. Her passions were swollen, captured inside of her, screaming to be released; and then, with the intensity of an explosion, they burst and bathed her in a sweet ecstasy.

* * *

Later, somewhere in the night, she awoke cold. She turned the blaring radio off, put more logs on the fire. Wrapped cozy in a soft comforter before the fireplace, she fell back to sleep.

# 10

## *WHERE THERE'S SMOKE ...*

In the early morning, in that early waking half-sleep, Dodge heard the storm returning. The wind was howling and making the tree branches scratch along the rooftop and against the side of the cottage. His eyes opened slowly and found their way to the skylight. For a moment he was disoriented as his focus brought in the pre-dawn twilight. He wasn't sure if he was in New York or Paris or somewhere else. Then the howling returned, and with it his consciousness. In an instant the happenings of the past couple days flooded over him and he knew where he was. He was in the sleeping loft in the cottage on Lake Wickaboag. He sat up, rubbed his face, stretched out his arms, and yawned. Below, the scratching took up again and then the howling. Dodge slid down to the end of the bed. He swung his feet onto the floor and sat a moment waking up. From the position he was in, he could just see through the top of the French doors, out to the deck and to the lake, also awakening in the soft morning glow. Again the howling, and then the scratching, but it was at the French doors this time. He leaned forward so he could see over the edge of the loft, and that's when he recognized the originator of the storm sounds.

"Hey! Willie!"

Another howl, and then scratching at the door. Willie was a cocker spaniel. He lived up on Wickaboag Valley Road with the Warrens. He liked to make his rounds first thing in the morning when his mistress let him out. Apparently Camp Nyla was on his route.

Dodge descended the loft ladder and opened the sliders. "You old dog, you. How are ya?" He bent down to give him a pat, but Willie brushed right past him. He hadn't been in here for a while, and he had a lot of sniffing to catch up on. Dodge Maddison stepped onto the deck and stood a moment breathing in the fresh new air.

There was a heavy mist on the lake obscuring the view to the western shore. Some invisible ducks were cackling in the distance. The sky was opening up behind him and it looked to be the beginnings of a nice day. *A little nippy though*, he thought, and turned back inside.

Willie had his nose stuck deeply into the crevice between the refrigerator and the wall, his tail was wagging furiously.

"What'dya got there, boy?"

Dodge peeked in and saw a deserted pile of split-open acorn shells. He bent down and scratched the dog's fanny. This got his attention, and Willie sat back on his butt and barked. He wanted a treat. Dodge rummaged through the cabinets but the only thing he could find was the mess his furry houseguest had left from the night before.

"Sorry, pal, there doesn't seem to be anything here for you."

As if he understood, Willie shuffled to the door and waited to be put out. That done, Maddison thought about making a fire to take the chill out, but then remembered the wine.

"Oh yeah," he said out loud, remembering what he had planned to do.

Gramma Emma had had a ritual she performed religiously for as long as Dodge could remember. Each morning she toasted in the day at sunrise with a glass of white wine. And each evening, she toasted sunset with a glass of red. That was it, two glasses of wine per day, each day, for as long as he'd known her.

In her honor, her grandson would toast the sunrise this morning, but he wanted it to be more symbolic. He wanted to row out to the center of the lake to do it, and then, with a small prayer, to toss the bottle of wine overboard.

He dressed and went outside to retrieve the faded wooden rowboat. It was on the side of the shed, perched upside down atop a pair of sawhorses. He righted it and dragged it down the bank to the shoreline, grabbed the oars from the shed, and went back inside to get the wine. Thinking about the chill, he grabbed a blanket to take with.

\* \* \*

Dodge rowed into the mist toward the hidden western side of Lake Wickaboag. When he figured he was about in the middle, he stopped rowing, pulled the oars inside, retrieved a corkscrew from his jacket pocket, and started opening the wine. *Shit!* He had forgotten a wineglass. But he made the toast anyway, and sat in the bottom of the boat at the stern and sipped from the bottle as the boat slowly turned with a mild wind skimming the water from the south.

The sun was creeping up, brightening the sky with bright pastel colors and burning off the night mist with its soft radiant heat. Casually he watched the day begin and the mist slowly dissipate. He noticed that the mist lightened before it lifted, becoming like a long piece of sheer fabric waving seductive glimpses of the distant shoreline. Most of it lightened anyway, except for a section near the point, which stubbornly remained a dark charcoal in the midst of the paling gray.

His focus was riveted on that patch of gray. It seemed to be out of place, not playing by the rules of the early day. Actually, it seemed to be getting darker, and as the mist faded, it appeared to be more of a cloud sitting on the shoreline and wafting stream-like upward into the horizon. Curious, he picked up the oars and rowed closer, keeping an eye over his shoulder as he went.

There was a log cabin sitting on the shore. Thick black smoke was gushing from the edges of the closed door and the closed windows. A huge black plume rested on top of the roof and seemed to spiral off one end into the skyline. There was a car parked on the side.

Dodge mustered all his strength and rowed hurriedly to the shore. The boat slammed onto the beach and he jumped over the bow and sprinted onto the porch. He yanked open the screen door and pulled on the front door handle. It was locked. Without a second thought, he backed up and kicked the door in. He was almost knocked over by a huge gush of thick smoke barging out of the confines of the cabin. Crooking his arm and coughing into his jacket, he plowed into the room screaming out to the inhabitants. He could hardly breathe. Quickly he opened the two front windows wide. No one was responding to his calls and he turned to move further in and tripped over something lying on the floor in front of the fireplace. As he bent down he caught a glimpse of embers burning in the fireplace and thick smoke curling upward over the mantel. There was a woman lying naked on the floor. Dodge scooped her up and carried her outside to the lawn. She wasn't breathing. Instinctively he began CPR, although he wasn't exactly sure how to do it. He pinched her nose, cupped his mouth over hers and blew deeply. He repeated the procedure three or four times. Running on adrenaline, his heart pumping wildly, he tried it again, wondering if there was anyone else in the cabin. One more time and then he'd have to leave her and go back inside. There may be kids in there.

Miraculously she coughed and began to breathe. She started coughing violently. Dodge screamed to her, "Is there anyone else inside?" She couldn't answer.

He raced back into the smoke. Luckily it was clearing out and he could see a lot better. The cabin was very small; just the front room where the fireplace was, a back bedroom, kitchen, and a bathroom. No upstairs. There was only her. He opened the back door, poured water from the sink into a large pan, and snuffed out the embers. He kicked the spent logs with his foot to make sure they were dead.

Outside he heard sirens approaching. The woman was sitting up with her arms clasped around her knees still coughing. Dodge ran to his rowboat to retrieve the blanket, and brought it to her and wrapped it around her. She tried to speak, but the coughing wouldn't subside.

The fire chief's red pick-up flew into the yard followed closely by the rescue van and a fire truck behind that. A neighbor had seen the smoke and dialed 911.

"Are you alright?" he hollered and Dodge nodded his head yes. The fire chief gestured to the rescue van and then ran into the cabin.

Immediately, with the practiced skill and commitment of Bryce Corner's volunteer fire department, the scene took on a professional atmosphere. Like clockwork the rescue squad descended onto the lawn and surrounded the woman in the blanket and administered oxygen. Hoses were rapidly rolled from the fire truck and a team of Firemen rushed into the cabin. Within minutes twenty or thirty professionals had responded and were busy going about their prescribed tasks insuring an expeditious and safe resolve to the emergency.

As it turned out, the fire hoses weren't needed. "There wasn't any fire damage," the Chief was explaining to Dodge as they stood off to the side, "Just a helluva lot of smoke. The flue was closed. Looks like it's faulty. Musta fallen shut sometime during the night. She musta had a fire goin' when she fell asleep. Looks like she got some wet wood mixed in there with the dry, either by mistake, or she don't know how to make a proper fire. At any rate, it probably burned half-decent 'til the flue shut. With that wet wood, it smoldered slow and long, just enough not to wake you, but just enough to slowly fill up your lungs with the smoke. Most fire deaths are from smoke inhalation, y'know."

They moved out of the way of the rescue van as it backed off the lawn to take its occupant to the hospital.

"Damn good thing you got here when you did, or she'd a been dead by the time we arrived. You saved her life, Dodge."

"You think she'll be okay?"

"Yeah, she'll be fine. Her color's returning - she's got plenty of oxygen back into her now."

A small group had gathered around them.

"We're just about done here, Chief," one of the firemen was saying, "We've got everything opened up and we put a couple fans in place to cross-vent, one at the back and one to the front."

"Good. Leave 'em going, I'll come back later to check on 'em."

"Hey! Everyone!" the fireman shouted to get his crew's attention. "Great job!" he applauded them.

"And special thanks to this guy, I hear," Chief Ben Benson had come up behind them and put his hand on Dodge's shoulder. "You know, Maddison, you're back in town not even a whole day and you're already causin' a stir," Ben teased. "You okay?" he added seriously.

"Yeah, I'm fine. Who is she?"

Big Ben flipped open a small notepad he was holding in his hand, "Annison Barrett, lives down in Connecticut. According to the next door neighbor she's a friend of the owner, a Nina Sanderson from New York City. She's been stayin' here by herself for a week or so." He closed the pad, "That's all I know about her."

A small group of the volunteers had circled around them, and one of them said, "I've seen her in town a couple times, and she's a real looker!"

"I guess Dodge got the best look at her," another one said and they all grunted in agreement.

"I was so panicked, I didn't have a chance to really notice her," Dodge said.

"Probably the first naked woman you never noticed," the firemen laughed.

"Man, I wish I had found her," the first one said.

"Hell, Chucky, you wouldn't know what to do with her anyways!" They laughed some more and then dispersed to return to their real life jobs.

"Well, we're done here," the fire chief said, "see you guys later."

"Dodge," Big Ben asked, "how'd you get to be over here in all this?"

Maddison told him the story.

"Okay, well, I'm gonna head back to the station and fill out my report. Want a lift?"

"No thanks, and Bennie, I'd appreciate it if you'd exclude my name from your report." The police chief's eyebrows asked why. "I'd rather not have the media get ahold of it, they'll make a big thing out of it, and I've got enough going on with the funeral and all. Be nice to have a little peace and quiet in my life, you know?"

"Okay. I'll put you in as an 'anonymous neighbor'."

"Thanks."

"Need the ride?"

"No, I'll row back."

"Looks like a nice day. 'Spose to get back up into the 70's again. What'dya gonna do today?"

"I'm going to open up the cottage and clean it up. Think I'll stay there for a few days. I've got to contact the water department and have them come down to turn the water back on."

"Don't bother, I'll stop by on my way back and let Ronnie know. I'll see if he can get to it this morning." The chief returned to his cruiser.

* * *

Dodge walked down the lawn, a wide green carpet sloping to the water. It felt longer than it had an hour ago. There were maple leaves strewn about, the colorful early ones of foliage, dropped off by the storm last night. They looked like little drops of paint - yellow and orange and red, lying on a blanket of forest green. As he rowed away, the log cabin, quiet and alone once again, seemed to be watching him making his way back across the lake, toward home.

# 11

## *ANNISON*

The Inn at Barrett's Bluff was built on the cliffs of the Connecticut coastline in the late 1700's by a seafaring gent named Captain Jonathan Barrett. It has remained intact and prosperous, passing from generation to generation, for the past two hundred plus years. It sits large and picturesque in its venerable grandeur on a meticulously manicured landscape. Save for necessary delivery vehicles, there are no cars or trucks allowed on property. Guests are coached to the Inn by horse drawn carriages from an offsite parking lot a mile away. To further authenticity, the cherished décor is steadfastly preserved, and the staff dresses in appropriate period costume. The Inn, an extremely healthy enterprise, offers a real eighteenth century experience, and is very popular and very busy year-round with dining, lodging, banquets, functions, and elaborate weddings.

Annison got involved with The Inn at Barrett's Bluff the night of her senior prom. She had been dating the handsome, popular, and notoriously promiscuous Jack Barrett. On that special night, they had been voted king and queen of the prom. Afterwards, in the exhilaration of that honor, mixed with the fun of the evening, the thrill of escaping high school, and the euphoria found in three quarters of a bottle of Jack Daniel's, they secretively made their way into the honeymoon suite back at the Inn, and let their passions run wild. Usually careful when they had sex, Annison chastised herself six weeks later for carrying that cute little black pocketbook with the long thin shoulder strap to the prom. It was too small to hold her diaphragm.

The escapades of the heir apparent Jack were well known by his parents, and in an attempt to bring seriousness and righteousness into his life, the pressure of responsibility was administered, and a formal marriage ensued. Jack's father held no regard for college, feeling it a waste of time and money. His son already had a vocation awaiting him as Innkeeper of the Inn at Barrett's Bluff - the sooner he got into the trenches the better. The elder Barrett would, as his father had done to him, stand over Jack like a Drill Sergeant, determined to shape up his wayward son and make a presentable businessman out of him. Besides, Annison was a lovely girl and would make a wonderful mother to their grandchildren.

Jack went along with the marriage, but resented the heavy-handed intentions of his father. Jack had worked at the Inn, pot-washing, busing tables, food-prep, you name it, since he was old enough to remember, and had wanted to get away from it all soon after high school. With parenthood, he saw his rebellious dream fading away and got even lazier, shrugging off whatever business ambitions his father had, and became devilishly comfortable in playing his self-proclaimed role of Prince Barrett. It was no surprise to anyone that Jack didn't change his ways.

The real surprise in all this was Annison. Not only did she become a great mother to the next generation, (first Jason Joseph, and then two years later, Sarah Marie), but she also dove headfirst into the busy day-to-day workings of the business. Over the years, by her hands-on approach to all aspects of the business, from waitressing, function coordination, sales and marketing, etc., she exuded a sincere sense of commitment and leadership, and gained the respect and admiration of both staff and management. When the time came for the elder Barrett's to retire, and for Jack to take the reigns as Innkeeper, it was well known by all concerned, that, although her husband held the title, it was Annison who held The Inn at Barrett's Bluff together.

* * *

The years rolled along. Annison tended the business and raised the kids while Jack did his own thing. The marriage slowly settled into what it began as, a marriage of convenience. Both children worked at the Inn as they grew up, as all of their ancestors had done, but when he came of age, JJ enlisted in the Air Force, became a pilot, and made it his career. Annison's daughter, Sarah, graduated from college with a degree in Political Science and accepted a position with a D.C. law firm where she could be closer to her dentist fiancée. Shortly afterward they had a fabulous spring wedding at the Inn, honeymooned in Europe, and returned to set up life in their new condo in Chevy Chase.

Even though her children were now essentially out of the Inn's picture, life moved on. Annison, with overseeing a ten member sales and management team and a staff of over a hundred (in addition to her various community endeavors), was never for want of things to keep her busy and occupied.

It hit her one morning as she sat at her vanity applying her make-up. She was lonely. This was the hard truth staring at her from behind those blank eyes in the mirror. With all the activity in her life, she felt alone and unfulfilled.

* * *

They were dining alfresco at one of the sidewalk tables outside GreenTrees on Christopher, Nina's favorite restaurant, located just a block away from her brownstone in Greenwich Village. It was a perfect August afternoon in New York City. Temperatures were comfortable at eighty degrees, no wind, and no humidity, sunny and pleasant. Colorful collections of summer fashions were passing by them on the brisk sidewalk.

"I don't know what I'm doing anymore," Annison was saying to her best friend, "I mean, I just sat there looking into the mirror and saying to myself, *What are you doing Annison? ... What are you doing Annison?*"

"Well sweetie, I think you've been doing *too* much for *too* long," Nina replied, "and I think it's high time you did something about it."

Nina Sanderson and Annison Barrett had grown up together in lower Connecticut, attended the same schools together, got into and out of trouble together, and were virtually inseparable until after high school, when Annison went into marriage and Nina went off to New York City to attend Business College.

Nina fell in love with The City. She found it exciting and cultural, more conducive to her lifestyle. She stayed on, acquiring her MBA from Columbia University, putting in her time at a leading realtor's office, getting her broker's license, and eventually branching off and setting up her own lucrative business, *Nina Sanderson Realty Specialists*. She was happy, well-established, and successful, having recently been featured in *New York Magazine* as one of the city's top ten *Women in Business*. She was used to, and good at, giving sound advice.

"You need to stand in front of that mirror a little more often, honey," she was saying, "you need to stop thinking about everyone else and start thinking about yourself."

Annison could sense that Nina was striking a chord close to home. She sat quietly letting the tone of their conversation sink in.

She knew she was depressed, ever since her daughter's wedding. No, before then. Way before then if she was honest with herself. The wedding had just been a diversion, something to focus on so that she'd trick herself into thinking she was okay, when she really wasn't. Now, with both children gone, she felt alone and empty. Annison could no longer hide her unhappiness in the therapy of being busy running the Inn.

"Mmmm, Sunshine Salad," Nina was reading from the menu, "Avocado, Orange, Fresh Corn, Red and Yellow Peppers, Sun-Dried Tomato, Red Onion, Glazed Walnuts, and Mixed Baby Lettuce all Tossed in a Shallot Vinaigrette ... sounds delicious! That's what I'm having," Nina closed the menu and picked up her iced tea, "What are you having, dear?"

"A nervous breakdown, but I can't seem to find it on the menu."

"Now that's the first humorous thing you've said since you got here last night."

The waiter arrived to take their order. Nina gave him hers. Annison decided on a Caesar Salad, which Nina called boring, and immediately ordered an appetizer for the two of them to split – Mini Crabcakes served with Remoulade Sauce.

The waiter took their menus and said he'd be back in a minute with their appetizer.

"My God, Annie, live a little! Caesar salad! When did you become so traditional?"

"Somewhere between motherhood and token wife and daughter-in-law, I think."

"There you go, getting melancholy on me again."

"I'm sorry, Nina," tears were welling up in Annison's eyes, "I just don't know who I am anymore." She lifted her pocketbook and began fumbling for a Kleenex. "I mean, look at you, you've done so much with your life – you moved to the city, you became successful, you're living the life-style you want to live ..."

Nina leaned forward and dabbed Annison's eyes with her napkin before the tears could do any damage to her makeup.

"Don't sell yourself short, honey, you're a special lady. You've got a lot going for you. You've been very successful yourself, don't forget. You put your blood, sweat, and tears into Barrett's Bluff. Without you that place would have crumbled years ago."

"Well it certainly hasn't been easy, and I fear it's taken its toll on me."

"Bullshit." Nina said. "You're still very attractive, still got one helluva body, you're intelligent and charming, a great mother, an admired and respected hard-working businesswoman, and *my* best friend … that's got to account for something hasn't it?"

This got a smile from Annison, "Yes it does," she took Nina's hand, "it accounts for a lot. I honestly don't know what I'd do without you. I love you for all that you are to me. You're always there when I need you."

"That's what friendship's all about," Nina said, "and you need me now, don't you?"

"Yes, probably more so than ever. I feel like I'm at a turning point or a breaking point, or something. I just don't know what I'm doing anymore, or why I'm doing it. Sometimes I feel like I'm not doing anything at all but just running in circles. I'm so confused."

"Well I knew something was up, you've been acting so different lately. At first I thought it was the pressure of Sarah's wedding, but then you seemed to get weirder after that, like more distant. Do you realize that this is the third time you've shown up on my doorstep since the wedding, and that was only three months ago?"

"I think it's all finally hitting me that they're both gone from Barrett's Bluff," Annison said, thinking of her children.

"I'm glad you're talking about it. It's good to let things out. You've always been too stubborn and closed about your feelings."

"I know, I know. And I guess that's why I'm here. You're the only one I can really talk to."

"Here we are ladies," the waiter said, placing their app in the center of the small table, "Crabcakes ala Remoulade. Enjoy!"

"Thank you."

Annison busied herself serving the tiny cakes onto the separate side plates the waiter had placed in front of them. Nina sat observing her and thought fondly of her friend. It hurt her to see her so unhappy. Her heart went out to Annison.

Nina tasted one of the little cakes, "Mmm, yummie! These are great."

Annison was staring at a point in the center of the table, her thoughts a million miles away.

Nina heard a ka-clop, ka-clop, ka-clop, coming from behind her. She turned just as a mounted policeman strode by on his huge horse. It was a beautiful Belgian mare. Sixteen hands high. She had a sheen on her dark coat glistening in the midday heat. The horse looked strong and powerful. You could see the outlines of the muscles on the body, and the legs looked long and fast. The NYPD insignia was embroidered gold onto a deep blue blanket sitting underneath the saddle.

"What a beautiful horse," Nina said.

Annison was oblivious.

The officer rode up close to the sidewalk beneath the tree shade, dismounted, and walked into a small open doorway at the back of the restaurant that entered into the kitchen. A minute later he emerged with a can of diet coke in his hands. Bernardo, the owner, dressed in his whites, was with him. He was carrying a white bucket. Nina watched them go over to the mare. Bernardo held the bucket in the crook of his left arm and let the horse drink from it. He stroked the mare's neck and patted it affectionately. When the horse lifted her head, Bernardo placed the white bucket onto the curb. The two men stood talking. Nina could hear their muffled conversation, punctuated every so often with laughter. The horse turned her head, slowly and elegantly, peering at the patrons seated along the sidewalk in the shade of the trees lining the curbside. Her big dark eyes stopped awhile at Nina and made her smile. Then, remembering her drink, the mare stretched her neck, long and shiny, down toward the white bucket of cool water.

"I feel like I've spent my whole life as a glorified babysitter, holding onto everybody's hand," Annison sat with her elbows propped on the table and her chin cupped in her hands, her crab cakes untouched before her.

"I mean, if it isn't Jack, it's the kids, or my freakin' overbearing in-laws, or the Inn ... oh my God ... I've got a hundred different people pulling me in a hundred different directions."

Annison sat back, slumped in her chair and looked Nina directly in the eye, "I can't take it anymore, I really can't."

"So don't."

"I'm tired of being responsible. I've been concentrating on too many people for too long, now I just want to concentrate on me, I just want to say to hell with it all, pack it up and head off to a deserted island somewhere."

"So, what's stopping you?"

Annison responded with a heavy sigh and lifted her shoulders as if to say *I don't know.*

"I mean it's not like I have to worry about the kids anymore," she said, "they're on their own now, away from Barrett's Bluff ... but the Inn ... I don't know how Jack would get on without me."

"Jack.? Fuck Jack!" He wasn't one of Nina's favorites. "What has he ever done for you? Except chase young waitresses and dole out perpetual heartache."

"I know, I know, but ..."

"The only good thing he's ever done for you was father those two wonderful kids – other than that, he's a shit." Nina reached for her iced tea glass and raised it towards her lips, but before it got there she added, "All men are shits. Once a shit, always a shit." and finally took a sip. "Thank God I'm a Lesbian."

"Well, at least I haven't had to worry about Jack chasing after you," Annison responded.

"I may be the *only* one of your friends he hasn't tried to bed."

"Listen," Nina leaned forward dabbing her lips carefully before placing her napkin back onto her lap, "I've got a great idea. Why don't you pack-up some things and move in with me for a while? It might be good to get away from things for a while, and the City would do you good."

"Oh, I don't know, Nina, I ..."

"No really. There's plenty of space, now that Carolyn has moved on, and I'd love the company. We could go out every night and raise hell, just like the old days."

"God, Nina, I've been so selfish throwing my problems all over you, I haven't even expressed how sorry I was to hear about you and Carolyn breaking up."

"Hey, relationships are tough, gay or straight."

"I'm sorry, Nina, you seemed so happy."

"We were happy. We had a good long-lasting relationship, the break-up was amicable, and we'll remain friends."

Annison gave her a small pout.

"Really. Don't worry about me, I'm fine. Life moves on and people change. I'm happy in Manhattan and she'll be happy in P-Town," Nina paused, "it's you we've got to find happiness for."

The waiter delivered their salads. Annison still hadn't touched the crab cakes, but said she would. He situated there plates before them, cleared Nina's appetizer plate and set down her Sunshine Salad, (which did look delicious), freshened their iced teas and turned to take an order from the table next them.

The police horse shook her head and whinnied. She was becoming impatient. Her hoof tapped at the ground.

The ladies found themselves famished and ate in silence. The food was good, the day was clear, even the NYC air seemed fresh and palatable.

Annison said, "I'm not sure I'd know what to do with myself. I've always had the Inn and the kids and, for better or for worse, Jack."

"He's a bastard, Annie, a charming one I will admit, but still a bastard. I honestly don't know how you've put up with him for so long."

"Old habits are hard to break, I guess."

Nina realized they'd had this conversation before – more than once. Annison would take Jack's indiscretions for only so long, they'd have a blow-out, she'd threaten to leave him, he'd cow-tow and make all the promises, and she'd always take him back. Remorse, pity, insecurity, stupidity, or a combination of all of the above, but she'd always give in and stick her head deeper into the sand by diving further into the business, determined to keep her world whole and organized and perfect (from the outside anyway) and he'd always return to his old ways. It truly was a marriage of convenience, Jack's convenience. *Maybe it's different now that the kids are out of the nest,* she thought.

"I don't know," Annison was saying quietly, "maybe I'm still in love with the bastard."

"Oh Christ, Annie! That's because you don't know any better. Who else have you ever been with? Since the prom, your whole life has been wrapped up in Jack and the kids and the Barrett's and the Inn. You need to live a little."

"I've been with other men."

"Who?"

"There's been others."

"Who? Who have you slept with besides Jack?"

"Well, I didn't say that, I just said there's been others."

"Yeah, in your dreams, maybe. Hell Annie, I've had sex with more men than you have."

"What?"

"You don't think I've been gay all my life, do you? I've tried men, I just happen to not enjoy them."

"Well, I've been close, that's all I'm trying to say. There has been an occasion or two over the years."

"Did you do anything?" Nina was surprised and curious.

Annison sort of snickered, "I wanted to all right ..."

"Annnd ..."

"And nothing. Guess one of us had to believe in fidelity."

Nina frowned.

"Annison," Nina said with her serious voice, "you're my best friend and I love you to death."

"Oh oh, here it comes."

"So I'm going to tell you how I see it. I mean, that's why you're here, right? No one knows you better than I do, so listen to me. You've spent your whole life satisfying others; from your children to your in-laws to your worthless husband. And you've been more than what they all could have possibly hoped for. But somewhere in there, you lost touch with Annison. It's high time you did something for yourself."

Annison was attentive. She knew Nina would tell it to her as she needed to hear it. They were both businesswomen and knew how to cut to the chase. Neither one was afraid to speak her mind. They loved and respected each other for this.

"Now, given my sexual preferences, I may not be the best qualified to offer an opinion on men, but, I am certainly qualified to give you my opinion on being a woman, having pride in yourself, and being brave enough to take the chance you need to be who you are, to be a woman, and to get back in touch with yourself."

"I'm listening," Annison smiled, "go on, Doctor Sanderson."

"I'm serious. You need to get away from it all. You can't keep running down here every month to shake off your self-pity and perform some sort of emotional exorcism - or whatever it is you do during these visits – and then go back into it and start all over again. Face it. You've got a big problem. You're wallowing in self-doubt, you're admittedly on the verge of a nervous breakdown, but most detrimental of all, you're not happy." Nina paused, "And that's what we need to focus on first.

"So, I've got a better idea," she continued, "forget about Manhattan, you're not ready for Manhattan. You need to take some solo time for yourself. Away from Barrett's Bluff and the Inn and the hundreds of people pulling at you in a hundred different directions. Time to be alone, to get back to being Annison again. I think you've lost her, honey, and it's time to go find her, and I've got the perfect spot."

"You do, do you?"

"Yes, I do. I think you need to spend some time alone where you can catch your breath and re-group. Some quiet time, for reflection and rebuilding your lost esteem. Why don't you take a sabbatical and move into my cottage on the lake in Massachusetts?"

Annison laughed out loud.

"What's so funny?"

"You're not going to believe this, but I've actually been thinking about that."

"Well it's perfect then. It's open and available. I think I've only gone up there two or three times this season. You know the place, and you'd feel comfortable there. You always enjoy it when you're there. You could take all the time you need. It's perfect for what you need now, which is a little R and R and R."

"RRR?"

"Rest, Relaxation, and Restoration."

"Sounds like a seminar."

"It should be. A seminar for one. That's what you need."

"Don't you think that's being a little too selfish?"

"No. Selfish is good. You need to be selfish, or ..."

"Or what?" Annison asked.

"Or, I'm afraid you're going to lose it, babe."

Annison knew she was right. She had the same fear. It was time to do something for herself. She needed to be brave and make a commitment. She was glad she came to see Nina, she had had a feeling she'd give her the push she needed.

They enjoyed the rest of their brunch at GreenTrees, finalizing things for what Nina was already calling "Annison's Retreat", and turning their conversation to a lighter topic as Nina excitedly revealed her plans for a complete makeover of her brownstone. "It's time to freshen-up," she said.

The mare sauntered past them, carrying her uniformed rider. Her hoofs were loud on the pavement, and broke into their conversation.

"Oh look, Nina," Annison pointed, "what a beautiful horse."

Nina smiled to herself and thought, *Gotta love this girl!*

# 12

## OPENING UP

Dodge spent the day opening up the cottage. It turned out to be a beauty. Bright and sunny, seventy-five degrees with just enough hint of a wind to make it pleasant. He opened all the windows, the French doors on the lakeside, and held the back door open with the small little boat anchor that had always been there for just that purpose.

He cleaned the entire inside, even washing the floors and doing the windows. He used the shop-vac to eliminate the mouse droppings in the cupboards and under the kitchen sink, and spent a good hour on the bathroom.

Outside, in his t-shirt and shorts, he mowed the lawn and trimmed with the weed-whacker. It felt good to sweat a little. He hadn't done any outside work in a long time; he found he was actually enjoying it.

Ronnie from the water department had come by to turn the water on. He flipped open a small cast iron cover sitting on the ground near the corner of the cottage and used a long T-shaped tool to access the underground valve located down beneath the frost line.

Ben stopped by around noontime carrying a lunch bag from Carlene and a tall cold beer. He sat on the deck talking away while Dodge ate, and then had to leave abruptly when he got a radio call from the cruiser.

In the afternoon, Dodge ventured into town to the hardware store to get a new hinge to replace the broken one on one of the window shutters, then over to the Corner General Store to stock up on food and supplies. He stopped by the Maddison farmhouse only long enough to grab a few tools from Grampa Jed's barn and then took the long way back around the lake to open up the coupe a little.

There's a smooth flat stretch along the valley road where he stretched through the gears, quickly getting her up to a high speed. He knew he was going too fast, but it felt good to be dangerous for a moment. He started tapping the brakes as he entered into the curve bending around McGreevy's farm, but was going too fast. The coupe strayed over the centerline and Dodge downshifted to third trying to bring her under control. *Expect the unexpected*, Jed had always told him about driving, and these words were actually going through his head as he caught his first glimpse of one of McGreevy's bulls standing dead-on-center in the bend of the road.

In that awful heart-stopping split second everyone's probably had an experience with, Dodge wrestled with panic and control, and frantically spun the steering wheel to avoid hitting the bull head-on. The coupe spun off the road and into McGreevy's cornfield sideways. The earth was still moist from last night's storm, and he stayed on the gas, downshifting to second, spinning back around through the cornstalks and back onto the edge of the road. He stopped, trying to catch his breath. The bull was standing still, in the same spot; he hadn't even turned around. Dodge looked in his rearview mirror and saw the damage he had done to the cornfield. His dormant teen-age responses kicked in; he put the coupe into first gear, and quickly sped off down the road, hoping old man McGreevy hadn't witnessed the destruction.

A couple miles later, as he pulled into the safety of his obscure little dirt road, he was feeling rather foolish, but had to admit, the whole experience was actually exhilarating. He felt great.

After putting the groceries away, he spent the balance of the afternoon putting the two short sections of dock into the water and securing the rowboat to it. He puttered around the cottage some more, washed the muddied coupe (cornhusks and all), and then grabbed a cold beer. He dragged an Adirondack chair from the deck out into a shady spot on the lawn and sat perusing his handiwork. He had to admit it was beautiful here. Peaceful. The lake was quiet, no boaters, no jet-skis. There was no one around. Only a statuesque great blue heron standing on the shoreline. Dodge sat there letting his mind go blank. A nearby mockingbird was entertaining him with its never-ending repertoire of songs, one right after the other, soft and soothing in the late afternoon air. The shade was cool and soothing, and the old weathered chair was worn and comfortable. His eyelids became heavy, and a moment later he was asleep.

He awoke near sunset and walked into the cottage. Looking at the clock, he was amazed, *must have dozed more than an hour, time for a quick shower.*

A few minutes later, refreshed, (and for some reason he couldn't quite pinpoint, feeling exceptionally good about himself), Dodge grabbed the bottle of red wine he had brought the night before (and a glass this time) and walked down to the dock. He wedged the red wine bottle into a life preserver at the bow next to the empty bottle of white, spilled during the commotion from earlier that morning. He situated the oars, unwound the rope from the cleats on the dock platform, and pushed away.

"Hey sailor! Where you shovin' off to?"

It was Harlow.

"Hey ... hi! What are you doing here?"

"Coming to get you." She made her way down the stairs and onto the dock carefully, minding that her heels avoided the spaces between the decking - she still had her New York clothes on.

"I've been sitting with Carlene for a couple hours, gabbin'," she said, "and seeing as how you don't have a phone down here, I decided to drive over and steal you for dinner. Carlene's got a casserole in the oven."

"You should have tried the cell phone."

"I would have if you hadn't left it back in the studio, remember? You wanted to be inaccessible?"

"Oh yeah ... and you know what, I think I'm starting to like that. Climb aboard," he offered his hand.

"Where you going?"

"Going to row out to sunset."

"Sunset?"

"Yeah, it's going to be a beauty, hurry up we don't have much time."

Harlow clutched his hand and started to lift her leg into the boat.

"Whoa! Wait a minute," he grabbed her foot and pushed it back onto the dock, "before you jump in, run back up to the cottage and get another wineglass from the kitchen cupboard, would you?"

"Sure, just one?"

"Yes, it's for you, I've already got one."

Dodge held onto the dock and a minute later, Harlow came running down the steps in her stocking feet, a wineglass in her hand, her heels in the cottage on the kitchen floor.

She sat on one of the boat pillows at the stern as Dodge rowed.

"I wasn't sure if you were coming or not," he said.

"Dodge, you knew I would. I'm not going to let you go through this alone, you need someone by your side tomorrow. I'm sure it won't be easy for you," she said, referencing the funeral.

He didn't answer, so she continued, "So, I went into the office this morning for a few hours, and then drove up this afternoon."

"How is everything?" he asked.

"Fine, just fine. You've got a million messages, and everyone wanted to come up, but I stressed how private you wanted the service, so they all send their love and condolences and hope you'll be back soon.

"And Dana! Oh my God, she's called a thousand times. She's actually called while she's been prancing down a runway. She's frantic, doesn't understand why you haven't called her. I've tried to explain to her what you're going through and how you're trying to handle it, but she thinks I'm intentionally keeping the two of you apart."

"Well, there's never been any love lost between the two of you," Dodge snickered.

"What? I love that little twit! Must be nice to be twenty and the world's most famous model hooked up with the world's most famous designer."

"Now, Harlow."

"I know, I'm being cynical. I'm sure she's sweet, but she's so clueless. She thinks the world is just one huge mall to play in."

"She's young."

"You should think about that, Mr. Maddison," she raised her eyebrows and gave a smirk.

"Alright, alright. Let's close that topic. I'll deal with her."

"You'd better, because she's threatening to drop her schedule and come find you."

"No. I don't want her here. That would cause too much commotion. I'll call her tomorrow after the service," he said, and continued his rowing.

Dodge rowed smoothly and steadily, the oars rhythmically creaking in the oarlocks, and making small swirling circles upon the glassy waters of the lake. Harlow, sitting comfortably in the stern with the dusking twilight colors a pink and lavender backdrop behind her, synopsized the business news and events since the successful Paris premiere just a few days ago. Orders were rolling in faster than they could handle them. *She looked fresh and radiant with the soft sunset washing onto her face.* The piece goods were already being dyed. *Her lips curved upward when she talked, with her ever-present smile.* Production on the dresses would start first, followed closely thereafter with the separates line. *The gold necklace Dodge had given her (on her birthday? No, a valentine's day, or was it one Christmas? and how long ago was that?) hung provocatively in her cleavage, tanned and glistening in the sunset.*

"I've got the girls scheduled to work this weekend," she was saying, "I think we'll be sold out by Monday, if we aren't already. It's the best line ever, Dodge," Harlow leaned forward and jubilantly squeezed both his knees.

*She's always so positive and upbeat, what a great lady she is.* He was finding the tone of her voice pleasant and soothing.

At the middle of the lake he pulled in the oars and went about opening the bottle of red wine. As he poured her glass, he told Harlow about Gramma Emma's sunrise/sunset ritual. They toasted Emma and Jed and sat in the tiny boat watching the sunset, enjoying the wine, simple conversation, and each other's company. They had always worked well together, and over the years had come to know each other's little quirks and nuances, and had become comfortably close in their platonic relationship. He was glad she had driven up, and quietly admitted to himself, glad that she was sitting in the boat with him. *How can she sit there all dressed up and look so much at ease? So striking?* An impromptu swirl of wind brushed her hair from behind. She tossed her head gently and combed it back with her fingers tousling the light auburn strands in the gentle colors of the sunset. *Has her hair gotten longer?*

"Is that it over there?" Harlow pointed to the log cabin sitting small on the darkening west shoreline. Dodge had told her about his morning adventure.

"Yes."

"Seems like someone's in there, there's a light on."

He saw the amber light coming through the windowpanes and faintly wading into the darkening lake. The memory of the early morning incident played quickly behind his eyes and then caught the present. He gazed at the small cottage and felt a kind of communion. He was happy it had turned out all right. *I hope she's okay.*

"Hey," Dodge said, "let's go out to dinner. Have you ever been to the restaurant at The Salem Cross Inn?"

"I don't think ..."

"Great food, great ambience, I'd love to take you there."

"But what about Carlene and Ben?"

"They'll be fine, knowing Ben, he's probably chowing down right now."

He returned the oars to the water and came about; pointing the bow towards the eastern shoreline. "Let's go out - just the two of us. We've both been through a hectic few days and deserve a break. Let's take the evening to chill out."

What does he mean by 'evening', she wondered, and then said aloud, "Well, from Paris to New York to Bryce Corner in two days is kind of culture shocking."

"Naw, it's kind of soothing, don't you think?"

She was actually thinking, *What's gotten into him?*

Dodge allowed the oars to lay steady in the water and poured the remaining few drops of wine into Harlow's glass and, grabbing the other empty bottle, gently slid both over the side.

"Sweet journey, Gram," he said in a tranquil tone.

He took up the rowing again with a new feeling over him. He smiled at Harlow and chatted actively all the way back; the two bottles bobbing together and quietly disappearing into the night.

\* \* \*

"Should I change?" they were back in the cottage.

"No, you're perfect. I'm the one who needs to change. Just give me two minutes," he went into the back bedroom.

"Okay then, I'll freshen up a bit." She took her pocketbook into the bathroom.

A short while later, they walked down to the cars. Harlow's was parked behind her boss'. "Want me to move it over?" she asked.

"Nope, we'll take yours." He opened the passenger door for her.

She placed her overnight bag and a floral tote into the back while he climbed into the driver's seat.

\* \* \*

Dinner was wonderful. Dodge had been right, Harlow loved the atmosphere; it was candlelit and quaint and very New Englandy. They sat in the rear corner of the main dining room opposite the open-hearth fireplace with the low fire. Beneath thick rough-hewn beams held together with age-old pegs, they nestled comfortably in twin high-back wing chairs at their table in front of the window overlooking the moonlit fields. But they were oblivious to the outside world. Seeing only what was directly in front of them. Each other.

"I'm glad you came," Dodge said.

Harlow moved the floral centerpiece to the side and reached for his hand. "Didn't you think I would?"

Of course he had. His look told her so. He let her pat the top of his hand in a comforting way. He was fiddling with a floral petal that had fallen from the small bouquet.

"I … you're the closest one to me now. You and Bennie and Carlene. Funny huh? A guy with so many people in his life and I've only got three people who are close to me."

"No, not funny, right. As long as they love you like *we* do." She took the flower petal from his fingers, turned his hand over and placed it into his palm. "Sometimes you only need *one*."

Her smile was captivating in the candle glow. The restaurant had emptied and the servers were quietly re-setting their stations for breakfast, being careful not to disturb them. They knew who the handsome guest with the pretty lady was.

It had been a long day for Dodge. A long couple of days. Too much had happened. Too quickly. He needed to forget for a while. It felt good sitting in the untroubled ambiance with Harlow. Different seeing her outside the hectic confines of the office. He refilled their wineglasses with a deep red Merlot and sat at ease letting the evening sink in, enjoying her company, listening to her soothing voice and childlike laughter as she carried on from topic to topic, keeping his mind away from his melancholy. Dodge had known Harlow for a decade. Spent almost all of his waking time with her. But tonight there was something different about her. He had noticed it in the rowboat earlier in the sunset. She seemed so … so much more …

"Would you like to take a look at our dessert menu?" their server said, extending two leather bound menus to them.

"Oh my God, no," Harlow said, "I'm full. Everything was delicious, thank you."

They passed on dessert and Harlow sat quietly finishing her wine while Dodge was figuring the tip and signing the receipt. She caught herself helplessly smiling at him, and in an instant, a swell of seductive thoughts rose uncontrollably from within her, rushing over her like an enormous impromptu wave at the seashore, taking her quickly by surprise and knocking her just as quickly off-balance.

*Oh my God*! She thought, *I've had way too much wine!*

"Ready?" he asked.

"YES," she responded too loudly, covering her mouth with an embarrassed hand. Then she rose too quickly from the table and felt the room wobble.

"You alright?" he asked reaching an arm out to steady her.

"Oh yeah, I'm fine and dandy," she giggled entwining her arm in his.

\* \* \*

They were the last to leave the restaurant and theirs was the only car in the parking lot. It had been fuller earlier when Harlow had parked off to the side near the rolling pastures surrounding the Inn. The night air was cool and refreshing, as they walked arm in arm together, the only sound, their footsteps upon the gravel way. Dodge inhaled deeply, to take in the scents of the evening but his nostrils filled instead with the perfume of the woman next to him. He lowered his head into the crook of her neck and said, "Mmmm." Harlow felt a stir and snuggled her head into his shoulder. Their pace, although slow, became slower, more intimate. Their bodies meshed side by side.

When they got to the car Harlow slid her pocketbook from her shoulder and fumbled for the keys. Dodge took her pocketbook out of her hands and placed it on the hood. He looked into her eyes and placed his hands on her hips, pushing her back onto the front fender and pressing the length of his body onto hers. She could feel his heat against her thigh. Harlow gasped. She felt lightheaded. She wanted to believe it was the wine but knew it was more than that.

He ran his fingers along the curve of her face, along the smooth angles of her neck. Harlow wanted to say something, needed to speak, but she was speechless, mesmerized by the hunger in his deep blue eyes.

Dodge was riddled with emotions. Too much had swept over him in such a short period of time. Paris, New York, home. Life, death, hurt. And now desire. Desire to feel needed, to feel loved, to give in to the unstoppable primal human emotions tugging at him, coaxing him to stay alive, to be alive. Harlow had come to be with him through this trying time. And she was there for him now.

Harlow could sense his need throbbing against her. It made her pulse quicken and her body shiver. She wanted him. She had always wanted him. But she remembered the silent vow they had made never to allow sex to jeopardize their working relationship. She breathed, "Dodge, we ..."

He pressed a finger to her lips and traced the outline of her mouth. Harlow closed her eyes savoring his electrifying touch. And when he tilted her head back she lingered in heated anticipation for his lips to claim hers. They kissed. Soft and dreamy at first ... and then harder as the rage swelled between them ... and then hungrily and careless.

Dodge was devouring her and Harlow was on fire. She felt her feet leave the ground and the cool of the hood against her back as she frantically pulled Dodge onto her. They were engulfed in the throes of ten years of pent-up passion. She felt him enter her and arched into the thickness of his lust, squeezing her thighs around him and clawing at the skin beneath his shirt.

Joined as one they moved heatedly and recklessly in wild abandon, oblivious to the world around them. And through the reeling rhythms of their passion an unrestrained ecstasy screamed across the dark parking lot and out into the fields of the moonlit night.

# 13

## SUNRISE SHADOWS

The colors were playing quietly in the treetops way off in the distance, in the dawn, out by the further edge of Jedediah's field. Old Percy sat rocking in his old chair on his old porch across the street watching them skimming the dark branches of the horizon, making way for the early sun to appear in the middle of their fun. A marmalade colored cat, not much more than a kitten, was purring and rubbing figure eight's around his legs. He didn't like cats, never had, too smelly. This one was kinda cute though.

"Whad'ya doin' little tiger? Hungry are ya?"

Old Percy leaned forward on the front edge of the rocker and bent over to scoop up the kitten. She came willingly onto his lap and sat content purring to the feel of his rough, weathered fingertips soothingly scratching her smooth underbelly. They rocked together watching the dawn, still far off across the street.

As the sun rose above the brightening treetops it stretched a ray of yellow gold, inching toward him and widening as it came across the field, dancing on the dew and making it sparkle as it came for him on the porch. It stopped a moment as it passed the barn and Percy rested his tired eyes on the barn and watched it lighten slowly and awaken in the nearing distance. The wide barn door swung open and Percy saw Jedediah standing there. He was holding the rope in his hands and the well-tied noose was heavy and hung down touching the ground. He let go of the rope and it fell in slow motion to the dirt, a small puff of dust rising from the dry earth at his feet. Jed took a step forward, stretching his figure, thin and long and dark, into the gravel way running between the barn and the house. Percy had to blink and rub his eyes before he realized it was only a shadow as the dawn crept slowly past the old barn, courteously closing the big door as it strolled by.

The old man and the kitten sat together, rocking, until the sunlight reached over the road and began illuminating the Van Ness' new mailbox, sitting atop the same old post Old Percy had set down how many years ago.

"Well little tiger, gotta be moseyin' along 'for your folks git up," he petted the kitten, still comfy in his lap.

Wrapping his big thin hands around her tiny ribcage, Percy carefully lifted the kitten up and over the wide armrest and placed her on the seat of the adjacent rocker.

"You sit here awhile with Jed and keep him cumpnee. I gotta go and git ready I guess."

He didn't look back to the porch nor across the street, as he gripped the handrail and descended the front steps. The next to the bottom one creaked beneath his feet.

"Gotta fix that one, one of these days Cora."

# 14
## DEARLY BELOVED...

The funeral service for Jedediah and Emma Maddison was held Friday morning at the First Congregational church on the common. It was the very church they were married in sixty years ago. The white steeple rose tall into the blue sky and held a shiny silver cross pointing to the heavens. Dodge remembered the teenage summer when he had helped his grandfather make repairs to it, climbing through the scaffolding like a gymnast and pulling their bucket of tools up with a rope passing through the block and tackle Gramp had rigged.

Dodge and Harlow got there early and to their chagrin found the local news van, along with one from Boston and another from FNN (Fashion News Network), parked out front adjusting their satellite dishes and testing their camera angles. They were used to fanfare, but Harlow could tell Dodge was upset at the intrusion; he didn't like the media invading his haven in Bryce Corner. They parked out back and entered the side vestibule unnoticed.

Reverend Blackmer greeted them and led them into his office where he discussed the eulogy and the manner in which he thought best to handle the details of a double service. Dodge had opted to forego the emotional strains of a wake and service at the funeral parlor for one memorial at the church, followed by burial at the cemetery. He had hired a caterer for the gathering afterward, which would be at the Maddison farmhouse. The details reviewed, Reverend Blackmer stood and excused himself. He opened a dark walnut door on a large armoire standing dark and huge, almost as an over-bearing intrusion, in the tiny office. He reached in and pulled out his robe, long and black with the fullness of a cape. He held it by the hanger and didn't notice it trailing on the floor as he exited. Dodge watched the fabric drifting away and felt an ominous shiver sweep over his shoulders. He suddenly realized he had never done any of his designs in black, not even the evening gowns, preferring the lighter, softer, and even brighter colors. He wondered if there was some inner meaning to this.

The coffins were positioned side by side at the base of the stairs in front of the altar. With her comforting hand in his, Harlow walked beside Dodge as he approached the twin boxes. There was a beautiful arrangement of flowers atop each with a white satin banner displaying gold letters. One said *Emma,* and the other, *Jedediah.* She bowed her head and said a silent prayer for them and then one for the man holding her hand beside her. Silently, she slipped away and took a seat in a forward pew, leaving Dodge alone to spend a pensive moment with his beloved grandparents. She sat peering at the back of this tall, handsome, gentle, man. The man she had made love to the night before, and again early this morning, this wonderful man standing forlorn and alone in front of her, with his head bowed and his arms spread, a hand atop each of the caskets. Tears welled in her eyes.

The church doors opened behind them and the mourners started to enter and fill up the pews. Chief Ben was the first to make his way to the front. He was wearing a black suit. He was a big man. He would be one of the pallbearers. He stood next to his best friend and placed his arm around his shoulders. She saw Carlene approach her husband and Dodge from behind and stand between them. They stood embracing. Harlow took a handkerchief from her pocketbook and patted her eyes. Carlene came and sat beside her and put her hand on Harlow's knee. They passed a silent smile between them.

Ben was saying something to Dodge. He was pointing his thumb backward towards the front of the church, and Dodge was nodding his head. They moved over a bit to allow the approaching mourners room to come pay their respects. The two men stood side by side as the people passed by offering a hug or a handshake to Dodge. There were quite a few. The Maddison's had been well loved. They were an active part of their town of Bryce Corner, Massachusetts. And they had a famous grandson.

Ben slid into the pew next to his wife and gave a nod to Harlow.

"What were you and Dodge huddling about up there?" Carlene asked.

"Oh, I was just telling him I took care of the pizza."

Harlow had a quizzed look, Carlene explained, "Ben calls the paparazzi *the pizza,*" turning her head back to her husband, she asked, "and just how did you do that?"

"Had the boys cordon off this side of the common and made 'em move their vans to the other side."

"You can't do that."

"Sure I can."

"Didn't they get upset?"

"Oh yeah. But I told them there was a town ordinance stating you couldn't set up any satellite equipment within a hundred yards of a church."

"There is not."

"I know that sugar plum, but by the time they send someone over to town hall to check on it, we'll be outta here."

Carlene shook her head from side to side, her common response to Ben's shenanigans. Harlow was laughing quietly, "The *pizza*," she said, "I love it."

"Besides, there's no one at town hall anyways, they're all here," Ben chuckled.

Reverend Blackmer took the pulpit. Dodge came around and took a seat next to Harlow. She placed her hand onto his and he laced his fingers into it.

"Dearly beloved ..." the reverend began "...let us pray."

* * *

The service was nice. Formal and short. Dodge had nixed Reverend Blackmer's idea of taking the pulpit and saying a few words. He knew he'd break down. It was hard for him to watch the pallbearers assemble around the caskets and walk them the length of the church. He followed behind them through the large ornate double doors at the church front and stood with Harlow and Carlene and the other mourners as they gently placed Emma and Jedediah into separate hearses. They would make a short journey down the road to their final resting-place on a knoll, beneath a stand of maples, at the edge of Restful Corner Cemetery.

"Mr. Maddison, how does it feel losing the last of your family?" A young blonde woman had come out of nowhere and was holding a microphone to her lips with the letters FNN attached to it; her cameraman behind her running a large video cam.

"Can you draw any similarities between the sudden loss of your parents and the questionable circumstances surrounding the deaths of your grandparents?" another asked.

Then another, "Is it true that your grandfather hung himself?" They were coming at him from both sides. Harlow asked, "Where the hell are they coming from?"

"They must have been hiding in the fucking bushes." Carlene replied.

In an instant a crowd of reporters had swarmed the front of the church. Dodge wrapped one arm around Harlow and shooed them off with his other as he made his way towards the limo parked behind the hearses.

Chief Ben caught the commotion just as he was pushing Jedediah's coffin into the second hearse. He slammed the rear door and bolted toward the *pizza* crowd. *Son of a bitch!*

"Mr. Maddison, is it true that your current flame, supermodel Dana, was not invited to the service?"

"Can you address the rumors of Dana's pregnancy?"

Big Ben barged into the crowd and lifted a large video cam one-handed off the shoulders of a cameraman and waved it like a shield into the paparazzi.

"Stand back!" He shouted and made a path for Dodge, Harlow, and Carlene to get into their limo.

The reporters were intimidated by his size, not to mention the anger in his voice. His friends safely placed into the limo, the chief turned to the stunned crowd and said in a low, but commanding tone, "Party's over children."

He gave each of them a scolding, scornful stare and said between clenched teeth, "I want you all to pack up and get outta my town right now. We are going to continue this memorial service, *that you are making a circus out of,* uninterrupted. PLEASE let me find ANY of you at the cemetery, or the Maddison's farmhouse, or anywhere in the jurisdiction of this town, so that I may arrest you for disturbing the peace and throw you into my dirty, scummy, unkempt little jailhouse, where you will be forgotten about over the weekend until Monday morning when the fumigators come to do their annual spraying."

No one spoke. They clearly got his message, and were clearly convinced that he was not kidding.

Ben was waiting for someone to bring up their first amendment rights so that he could make an example out of them by arresting them for preaching without a permit or inciting a riot or something like that, but they began dispersing.

"Hey, that's my video cam," the scruffy-faced cameraman said.

*Too cool to shave,* the chief thought. Ben held the heavy camera out to him at arm's length. Just as he reached for it, the chief let go his grip and the video cam crashed onto the sidewalk.

"Oops." he said and turned and walked away.

Ben joined the pallbearers in their limo and the procession started off.

In their forward car, Carlene said, "Dana's pregnancy?"

"She's not pregnant, trust me," Dodge answered. He looked at Harlow and shook his head, "just another tabloid rumor."

"I'm sure she's not," she responded, "she'd have to gain more than one ounce of weight if she were pregnant." The girls laughed.

There were quite a few cars in the funeral procession and it took a while for them all to loop single file around the narrow way of the cemetery. Finally, all gathered, they sat motionless in the morning sun as the pallbearers performed their solemn duty, twelve silent men carrying the last of Dodge's lineage to their final resting-place beside his parents. Somber. Yet through the curtain of the circumstances, the sky bestowed a promise of another nice day, the sun bright in the breezeless mid-morning.

Standing at the gravesite beside her husband while the group assembled around them, Carlene whispered, "Ben, where's Percy?"

"I don't know. I expected to see him at the church, but ..." he shrugged his shoulders. "I called the nursing home early this morning, but they said he'd already left."

"Do you think he's alright?"

"Yeah, I wouldn't worry 'bout him, he's probably sittin' on his porch rocking away."

"Aren't the new owners, what's their names?..."

"Van Ness."

"The Van Ness's ... aren't they bothered by that?"

"Naw, I don't think so. Actually, I think Mrs. Van Ness has taken a liking to him."

"Well, I'm not so sure I'd like an old coot sitting on my new porch every morning."

"'Lene, it's not an old coot, it's Old Percy you're talking about, he's harmless."

"Why wasn't he at the church? And why isn't he here? Jedediah was his best friend for chrissake."

"Don't know. Gotta handle it in his own way I guess."

Reverend Blackmer once again led off with a prayer, and they all bowed their heads.

\* \* \*

Off in the distance, on the far hill at the edge of the cemetery, stood a solitary figure, dressed in black, watching the proceedings. He would come down and pay his respects later, alone, after the crowd had gone.

# 15

## *FARMHOUSE*

Salem Cross Inn had set up catering for a hundred and fifty people. They had pre-cooked everything at the restaurant, loaded it into their step van, and traveled the mile and a half down the road to the Maddison farmhouse earlier that morning. They took over the kitchen, rearranged the dining room by adding two eight-foot banquet tables to Emma's long dining room table (the one she'd used years ago to lay out her fabric and sew Dodge's early designs into dresses) and spread out a beautiful buffet. The catering chef stood behind one of the tables carving roast beef, ham, and turkey; his tall puffy white hat occasionally touching the large rustic beams of the low eighteenth-century ceiling. There were big stainless steel pots of New England clam chowder and French onion soup; mashed potatoes, sweet potatoes, a medley of fresh vegetables, scrambled eggs, bacon, sausages, baskets of fresh baked breads and muffins, and several pottery bowls of local jams and jellies. They had coffee and tea, both hot and iced, juices, milk, sodas, bottled water, and had even set up a portable bar. They were ready when the procession began arriving just before noon.

The gathering of townsfolk and neighbors mingled about the house and outside on the back lawn. The men seemed to gravitate more to the outside, and the women seemed comfortable in the living room and parlor. Inside, Harlow assumed the role of hostess, not because she was appointed, but because she was just that way. She was used to directing the functions of Dodge Maddison and just naturally immersed herself in the overseeing of the caterers. Being an integral part of Dodge's business life, Harlow had gotten to know Emma well over the past ten years. She had accompanied Dodge to the farmhouse on many occasions. Dodge liked to stay in touch with his grandparents and tried to visit as often as possible. However, he was also a workaholic at times and carried his business with him wherever he went. Harlow was part of that business, hence her accompaniment on the Bryce Corner visits. Emma liked Harlow, not only for her company, but also for the way she took care of her treasured grandson. The two women would sit for hours in the sunroom talking about fashion. Emma liked the way Harlow kept her abreast of Dodge's world. Harlow thought that Emma would be happy with the way things were going today, but she wanted to be sure the afternoon went perfect. Carlene was at her side in the kitchen, greeting everyone as they came along to the buffet and making sure everyone had a full plate and a comfy spot to light upon.

Carlene leaned over and whispered to Harlow, "I guess I didn't have to leave the back light on for you last night," she was holding a little smirk on her face that said *I want to hear all about it.* Then she added, "What'd you two end up doing for dinner?"

"We went to The Salem Cross Inn."

"Oh, I love it there. What did you have? I usually get the lobster pie casserole, it's delicious."

"I had the salmon almandine and Dodge had the prime rib."

"He's just like Ben, a meat and potatoes man."

"It really is a lovely place. We sat at a quaint little table near the fireplace. The service was excellent."

"Sounds kind of *romantic.*"

Harlow felt a blush coming to her cheek and tried to hide it from Carlene. It wasn't effective. It's hard for women to fool other women, men are easy, but women have this sixth sense of things that you just can't get around.

Carlene gave herself a satisfying *mmm hmmm,* and then took the heat off. "Were there a lot of leaf-peepers?"

"Huh?"

"You know, leaf-peepers, tourists, they come this time of year when the leaves start to change."

"No, it wasn't too crowded," Harlow realized she had no idea how many people were there, she had been too engrossed in the enchantment of the evening, "but I think we may have been the last to leave, the parking lot was empty when we left." Or at least she hoped it had been. *I can't believe we did that!*

87

"Probably too early, the foliage doesn't peak for a couple weeks yet," Carlene watched Dodge in the hallway accepting condolences. She saw the sadness in his eyes.

"So, how is he doing with everything? He seems to be taking things well, but I worry about him, he tries to hold too much on his shoulders sometimes."

"We didn't really talk about it last night. I guess he just needed to break away from the melancholy for a while. I was trying to keep his mind off of it."

"And I'll *bet you did*!"

\* \* \*

It was a lovely late September day. Cool in the morning, but by noon, the temperature was hovering near the seventy-degree mark, and climbing. The leaves in the trees lining the yard and spreading out into the field were starting to show their bright colors of autumn. A group of men holding their heaping plates were gathering out back in the barnyard next to the corral fence.

"Helluva nice day we got here, Bob," Dave Bean of D.L. Bean, Land Surveyors said.

"Yup," Bob Pouliot, local insurance agent answered. "Supposed to hit seventy-five or eighty today and I'll take it. The longer it's warmer, the better. I remember that damn awful winter last year. Snow on the ground from the first of December 'til three weeks past Easter."

"Great snowmobiling though," Bean said. I must have put a couple thousand miles on my new sled last season."

"Well, you can have it. This is the kind of weather I like, seventy degrees, sunny, just like Florida in the winter. Been thinking I might get a place down there."

"Oh yeah, whereabouts?"

"Not sure. My sister's got a condo down in the Tampa/St. Pete area, nice spot, maybe there."

"How ya doin' gentlemen?" Jack Patterson, one of the local builders joined them. He placed his beer on the top of a fence post, leaned against it, and dug into his overflowing plate.

"Little early for a beer isn't it, Patterson?"

"Shit, it's past twelve o'clock ain't it?" he mumbled through a mouthful.

"No wonder your houses come out crooked," Bean chuckled.

The men got busy eating. A crow, perched on the high peak of the barn, was watching them. He cawed, his shiny black head twisting and turning, his sharp eyes capturing their every movement. Bean pulled one of his rolls in half and threw it out toward the barn. The crow raised his wings, gave a quick glance for enemies, swooped down, grabbed the bread, then flew off low over the calm of the yellow hayfield, his pointed wings glossy-black in flight.

"Wonder what Dodge's gonna do with the farm?" Pouliot asked.

"I suppose he'll sell it," Bean said. "I don't think he's got farming on his agenda."

"This'd make a great sub-division," Patterson, the builder, said, "I'd like to buy it off him, bet I could put a dozen houses in here."

"Naw, not this close to town," Pouliot said, "it's in the historic district."

"Just as long as I build 'em on two-acre parcels, it's allowed, ain't that so Dave?" he asked the surveyor.

"It's allowed, as long as the historic commission signs off on the style of architecture."

"What's this pow-wow all about over here?" Dodge joined in.

"Oh, Pouliot's talking about moving to Florida to avoid our beautiful winters," Dave Bean said, "and Patterson's got an itch to build more of his crooked houses."

"Hey, fuck you, Bean," Patterson said, "my houses aren't crooked, your dick's crooked!"

"Chief, get over here, there's gonna be a brawl!" Pouliot hollered through his laughter.

Big Ben was walking towards them with two drinks in his hands. "Here, drink this, slowly," he offered one to Dodge, "scotch, single malt, it'll settle your nerves."

Dodge took a sip. "Whew! Tastes like gasoline."

"Almost as good," Ben grinned.

\* \* \*

Carlene grabbed a glass of wine and motioned *follow me* to Harlow. She led her upstairs and down the hallway to the front of the house to the tiny sunroom Emma would sit in and read. Harlow stopped momentarily at the bedroom door, looked in, and felt a slight tinge of sorrow. She noticed how perfect the room was. The oak bed with the high headboard was neatly made. She had a pure-white George Washington spread on it that showed off her hand made floral pillows. A beautiful patched quilt fell over the footboard and cascaded onto an antique chest. There were a variety of colorful scatter rugs laying in random orderliness atop the dark, wide floorboards. The set of oak bureaus were both neatly cluttered with framed pictures, Emma's held a few more than Jed's. The room had a high ceiling and white lace curtains covered the tall windows and fell to the floor. It was a lovely room, bright and cheerful. Harlow smiled in approval. She knew Emma would be pleased with the way her house looked and with how well things were going with all her guests, and felt her saying *thank you* for filling in as hostess.

At the end of the hall, the sunroom was like a tiny turret with windows all around. There was a deeply padded sitting bench cluttered with pillows of all sizes wrapping around in the circular formation of the room. A small narrow table was squeezed in the center with barely enough room for your legs to fit. The most comfortable position was to lounge on the deep padded benches and prop yourself up against the pillows with your back against the doorway side. This way you could gaze out the windows and catch the view of the goings-on along the street-side out front, or just repose in the sunlight. Carlene placed her wine on a coaster on the tiny table, hiked her skirt up, and walked on her knees around the fluffy horseshoe bench, opening the high windows; that brought a nice breeze into the room.

"Ahh, much better," she said as she kicked off her shoes and brought her legs up Indian style. She leaned forward, picked up her wine, fluffed a couple pillows behind her, then leaned back and waited.

Directly across from her Harlow mimicked the lounging-preparation routine, except she opted to stretch her legs out. They reached easily across the table and found the softness of the opposite bench. She sat unconsciously spreading and curling her toes into the spongy cushions; like a cat would do when she's purring in the comfort of your lap, pushing her legs into your velvety cotton sweater, spreading her paws, then curling them in a relaxing and soothing grabbing motion. Harlow was at ease, holding her tea saucer in the fingers of one hand, and the handle of her floral teacup in the other. She took occasional sips as her mind drifted to other places, her ruby-red lipstick blending with the colors of the roses on the teacup.

Carlene sat quietly watching her until she was unable to maintain her silence a second longer - she hadn't come up here to be quiet.

"Well ..." she said.

"Well, what?"

"You *know* what. Come on, I want to hear all about it."

Harlow hesitated, looking over her teacup at Carlene, "I knew you had a reason for getting me alone."

"So, what happened?"

"So, we had a nice evening, that's all."

"How nice?"

"Nice, it was nice," she sipped. "We went for a sunset ride in the rowboat, then went out to dinner. I wanted to call you and let you know, but Dodge insisted it was alright."

"Don't worry about that ..." she said impatiently, "then what happened," she raised her drink to her lips.

"Then I fucked his socks off."

Carlene almost spit out her wine.

"Well, that's what you wanted to hear, wasn't it?"

"Oh, come on Harlow, I'm just wondering how things are going for you two, that's all."

"And being nosy."

"Yes, and being nosy, but it's a sincere, caring kind of nosy. I mean, you two have been so close for so many years now, and I just think it'd be nice if you stopped dancing around the issue and got together."

"Geez Carlene, I wish you'd get to the point." Harlow chuckled.

"Ben's always saying I wouldn't be able to talk without my foot in my mouth."

Harlow placed her tea onto the tiny table, put one of the small-fringed pillows onto her lap and drew her legs up, pressing the pillow between her thighs and her breasts. She wrapped her arms around her knees and lowered her chin into the pillow. She thought.

"Does he know?" Carlene asked.

"Know what?"

"That you're in love with him."

She pondered this for a moment. "I love him, I truly do, but I'm not sure it's in the way you mean. We've been close to each other for so long, gotten to know each other in a special way, not only in our work, or maybe because of it, I think that we, that we're, I don't know, maybe it's that we ..."

"Harlow, what the hell are you saying?"

"I mean, I don't know, I'm not sure how I feel anymore. I think last night may have changed everything, or kept it the same, I'm not sure."

"You're a little confused, that's all. Sometimes love does that."

"Hmm, maybe, I don't know. Maybe I'm comfortable in the role that I play in his life, in the roles we both play in each other's life. I stepped outside of that role last night and I'm not sure it took me to where I thought it would."

They sat quiet, Carlene letting her words sink in, "I guess I've always felt that you were in love with him, and that sooner or later he'd wake up and come to his senses and realize that he was in love with you too."

"He is in love with me Carlene, in his own way. We've been through a lot. We've shed our share of blood together in this business. Believe me, fashion is a "dog-eat-dog" business, one bad line and you're history. Dodge is a very talented man who has a knack of surrounding himself with other talented, loyal people who will go the extra mile for him, and have, season after season. I'm lucky to be a part of it, a part of him, and I know how much he appreciates me, and that makes me feel good. But part of what makes our relationship work, and has for such a long time, is the mutual respect we have for each other." Harlow stretched her legs across the tiny table and took up her cat kneading again with the cushion on Carlene's side. "So, to be honest with myself, I'm there when he needs me, and I feel comfortable with that. And last night? I guess I was there when he needed me, and I feel comfortable in that too." She looked directly into Carlene's doleful eyes, "And I'm too old to kid myself, I'm not expecting flowers and candy out of this."

"Hey, there's nothing wrong with flowers," Carlene grinned into the conversation.

"This has been a terrible blow to him," Harlow continued, "you know as well as I how important Emma and Jed were to him, they were the solid foundation in his world. I'm not sure what direction he'll go in now, but I do know I want to be there for him no matter what. He's a very creative, loving, and talented man, yet even with all his successes, I don't think he knows quite what he wants."

"I know what you're saying, Harlow, and I understand where you're coming from. Dodge is very special to Ben and me. We want only the best for him. If you two work out, we'd be thrilled that's all. Maybe it's the mother in me that holds out hope."

"I've never held any illusions Carlene; he needed me, he reached out for me and I was there for him, like I've always been, and hope to always be. Where it goes from here …" she shrugged.

"Carlene?!" Someone was calling from the foot of the stairs, "Carlene, you up there?" It was Sadie Gilbert, Emma's next door neighbor. Not waiting for an answer she continued, "There's someone down here I'd like you to meet."

"Okay Mrs. Gilbert, I'll be right down," she hollered back.

"Well, I guess where it goes from here is back downstairs," Carlene rose from her seat and slid back into her shoes. She reached over and grabbed Harlow's hand, "Anytime you need to talk, I'm available."

"Thanks. You're a good friend. Don't worry, I'll be fine."

"You coming?" Carlene asked.

"I'll be down in a minute."

Harlow sat in the sunlight, in the breeze coming in from the open window. She held the teacup in her hands. She was warmed by Carlene's words. She understood her implications, her hopes, and her concern. She'd been asking herself much the same questions all day. But she thought she had explained it well to Carlene. Hadn't she? She was fine with the way things were. Nothing's changed between them. They were two grown people who shared a common interest, who'd, by the very nature of it, grown close to each other. Grown to know one another and to rely on each other. Why should anything be different now? Just because they'd crossed a line - that didn't mean that their lives should change. She took a sip of tea. It had cooled. She needed a fresh cup.

Sadie Gilbert was at the bottom of the stairs with Carlene and another woman. She saw Harlow descending the staircase and said to Katelyn Van Ness, "Oh, and this is Harlow, the woman who ensures the success of *Maddison Designs*."

"Well, I wouldn't go that far, Mrs. Gilbert," Harlow replied. "Hi," she shook Katelyn's hand.

"Nonsense," Sadie Gilbert said. "Every successful man has a strong woman behind them," she squeezed Katelyn's elbow bringing her new neighbor into her confidence and said, "Isn't she lovely?"

"Katelyn's from across the street," Carlene said, "the Van Ness' bought Cora and Percy's house."

"Oh, how lovely," Harlow said, "you're very lucky, it's a beautiful house."

"Yes it is. We're thrilled to have found such a lovely house in such a lovely town. Are you from Bryce Corner also?"

"No, Long Island."

"Well, you young ladies chat," Sadie Gilbert said, "I'm going back to the living room."

"She's sweet," Katelyn said, "I'm looking forward to having her as a neighbor."

"You'll love her," Carlene said, "She's a real character."

"Actually, Mrs. Benson, the reason I ..."

"Oh, please ... just call me Carlene."

"Carlene ... I didn't mean to intrude, but I thought you'd like to know that Percy is on the porch and he's acting kind of funny."

"How so?" they headed down the hallway to the front door. Carlene saw him rocking in his chair.

"I said hello to him, but he didn't answer. I brought him out a cup of coffee, but he wouldn't touch it; he's just very quiet, staring across the street. I asked if he was going to join you all, but I couldn't get him to say anything."

"He probably hasn't eaten anything yet, that'll mess up his blood sugar," Carlene said, "I'll fix him a plate and bring it over." She disappeared, leaving Harlow and the new neighbor to chat idly about her new house and new town.

A few minutes later, Carlene rejoined them with a plate in her hand and a can of seltzer water, "I'll be right back," she exited.

Katelyn Van Ness was telling Harlow about her relocation, her husband, her plans for a dance studio, and how happy she was that they settled in Bryce Corner, "It's such a perfect little town and everyone's been so nice in welcoming us."

Carlene was back with the seltzer can in her hand, "He's fine. He wants a beer. Yelled at me for bringing him 'F'ing water!'" she laughed on her way into the kitchen.

She reappeared a moment later as the two ladies were saying good-bye.

"Carlene, I'll take the beer over if you'd like," Katelyn said.

"Sure, but don't let him bite your hand off."

"I won't," she smiled, "I'm glad we met, I met your husband on our first day here and he's very nice. Hope to be seeing you again. Bye."

"She seems nice, wants to open a dance studio for tap and ballet."

"Really? Does she have a background in dance?..." They made their way back into the gathering.

\* \* \*

The day was nice, forgoing the circumstances. Actually, even with the circumstances; for Dodge had the opportunity to reconnect with old friends again, something he realized he hadn't done for quite a while. He found it to be not only heartwarming, but also rejuvenating. It was good to feel the outpouring of genuine concern and support for him. Genuine, that was what it was, not like in his business world, where pretense played an everyday role, weaving into his life like an ineludible pattern on one of his designs. It was part of the fame. People just wanted a part of you, your limelight, your "friendship", and your money. But how many of them would be there if you bombed? How fast would they turn away? Like colors running. It's great to be on top, but so much more work. So many new pressures, so many more demands taxing your time and your creativity. *Am I being too cynical? Too distraught over the loss of Gram and Gramp?* They had always been sincere, had believed in him, had supported him, had been proud of him. He'd always carried that feeling in his heart, why was he questioning it now? He had plenty of sincerity in his life, right? Or was it plenty of pretense? Had he drifted too far? Maybe he was starting to see his life in a different light. For the first time in a long time he felt like he belonged to something again, this house, these people, this town, Bryce Corner. The events of the past few days and especially today seemed to wrap around him like a cocoon. Were Emma and Jed trying to tell him something?

Dodge found himself alone. He had wandered out by the barn lost deep in his own thoughts. He entered the barn reluctantly; a little fearful of how he'd feel. There was the beam Jedediah had hung himself from. Dodge remembered hoisting the engine from the old Ford with the help of that very beam. Gramp had helped him. They had lifted the engine and left it swinging there from the strong cherry beam while they pushed the car backward, out of the way, and then moved a bench underneath it and carefully lowered the engine onto it and propped it so that Dodge could work on it. He'd started by taking the carburetor off, then the intake manifold so that he could remove the heads. He spent weeks rebuilding that motor, and then started on the car, doing the bodywork, grinding out the rust spots and filling them with Bondo, and then sanding that down smooth enough to paint over. He'd borrowed a paint gun and compressor from Wright's Garage, and with Ben's help they put on a coat of primer and then shot it in "candy apple red". By the time he was ready to place the rebuilt motor back in three months later, Dodge and Ben had been joined by Jed and Old Percy in the restoration project and the four of them had a helluva good time out here in the barn working together. They shared some good laughs too. In the evenings, they'd pop a few beers and celebrate their handiwork. The boys had to promise not to let on that their grandfathers were letting them drink, and were mindful not to get drunk. That is, until the night they fired it up. With the motor back in, the bodywork complete, and everything ready to roll, Dodge ceremoniously started it up. (Old Percy had wanted to crack a bottle of beer on the hood ornament, but Jed talked him out of it.) It sounded great! Gramp got under the hood and twisted and turned the settings on the carb until it was purring like a kitten. They all jumped in, Jed and Perce in the back and Ben up front with Dodge driving. Didn't have his license yet, but what the hell, they were celebrating. They cruised around town making sure everything sounded right. Ran like a charm. Jed and Percy were hootin' and hollerin' in the backseat, Ben was shoutin' out the window, and Dodge was driving *his car* with a hard-on. He felt great! They lucked out and didn't rouse the attention of the town cops, but they weren't too worried about that anyways - the chief at that time was Percy's son, Ben's Uncle Bob. Exhilarated, they pulled back into the barn an hour later, and spent the rest of the evening sitting in the car drinking beer and telling car stories.

Dodge stood in the middle of the barn laughing out loud.

"Hey, what's so funny?" Ben had come in behind him.

"I was just thinking of the time you and me and Gramp and Perce were sitting in here in the Ford after we took it on its maiden cruise, remember that night?"

"Are you shittin' me? Never forget it. My first damn hangover came from that night."

Ben looked up at the beam and then back to Dodge, "Are you alright?"

"Yeah, I'm okay, just had to get away for a minute, I guess."

"Folks are gettin' ready to leave and want to say good-bye."

"Alright."

They left the barn and walked towards the house.

"People've been asking me what you're gonna do, y'know, with the house, the land, and everything. Are you keepin' it, are you staying in New York, are you gonna move back to town, stuff like that. I've been tellin' 'em it's too early, that you're probably not sure yet." Dodge didn't respond, so the Chief continued, "There's already talk about building some houses in here," he looked off into the accompanying fields, "that'd probably look like shit."

"I think you're right, it's too early yet. I'm not sure what I'm going to do. For now, I'm thinking I might stay at the cottage for a while. The line is in and New York's got a handle on that, and I've got time before I've got to start putting the next one together, and you know what?"

"What?"

"I haven't taken a vacation, a real 'just hang out and relax' kind of vacation in a couple of years. I think I might just do that."

"That'd be great, ole buddy! We could go fishin', go campin' up to the old shack, drink some beers …" Big Ben was getting excited. Plans for fun and frolicking were forming in his head.

"Yeah, maybe I'll take a week or so for myself."

"A week? Hell, take a couple, take a month. You can afford that. It'd be good for you. This is a great time of year. Indian summer's always been my favorite, I love the season changes, perfect weather. Leaves a changin', fish are bitin', October Fest is just around the corner, great beer-drinking …"

They walked shortening the distance to the house, quiet in their own respective thoughts.

"Oh, by the way," Ben said, "old man McGreevy was tellin' me that someone tore up part of his cornfield yesterday."

"Oh yeah?"

"Said something about a flashy red hot-rod spinnin' through his corn stalks. You wouldn't know anything 'bout that, would you?"

"Me?" Dodge kicked a stone across the gravel way, it bounced into the grass beneath the barnyard fence, "Nope, don't know nothin' about it."

"Didn't think you would."

They entered the house through the back door.

By midafternoon the caterers had packed up and Dodge was out front of the house saying good-bye to the last of the guests. Chief Ben had left to go check on things at the station, Mrs. Gilbert was inside helping Carlene with clean up, and Harlow waited for Dodge at the top of the stairs on the front porch.

"Well," he said as he approached her, "I think everything went okay, don't you?"

"Yes, it was very nice."

He climbed the steps and stood next to her.

"Dodge, I'm going to leave, I'm going back to the city tonight."

"What do you mean?" There was confusion in his voice, "I thought you'd want to stay."

"I do want to stay, that's why I'm leaving."

He was looking into her eyes asking for a reason, unable to verbalize his feelings. Harlow said, "You know, last night was nice, really nice. We shared something very special," she spoke tenderly into his sky blue eyes, "something I'll cherish forever."

"Is there a 'but' coming up?"

"No, no buts."

She drew close to him, "Listen, Dodge," she reached her hands up and began loosening his tie, "I've got to say something here and I need you to just listen and let me get it out." She tugged his tie open an inch or two, then unbuttoned his shirt collar. She was trying to make them both feel a little more comfortable. She reached down and clasped his hands hanging loose by his sides. She held them with her fingers. "We've known each other for a long time and we've always been honest with each other, we don't pull any punches, right?"

He nodded.

"So," she took a deep breath, "I don't have any regrets about last night, in fact, I've dreamed about last night for years, so I should have been prepared for it, but I wasn't, it's taken me completely off guard. And I'll be honest with you; I'm not sure how I'm feeling about us now that it's happened. That didn't sound right, I don't mean that in a negative way, it's just that I want you to know I'm not expecting flowers and candy out of this, I'm really not expecting anything, well that's not true either. I guess what I'd like to happen, is that we remain the same way as we were before. I don't want you to feel any schoolgirl pressures from me and feel like you have to change the way you feel about me, about us. I love you, Dodge, I really do. We've got a special relationship and I don't want to lose that."

"We're not going to lose that."

"I know."

Dodge sensed her seriousness. He felt as if he should say something, maybe she expected him to say something. He was uneasy.

"Hey, it was only sex, right?" He teased.

"Yeah, but great sex!" She had a comeback.

"Come on, let's do it again, right here on the porch."

"Okay," she hopped up on the railing and pulled him by his belt, "but you've got to get naked first," she began playfully tugging at his buckle.

"Right here in broad daylight?"

"Oh, that's right, I forgot, you're the shy 'empty-dark-parking-lot' kinda guy," she smirked.

The front screen door squeaked open. It was Mrs. Gilbert, closing up her pocketbook and slinging it onto her shoulder, "Well, that's done, things are back to normal in the house again and I'm ... oh, excuse me, am I intruding?"

"Nope," Dodge said, "we were just going to have wild sex right here on the front porch in broad daylight."

"Oh, that's nice," she descended the stairs, "you go right ahead." Without stopping she said, "But you know what I always say?...."

They chuckled, "What's that Mrs. Gilbert?"

She turned her head and gave them a big grin, "Use a condom!"

Harlow and Dodge laughed. Sadie Gilbert was laughing too.

"So," Harlow continued, "I think what would be best for me would be to get back to the office and stay focused on getting this line out."

He knew she had her mind set, she was like that, "Harlow, I don't know what I'd do without you, without your honesty. I'd like you to stay, but I will respect your wishes. But, I want you to know that last night was very special for me also." She liked that, she smiled. "And," he said, "I love you too." They embraced.

"I'm glad," she said. "So, no expectations, right? Whatever happens happens, we're going to be ourselves, that's the most important thing."

"Yes."

"Good."

"And, I also think that you could use some time for yourself, you've been working like a madman lately and it would be good for you to get away from it all and just chill out." She was back to her motherly, executive assistant role, "When's the last time you took a vacation?"

"Funny you should ask that, I was just telling Bennie I haven't taken a vacation in a couple of years."

"Then do it. You need it, believe me, I know. You've been pushing yourself to the limit lately, and now this thrust upon you. You've got a lot to take care of here. So, I'll handle things in New York, and you take some time for Dodge Maddison. Deal?"

"When have I ever argued with you?"

"Always, but you can see I'm right, can't you." This wasn't a question.

# 16

## *WAITIN' ON A TRAIN*

There's a spot at the further end of the Maddison property, way past
the fields, hidden by a thick copse of oaks and maples and elms,
where the railroad tracks stand on a manmade mound of earth
overlooking the Wickaboag River - bending and twisting its way from
the far off hills of the Mohawk Trail onward to the Boston Harbor. You
can look either way and see the rails appearing and disappearing, riding
the ledge above the river, like satin piping trim accenting the curves on
the lapels of a silk blazer. When he lived on the farm, Dodge used to
come here and sit on the rails and watch the sunset. You could see the
river changing colors as it flowed in the shadows of the tall trees on the
other bank, streams of long flowing colors, like a windsock in the wind,
chasing after the giant fading trains.

Sitting on the rail you could feel the rumble of the trains in the seat of
your pants long before you could hear them. It started as a tingling, almost
as an itch, except it got stronger and stronger as it grew into a steady
vibration. Then the sound, starting as a low hum, like how your music
teacher prefaced a class song, blowing into her pitch pipe. Steadily it
progressed to a loud roar and you had to get up off the rail and stand back
to let the train thunder past, wildly trying to blow you off the ground.
Dodge sat here now, waiting on a train and watching the sun drop.

After everyone had left, and he found himself alone in his old
house, he had gone to his room to change into jeans and a long sleeved
tee shirt. Harlow had driven off earlier with Carlene to pick up her things
at the cottage and get her car to return to New York. He was relieved
actually. *Maybe she's right, our relationship's too important to let love
and commitment screw it up.* He loved her, he really did, but not in a
man/woman sort of way, it was more than that. He couldn't quite

pinpoint it, but he had the feeling that she felt the same way. They'd always shared an unexplainable understanding for each other. He was very glad she was in his life.

He sat on the cool steel rail overlooking the river thinking about everything; the events of the past few days passing through his mind like the rolling ripples in the river below him. The Paris premiere, the call from Old Percy, New York, Bryce Corner, being with his good friends Bennie and Carlene again, the cottage, rescuing that lady on the lake, making love to Harlow, Gramma Emma and Jedediah, the funeral, all the caring folks who came to the house afterward, *the house, what am I going to do with that?* And the property – what would he do with the land? It'd be a shame to sell it off so that some developer could parcel it into monopoly houses. He could sell it as a farm, although it hadn't been used as a workable farm for many years. Gramp had turned the fields into haying, and anyways, people just weren't interested in farming anymore. The house was big, too big by today's standards. Even when the three of them were living there together, they'd never been able to use all the rooms. He could rent it out – no, Emma wouldn't approve of that. Jed'd like to keep it a farm. Maybe he could find some young guy with dirt in his veins crazy enough to want to be a New England farmer. He'd stop by Cregan Realty and talk to Jack about putting it on the market. *I've got no use for it. Who would I share it with? Dana?* No, that wasn't real, he knew that. *Harlow?* He had a whole new feeling for her. He'd never made love in quite that way before, especially in the morning at the cottage. It was nice, different. And hell, they've known each other long enough to be married - but she doesn't want to change their relationship - she'd even said so. *Damn! Why are women so hard to figure out?* He sat thinking for a long time. A train never did pass by, but the sun did set.

\* \* \*

Dodge didn't feel like staying at the big house alone any longer, Ben and Carlene had driven into Boston to attend an annual policeman's awards ceremony, and he wasn't ready to head back down to the cottage. He decided to visit The Tavern. It was Friday night, they had a band playing up front in the old ballroom, and the usuals were at the bar in the back. Eggman was at the door collecting cover fees from the crowd coming in. He wouldn't take any money from him, so Dodge went to the bar, got a couple beers, then returned to the door and stood there talking with Eggman. He was the source of town gossip. He was a "townie" and had grown up with

Dodge and Ben. His dad had had a chicken farm, and Billy helped him deliver eggs since he was a kid. Later on he helped expand the business by establishing routes into Boston and Connecticut; it became very lucrative and provided for the family quite well. They eventually sold the routes to a competitor, Billy's parents retired south, and he now was content with his solo handyman/carpenter business where he could work when he wanted and not when he didn't. He did work for just about everyone in town at one point or another and was thus the unofficial town crier. Although he'd had nothing to do with the egg business for years, the name Eggman had stuck. Most people couldn't tell you his real name.

"You gonna stay in town awhile?" he yelled over the loud music.

"Yeah, I think so."

"Staying at the house?" Eggman was filling his gossip portfolio.

"No, at the lake. Are you still doing carpentry?"

"Oh yeah."

"Might need your expertise."

"At the lake cottage?"

"No, at the house."

"You gonna move back in?"

"No, I'm probably going to put it on the market and it needs a little attention."

"Like what?"

"Well, the front porch is rotted out on one side and should probably be replaced, and I think the roof is starting to leak. I noticed a few spots on the ceilings upstairs."

"How old's the roof?"

"No idea. Maybe twenty years or so."

"Should be replaced then. Give ya a good price on a new roof."

Eggman had to check ID's on a group of girls coming in. Dodge unconsciously scanned their attire. It was a habit; he was forever finding new ideas for his designs wherever he went. One of the girls with a short leather skirt and long legs had a scarf wrapped around her neck and thrown off to one side over her shoulder. It was long and sheer and looked like silk. As she passed him he saw that she had it tied in an unusual way so that it fell down her back, provocatively accentuating the shortness of the leather skirt as she moved into the crowd. It was sexy. He wondered how she did that; a new design was formulating in his head.

"I can stop by tomorrow and take a look at it if you like," Eggman said.

"Sure."

"Nine o'clock good?"

"Fine with me."

Dodge spent the next couple hours alternating between the live music up front and the loud bar banter in the back. He joined in some doubles at the pool table and even managed to play a few games with Lindsey when she took a break from tending the bar. She beat him bad, four in a row.

"You'd better stick around and sharpen up your cue skills, city boy," she teased. "Want another beer?" she was heading back behind the bar.

"Naw, I'm beat. Think I'll call it a night."

"Coward."

"I'll take a rain check though."

"You're on." She gave him a nice smile, "I'll play you left-handed next time."

"Oh no, next time I'm going to whip your ass."

"You're such a tease!" she snickered and returned to her duties.

He confirmed his appointment with Eggman on his way out and climbed into the Coupe and headed home. He was exhausted. The short ride out of town and around the lake seemed to take an hour. He pulled into the cottage after midnight. The lake was calm and asleep. The sky above it was crystal clear, ebony blue with millions of white rhinestone stars. When he got to the back door, he noticed a note rolled into the handle. He smiled to himself, *must be a note from Harlow.*

*Dear Mr. Maddison:*

> *I hope you get this note before you return to New York. I am so grateful that you were out rowing the other morning - you saved my life.*

> *Please let me express my gratitude in person. Could I buy you a cup of coffee tomorrow morning? Say, 10:00 a t Dot's Diner?*

> *If you can't make it, I understand, please don't feel obligated. I just wanted to say thank you, I am indebted.*

> *Fondly,*
> *Annison Barrett*

103

# 17

## DOT'S DINER

Eggman was sitting on the tailgate of his pick-up truck in the Maddison driveway. He had a coffee in his hands and another one sitting beside him. Dodge pulled in punctually at nine a.m.

"Good morning."

"Mornin'. Brought you a coffee. Black. Got sugar and cream in the truck if you need it."

"No, black's fine, thanks."

They sat awhile enjoying the morning; sunny, but cool. Dodge wore jeans and a chambray shirt covered with a fleece-lined denim jacket. Eggman was in shorts and a tee shirt – hard core New England construction attire until at least December. He synopsized the rest of the evening at The Tavern. Things had gone pretty smoothly except someone had passed out on the pool table right in the middle of a decisive game-winning shot. The girl in the leather skirt fell on the dance floor and had to be escorted out to her car; luckily she was with a designated driver. Eggman's old girlfriend had come in, stoned out of her mind, hanging all over him, wanting to get back together, and then his new girlfriend showed up and got pissed off at him (which he couldn't figure out) and then both women left together (which he really couldn't figure out). Typical Friday night at The Tavern, he said.

They spent about an hour checking out the house. It would need some minor repair on the front porch, a half dozen or so replacement windows, and definitely a new roof. Dodge didn't haggle over price, he knew Eggman was fair, and his work was impeccable. But he couldn't get to it for two or three weeks, which put off Dodge's idea of listing it on the market asap. No matter, fall was a good season for real estate, houses showed well in the bright foliage, and he didn't think it would be on the market long, it was a great house with enviable property; some dot-commer from Boston would scoop it up.

"Alright then," Eggman was saying, "I'll go ahead and order the windows, that'll take a few days anyhow. Maybe I can start replacing them at night and get that out of the way before I start on the other stuff."

"Whatever's good for you. Come and go as you need to, the key's up over the back door. Need some cash to get started with?"

"Nope, we can square up at the end." Business done, they shook hands and departed.

\* \* \*

Dot's Diner is a converted railway car leftover from the days after the Second World War when train service was popular, strong, and necessary; when many men found the production of their small New England factories diminishing and the larger cities booming in the post war economy. Train travel to and from their newfound jobs was fast and affordable. A short generation later, expanding industry had spread back to the towns, houses were being built, and the growing middle class was enjoying their money buying new Frigidaires, TV's, and shiny new cars. Train schedules disappeared and diners were born. Or at least that's how it had happened in Bryce Corner with Dot's Diner.

Located in the center of town, directly across from The Tavern and next to town hall, Dot's Diner was the best breakfast spot in town, and the only one. Dot opened her diner every morning, six days a week (closed on Mondays), early, five a.m., and fed the first wave of customers - hungry construction workers. They'd be gone in an hour, and another wave would arrive between seven and nine; initially the early-rising retired townsfolk talking about the day before, plans for today and of course, the weather. Then the business people; shop owners, town hall personnel, Real Estate agents, the girls from the bank and the insurance agencies, and just about anyone out and about would stop in for their morning coffee, either to stay or to go. With no *Dunkin' Donuts* or *Starbucks* around, you had to get your java from somewhere, and Dot brewed a mean cup of coffee.

Business was still brisk when Dodge came in at ten. He made his way along the counter, stopping briefly to say hey to a few of the occupants on the mushroom-like swivel stools. Dot passed him a mug of coffee over the shoulder of Orton Bailey, the postmaster. Dot's husband John waved hello from the grill in back.

She was sitting in a booth at the window, fashionably dressed in a casual manner. She wore a brushed cotton v-neck top, rose pink, with the vee cutting tastefully into her cleavage and accentuating a cluster of tiny freckles. It was tight and fit her very well, not slutty, but natural like. Some women could wear tops like that and look elegant. She was holding onto a silver pendant with her slender fingers and see-sawing it from side to side along its chain, the Boston Globe lying open before her. The steam from her coffee cup was wafting lightly into a myriad of long dark curls hiding her face and spiraling down on her shoulders like freshly popped party streamers; her hair rich in tone and lending a startling shine to her countenance.

"Hello," he said.

She looked up from her paper, her eyes a deep emerald green, a gleam of morning sunshine illumining them with a bright golden sparkle, like lifting the top on a gold-laden treasure chest.

"Oh, hello," she said. Their eyes held onto each other for the briefest of seconds, her emeralds swimming in his deep blue ocean. "Please, sit down."

She folded the paper up and placed it on the seat next her. "I wasn't sure if you'd come, but I'm glad you did," she looked at him sitting opposite, her demeanor serious. "Mr. Maddison, I ... I don't know what to say, I don't know how to properly thank you, you saved my life and I'm very grateful."

"I'm glad I was able to get you out in time. How are you feeling?"

"Fine, just fine. My throat's a little raw but other than that I'm okay."

"What about the cabin?"

"It's fine, no damage really. The smell was pungent for the first day, but the weather's been pleasant enough to leave the windows open day and night and I've been burning some Yankee Candles to freshen it up."

"You're brave."

"What do you mean?"

"Burning candles?"

"Oh," she laughed, "but they're jar candles and I'm keeping an eye on them. The whole thing was stupid really. I shouldn't have been building a fire so late at night."

"I don't think it was your fault, the fire marshal says the flue was faulty."

"Well, I guess so, but I still feel foolish."

He pictured her lying naked in front of the fireplace, it was a pleasant thought. He wondered why she had been lying there.

As if reading his mind, Annison said, "It was a nice night early on, but then it turned chilly. There's no heating system in the cabin, so I started the fire and curled up in a comforter in front of the fireplace. I had brought in some wood from the pile out back, but I guess some of it was damp. I was reading and fell asleep." (A little white lie)

"That's when the flue must have closed, while you were asleep."

"Yes, and the next thing I remember was sitting on the lawn coughing." She thought of herself sitting there in her nakedness and blushed. "I'm so embarrassed."

He wanted to ask her why she was naked, but thought better of it. "Don't be, I'm just glad I got you covered up before the rest of them got there," he smiled, "knowing some of those guys, they may have just let you stay that way."

She took a sip of her coffee to help settle the blush. She set the cup down, raised a napkin from her lap, and gently patted her lips. He was watching her. She returned the napkin to her lap and met his gaze with those colorful eyes. "I'm sorry, I think I've gotten ahead of myself," she extended her hand. "I'm Annison, Annison Barrett."

"Dodge Maddison," he squeezed her soft hand. "I'm really glad you're alright, you gave me one helluva scare, I wasn't sure you were going to start breathing again. I was running on adrenaline. I'd never given CPR before and I had no idea if I was doing it right or not. Then I thought there might be someone else in the cabin, like kids, so I gave it one last try and was going to go back inside … thank God you started breathing."

"Thank God you were there." Their hands were still linked. "The doctors at the hospital said it was very close, another minute or two and it would have been too late to resuscitate me. I truly owe you my life, and I must do something to repay you."

"No, please don't feel that way, it was fate," his eyes started to fade away, "I'm a true believer in fate, and I think I was guided there."

Dodge got quiet. Annison could see he was slipping deep into thought. His eyes were fixed on their clasped hands, he wasn't blinking. She was concerned. She placed her free hand on top of his, "Are you okay?"

They were total strangers who had been brought together by a life threatening circumstance. They had been in a harrowing situation, profound in its severity, intimate by its very nature, and instantaneously rendering them close and special to one another. "I was going to stay at the house," he was talking low, almost to himself, "but something made me drive down to the lake that night." He looked up. "I lost my grandparents, we were very close."

"I was just reading about it in the newspaper, I'm very sorry."

He leaned closer to her and placed his free hand now on top of hers. In the short solemn moments of that daybreak morning they had shared a communion transcending normal protocol, a depth beyond pretense and social role-playing. They felt as if they knew each other deeply and felt intrinsically comfortable with one another. He spoke quietly to her, "I haven't stayed at the cottage in years, but something called me down there that night, you're going to think this is weird," he paused.

"No, go on, please."

"I think it may have been my grandmother. She had this sort of ritual she performed each day. She had two glasses of wine each day; one glass of white in the morning, at dawn actually, and a glass of red at sunset. I grew up with them, my parents were killed when I was very young, and they brought me up, and as long as I can remember, Gramma Emma performed her little homage to the beginning of the day, and to the end of the day. So, I decided to stay at the lake and row out to the middle at dawn with a bottle of white wine and make a final toast to her and then ceremoniously slip the bottle over the side. That's what I was doing that morning. Crazy, huh?"

"No, I think it's sweet. I guess I have your grandmother to thank too."

"Maybe. I don't know, but something definitely happened to me that morning, I've been thinking about it a lot. It was like breathing life back into you somehow was giving a gift from her. Passing something on. I really don't know how to explain it, it all happened so fast; it was all so surreal to me. I felt something at that moment that I can't quite explain. But whatever that feeling is has stayed with me." He paused letting the deep thoughts of the past few days come to the surface.

"Since I received the news of their deaths, I had been wallowing in my grief, lost in lament and ridden with guilt, and then, after that morning, I felt exhilarated, actually stimulated, as if I had somehow met death head-on and had beaten it." He looked up at her, "Does any of this make sense?"

Annison reflected, "Yes, I think I have an idea of what you mean. I've never had an experience that I can draw upon that comes anywhere close to what I went through that morning. It was surreal for me also. I remember dreaming. I was floating, someone was whispering my name, I was drifting towards that voice, it was a peaceful voice, calm and soothing, calling me toward it. I was flying, there were people all around me, familiar people, yet I couldn't actually identify anyone. They were warm to me, extending me a feeling of welcome. I was pleased to be amongst them and happy to be getting closer and closer to that comforting voice. It was a feeling of excitement that I can't explain. I knew I was dreaming, but it was so real and I didn't want to wake up. And then, there was this jolt and I was suddenly falling, falling fast. Everything disappeared and it got all black and cold, like falling through a black night. I could feel the ground coming up fast and I could see it coming at me hard, and there was water all around. I panicked, trying desperately to stop, flailing my arms wildly and calling out to that voice to help me. Then a second before hitting, I screamed. And then I was on the lawn, curled up and coughing, the air rushing into my lungs, cold and stinging, and someone beside me, wrapping me in a blanket making me warm."

"I'm glad I brought a blanket. Everything happened so fast. When you started breathing again I got up to run back into the cabin, and that's when I noticed you were naked. I ran down to the boat and got the blanket and put it over you."

"Dodge, I don't remember you doing that. I distinctly saw a woman, an old woman, wrapping it around me, I even tried to say thank you to her, but I was coughing too hard, I couldn't speak."

They sat in silence, neither one knowing what to say. They wanted to give each other an explanation, but decided to let it stay the way it was, maybe there was a plausible explanation, maybe not. The important thing was that Annison was all right. She knew this and Dodge knew it too. He was looking at her. She was a beautiful woman. Her smile was wide and bright and touching, illuminating her face and making her green eyes shine.

Dodge said, "You know, I'd ..."

"Well hello there!" bellowed Chucky. He was one of the firemen who had been at the cabin that morning. "How ya doin'?" He grinned at Annison and looked at their intertwined hands. They had forgotten they had been holding hands, and with the intrusion became suddenly aware of it and released each other as if they were secret teenage lovers caught by a nosy body classmate.

"Hey, Chucky," Dodge introduced Annison.

"Hi," he shook her hand, "nice to see you out and about." His eyes were scanning her breasts, he was the proverbial short, squatty, balding pervert, harmlessly endearing once you got to know him, which every girl in town unfortunately did. "I was one of the firemen that came to your rescue."

"Well then, I thank you very much, Chucky."

"Lotta smoke in there that morning, but we got it out for ya. I was the one who set up the fans in the doorways for ya."

"Oh? I'm glad you did." His stare was off her breasts by now, but Annison could see why Dodge said he was glad he got the blanket around her before the rescue team arrived. Annison was used to the male responses that her appearance brought, she dealt with businessmen on a daily basis at The Inn at Barrett's Bluff. Chucky's glances seemed harmless, but she thought he could use some lessons in discretion.

"Yeah, and then I re-conned the whole house, just ta make sure everything was okay. Sometimes if you're not thorough things get overlooked, and a fire can start up again hours after we've left," he was showing off, trying to look important.

"And then I ..."

"Move out of the way, Chucky." Dot pushed him with her hip. "And leave these fine people alone." She set down two menus with one hand, and refilled their coffees from a pot she held in the other. "Specials are on the chalkboard." She grabbed Chucky's elbow and ushered him away like a teacher rounding up her pesky student.

"Nice to meet you," Chucky said to Annison over his shoulder.

"You too, Chucky."

"He's a decent enough guy," Dodge chuckled, "but Chucky can be a pain in the ass sometimes."

"Oh, I think he's cute."

"Don't let him know that, he'll have that comment blown up into a full-fledged romance and all over town in two minutes."

Dot came back and took their orders. Annison ordered the #1, over easy with whole-wheat toast and hash browns. Dodge got the 'Big Bad John' blueberry pancakes. Dot stayed at the table for a minute chatting with Dodge, which gave Annison the opportunity to 'discreetly' check him out. He was as handsome as he appeared in the magazine ads and the TV clips she had seen of him. But up close and personal like, there was a settled warmth about him. He seemed very real, not like some of the personalities she knew who visited Barrett's Bluff just to be noticed and pampered. Compared to the famous sitcom and Broadway people, the Hollywood and music stars, and the pompous talk-show personalities, Dodge Maddison seemed unpretentious and easygoing. She felt at ease with him, as if she had known him all her life. She watched him conversing and laughing with Dot.

Annison had seen him come in and had watched his nicely fitting jeans walk over to the counter where he had said hello to the patrons and had gotten his cup of coffee. She had buried her head in the newspaper as he approached her, but now, she could take a free look at him sitting there in his light chambray denim shirt with the first two buttons undone. The blue shirt perfectly complementing his blue eyes, oh those blue eyes …

"You two just sit and relax," Dot was saying, "I'll be back in a few with your breakfast," and she spun on her heels and was gone.

"She's nice," Annison said, "is that her husband in the kitchen?"

"Yup, Big Bad John. They've owned this place forever."

"It's very nice, you seem wholly at ease here."

"Well, it's my home town. I don't get any special treatment here; I'm just another townie. I like that. People respect your privacy."

"Tell me about your grandparents, your grandmother sounds like an interesting lady."

"She was. She was a very fashionable lady. She wore fashion well. She's actually responsible for my career."

"Really?"

Dodge told her about watching the old movies with her and sitting on the couch sketching and how it progressed to her sewing together his designs to sell to her friends. And how Emma and Jed had sold off part of the farm to send him to be educated at London's R.A.F.D. He continued his story during their breakfast, telling Annison how he had trudged all over New York City with his illusions of working for the big name fashion designers. How he had ended up down in SoHo sketching hats; his relationship with his 'mentor' Stanley Silverman; the tragedy and Stanley's gift that had gotten him started in manufacturing; how he began alone, sewing his own dresses at night and selling them by day out of the storefront.

"It was slow and tedious at first, for a long time actually, but then it caught on, and wham! it took off like wildfire. I was scrambling to hire more people and buy more machinery."

"And you live in the City now, right?"

"Yes, in the same building, actually." He told her how he had eventually bought the old building and gave her a descriptive tour from the top down. Starting at his penthouse, to the Level 5 Studio, to the manufacturing floors, the second floor loft, and down to the street level shop and storefront windows of *Lady Maddison*.

"So, is there?"

"Is there what?"

"Is there a Lady Maddison?" She couldn't believe she had just asked him that.

"Now or ever?" he grinned.

"Both," she said coyly. What the hell, she was brave.

He thought of Dana, and then of Harlow, "No, not at the moment." He wasn't exactly sure about Harlow, he was still wondering about those feelings, "but I was married once, a long time ago."

"Oh?"

"It didn't last long, less than a year actually. "

Annison was adding sugar and cream to her coffee that Dot had freshened after clearing the table, "What happened?"

"Young, successful, and foolish," he laughed. "She was a model, I was feeling my oats, it seemed like the thing to do at the time. But the novelty of it wore off quickly, and our goals became different. She wanted to settle the pace down, have kids, raise a family, but I was too much into the business, not ready to share my time. So, we called it quits."

"Do you regret it?"

"The marriage?"

"Not having children."

Dodge hadn't really thought about it. That's not true, he had, subconsciously, and now even consciously. With Emma and Jed gone, he had no family, he was alone. Successful and alone. Kids; he had Penny and Brent, but they were Ben's kids. What was all of this work work work for? Who did he have to share it with? To pass it on to? Where was his mindset? Was he afraid of having children? Afraid something would happen to him and his kids would have to grow up without him?

"Do you still see each other?" Annison broke into his silence.

"No, not in many years. I heard she's happily married to a movie producer in L.A., got two or three kids."

"Oh, I thought maybe she was the one you've been photographed with recently."

"Photographs?"

"Well, I *do* read magazines occasionally," she needled him.

"Oh, that's mostly rumors."

"Mostly?"

He smiled at her teasing tone; he was enjoying their bantering. "Hey, enough about me! I've told you my life story, you've got me at a disadvantage already."

"Woman's prerogative," she kidded.

"That's not fair, I don't know anything about you." He looked down at her pendant resting in the nook of her cleavage and then back up into her eyes. Thinking about that morning they first met, he said, "Well, that's not exactly true is it?" He could tease too.

"Touché, Mr. Maddison," she said. "See, you already know more about me than I'd like you to."

* * *

They didn't notice as the lunch crowd shuffled in and the diner got loud and busy, they sat engrossed in their conversation learning about each other and liking what they learned. The day outside, cloud free and baking in the strong autumn sun, had heated up into the mid-eighties. Ceiling fans whispered above them, stirring the air and keeping it pleasant.

"So," Dodge said, "how about you? Ever been married?"

"Umm," she didn't know why this took her off guard, "I ... I am, am married," she struggled.

"Oh, I didn't realize. You're not wearing a ring."

Annison was unconsciously rubbing her ring finger with her left thumb, "I just took it off recently, the other night actually."

"I'm sorry, I didn't mean to pry."

"No, that's alright. I guess it would only be fair, I've certainly pried enough into your life history," she stopped the finger fidgeting and sank back into her booth. "That's part of the reason I'm here, maybe most of the reason, I'm not sure."

He gave her a look that said you don't have to get into it if you don't want to. "We can change the subject if you'd like."

She thought for a moment and then began, "A close friend owns the cabin and I needed some time for myself. I run an Inn down in Connecticut. Things have been weighing on me of late and I had to just 'get away from it all' for a while."

"Whereabouts in Connecticut?"

"Barrett's Bluff."

"The Inn at Barrett's Bluff?" he said with a knowledgeable slant.

"Yes, do you know it?"

"I've been there. Couple times; once attending a wedding, and then another for a getaway weekend. It's a very nice place."

"Thank you. Funny, I don't remember seeing you there."

"I'm sure we missed each other," he said matter-of-factly, "I know I would have remembered seeing you."

"Is that an ounce of flattery I detect?" she asked.

"A pound or two at least," he smiled. "How long have you been there?"

"Oh God, all my life! That's got to be part of my problem."

"Annison Barrett," he pondered her name, "so does that mean your ancestry founded the town?"

"My husband's ancestry. Old Captain Jonathan J. Barrett himself; renegade pirate and seafaring scoundrel ...Arrr!...blender of the rascally Barrett bloodline."

Dodge laughed. "Sounds like an interesting character, how'd he get a town named after him?"

"Won it in a card game."

"Huh?"

"Do you really want to hear this story?"

"Yes, please go on." He wanted to hear all about this Annison Barrett, this charming, funny, charismatic woman sitting before him and making his morning more than a pleasant one. She could tell him about the origins and history of crocheting and he'd be enthralled. Her voice was pleasing to him, and looking at her wasn't bad either.

"Way back when in the days of 'yor,'" she began in a bedtime-story voice, "for unknown scandalous reasons, Jonathan J. Barrett, a British Naval Captain, got himself decommissioned and kicked out of jolly old England. So, he loaded up his schooner with all sorts of pillaged goodies and set out across the Great Pond. Stealing the boat of course. As the story goes, he landed rather hard, one stormy night, upon the craggy shores of southern Connecticut. Not one to let a mere shipwreck disturb his thirst for a good time, the ole pirate wandered into the nearby town in quest of a frothy pint." Dodge was enjoying this, she's a great story teller. "He joined in a game of poker with a few of the local dignitaries, one of whom happened to be the landowner of the cliffs whereupon the captain's schooner now rested. One thing lead to another, the beer was flowing, the night got longer, the men got drunker, and the cards seemed to play in the captain's favor. The conniving captain kept raising the pot until it was just he and the squire left in the game. The pompous landowner, so used to controlling the game and winning by shear intimidation, wasn't about to be embarrassed by some ruffian sailor who couldn't steer a ship properly. The stakes climbed higher and higher. Then Barrett reached inside his shirt, pulled out a hefty bag of gold doubloon and tossed it onto the table. The crowd was transfixed; they were enjoying the landowner's predicament. He was significantly challenged for the first time. But, not to be outdone, he matched the bag of gold with the title to the land the ship rested upon. The crafty pirate then put up his ship's entire bounty – supposedly worth a hundred bags of gold – against all of the properties the squire held. The air got thick and quiet, and, in a moment of stale sobriety, realizing he was out-matched, the landowner backed down and folded."

"Then what happened?"

"Well, the dethroned squire wanted to see the pirate's winning hand. Barrett refused of course, because he had been bluffing all along, and a brawl ensued. Much to everyone's delight, the pirate easily KO'd the landowner, and, devil be with him, ole Jonathan J. Barrett bluffed his way into a piece of America."

"Hence, Barrett's Bluff?"

"Hence, Barrett's Bluff."

"That's a great story."

"Did you like it?"

"Yeah."

"I made it up!"

"What?! You did not!"

"No," she snickered, "I didn't, but I had you though."

"Very funny," he liked her sense of humor. "It's a big place, it must be a lot of work."

"It is, it's very demanding, and now ..."

"Now?"

Annison couldn't believe how easy Dodge was to talk to, she had no reservations opening up her life to him. "Now I think I've lost my drive."

"How so?"

"I have a son and a daughter. They grew up at the Inn and worked there since they were young. All along I was assuming they would take over the business, but neither of them has expressed an interest. In fact, they're both out of the picture. JJ, my son, is a career pilot in the Air Force, and Sarah just got married this past spring and is living in D.C. So, all along I've been busting my hump more so for them than myself, and now I don't see any reason for continuing on."

"What about your husband?"

"He's never been involved, really. He fell into it by heritage and was pushed by his demanding father to run the Inn, but he always resented it, still does. And, he's got too much of the pirate's mischievous blood in his veins, too much of a playboy and not enough of a businessman. To tell you the truth, if it wasn't for me I truly believe the Inn would have collapsed years ago. And now, with the kids gone, I don't think I can do it anymore, just don't have the will."

"So you've taken a sabbatical to figure things out."

"Essentially, and at the urging of my best friend. You might know her, Nina Sanderson? She's owned the cabin here for years and she's a Real Estate broker back in the City."

"No, I don't know her from town, but I think I may have seen her ads in New York, Sanderson Specialty?"

"Sanderson Realty Specialists. She's been my best friend since we were little girls. She grew up in Barrett's Bluff. She probably understands me better than I do. She's the one who suggested secluding myself at the lake."

"That's a nice spot over there, I like that part of the lake."

"It's a perfect little getaway. I'm really quite enjoying it."

"Have you come up with any solutions yet?"

"Hell no! But it's nice spending time just for myself. No one knows where I am, except for Nina. I just had to face my demons alone. I knew I needed to, and now that I'm into 'Annison's Retreat', as Nina calls it, I'm realizing how much I needed it, and how long overdue it's been. I've been here only two weeks and I already feel like a new person."

"That's a brave thing to do, I commend you."

"Thank you."

"How long are you staying?"

"Forever! Or at least I wish I could. I'm not really sure. To tell you the truth, it hasn't been easy. The first few days were tough, I think I cried a river of self-pity, and almost got in the car and drove back home several times. But I made a promise to Nina to stay at least two weeks. She said it wouldn't be easy. It's been so long since I've spent time alone for myself. I guess I had to get through the initial first days of loneliness or guilt or trauma or whatever. But now, I feel great. I'm feeling good about myself again, rejuvenated, doing things for myself again. Creative things like revitalizing my long dormant artwork. I've actually surprised myself with a few halfway decent sketches."

"That's great. I always enjoyed my artwork. It's peaceful and gratifying, I'd love to get back into it."

"But aren't you? As a designer, I mean?"

"Not as much anymore. *Maddison Designs* has become its own animal, with a huge clientele to dress and stockholders to satisfy. Production is so high and the designs changing so fast that we've got a studio full of young designers that do most of the work."

"Oh."

Dot caught their attention from behind the counter and lifted a fresh pot of coffee. The both shook their heads.

"So," Dodge asked Annison, "what else have you been doing?"

"Well, I've been doing a lot of walking. Walking and thinking. The weather's been beautiful and there are a lot of neat little trails around here, and the foliage is spectacular."

"Wait 'til it peaks, the colors around the lake and the surrounding mountains are really breathtaking."

"And you?"

"Me?"

"How long are you staying?"

"Oh, a couple more days I guess. There are a few things to be done with the estate and probate and all that legal mumbo jumbo. And I've got to get back to New York, we just broke our new line and there's a lot to do."

"It must be very exciting, the fashion world."

"It's probably pretty much like any business, only lots of hard work keeps it running, you know what that's like. With fashion, most people see only the glitter and glamour of the runway models and the extravagant designs, but that's only ten percent of it. The other ninety percent is damn hard work, and pretty boring at times."

Dot was mopping the floor. She had already flipped the "closed" sign in the window and upturned the chairs onto the tables. Her husband John had cleaned his grill and put things away in the kitchen and had already gone. It was past their two o'clock closing time.

"Wow," Dodge said looking at his watch, "I can't believe we've been sitting here for over four hours."

"Oh my God," Annison said looking at her wrist. "Have we? It seems like it's only been no more than an hour."

"You two can sit's long as you like," Dot said as she dragged the mop past their table, "I'll be through here in just a minute and you can have the place to yourselves. The front's all locked up and you can leave out the back, just turn the lock on the door as you leave," and she was past them and mopping around the counter.

"Would she do that? Just let us stay in here?" Annison asked.

117

"Knowing Dot, she probably would."

"Boy, this is a small town."

Dodge went over to the counter to pay up and Annison took the time to check her face. She got up and went to the counter. "I'm going to the ladies room," she said as she passed by Dodge. "Now, please don't lock me in here." She smiled at them.

"Seems like a nice lady," Dot said handing Dodge his change.

"Yes, she does, doesn't she? She's visiting down at the lake."

"I know. She's the one you rescued the other day."

"Nothing gets by you, huh Dot?"

"Not in this town it don't," she grinned. "Hear you opened up the cottage again."

"Yup. It's been a long time."

"You stay there awhile, it'll do you good," and she turned from him and went into the kitchen.

He went over to the table, left a tip, and stood looking out onto Main Street. It was a beautiful Saturday afternoon. The shops across the street all had their doors open and their wares were gracing the storefronts. The antique shop even had an oak dining room collection set up on the sidewalk. There were two white limos parked in front of The Tavern, there must be a wedding reception going on, he thought. Traffic was light and some boys on skateboards were jumping the curbs, their feet hidden beneath their elephant bell-bottoms.

"She didn't leave did she?" Annison walked back to the booth.

"No, she's out back, but we'd better go before she goes, I wouldn't feel right being in here alone."

"Me either, although I feel like I could just go on talking to you, you're very easy to talk to, and you're a good listener. I hope I didn't burden you with all my jibber-jabber."

"No, not at all, I rather enjoyed it. The time really flew by. You're an interesting lady."

Annison gathered her things and they headed for the door.

"We're going out the front, Dot!" Maddison hollered.

"Okay, I'll lock it up," her voice bellowed. "You two have a nice day ... and you remember what I said Dodge Maddison."

"Yes ma'am," he replied respectfully.

"What's that all about?"

"Oh, nothing. Dot just playing mother hen."

They spent an awkward moment on the sidewalk in front of the diner, neither one wanting to end their time together, but not knowing what to say. Annison spoke first, "I really do thank you for all you've done for me and for meeting me this morning, I really enjoyed our talk. It was very nice meeting you," she extended her hand.

"The pleasure was all mine," he replied and he meant it.

They shook hands and then stood again in another awkward moment. "I must do something to repay you."

"No, please don't feel that way." *How about dinner tonight* was what he really wanted to say. *Why am I suddenly so shy?*

"Well then, at least let me extend a welcome to *Barrett's Bluff.* Anytime."

"Thanks, but will you be there?"

"Hmmm, right now I think not, but I'll probably end up back there in some way or another."

"A positive one I hope."

"Oh, I'm sure it will be." Awkward again. "Well, I think I've taken up enough of your time, Mr. Maddison, but please, let me know if there's anything I can do, I am truly indebted to you."

Again a handshake.

"Good-bye, I've really enjoyed talking with you."

"Good-bye, Annison Barrett. I hope your time in Bryce Corner is fruitful. Good luck with your 'retreat'."

"Thank you, good-bye."

They parted and went their separate ways. Dodge got only a few yards before he turned to speak to her, but she was already gone. He stood a moment in the hot sun soaking up the feelings of the past few hours.

*What an interesting lady.*

She had made quite an impression on him.

# 18

## *TWIGS OF BITTERSWEET*

Annison rounded the corner by town hall and walked along Cottage Street. The maples lining the long sidewalk down to the town beach were dropping early leaves of foliage, like intermittent lollypops floating down to the trim green lawns fronting the Victorian houses, warm in the bright afternoon sun. Another perfect lazy-day New England afternoon. A perfect complement to her wonderful morning. She had been skeptical on her earlier walk into town. She didn't really think Dodge Maddison would take the time to meet with some loony woman who almost burned her friend's cabin down. She felt embarrassed and wished she hadn't left the note on his back door. But it was too late and she was obligated to show up or look even more foolish. She had almost walked right on by Dot's Diner, but now she was glad she had gone in. Very glad.

She was smiling as she passed by the football field across the narrow street from the beach. She heard the coach yelling commands to the little elementary kids all dressed in their bright uniforms, practicing their plays. They looked top heavy in their helmets and big shoulder pads, like they would fall over just standing up. They were so cute. The coach barked at them, ordering them to lap the field in single file, and she heard them singing a school song as they ran towards the far goal posts.

She was still smiling, walking along thinking of the conversation with this interesting man. She was surprised at his demeanor, not expecting him to be so down to earth, so pleasant, so intriguing. And charming, *God he's charming! I wonder what Nina would think of him?* She stopped dead in her tracks, *What the hell am I thinking? Where did that come from?* She moved along, going off the roadway and onto the shortcut through the woods that would bring her up to the bluff on the southern side of the lake. *You're supposed to be figuring out your life, setting goals, and deciding your future. Not getting schoolgirl butterflies in your stomach over some hotshot fashion designer.*

She had pretty much resolved to get a divorce from Jack. And this time she had to be steadfast and not let Jack sweet talk her into one more reconciliation sugared with promises to change his ways and become '*a man you can respect and still be in love with.*' It was over. That was one thing she knew for sure. What to do with her life beyond that, no idea, but one step at a time. She wasn't sure about the Inn. It was all she had done, ever, and she was tired of it. Time for a change. Maybe getting away from Barrett's' Bluff would be best too, move down to the City. *I could stay with Nina until I found something. Advertising or marketing or get my Real Estate license and join her firm, she's always said she'd love to have me, that with my personality I'd enjoy it and do very well.* Her options were open, so she felt a security in that respect. The kids? They were grown and on their own. They probably wouldn't be surprised. They had, after all, grown up in the atmosphere of a troubled marriage. They weren't stupid. Sarah had even asked her more than once how she put up with it for so long. They knew. *I hope they're marriages are long and happy ones, not like mine.* She chastised herself for not being strong enough to get out of it earlier, but felt that she had done the right thing. For better or worse, JJ and Sarah had grown up with both their parents there for them. Most of their friends had had to deal with step-moms and step-dads and visitation rights. Annison didn't want that for her children, no matter what, and she had sacrificed. Sacrificed her happiness, her twenties and thirties, and even her dreams. But now it was time. If she had learned nothing else during these past two weeks of forced introspection, it was that now was her time. *I need to be me again!*

She was on the ridge that overlooked the lake from south to north. The Ottauquag Indians used to hold their councils here. It was a safe spot with a long view of the entire lake and they could see to the reeds at the northern point where the narrow river entered and where their enemies might attack from. The Maukaquee from Vermont or the Sasquats from Canada, slithering through the tall reeds in their war canoes. The view was spectacular and Lake Wickaboag lay calm in the heat of the day. It was cool in the shade of the tall pines as she sauntered along with a new sense of self. She found herself smiling again. She was thinking of when she was telling Dodge the Captain Barrett story and how she had gotten him at the end. She laughed. He had listened to her story with obvious interest. Actually he had listened to everything she had talked about.

Really listened. *There's a novelty*, when was the last time Jack had listened to anything she was saying? *Oh Jack, you're not going to take this well are you?* She wondered how he was holding up, how things were going at the Inn. She was sure he was pissed off. She had left him a note, not wanting to face another yelling spree by attempting to talk to him, to let him know her feelings and how much she needed to take some time for herself, alone, where no one knew where she was, to sort things out. He wouldn't care. He wouldn't understand. "Who the hell's gonna take care of things!?" he'd yell. "What about the functions? The damn staff? We're coming into foliage season! We've got weddings up our ass! You can't leave!" God forbid *he'd* have to do anything. Actually work a day in his life.

Annison hadn't wanted to leave the diner. She could have stayed all day long chatting with handsome Mister Maddison. *He has such beautiful blue eyes. I wonder if he's happy. He must be, how could he not be? Good looking, successful, rich. Women falling all over him. But he seemed withdrawn at times, almost sad. It was probably the grief over losing his grandparents. It must be that. I'm sure he's happy with his life ... and why would you be wondering that, Annison?*

Below the bluff, you picked up the gravel road snaking along the western shore. It is lined high with pine trees and white birches and hedged with bittersweet popping with little red and yellow berries. Annison picked a few branches and watched the squirrels gathering acorns in their cheeks and running them up the pines to lofty nests insulated with freshly fallen leaves and pine needles and thickened with bramble. Another sure sign that autumn was here and the inevitable winter was approaching. *Maybe I should go somewhere warm this winter, stay four to six months in Florida, in the Keys, or maybe the Bahamas. Where does Dodge Maddison winter? Dammit! There you go again. Forget about him. It was a nice brunch, we had a lovely talk and that's that.* But she did want to see him again, at the Inn perhaps if he came for a visit this season. But she wasn't sure she'd even be there. Her new plans seemed to be telling her not to go back, not to get wrapped up in it again, not to succumb to everyone else's wishes, to remain strong like she was feeling now and be selfish. Nina had said selfish was good. *Remember? That's the mantra, selfish is good ... selfish is good.*

Nina's little log cabin came into view sitting at the very end of the lane. She was thinking she'd place the bittersweet along the mantel, and maybe a twig or two in the kitchen. Consciously, these were the thoughts going through her mind. Subconsciously, she was wondering if she would see Dodge again before he left town. She wanted to see him again right now, but she didn't allow those thoughts to reach the surface. But her insides knew. Her heart had a new throb to it.

*How could you know that? How could you have such feelings after spending only four hours with someone?*

\* \* \*

Annison spent the rest of the afternoon fussing about the cabin. The twigs of bittersweet she had placed here and there freshened the main room and brought a feeling of autumn inside. The open windows had eliminated the acrid smell from the smoke and the air was clean and renewed again.

She grabbed a book to read and wandered down the slopping lawn to a set of Adirondack chairs near the water's edge. She could see across the lake to the cottages on the eastern shoreline. The Maddison cottage was sitting tiny in the distance across the water. *What had he called it? Camp Nyla? Named for a Scottish ancestor? A reference to family from a man who now has none.* Annison felt pity for him - a twitch of a motherly instinct. And a desire to hold him. Ohmygod! *Where is this coming from?*

The day before, she had gotten directions from Chief Ben and had gone over to Camp Nyla to pin her note to the back door. Now, sitting across the lake, Annison watched Dodge Maddison's cottage being washed with the soft colors of the approaching sunset. All afternoon she had tried to keep her mind busy and occupied, but no matter what she did, it wandered back to Dot's Diner.

She had been reading and now, as the twilight shadows crept up behind her stealing her light, she sat with her book open and upside down in her lap, watching the opposite horizon in its autumnal foliage, so quiet and calm and serene before her. The colorful scene like a still painting, framed by pink clouds above and below in the mirror of the lake. She wondered if Dodge had been thinking of her all day. *That would be a little presumptuous of you, now wouldn't it Annison?* She heard the sound of a small motor and saw a boat coming close to the shore to her right. A figure sitting in the stern was steering the boat with his hand on the motor. He waved as he passed by. She didn't know who it was, but returned the neighborly greeting. Again for the thousandth time her eyes found Dodge's cottage. It was darker than it had been even a moment ago, the sun falls faster in autumn. A light came on. Clearly she had just seen it. She stared to be sure. Yes, it wasn't there a second ago. He must still be here. *What is wrong with me?* I feel like a stalker. But she had so enjoyed the time they had shared. She wanted to call him to say thank you for their conversation. To let him know how much she enjoyed it, how touched she was that he had taken the time to be with her. Maybe drive over and do it in person. *What?! Are you crazy? What are you thinking? What's wrong with you?*

A phone rang. She snapped out of her illusion. It rang again. It was definitely coming from the cabin. She sat frozen to the chair, her eyes glued to the cottage across the lake. It rang again and she jumped up and flew into the cabin. Annison placed her hand on her cell phone on the counter and hesitated. It rang again and scared her so that she actually jumped. She closed her eyes and an unexpected sultry voice came out of her mouth, "Hello?"

"Well that's an interesting tone of hello. Who were you expecting a call from?" It was Nina.

"Nina, ohmygod," she shrieked. "I'm glad it's you."

"Were you expecting someone else?"

"No, no, I guess I'm just a little stir crazy." The phone scared me, it's the first time it's rung."

"You haven't called the Inn have you?" Nina asked sternly.

"No, doctor."

"Good. You're supposed to be stress free and introspective, remember?"

"Yes doctor, Sister Annison here."

"Very funny. But it's working, right?"

"Actually I have to admit it was kind of tough the first week, but since then it's gotten better each day. I've been doing a lot of soul searching."

"That's a perfect spot for it, isn't it? It must be beautiful this time of year, I should be there with you, but you need the time to yourself. I'm glad my little cabin is there for you. I've been meaning to call you earlier but it's been so hectic around here lately ..." Nina trailed off going into a long non-stop dissertation about the remodeling dilemmas she was going through on her brownstone in the Village. The good news was that the painters had completed the living room and foyer, including the ornate woodwork, while she was away in Atlanta at a real estate conference. The bad news was that they did it in the wrong color. And she hadn't wanted the woodwork touched.

"What a fiasco that turned out to be! I made them re-do the walls and strip and stain the woodwork back to its original state. They of course fought me on everything 'cuz they didn't want to correct their own damn mistakes, the jerks!" Annison laughed, it was good to hear from her close friend, she was lifting her spirits and bringing her back to reality, she recognized that perhaps she'd been doing too much day-dreaming.

"And then ..." Nina went on and on. Annison placed her cell on the counter and put it on speaker so she could move about the kitchen fixing herself a cup of tea.

"But enough about me, how are you doing?"

"Well," Annison picked up her phone and sat on one of the stools, took a sip of tea, and began, "Initially I felt guilty about running off and secluding myself, but I kept repeating your mantra ..."

"Selfish is good ..."

"Uh huh, and I've been doing a lot of walking, taking little drives into the countryside, and I've actually started sketching again. I was thinking I might pick up some brushes and paints and attempt watercolors again."

"Oh that would be so good for you. I remember your paintings from school, they were always so nice. You've always had a knack for color, even in how you decorated the Inn."

"Well, we'll see, it's been over twenty years since I've painted anything more than a guestroom," she laughed, "but the sketches have surprised me and I feel quite good about it."

"That's because you're feeling good about yourself again! Listen, I'll bet you could find all the art stuff you need in Amherst. It's not far and it's an artsy college town, and there's an art supply store right in the center of town. I think it's in the bookstore building."

"I'll have to go check that out," she sipped her tea.

"So, how's Bryce Corner been treating you? Quaint little town isn't it?"

"Yes it is. It's very relaxing."

"Yeah, not much ever happens up there."

Annison bit her lower lip. She hadn't told Nina about the fire. She didn't want her to know how stupid she had been. She still felt it was somehow her fault no matter what anyone said. *Like if I hadn't been so damn drunk and passed out! She'd never tell her.* There was no damage done, she'd gotten the flue fixed, and Nina rarely visited anyways. What she didn't know wouldn't hurt her.

"I met the Chief of Police."

"What?"

"And the Fire Marshall." Women can't keep a secret.

"What are you talking about?!"

Annison told her the story, including the part about dancing to her newfound freedom and passing out in front of the fireplace. *What the hell, if you can't tell your best friend things ...*

"Oh Annie, I'm sooo glad you're alright. I feel so bad! I'll have someone come out and fix the chimney and make sure everything's safe."

"Nina, don't worry about it. I've already done that. It was just a faulty flue, that's all. That and a drunk girlfriend. The contractor replaced the thing and everything works perfect. In fact, I had the fire going last night and everything's fine, really."

"Are you sure you're alright?"

"Yes, I'm fine. Please don't worry about me, if anything I'm more embarrassed than anything else."

"Embarrassed about what?"

"Not having my clothes on when I got rescued."

"What?"

"I was naked."

"Naked?" Nina snickered.

"Bare ass naked."

"Do I dare ask why?" the snicker grew to a giggle.

"I got so hot in the cabin dancing around ..."

"And drinking a whole bottle of champagne ..."

"And drinking almost a whole bottle of champagne," Annison was beginning to laugh now too, "that I ripped all my clothes off and ended up falling asleep ..."

"Passing out ..." Nina was laughing hard picturing the upcoming scene.

"And when they rescued me ..."

"You were naked as a jaybird!" Nina finished, and they both laughed hysterically, Nina the loudest, wiping the tears from her cheeks. "Oh my God, Annie, I would have loved to have seen that! I'll bet the firemen were falling all over each other to give you CPR."

"Well actually I was covered up by the time they got there."

"With what?"

"A blanket."

"I thought you said you were out cold." Nina was confused.

"I was, but there was this man in a rowboat who happened by and broke the door in and actually pulled me out."

"Huh?"

"He was the one who pulled me out of the smoke and gave me mouth to mouth and wrapped me in a blanket."

"A man just happened by at dawn in a rowboat? What man?"

"You're not going to believe this ..."

"I'm not sure I believe any of this."

"Dodge Maddison."

"Dodge Maddison? The designer?"

"Yes," Annison smirked to herself wishing she could see Nina's face.

Nina hesitated, "Annie, now I know I don't believe this. Are you putting me on? What the hell are you talking about? Are you still hungover?"

Annison laughed, "No, really, he has a cottage on the other side of the lake and was out rowing that morning and saw the smoke."

"Are you shitting me?"

"No, not at all."

"I don't believe it," Nina said, "and if I knew you to be a practical joker, I wouldn't. That is amazing! I didn't know he lived in Bryce Corner."

"Actually, he lives in the City down in SoHo, but he's originally from Bryce Corner, he was born here."

"So was he just up there vacationing?"

"No, his grandparents died, and he's here for the funeral."

"Together?"

"Huh?"

"His grandparents died? In a car crash or something?"

"No, his grandmother had a heart attack and his grandfather died."

"How?" Nina, as inquisitive as always.

"I don't know, it didn't say in the newspaper, and Dodge didn't get into it."

"That's odd."

Annison thought for a minute and realized Dodge hadn't mentioned how his grandfather had died. "I don't know."

"So what's he like?" Nina, moving the conversation right along, "I can't believe Dodge Maddison rescued your naked ass - that's hilarious!" she was laughing hard again. "So, what's he like."

Annison synopsized her breakfast meeting at Dot's Diner to an attentive Nina.

"A four hour breakfast?" Nina said, "Wow, he must be something to look at."

Annison said he was and mentioned his well-fitting jeans.

"I love a man with a nice ass," Nina sang.

"You don't love men, remember?"

"A cute ass is a cute ass. Besides, I'm thinking of swinging back the other way."

"What? Are you serious?"

"Probably not, but it's becoming trendy, and you know how I like trendy."

There was a click on the phone line. Nina said, "Hang on a second, I'm expecting a call, I might have a dinner date, let me see if this is her." A moment later she clicked back in, "Gotta go babe, but I need to tell you something first. I wasn't going to because I don't want you to get upset, but you need to know. Jack's going bugshit trying to find you."

"That doesn't surprise me, Nina."

"He's left umpteen messages at my office and last Sunday he showed up on my doorstep."

"Now *that* surprises me. Why the hell would he do that?"

"He thought you might be here and he misses you and wants to apologize for being an asshole his whole life."

"That's a laugh."

"His male ego is hurt, that's all. He tried to use his boyish charm on me. Says they all miss you at the Inn and want you to come back asap. Which translates into Jack's clueless on how to run things without you and he's desperate to get you back. He tried to get me to tell him where you are, so I told him you went out of the country for a sabbatical."

"Did he believe you?"

"I don't know, our conversation was civil for only about five minutes before we got into an argument. He tried to tell me how he realized he was a fool at times and how much he really loved you and how much he needed you, yah da yah da yah da. I told him he was a no-good-lying son-of-a-bitch and it went off from there."

"Then what?"

"He called me a 'fuckin' dyke', I told him to go suck-a-big-one and he left."

"Nina, I'm sorry I got you in the middle of this."

"Don't worry about that. I've known Jack as long as you have. We understand each other, he doesn't like me and I don't like him. I'm only telling you this to reassure you that what you're doing is right. Give yourself all the time you need. You sound a helluva lot better than you did a couple weeks ago. Don't give up. Stay strong. If you need me, call, otherwise, I'll give you a buzz next weekend for a progress report, okay? Gotta go, love you!"

"Okay, I love you too, take care."

"Oh ... say hello to fashion Maddison for me," and she was gone.

It had been nice hearing from Nina. Annison was glad she had such a wonderful, caring friend. She was one of a kind. Fashion Maddison; cute; only Nina.

Jack's behavior didn't really surprise her, but she was a little concerned that he had driven into the City to pester Nina. Her first reaction was to call him and tell him to chill out, that she'd be back when she got back. But she thought better of it. She knew it'd only be one more argument. Jack had grown up a spoiled little boy used to getting his way by whining and throwing tantrums. When they argued you couldn't get a word in edgewise, it was a one-way conversation. Jack was right and that was that. He'd say his piece and then storm off, usually to a bar. Annison would hide her feelings in the business of running the Inn. But not anymore. She felt stronger. She felt like calling him up and calling him a 'no-good-son-of-a-bitch' herself. Dammit! She had gotten the Jack thing resolved in her mind, and now it was back on the surface. She was concerned about the Inn. She knew how the staff relied on her and she started feeling guilty again for abandoning them. She could drive back, spend a couple days checking on things, reassuring everyone that things would be okay, and then drive back to her 'retreat'. No! That wouldn't work. She'd get caught up in everything again and before she knew it, she'd be going through another holiday season, then another spring, summer, and right back into fall again. It'd be a year later and she'd be right back to square one. Only she'd probably be worse off, even further over the edge. She'd never been a quitter and she had promised herself to do this. Selfish is good. Stay with it girl!

Annison decided to get her mind off things. Drive into town and rent a movie. A sad girlie movie. All of a sudden she felt she could use a good cry. Maybe get some popcorn. It was too late to eat dinner, she'd been on the phone with Nina for almost two hours. She remembered her book and went outside to retrieve it. The ebony sky was clear and full of bright stars. There was dew beneath her feet as she bare-footed down the lawn to the Adirondack chair, muted white against the black lake. The book jacket was slippery to her touch. She folded over the jacket flap to mark her place. Instinctively she looked across the lake. The sky blended into the night-water making it difficult to tell the difference and find the horizon. It looked like one big ocean. It took her several seconds to discern the tiny yellow light hovering out there in the darkness like a lantern on the bow of a faraway ship. *Guess he's still here. She felt better.*

\* \* \*

The Bryce Corner General Store was an old building in the center of town across the street from Dot's Diner and adjacent to The Tavern. Originally home to the town doctor in the early eighteen hundreds, it went through several transformations: town hall offices, coffeehouse, bookstore, package store, coffeehouse again, and now a general mercantile which, in addition to groceries and sundries, offered a nice selection of DVD's for rent.

Annison pulled her white Lexus into the short parking lot next to a bright red antique car. She got out and walked between them and ascended the three quick steps onto the veranda and reached for the door. It unexpectedly swung open at her and she was almost knocked backwards.

"Oh, I'm sorry, I didn't ..." Dodge said apologetically, "Hey, hi! How are you?"

Annison was more taken aback by the sudden appearance of him than she was by the near collision, "Hello," she mustered and they stood a moment on the porch, Dodge still holding onto the door.

"Getting some groceries?" he asked.

"Um, yeah, I mean no," she stumbled. "I was thinking of renting a movie. Something romantic for a quiet evening. *" Why'd I say that? What does that mean?!* "And you?"

"Already got one. Gonna fizzle out in front of the tube and take it easy."

She felt silly. As if he knew she had been thinking of him all day and that she had wished they'd meet again, only she had no idea it would be this soon. She was unprepared, she had just slipped into her shoes and driven into town. *What does my hair look like?*

He almost asked her if she'd like to join him and watch a movie together, but thought better of it. After all, he didn't know her well enough for that kind of an easy friendly evening. And besides, she was here to be alone, and she had just said she wanted to spend a quiet evening. Don't be obtrusive. So, Dodge, misreading her uneasiness and feeling a bit awkward for almost hitting her with the door, said something stupid like, "Good evening for it."

"Yes, I guess it is," she was uneasy, still pondering her appearance, she absolutely hated to be caught off guard.

They stood in an awkward silence.

"Well," he held the door for her, "I do hope to see you again. Have a nice evening."

"Thanks, you too," she said as she shuffled by him. She heard the door slowly swing shut as she walked over to the wall of 'new releases'. *Well, that was brilliant, Annison! Could you have acted any more foolish than that?* She grabbed the closest DVD and stood with it in her hand meaning to read the back but only being able to think of how she'd blown an opportunity to ... *to what? Shit! Why did that all have to happen so fast? I wish I had ...*

"Hey," he said softly. She turned and there he was standing right next to her, "Does your earlier offer still stand?"

*What offer?* "Sure, absolutely," she said with a smile.

Dodge sensed her bewilderment. "You offered to repay me for rescuing you."

"Oh, yes, absolutely." *What am I getting myself into?*

"Good, are you an early riser?"

"I can be," she responded, having no idea where this was going.

"Great, I'll pick you up at 7 am," and he turned and walked away. At the door he added, "Wear something real casual, like jeans and a sweatshirt. It might get kinda messy," he grinned and was out the door.

Messy? She said to herself and went to the counter with the movie.

She had no idea what movie she had rented. She wouldn't realize that until she got back to the log cabin. No matter, she wouldn't watch it anyway; she had to figure out what she was going to wear tomorrow.

# 19

## GOIN' CHOPPIN'

Annison stood in the doorway of the log cabin facing the lake brushing her hair and watching the Sunday morning sunrise. Pretty. There wasn't a cloud in the sky. Temperatures had stayed warm during the night with a mild southern front and were already quickly climbing through the sixties on the last Sunday of September. *It's going to be a warm one.* She decided to change out of the cotton crew-neck sweatshirt that she had just put on and into a v-neck tee shirt. She'd cover that with a lightweight button-front top that she could shed later. The jeans and sneakers were okay for now, but she thought she'd throw a pair of shorts into her tote bag and maybe her sandals too. She wasn't sure what Dodge meant by messy, she had no idea what he had in mind, but she didn't care, she was sure she'd be happy just being with him. She was more than looking forward to it, whatever it was. She'd hardly slept a wink last night.

It was almost seven and he'd be here shortly. Annison went into the bathroom and debated putting her hair into a ponytail or leaving it down. In the mirror she saw a flush upon her face. She was excited and nervous at the same time, but it was a happy anxiety. She felt good about herself. She heard a car coming into the drive. She pulled her hair back and twisted a Scrunchy around it and added just a touch of lip-gloss to her lips. Checking, the image in the mirror met with her approval. No it didn't. *Oh God.* She pulled her hair down, sliding the Scrunchy onto her wrist and shaking her head, running her fingers through her long dark curls. There came a knock upon the front door. Annison looked herself straight in the eye, *okay girl, here we go.*

Dodge was standing by the side of the coupe reaching into the open window on the passenger side, his back to Annison as she came off the porch and walked along the cobblestone path to the gravel driveway. He had on well-worn jeans, equally worn construction boots, a black sweatshirt with the sleeves pushed up on his forearms, and a straw cowboy hat. He looked more like a farmer than a fashion designer. He pulled out a white bag that said Dot's Diner on it and set it on the fender.

"Howdy cowboy," Annison said with a twang.

"Mornin' ma'am," Dodge nodded pinching the brim of his hat, giving her a wide smile.

"We going to the rodeo?"

"Not quite," he said, taking her tote bag from her hand and placing it into the open window, "but," he reached further in and pulled out another straw hat and handed it to her, "we will be out in the hot sun."

Annison took the hat in both hands, leaned her head back, shook her hair out of the way and put it on.

"How do I look? Am I dressed for the occasion?"

"You look great. Does it fit you okay?"

"Yes, it fits fine." She adjusted the dangling chin-strap and pushed the hat over her head, resting it on her back, "I feel like Annie Oakley."

He smiled at her as he went about opening the paper bag.

Annison walked around the coupe, bright red and shiny in the rising sunlight, and peered in the open window, "Wow, this is sharp. What year is it?"

"Nineteen forty." He handed her a coffee.

"So, you're a fashion designer *and* a hot-rodder. Let me guess, we're going to a car show."

"Ahh, nope. Blueberry or blueberry?" He dug out two muffins and handed her one and sat on the running board facing the sun hovering low over the lake. It felt good. Annison disappeared, taking another tour around the car and then reappeared from the other side and stood in front of him.

"It's a beauty, how long have you had it?"

"It's my first car actually."

"Really?"

"Belonged to my grandfather. He gave it to me when I was sixteen, actually a few months before my birthday. Didn't run and didn't look anything like she does now. She'd been wasting away in the backfield on the farm for years. I kinda rescued her and brought her back to life, in a roundabout way." He took a bite of his muffin and thought of the story that had played through his mind just a few days ago back in New York, when he was having breakfast with Harlow. *Harlow.* She came into his mind. He realized he hadn't thought of her since Saturday, since he'd been at Dot's Diner with Annison. He wondered if that was conscious or sub-conscious. He thought of their love-making and even …

"And you've kept it all these years?" Annison was saying. "That's really nice. Did you do the restoration yourself?"

He looked up at her. He liked the way she was standing, the way her faded jeans clung to her legs standing long before him.

"Well, initially all I wanted to do was get it running and on the road. I had a goal of getting my license on my sixteenth birthday and picking up my friends and going for a ride."

"Did you make it?"

"Yeah, I did actually. I had some help though. My grandfather helped, and Old Percy, his best friend, and Bennie, you know Ben, the chief of police?"

"Oh, yes."

"We had some good laughs, the four of us out in the barn working on the coupe."

"It came out beautiful."

"Well," he stood up next to her, both of them looking at the car now, "it didn't look quite this good by the time we got through with her, but she ran. Luckily I held onto her, and years later when I was finally able to afford it, I sent it out for a full frame-up restoration."

She wondered what that meant, "Funny, I would have pictured you in a Mercedes or a Jag or something like that."

"Naw, I've had a few 'success cars' over the years, but living in the City I really don't need one, so I guess I've come full circle. Now it's only me and her," he smiled at Annison, "my first true love."

A large vee of ducks flew over them, squawking and jostling for position as they made their way south over the water, their wings flapping fast like hummingbirds as they headed into the warm wind.

"Ready to go?" he asked, popping the last bit of muffin into his mouth.

"Sure," she answered, picking the bag up from off the fender, crumpling it, and walking it over to the trash barrel on the side of the cabin.

Dodge got behind the wheel and fired up the coupe. Annison opened her door and got in. "So, is it top secret, or are you going to tell me where we're going?"

"We're goin' choppin'."

\* \* \*

The coupe throttled off low in first gear, wound along the gravel road and then found the smooth tarmac of route 9 and opened up, stretching through the gears, the needle on the tachometer rising and falling, and the wind screaming in through the open windows and tousling their hair.

They made their way around the lake and Dodge was telling his passenger about the other day, "I was letting it all out, I guess; the remorse, the anger, the desperation I was feeling, and I was driving too fast."

"Faster than this?"

"Quite a bit."

He double-clutched from fourth gear down to third and slowed into the curve by the McGreevy farm. Dodge was telling Annison about the bull, "He was standing right there, smack in the middle of the road, big as a house."

"Oh my God, that must have been frightening."

"Scared the shit outta me," he pulled the coupe over to the side of the road, "and that's where I went, sideways into the cornfield." Dodge snickered, looking at the leveled cornstalks. "I felt so damn foolish I just spun out of there and kept going. Old man McGreevy must have seen me and contacted the chief about some bright red hot-rod tearin' up his corn."

Annison was laughing, "That's pretty funny."

"So, I figure I owe him." He lifted his coffee from the cup holder on the floor next to the shifter and took a sip from the small opening flipped back on the lid. He was looking out over the vast field of corn standing tall and ripe in the morning sun, "That's the last of his corn for the season, silage corn. They'll harvest it and keep it on the farm, ferment it and use it for feed." He placed the coffee cup back into the cup holder and smiled at Annison. "But first it has to be chopped."

Dodge drove across the road and entered the long driveway curling up to the McGreevy farmhouse. "And that's where you come in. You can repay your debt by helping me repay mine, sound okay to you?"

"Sounds like I might be getting off easy," she smiled.

"You may not be saying that after the first hour," he grinned.

"Hey, I'll bet you I can chop more corn than you."

He thought of her stories about running the Inn and knew the hard work she put in. "I don't doubt it for a minute, but can you drive a tractor?"

"Actually, I can, smart guy," she teased, "I've done my share of haying the fields behind the Inn."

"Oh yeah?"

"Yeah."

"Good. Then you can run the tractor and I'll follow along in the dump truck."

"Sounds okay to me."

"I figure we can work 'til noon then break for lunch. I'll treat you to a sumptuous hot dog at Howard's Drive In."

"Oh boy! Can't wait!"

Dodge was having a good time enjoying her company and the bantering they were sharing. It was easy being with her. She was an interesting lady, good humored and fun loving.

"Are you sure this is alright with you? I mean if you'd rather …"

"No, no. I'm fine. It's a beautiful day, perfect for choppin'. It'll be fun!"

They pulled up to the huge barn; faded red, well-worn and well used. It had a large, lop-sided silo attached. Beside it lay the pickling pit where you would drive the dump truck up to and dump in the chopped corn. The farmhouse was white, also well-worn and well used. The McGreevy's had been around for a few generations. Once, one of the many working farms in this fertile area of Central Massachusetts. Now, one of the few farms that had not been harvested into a sub division or a field of condominiums. Like most of the younger generation the McGreevy kids showed little interest in farming. They had taken the education offered them by their proud parents and had run off to the big cities, opting for faster cash with shorter hours. Dodge felt a tinge of guilt. Hadn't he done the same? He thought of his grandfather, Jedediah, and how he had loved farming. Suddenly, second thoughts about selling the Maddison farm came into his head. He didn't want to become a farmer, but he didn't want the property to fall into the hands of some heartless developer. He made a silent vow to hold to his idea of selling only to a young farmer who would appreciate the land. And hoped to God he could find one out there.

A dusty ten-wheel dump truck sat off to the side of the barn near the house. The passenger door squeaked as Dodge opened it for Annison to get in. She put her left foot on the doorstep and reached with her right hand for the grab handle. Dodge put his hands on her waist to help guide her up into the lofty cab. It wasn't a big deal, just a gentlemanly thing to do, but Annison felt a tingle shiver throughout her whole body. He shut the door and made his way around the front. It had been a long time since she felt the hands of another man on her, even in this slight a way. She wanted to dismiss the feeling as something as simple as a handshake, but couldn't deny the spark his strong hands had ignited within her. *Jesus! What is this all about?!*

"Keys in the ignition?" he asked from the driver's door.

"Yes."

Dodge jumped in and rolled down his window and started the truck.

"Okay, here we go," he put the shifter into drive and made a loop in the gravel driveway by the house. The curtains in the kitchen window parted and Dodge tipped his hat to Mrs. McGreevy as he wheeled by.

They rambled out along a double-rutted path bordering empty fields. Most of the corn had already been harvested earlier in the season and sent off to supermarkets and farm stands. New England 'butter and sugar' corn; like no other. The remaining acreage of the tall green cornstalks sporting their long pointed leaves lay out on a rise in the northwestern section of the farm and sloped gently in the sun down to the road. McGreevy's big John Deere tractor sat at the end of a row where he had left off the day before. Attached behind it was the chopper. It had a tall red shoot like a giraffe's neck.

"Does he know you're doing this?" Annison asked.

"Naw, but he will. He's probably at church already. He's a deacon. Sunday's about the only morning he doesn't farm."

"So he'll come home and be surprised. That's nice of you."

"Men work together, whether they work together or alone."

"Robert Frost."

"Hey, I'm impressed."

"A Tuft of Flowers."

"Whoa, even more impressed."

"He's my favorite poet, along with Emily Dickinson."

"Ah, a true New England girl."

"That, and a lover of poetry."

Dodge smiled to himself.

"What?" she asked.

"Nothing," he laughed, "it's just that you continue to amaze me."

"Me! What about you? Not many men can recite poetry."

"Oh, I don't think that's true. There are still romantics out there. My grandfather loved Frost. Fellow farmers."

It was Annison's turn to smile to herself.

Dodge pulled alongside the tractor then backed down beside the chopper so that the shoot was positioned in the middle of the dumpster.

"Let's go fire up the tractor. It's automatic, so all you've got to do is go right along the rows in a straight line and I'll follow along behind you. When the truck is full, I'll flash the headlights."

"Then what?"

"Then you can kill the engine and jump in with me and we'll go dump it in the fermenting pit."

"Sounds like a plan, farmer man," and she opened her door and jumped down.

Temperatures climbed steadily throughout the morning as the day remained calm; there wasn't even a hint of a breeze. On the tractor, crawling along at its slow pace with the heat of the engine in front of her, Annison felt like she was in a sauna. She was appreciative of the straw hat Dodge had brought for her, that was thoughtful of him. She was having a good time. They had made a few trips to unload the dump truck and had decided to alternate driving responsibilities in order to give each other a chance to be in the shade of the truck while the other was out baking in the sun. She had luckily found sunscreen in her tote bag and they had applied some last time they exchanged driving chores. They were both in their tee shirts, the heavier tops laid on top of her bag in the truck riding next to Dodge. He was following the John Deere and smiling to himself, watching her hair, now pulled back in a ponytail, bouncing gently beneath her straw hat as she rolled along just in front of him. She kept a keen eye to the stalks and he was impressed that she was doing such an excellent job. They hadn't had an opportunity to talk much, but it was nice just being together, doing something different together, and they were both pleased and comfortable with their day.

By eleven o'clock, they had made a substantial dent in the final acreage of corn. Dodge figured another hour would be plenty to satisfy his self-imposed penance. That would leave old man McGreevy and his farmhands only about another half-day's work to complete the job. He was thinking he'd ask Annison if she'd like to go for a swim after lunch, and wondering what she looked like in a bathing suit. He had seen her naked that other morning, but had been so consumed by the crisis that it hadn't actually registered. He was trying hard to recollect her naked image sitting on the lawn as he wrapped the blanket around her. He didn't notice that the chopped corn had overfilled and was spilling off the sides of the truck and reflecting in the side mirror. *Shit!* Dodge flashed the headlights. Annison slowed the tractor to a halt, climbed down and came into the truck.

"What's all that spillage? You leaving a trail so we can find our way back?" she teased him as she jumped up into the cab.

"Got lost in a daydream."

"Sure you weren't taking a snooze?"

"No, but it's getting too hot to do much more. You doing okay?"

"Yes, I'm doing fine. A little thirsty though."

"We'll go dump this load and go into the house for a drink." Dodge pulled away and headed towards the barn. "I figure if we do one or two more loads, that'd be enough for the day. Then we can grab a bite to eat."

"Okay."

"You feel like taking a swim after?"

"I feel like taking one right now!" She was fanning herself with her hat, "What's that?"

An ATV was approaching them over the crest in the open field. As it got closer, Dodge recognized one of the McGreevy grandsons and shifted into neutral and let the truck roll to a stop. The boy pulled up next to the driver's side window.

"Gramma sent me out with this for you." He turned on his seat and unhooked a bungee cord from a plastic cooler on back and set it on the ground.

"Sandwiches and iced tea, and she even put two pieces of her apple pie in too!"

"Wow, that's great." Dodge said. "Tell her we appreciate it very much."

His job done, the boy spun his ATV around and shot off into the farmland. To Dodge it sounded like a sewing machine whirring at high speed as he raced through the gears, showing off like little boys do. The sound instantly brought him back to New York and onto the manufacturing floor, he wondered how they were all doing, how the line was coming, how many orders were being placed.

"Look at this!" Annison was already opening the lid on the cooler. "Boy, she must think we're big eaters."

Dodge shut the truck off and climbed out of the cab. He removed his work gloves and stuck them in his back pocket as he squatted next to Annison, "Wow," he said, looking into the cooler, "this looks great. Let's move it over to the other side of the truck, there's a little bit of shade there."

"Alright."

They both grabbed onto the side handles of the cooler at the same time as they were getting up. Dodge twisted one way and Annison the other and he lost his footing and fell over onto his butt. The sudden shift in weight of the cooler foiled Annison's attempt to catch it and she fell on top of Dodge, cooler and all. The lid fell open and the contents tumbled out. They were laughing; it was funny, playful. They lay in one of those positions that life throws you into on the spur of a moment that you feel awkward about but secretly enjoy. Their eyes met and the giggling stopped. Time stood still. The air was filled with the pleasant scent of the fresh chopped corn and held an enchanting waft of Annison's light perfume. The sky was picture perfect above them and the fields surrounding them lay calm and quiet. The birds, hiding from the heat, were perched soundless in their lofty trees standing motionless and still in the breezeless day. They were face to face, lips just inches away, frozen, like in that 'Simon Says' game when Simon says stop.

Annison was on top of Dodge, her mind so filled with a combination of embarrassment, excitement, and anticipation, that it went completely blank. Dodge could feel her heart beating strongly against his chest, or was that his? He had his arms around her, his hands spread wide onto her back where they had ended up after the tumble. He could feel her skin, hot and smooth, beneath her light tee shirt, moistened by the sweat of her toil and the blazing sunshine. His urge was to press his lips hard onto hers and to draw her into him, to devour this sweet beautiful lady right here, right now, to take advantage of this unexpected instance that fate thrust upon them. And she was ready. Her breathing (which she was sure had stopped) became heavy, and she felt her breasts rising and falling rapidly, her nipples swelling and pressing hard into his chest.

"I think I've seen this movie," he said.

"Oh, and what's the next scene?"

His eyes looked deep into hers and his lips curled into an impish smile. "A huge hawk swoops down and snatches the sandwiches ... look out!" He squeezed her tight, rolling them over and over until they fell away from each other and lay on their backs laughing like two little kids on a playful romp.

"I think I'm lying on a squished sandwich," Annison giggled and got up brushing herself off.

"Nope," Dodge said, rising, "it's a huge piece of cow-flop."

"Eeuuu!" she shrieked.

"I'm only kidding," he laughed, "it's just some corn husks stuck together." He pulled them off her shirt.

"You're evil."

"You ain't seen nothin' yet!"

"Ouuu, is that a threat or a promise?"

"Both."

"Hmmm, come on big boy," she said in a Mae West tone, "let's go have a sandwich."

The iced tea was delicious, and they were thankful Mrs. McGreevy had given them a big jug full. They sat beside the truck against the big rear tire, leaning into the sparse shade enjoying their lunch. They chatted about nothing in general, just easy talking, like they had done yesterday at Dot's Diner. A comfortable bond was growing between them, the beginnings of a relationship. Something exciting and out of the blue, when you least expect it. They didn't acknowledge it; it was growing there on its own, with or without their permission. Invisible. Love does that. It's kind of like a storm, sometimes you see it moving in, sometimes it appears out of nowhere. Invisible, to even the wind. The end result is still the same, you can't do a damn thing about it.

After a while, after they had finished the delicious apple pie, they got up and put things away in the cooler, and climbed back into the cab.

"I think this is enough for today," Dodge was saying, "it's too damn hot for anymore choppin'. I say we dump this load and head down to the lake and jump in, whad'ya think?"

"An absolutely perfect idea!"

"Great. Let's get outta this heat." He started the truck and made for the barn.

* * *

The Chief's vehicle was a big 4x4 Ford Excursion. Four doors with two more in the back that swing open. Gunmetal gray with tinted glass all around. POLICE graphics on the front and sides in vivid blue with silver accents and *Bryce Corner Massachusetts* on the doors circling the town emblem. There was a large airbrushed American flag covering the entire back, like it was waving in the wind. Below it in white letters it said, *9-11-01 ... We will never forget!* The engine was the biggest most powerful V-8 Ford made and Big Ben had his foot into it. From the high cab in the dump truck Dodge and Annison could see the cruiser a hundred yards off, coming straight for them, cutting across the freshly sheared rows, the four-wheel-drive tires spitting out remnants of the cornstalks in a huge rooster tail. *This doesn't look good,* Dodge thought. He killed the engine and leaned forward resting his arms on the steering wheel, holding his work gloves in his hands, he waited.

# 20

## *THE SEARCH FOR OLD PERCY*

Chief Ben slid the big cruiser to a halt within inches of the truck. He was out of uniform. He was wearing a tee-shirt. His elbow stuck out the window. He said, "Old Percy's gone."

"What do you mean gone?"

"Missing. No one's seen him since Friday. The nursing home called Carlene this morning to ask if she was going to stop by and pick up his medicines for the week. They thought he was staying with us since the funeral. So he hasn't been at the nursing home for two days."

"Where do you think he is?"

"Don't know. But Doc Keenan says if he doesn't get his insulin every twenty-four hours he could slip into a diabetic coma. The senile old bastard."

"Did you check the porch?"

"First place. Mrs. Van Ness says the last time he was there was Friday afternoon when we were all at Jed and Emma's after the funeral. I even checked over there. Thought he might be in the barn or something. Even went way out back into the fields."

"You try Dot's?"

"Yup."

"The senior center?"

"Yup. We've been looking all morning. Someone said they thought they saw him at the cemetery, so I've got some of the boys scouring the woods around there. Carlene's worried as hell. Pissed off and blaming me for not paying closer attention to him. She's driving all over town with Penny. Brent and his buddies have taken their ATV's and gone out along the railroad tracks at the further end of town. I even thought he might a gone down to the lake with you, but I just came from there.

Nothin'. Saw your car as I was rounding the bend here and figured that was you out in the field. I could use your help, ole buddie."

Annison could feel the concern in their voices.

"Who's Old Percy?" she asked quietly.

"Ben's grandfather."

"Reverend Blackmer got wind of it," Ben was saying, "and cut his sermon short. He's got the whole damn congregation out lookin' for him."

Dodge sat thinking of places where Percy might be. "How about the gas station?" Percy was known to hang around there and pester the mechanics.

"Nope," Ben was shaking his head. "I don't know where the old bastard is. It's not like him to just wander off, least not overnight. All I can think of is his mind's snapped, maybe the funeral put him over the edge, I don't know. I've alerted the adjacent towns and they're sending out search parties. Hell, if I don't find him soon, I'm gonna have to call in the State Police."

"He's somewhere, Ben, don't worry, we'll find him," Dodge opened his door and jumped down from the truck.

"Is there anything I can do?" Annison asked from the open driver's side door.

"Shit yes," Ben said, "calm my wife down. She's freakin' out." Ben grabbed his handset, "Sugarplum, come in, this is Big Bear." He repeated the call again.

Annison grabbed their tops and her tote bag from the truck and came around to the Excursion to where Dodge was holding the door open for her. She slid into the front next to Chief Ben and Dodge got in and shut the door.

Ben stepped on the gas and the SUV bolted forward. He spun around and headed back along the leveled rows he'd entered on. "Sugarplum, come back, this is Big Bear, over."

"Big Bear, my ass!" Carlene's voice barked through the radio.

"Ahh, I love when she talks sweet to me," the Chief winked at Annison, "Any luck?"

"No, you?"

"No, but I've at least found Dodge. What's your six?"

"I'm north on the valley road heading back home. I'm going to drop Penny off at Joanne's."

"Sit tight, I'll meet you at the house … out."

\* \* \*

On the ride to the Benson house, the chief kept busy on the radio checking with his people and the cops from the surrounding towns. Dodge brought Annison up to snuff on Old Percy; the two boys growing up with the two grandfathers, the friendship of Percy and Cora with their life-long neighbors Jed and Emma across the street, Percy's morning porch ritual with Jedediah, his forced and resented residence at the nursing home, Percy's phone call to Dodge in Paris, his absence at the funeral and his subsequent appearance in his rocking chair at the Van Ness's, and lastly, his strange behavior of late.

"But this doesn't fit," Dodge said, "he's crazy at times, but to just disappear..." Dodge shook his head, "I don't know."

A few minutes later they pulled into Ben's driveway behind Carlene's car. The wash bucket was still sitting in the midst of the lime green hose strewn across the lawn. The nozzle reached to the edge of the driveway and was leaking water into small puddles that stretched into tiny rivers all the way out to the street. Ben had hurriedly dropped his car washing when the call from the nursing home had come through.

"Jesus Christ, Ben! How could this have happened?" Carlene said coming out the back door. She held a cup of coffee. Even with both hands wrapped around it, you could see the coffee mug shaking. She was nervous. Ben went up to her, took the cup from her hands and wrapped his big arms around her.

"It's gonna be alright, babe, it's gonna be alright. We'll find him. He's okay. There's been no accidents reported, no mischievous behavior, nothing out of the ordinary. He's somewhere by himself, that's all. We're talking about Old Percy here. He's too ornery to let anything happen to him." He pulled his head back and took her chin in his big right hand. "Okay?"

"Oh Ben," Carlene hugged him. "I'm sorry. I don't mean to overreact. There's just been too much lately. First Emma and Jed, then the funeral, and now this ..."

"It's gonna get better, you'll see."

She looked up into his big comforting eyes and remembered why she'd married the big oaf. He was her teddy bear. He always made her feel safe. She loved him very much.

"Alright," she said, with her composure returning. "What do we do next?"

"Next we say hello to Annison Barrett," Ben turned his wife around and they walked over to where Dodge and Annison stood on the front lawn.

"Annison, this is my pretty bride, Carlene."

"Hi."

"Hello, nice to meet you." They nodded to each other.

"I've got some coffee on, would anyone like some?"

"I'd love a cup," Annison replied.

"Dodge?"

"No thanks, 'Lene."

"Bennie?"

"No, I've gotta get back on the trail. How 'bout you two stayin' here and manning the radio," he said to the girls, "everyone's out of the station so I'll center everything through here." As chief, Ben had a mini command center set up in the house. Carlene had, on occasion, handled the 'ops center' before.

"You coming, Dodge?"

The men got into the SUV and backed out of the driveway. Carlene escorted Annison into her home. "Do you take cream and sugar?"

* * *

Ben drove over to the nursing home on route 9 on the south side of the common. It was an old Victorian house with twenty rooms that had a modern addition jutting off the east wing looking like a two story motel. It didn't fit with the architecture, nor the taste of the historical committee, but it had somehow passed permitting ten years ago because of its distinction as a 'medical facility'.

"I'm gonna start at the beginning." Ben said.

They entered the tinted glass doors that had replaced the original ornate wooden ones hand-crafted there in the early eighteen hundreds. The Administrator's office was just off the foyer. Ben marched in and found Alice Shaw at her desk behind her trademark gold-rimmed glasses, stuck permanently on the tip of her nose.

"Morning, Alice."

"Good morning, Chief." The stately woman in her early sixties in a flowered dress got up and came around the front. "Morning, Mr. Maddison, how are you?"

"Fine Alice, nice to see you again."

"Sorry to hear about your folks ... grandparents, I mean ... sorry."

"That's okay. Thanks."

She looked over to Ben, her chin down so she could see over the rim of her spectacles, "Did you find him?"

"No ma'am, not yet, but we will. I'd like to ask you a couple questions if I could. Tell me, when was the last time you saw him?"

"Well, t'was Friday morning. He got up early, as he always does, made his bed and came out to breakfast. He was all dressed up in his suit to go to the funeral."

"Had he had his medication that morning?"

"Yes. I checked the chart and his meds had been administered."

"When were they due again?"

"Saturday morning. He gets them once a day, each morning. He's very good about that too."

Ben calculated in his head, *today's Sunday, so he's forty-eight hours overdue.*

"What happens if he doesn't get them?"

"Well, he's on daily insulin injections. If he doesn't maintain his insulin, his blood sugar will shoot up."

"Then what?"

"He'd get fatigued, confused, then ..."

"Go ahead, Alice, I need to know."

"Next would come the shakes and seizure."

"Diabetic coma."

"Yes."

Ben stood large in the tiny office, as still as a statue, thinking. Dodge shifted his feet on the Oriental rug. Alice Shaw said, "I'm awfully sorry Ben, we thought he had gone to the funeral with you folks and assumed he was staying with you. I thought the head nurse had given out his medication to you or Carlene. When I asked her this morning if she had, and found out she hadn't, that's when I called the house. It's clearly my fault, I should have followed through earlier, I'm so sorry. I hope nothing has happened to him."

Ben put his hand onto her shoulder, "Don't worry, Alice, it's not your fault. He's just a damn ole fool. He's all right. We'll get him back. Could you get me whatever he'll need when I find him?"

They left the nursing home with a cold pack of insulin and syringes. Ben hadn't needed directions, he'd given Old Percy insulin shots before. The Administrator was clearly worried and although he had comforted her, Ben was worried too. It was a race against time, and he knew time might have already won. He pictured Percy alone, laying in a coma on the side of the road somewhere. Worse, he could already be dead. He pushed that thought out of his mind, trying to not let it be personal, just another cop case, some old fool nursing home patient run off and missing. *Stay focused*, he said.

\* \* \*

"You have a lovely home," Annison said, perusing the country kitchen.

"Thank you," Carlene poured two fresh cups of coffee. They stood at the island counter preparing their coffees to their liking. Carlene's mind was overburdened and anxious. She was silent and distant, unconsciously swirling her spoon in her cup.

Annison felt odd, inconspicuous. She hoped Carlene wasn't intentionally being cold to her, but she couldn't help but feeling outside. Ben had asked her to help calm his wife, *she's freakin' out* he'd said. She didn't know this woman, but she wanted to be her friend. "Coffee's very good," she attempted again to stir conversation, "there's a light taste of flavor, is it French Vanilla?"

Carlene looked at her slowly for a moment, "Hazelnut, I put a dab of syrup into the grounds before it brews."

"Oh, it's very good," Annison sipped. "Have you lived here long."

"Um, we bought the house when I was pregnant with Penny, so I guess we've been here about thirteen, almost fourteen years. Wow, doesn't seem that long."

"Do you have other children?"

"Brent, he's seventeen."

"Seems like a nice town to grow up in. Are you from Bryce Corner?"

"No, originally Vermont. My family moved here when I was a teenager. Ben's a townie though."

"He seems very nice. Must be tough, married to the chief of police."

"It certainly has its moments, like the one we're having now," Carlene glanced out the window to the back yard. "Damned Old Percy!" she said.

"He's Ben's grandfather?"

"Yes."

"Why do they call him Old Percy?"

"I guess that's what Jedediah called him. Jed is ... was, Dodge's grandfather. He and Percy were best friends since their childhood. Percy's less than a month older than Jedediah and Jed used to rag on him, on how much 'older' Percy was than he was. He called him Old Percy since they were kids and it stuck." She added a touch of hot coffee to her cup and gestured to Annison.

"No thanks, I'm all set for now."

"Let's go into the den."

Carlene gave Annison a brief tour of the downstairs as they made their way through the neat dining room and tidy living room, out through the hallway along the staircase and into what she called Ben's Den. It was a small room that held a corner-style shelving unit with a desktop, adequate for Ben's computer and police radio equipment. The walls on either side were shelved and held books and pictures and plaques and framed commendations and other cop memorabilia. Ben was proud of his accomplishments, and his wife was proud of him. He was good at what he did and she knew he'd resolve this current situation, she just hoped it would end well. With all that had happened in the past week, losing Percy on top of it all was just unthinkable. She couldn't go through another funeral. She said a silent prayer as she went over to the large chrome microphone sitting on its pedestal on the desk, pushed down a toggle switch on the face of the command center and said, "Big Bear, come in."

A second later, Ben returned, "I'm here, Sugarplum."

"I'm at the desk."

"Okay, get ahold of the guys one by one with a progress report and then call me back. I'm on my way to the Van Ness'."

"Will do."

"This'll take a few minutes, please make yourself at home." Carlene addressed Annison.

"Don't worry about me, I'm fine," Annison replied. She took a seat on the settee against the opposite wall and watched Carlene get comfortable in Ben's desk chair. It had a tall back with armrests, all done in cordovan leather with gold upholstery tacks. There were wheels on the bottom and Carlene positioned herself right up against the desk and quickly got about her work on the radio. Annison held her coffee in both hands and blew across the top of the cup. It was hot, but they say hot coffee's good on a hot day. She wondered how that made sense and let her gaze drift out the window and out across the lawn. A huge maple tree took up most of the side yard. There were dying maple leaves, colorful and dry, scattered randomly on the green grass. A small yellow finch fluttered its wings in the shallow water of a birdbath in the flower garden just in front of a white picket fence. It was cozy here. Like home in Barrett's Bluff. No, not really. It had the same New Englandy feel, but Annison's home was set on the far end of the Inn's property and even though it was a separate house with its own two acres of lush landscape, it still seemed part of the Inn; inescapable. This felt like a real home. It had its own personality, its own entity. She realized she'd never had that feeling before.

"Okay, I'll do another call around in thirty minutes and get back to you," Carlene ended her callback with Ben and swiveled around to face her guest.

"Now we cross our fingers and wait." Carlene leaned back in the chair and drew her legs up Indian style. "So, Ben tells me you own an Inn down on the Connecticut coast?"

Annison told her all about Barrett's Bluff, a recitation she had given many times. She feared she sounded like she was giving a sales presentation to a prospective function guest, but Carlene was attentive, asked polite questions, and seemed to become more relaxed and hospitable than before.

"And do you have any children?"

Annison spoke about JJ with his Air Force career and Sarah with her recent marriage and relocation to D.C. She didn't get into her dismay with their decisions to no longer be involved with the Inn.

"And I hear you had quite a scare at the lake the other day," Carlene said.

"Yes. Thank God Dodge happened by, I probably wouldn't be sitting here now if he hadn't."

"You're very lucky. Ben says that cabin would have lit up like a book of matches if the fire had caught."

"I feel very lucky."

"So, I'm curious, and please forgive me if it's none of my business, but how did you come to be with Dodge this morning?" Typical Carlene, not afraid to be nosey.

"We were chopping corn at the McGreevy farm."

"Oh? Do you know the McGreevy's?"

"No, actually I don't." Annison smiled to herself thinking of how the morning's activity had come about. She was thinking about their chance meeting at the general store, and the coffees and muffins she had shared with Dodge that morning. *That was so thoughtful of him.*

Carlene wasn't sure she liked Annison's private little smile.

"It's a little complicated," Annison continued, "I was paying off my debt to Dodge who was paying off his debt to Mr. McGreevy." She left it at that.

"Oh," Carlene was confused.

\* \* \*

"Is there anything, anything at all you can remember that he said when he was here Friday afternoon that might be significant?" Ben asked Katelyn Van Ness. They were on her front porch next to the two rocking chairs.

"No, I've been thinking about it since you were here this morning. I remember I was inside the house and I heard the rocker squeaking and came out here to find him. I thought he had walked over from the Maddison's house," she looked at Dodge, "I just figured he was with you all."

"Did he say anything?"

"No, he was acting kind of weird. Usually I come out and say hello, you know, offer him a cup of tea or something, and he's very polite and chats awhile. But he didn't say a word, just kept staring across the street."

"Did he acknowledge your presence at all?" Dodge asked.

"No, he was just sitting here rocking and staring, like he was in a trance." She said to Ben, "That's why I went across the street and told your wife about it, and she brought him a plate." Katelyn Van Ness chuckled, "He did act up then though."

"How so?"

"He didn't take kindly to Carlene bringing him a soda, and he asked for a beer."

"So we know he still had his sanity as of Friday afternoon," Dodge said to Ben trying to lighten up the predicament.

"Mmh," Ben replied. "What time did he leave?"

"I'm not sure. I came out to the porch when it was getting dark and he was gone. There seemed to be nobody left across the street, so I assumed he'd gone with you folks. He'd left his plate and empty beer can on the floor."

Ben stood with his big hands on the railing looking over to Jed and Emma Maddson's place trying to piece together where Percy might have gone from here. "This was the last place anyone saw him. Near sunset Friday, almost two days ago. He didn't go back to the nursing home ..." he gripped the rail tight, Dodge could see his knuckles whitening, "...didn't return to the porch either Saturday or Sunday morning ..." off his normal routine. "Where the hell are you, Percy!"

He turned around, "Katelyn, there's a good chance that this is the place he'll show up at." Ben said. "If and when he does, call 911, Carlene will answer and get ahold of me."

"Okay."

"Come on Dodge, let's check out the farmhouse."

"I hope you find him," Katelyn Van Ness said to them as they walked down her steps to go across the street.

They checked the house, Ben calling out in a loud roar as if he could make Percy appear just by the power of his voice and Dodge following along behind him in silence as the chief stomped from room to room. Ben did the same routine out in the barn, screaming into the horse stalls, yanking the tack room door almost off its hinges, climbing the ladder into the loft.

"He's not here Bennie."

"Percy!" Ben called out.

"You're going to have to call in the Staties."

Ben stood looking out the hayloft door, his arms spread across the wide beam above the opening. "Let's go check out the fields."

"Bennie, you've already done that. You're taking this way too personal," Dodge spoke up into the loft. "If it wasn't Old Percy, you'd be acting differently." No answer. "Come on, it's time to get more help. Call the State Police."

"God DAMN it!" The chief kicked a bale of hay, hard enough that it toppled over the edge and fell with a loud thud onto the barn floor just inches from Dodge. He climbed down and stormed out of the barn and climbed into his SUV, "Come on, I'll do it back at the station."

* * *

"... and she was just standing there soaking wet, absolutely drenched to the bone, happy as a clam." Carlene was feeling more relaxed now, she was telling stories. "She thought it was hilarious, dancin' in the rain, but I marched her little fanny right upstairs and got her out of those wet clothes and made her take a hot shower. She could have caught a death of cold ...kids!" Carlene snickered with a wide smile. She dabbed a celery stick into the bowl of herb dip she'd placed on the table in front of the settee. She was sitting next to Annison now, the late afternoon sunlight streaming into the room and settling comfortably onto their laps. Annison was more at ease too; the tension of the crisis momentarily absent and the room warm and peaceful, as if nothing could be wrong in the world.

A call came crackling through on the radio. Carlene picked up two celery sticks, dipped them together into the creamy sauce and chomped down on them as she made her way over to the desk, the celery making a popping sound with the radio's crackling.

Ben and Dodge had been at the Police station for a couple hours, Ben coordinating with the Mass. State Police, and Dodge busy on the phone calling the residents on the outlying roads of Bryce Corner, hoping

151

to find someone who had seen Old Percy. He checked back with Katelyn Van Ness, no sign of him yet.

"Bennie," Carlene's voice came over the radio, there was a shaky tone to it.

"Yeah, Babe," Ben answered.

"I've got a call from Doug Richards. He's in his plane out over Craggy Hill Orchards, I think you need to speak to him."

"Okay, patch me through to him."

A moment later the air inside the police station was filled with the sound of the single prop Cessna and the rough voice of its pilot straining above it. "Can you read me, Chief? Come back."

"I read you clear, Doug."

"I'm out over the ridge in the orchard and I've spotted something on the ground."

"What've you got?"

There was no immediate response.

"Doug, can you hear me?"

"It looks like someone's lying on the ground next to one of the apple trees."

Dodge got up and stood next to Bennie.

"Is it him?" the chief asked the pilot.

"Can't get in close enough to tell."

"What's he wearing?"

"Dark clothing." Ben could hear the plane banking low. "Looks like a dark suit."

"Does he see you?"

Again a hesitation on the airwaves.

"Doug?"

"I've circled several times and gotten in as close as I could, trying to rouse him, but he's not moving. He's face down in the grass at the base of the tree."

A chill came over both Ben and Dodge. They looked at each other.

"Doug, can you set down?"

"No, the terrain's too perilous, too many trees, there's not a spot anywhere."

"Okay, listen," Ben said, "we're on our way. Keep circling right above him."

# 21

## *A FAVOR*

"**O**ld friend, I got a favor to ask ya."

The two men sat on the porch, rocking next to each other, enjoying the early morning together, as they had for so many years.

"Sure Jed, whad'ya need?"

"We've sure done a lot of things together this time around, ain't we?"

Percy wasn't sure what his old friend meant.

"It's about Emma." Jedediah Maddison felt a lump forming in his throat. He tried to swallow it but it wouldn't go away. His old eyes watered.

"What about Emma?"

"She's tired."

They sat awhile talking about things, time on their side. Birds chirping in the distance.

Jedediah told Old Percy of their plan and expressed his trepidation.

"She's worried about the boy. I think he'll be okay in all this, but she's worried. Wants me to be the one who tells him. She made me make a promise to her, and I did. But I can't keep it. So I'm coming to you."

Percy had known Jedediah all his life, they were more than friends, they were kindred spirits. They would do anything for each other, and had over the years. But this was different. Percy felt a twinge in his stomach.

"I tried to put it all into words, write it down on paper, but I can't seem to get it out right, never been any good at writin' anyhow. And I won't be able to tell him. So, I'm asking you to. You're near as close to him as I am. One last favor, my friend. I wouldn't ask it of ya if it twasn't important to me and Emma."

Percy wanted to ask Jed a few questions. He knew what they were, they were in his head, but he couldn't form the words in his mouth.

Percy thought of his loving wife Cora. God he wished she was still here. He didn't know what to say. Maybe he didn't need to say anything.

They spent awhile longer, rocking gently on the worn wooden floor, the chairs softly squeaking. When there wasn't anything more to be said, Jedediah rose. He patted Old Percy's knee and, without saying anything further, walked down the length of the porch, descended the short steps, and walked across the lawn, heading home.

* * *

As he lay with his back settled against the tree, Percy wished he'd said more to his old friend than he had. Maybe it would have made a difference, maybe not, he'd never know.

# 22

## *IN THE ORCHARD*

Big Ben barged through the front doors of the police station and descended the town hall steps two at a time, Dodge running behind him to keep up. The rescue squad van was parked in front on stand-by and the chief beckoned them to follow. He flipped the switch on the overhead console and the siren and blinking blue and red lights snapped on, all at the same time. The Excursion spun around in the middle of Main Street and they sped out of town, passing the cars traveling east on route 9 like they were standing still. It would take them several minutes to get out to the apple orchards on the further end of town.

"What the hell is he doing way out there?" Dodge asked.

"I don't have a goddamn clue!"

Ben got on the radio to the State Police captain who was coordinating his search from the Van Ness property, the last place Percy was seen at, and gave him directions to Craggy Hill Orchards. "Can you get the chopper up there? We'll probably need to air-lift him to UMass Hospital."

"It isn't here yet, they're all down at the Cape at the air show in Woods Hole."

"Jesus Christ!"

"I've got one coming, but it'll be at least another hour or so."

"That'll be too late! Fuck!" Chief Ben slammed the handset into the dashboard.

"Take it easy, Bennie," Dodge said.

The SUV was in the opposite lane of traffic coming up on an eighteen wheeler. It had nowhere to pull over to. Cars coming the other way were quickly pulling onto the shoulder. Dodge caught a glimpse of the speedometer; they were doing over 90 mph.

"Fuckin' Staties!" Ben flew past the truck and sped down the center of the road, keeping the hood dead-center on the double yellow lines.

"Carlene!"

"Yes, Ben," she came back over the radio.

"Call UMass Med and see if their chopper's available, if it is, get it out here right away."

"Will do."

Annison, standing by the window in the tiny den, was feeling the tension from the radio conversations overcoming her, feelings of deja-vu were sweeping over her and rousing the dark anxieties of her harried ordeal of the other morning. "May I use your bathroom?" She had to get out of the room for a minute.

"Upstairs, down the hall."

The speeding SUV left the smooth tarmac of route 9 and headed up the windy dirt way of Craggy Hill Road.

"You with me, Chucky?" Ben asked.

"We're right behind you, Chief," came the response from the EMT driving the rescue van, a mile behind.

"You got the insulin?" Dodge asked.

Ben took his right hand off the steering wheel and opened the lid on the center console. He took out the packet Alice Shaw had given him at the nursing home and handed it to Dodge. He held onto it with both hands in his lap.

They twisted and turned ascending the curvy road to the top of the hill.

"You see Doug's plane?" Ben asked.

"No."

"Doug," Ben said into the handset, "you still up there?"

"Yup, I can see you coming up the hill, I'm just on the other side, take the gravel road at the top, it'll be to your right."

Ben found it readily and spun onto it heading along the ridge. The trees were thick, still full of leaves hanging in their brightening autumnal colors along the narrow gravel way with their droppings.

"Chucky, take the gravel road to your right at the top of the hill," Ben instructed the rescue van.

"There he is," Dodge spotted the plane circling ahead just over the crest.

Ben cut into the apple orchard, slammed the floor shifter into 4-wheel-drive and snaked through the apple trees at full speed, the windshield taking on the appearance of a video screen at the arcade, trees coming at them like they were a magnet.

"Doug, swoop as close as you can get to him so I can see where he's at."

The Cessna dipped a wing and fell towards the ground only fifty yards away. It pulled up just above the treetops and flew right over them. So close, Dodge actually ducked.

"Got it!" Ben said.

*  *  *

Percy's body lay crumpled in a heap beneath a ripe apple tree, the red apples hanging above his dark figure like red bulbs on a Christmas tree.

The SUV slid to a stop, the doors popped open, and Ben and Dodge were at his side in a split second.

Ben fell to his knees and grabbed onto Percy's shoulders to turn him over.

"What the fuck?!" Ben said.

"Oh, Jesus," Dodge said softly.

It was only a scarecrow. Blown off its stakes by an earlier wind, settling upside down beneath the tree.

Ben rose slowly, still holding onto it by the shoulders, the potato-sack head, with a painted clown-like face, tilting to one side. He looked at Dodge with a blank look of desperation on his face. Dodge could feel his heart pounding like a drum.

The rescue van pulled up and the two EMT's jumped out, one carrying a black bag and the other opening the back doors to pull out the stretcher. Three State Police cruisers were coming full speed across the orchard with their lights and sirens blaring. Behind them would follow the remaining two town cruisers and a satellite van from the local news station, all gathering at what they thought to be the scene of the rescue.

The crowd of emergency officials assembled around Chief Ben Benson, still holding onto the scarecrow in utter disbelief. No one said a word. In another context it would be a hilarious situation, and if Percy was found alive and well, this moment would be fodder for great laughter at The Tavern, over celebratory cold beers. But not now. Now was a time for gravity, to stay focused, to shake off this unfortunate diversion and re-group. It was the State Police captain who broke into the silence.

"Alright, let's all get back to our previous positions, and be quick about it, the sun's going to set pretty soon and we're wasting daylight."

He walked over to Ben and said, "You okay, Chief?"

"Yeah, I'm okay." He dropped the scarecrow on the ground and turned to walk away from the dispersing crowd.

The Captain said to Dodge, "Tell him we're going to find him," and returned to his cruiser and led the way out of the orchard.

Dodge walked over to Bennie, standing near the ragged ledge of the hill with one foot perched on a large rock, his elbow on his knee and his chin resting on his clenched fist.

"You okay?" Dodge asked.

"I thought it was him. When I saw him lying there, I thought it was him, and I knew he was dead. In those few seconds it really hit me," he turned to Dodge, "he's dead. We're gonna find him dead."

"Hey," Dodge placed a hand on his best friend's shoulder, "don't get negative on me. We're going to find him, and we're going to find him alive. He's probably watching us right now from somewhere and laughing his ass off."

Ben looked straight into Dodge's eyes and said levelly, "That would be just like the old bastard wouldn't it?"

"Damn right."

The radio was squawking from the cruiser and Ben went over to it. Dodge stood looking across the valley. From this height you could see most of the town, the white church steeples and the gold cupola of town hall poised amongst the orange and yellow and red leaves of Fall, spread all around them and ringing around the lake. You could see the entire lake from here and then clear off to the top of Crow Hill, on the far horizon across the valley, with the sun starting to set on it.

"What the hell happened?" Doug Richards asked the chief from his plane.

"It was only a scarecrow, a scarecrow dressed in a dark suit."

"Son of a bitch! I thought for sure it was him, Chief."

"Don't worry about it, Doug. It was a good call. Good eye. Keep looking will ya?"

"I ain't got enough fuel left, I'm gonna have to head back to the airport."

"Bennie," Dodge said coming up behind him, "have him fly over Crow Hill up by the shack."

"What? Are you fuckin' crazy?"

"Maybe not."

"What the hell would he be doing way the fuck up there?" He looked off to the distant horizon. "It'd take him two days to get up there."

"He's been gone two days."

"You're crazy."

"We've looked everywhere else, it's worth a shot."

Ben shook his head and clamped down on the send button on his hand held, "Doug, you got enough fuel to fly out over Crow Hill?"

"Yeah, I gotta pass over it on my way back."

"You know where the old shack is at the southern peak?"

"That thing still standing?"

"Far's I know. Could you give it a look see on your way out?"

"You bet."

# 23

## THE SHACK

It had been a beautiful day and the upcoming sunset would be spectacular. Percy was sitting against an oak tree high on the top of Crow Hill next to the old shack that he and Jedediah used to frequent when they wanted to get away from it all and rough it. It was peaceful and quiet here, except for that pesky, hot-dogging airplane that had been showing off doing circles over the further hill for the past forty-five minutes. *Noisy bastard.* Now it was coming across the valley directly at him. Old Percy flipped it the bird as it flew by, circling once, and thankfully flying off out of earshot. *Good riddance!*

Doug Richards didn't see Percy's gesture, the trees were too thick to see the shack, sitting small and broken down and blending into the terrain.

"Nothing up there, Chief," Doug radioed, "I don't think that old shack is still standing."

"Thanks, Doug," the chief returned, "thanks for all your help, over and out."

"He might be right, you know," Ben said to Dodge as they were traveling back through town, "nobody goes up there anymore, not even the teenagers. It's so overgrown it's barely accessible. I don't think it's worth our time to go all the way up there, Dodge. Even Percy and Jed stopped going to the shack years ago."

"I've got a hunch."

The chief wasn't convinced. "That's a hell of a hike for even a healthy man. I don't see how he could get way out to that mountain without anyone seeing him along the way."

"Maybe he went at night."

"There's still traffic."

"Could have gone through the woods all the way from the farm. Remember that time we all did that?"

"Shit, that was twenty years ago and that took us damn near a whole day."

"That's the only place we haven't looked, Bennie."

"Alright, alright. Against my better judgement as a trained police officer, we'll go - to satisfy your hunch. But I'm telling you buddie, I'm getting real worried. I don't know where the son of a bitch is, and I don't have a good feeling."

They jostled along the rocky road beneath the power lines cutting a perilous path up the side of Crow Hill and put the SUV through some real 4-wheel-drive testing. Ben kept hitting his head on the roof as they bounced over the steep rough terrain climbing higher and higher toward the far southern end of the mountain where the shack stood, or at least had once stood. At this time of day they were in shadow, the sun beyond them, sinking fast on the other side. They couldn't reach the very top by vehicle, so they went as far as they could, then got out to climb the rest of the way on foot. It was treacherous and steeper than he remembered and Ben was clearly unhappy with the whole idea.

"You don't think ... he'd leave town, do ya?" Ben asked, catching his breath, the physical climb up the craggy side of Crow Hill getting the best of him.

"Huh?"

"I mean ... you think he'd a gone ... off to Connecticut ... or something?"

Dodge was in the lead, ten yards ahead of the chief. His footing slipped on some leaves and a chunk of earth and rock slid down just missing Ben's head.

"Goddamnit! Be careful!"

"Sorry."

"Didn't we used to have an easier way of ... getting' up here?"

"Yeah, it was called youth."

"Very funny."

They made their way slowly, clutching onto branches and brambles as they neared the top.

"I feel like ... Butch Cassidy and the ... fuckin' Sundance Kid," his foot slipped and Ben slid back a couple feet, grabbing onto a boulder.

"You alright there, Butch," Dodge chuckled.

"We get to the top ... of this hill ... and I'm gonna kick your ass!"

"You may never make it at the rate you're going."

"I aughtta sit right here and just let you go the rest of the way alone. Fact, I think I will. Ain't gonna find anything anyhow. Whad'ya think of that smartass?"

"Come on, get the lead out. Man, are you out of shape!"

The chief got up, continuing his climb, "I am gonna kick your ass."

* * *

Dodge was at the top, on the flat of the ridge where the earth settled smooth and the trees were the thickest. He turned looking for something familiar. It had been quite a while since he'd been up here. The trees had grown and the overgrowth was plentiful, he couldn't get his bearings. Ben finally ascended and stood next to him, bent over with his hands on his knees, catching his breath.

"Which way from here, Bennie?"

The chief stood erect and wiped his brow, "Over there," he pointed and Dodge could barely make out the tiny weather-beaten shack nestled amongst the wild foliage. It was much more dilapidated than he'd remembered. The roof had lost most of its shingles over the decades of wind and storms and showed wide expanses between its rough tongue and groove planks. There was an open section with the remnants of a fallen oak branch sticking into it. The front door lay flat on the low flimsy porch as if some giant had yanked it off its hinges with his giant hand and left it there. It was covered with old leaves and barren acorn shells. The whole place was far beyond rundown, as if one more gust of wind would take it apart and blow it easily off the mountain and out into the valley, scattering the aged wooden boards like toothpicks into the wind.

Ben's heavy foot on the porch broke through a weathered floorboard and it made a loud snap in the quiet twilight air.

"Little heavier than you were the last time up here, Butch?" Dodge laughed.

Ben pulled his foot out, "Shut the fuck up."

The inside looked remarkably different than the outside. It was clean and organized; no dust, no leaves, no animal traces. In one corner of the open room stood a wooden booth. It had a clean top with an empty liquor bottle on it. Ben went over to it. The bottle was dusty, but he could see where the neck was clean, the dust worn off by someone handling it.

The shelf on the adjacent side of the shack (where there might have been a kitchen sink if the shack had ever had one) held a few cans of non-perishable foods, with a can opener dangling off a nail on the right edge of it. Below that, in the corner, was a hackneyed straw broom holding down a swept-up pile of dust and leaves and animal droppings. Nailed to the opposite wall was an ill-constructed bunk bed. No mattress, just flat boards grouped together to make a platform. There was a nap-sack on the bottom section.

"Someone's definitely been here," Ben said as he went over to inspect the nap-sack.

*Arrrroouuughh!* A high-pitched shrilling cry came into the shack.

"What the hell is that?" Dodge said to Ben.

"Sounds like a coyote."

"Are there coyotes around here?"

"We're on a mountain, Dodge."

"I thought they were nocturnal, didn't come out 'til the dead of night."

"They are. Unless they're rabid."

"Great! You got your gun?"

"Nope, it's back in the truck."

"Wonderful."

*Arrrroouuughh!* Louder.

"That's close," Dodge said in a distressed tone, "Do they attack people?"

"Not usually, but I hear their favorite snacks are fashion designers." He dropped the empty nap-sack back onto the bunk.

Dodge was peeking around the corner of the open doorway seeking the source of the frightening sound.

*Arrrroouuughh!* It came again, only this time it was real close, coming from the trees not twenty yards from the shack.

"Chief," Dodge said, motioning his friend to the doorway, "you'd better have a look at this."

Old Percy sat at the base of a tree near the mountain's edge, the setting sun back-dropped behind him. "*Arrrroouuughh!*" he waved at them.

"Scare ya?" he said as the two men approached him.

"Percy, what the hell are you doing?!" Ben asked angrily.

"Takin' in the sunset."

"Are you alright?" Dodge squatted beside him and put his hand on his shoulder, checking him out.

Ben stood before them with his hands on his hips, he was probably glad to finally find his grandfather, but he didn't show it. He was clearly upset with him.

"Have you gone out of your fucking mind!? How the hell did you get up here?" Not giving him a chance to respond, "Do you realize the whole goddamn town is out looking for you? Carlene's out of her mind with worry, the kids are out looking for you, the fucking Mass State Police are here! The media's here! For chrissake Percy, what the hell's gotten into you?!"

"Why the hell'd ya do all that?!"

"You've been missing for two days!" Ben paced around in a circle, coming back in front of him, "No note, no message, no communication with anyone, you just take off and figure no one's gonna notice you're gone? Geesus!" he kicked the ground, "What's wrong with you?!"

"Didn't figure'd it take you two days to git up here."

Ben walked away and stood a few yards off, letting the heat of his anger subside in the cooling temperatures of the end of day. He could hear the muffled conversation his best friend was having with his grandfather. He walked back over to them and said in a calmer voice to Dodge, "How is he? Is he alright?"

"Seems to be fine."

"You got the insulin," Ben asked Dodge.

"Don't need it," Percy said.

"Don't be a goddamn fool, Percy!" his grandson said sternly.

"I'm not a goddamn fool," Percy reached into his suitcoat pocket and pulled out a packet similar to the one Alice Shaw had given the two men.

"Where did you get that?"

"From that hell-hole of a nursing home you stuck me inta!"

"How'd you get it?"

"Stole it."

"Stole it?"

"They never keep that medicine cabinet locked up like they're 'spose ta. They think we're all too senile to be clever anymore."

"Those cans of food in there and that nap-sack ... yours?"

Old Percy nodded to Ben.

"You planned all this, didn't you?"

Old Percy stared off over the horizon, "Look at that sunset. Purrty ain't it?"

"You planned all this and didn't have the courtesy to tell anyone?"

"You all would'nt a let me go."

"Damn right!"

Dodge, satisfied that Percy was fine, sat back against the wide tree-trunk with him, "Only you, Percy," he shook his head back and forth, smiling, "only you." Ben was still pacing and fuming.

Old Percy reached into the inside of his suitcoat and pulled out a bottle. He held it out for Dodge.

"Gimme that!" Ben snatched it out of his hands. "What the hell is this?"

"Single malt scotch," Percy smiled, "good stuff."

Ben shifted the bottle into his left hand and pointed with his right forefinger, "You're not supposed to have any booze, you know that!"

"Ah, hogwash! Single malt cain't hurt ya."

"Where did you come up with this?"

"Floorboards," he pointed his nose at the shack. "Sixteen years old when it come over from Scotland, probably got 'nuther twenty on top of that." He poked Dodge in the ribs, "Rrreal smooooth."

Ben held up the bottle and dusted off the label. He looked down at his wily old grandfather, then over at his friend. Dodge was unable to contain a snicker.

The chief pulled off the cork top and took a swig.

"Atta boy!" Old Percy said.

Ben grimaced as the scotch stung into his insides. He held the bottle at arm's length and took another look at the label, then took another swig. Much smoother the second time. He sat down in front of the two of them. "You are one cantankerous old bastard, do you know that?"

Percy just stared at him with a grin on his face, "Good stuff, huh?"

"You think you're so damn smart," Ben said, "food, booze, your insulin shots, you think you thought of everything." Ben looked at Percy's dusty suit and scuffed dress shoes, "but you didn't think enough to wear better hiking clothes did ya?"

"Well, I can't think of everything, what'd be left for you to think about?"

They looked eye to eye at each other in a sort of stand-off and then Ben set the bottle down and reached over and gave his grandfather a hug, "I'm glad you're okay."

"And I'm sorry I caused such a disturbance," Percy patted Ben's back, "I didn't set out to."

Dodge lifted the bottle of well-aged scotch, "What the hell," he said, and took a swig.

\* \* \*

The three men sat on the earth at the top of Crow Hill passing the bottle and watching the sunset. There was an air of relief, the anxieties of the ordeal dissipating with the scotch. Colorful streams of clouds wafted over the western hills, painted by the reflection of the sun, falling far off and deep into the waters of the Quabbin Reservoir. Behind them the Ottauquag Valley was already dark and quiet, a few early stars appearing above the eastern horizon as the evenings arrived faster now that Bryce Corner was beyond the autumnal equinox.

"Why'd you do it, Gramps? Why'd you come all the way up here?" It was the first time Dodge had ever heard Ben call his grandfather anything but Old Percy.

"Is it because of Jed? And Emma?" Quiet, no response. "The funeral, the nursing home? What?"

"Well, that hell-hole nursing home's one thing. I don't like it there one damn bit! Fact I'm thinkin' a stayin' right here. Fix the hole in the roof and it'd be just fine right up here."

"What about electricity?" Ben teased.

"Naw."

"Bathroom ..."

"Naw, I'll just piss and shit in ta woods."

"Running water?"

"Yeah, Perce, you're smelling a little gamey, you could use a hot shower," Dodge waved his hand in front of his nose. "You know what I mean?" he laughed.

Ben took the bottle from Dodge and took a sip, "Okay, okay, we'll get you out of the nursing home."

Percy gave him a look of disbelief.

"No, really. If you're that unhappy there, we'll move you out."

"Ta where?"

"To our house. I'll set you up in the den."

Old Percy looked to Dodge as if to say, is he serious?

"Naw, I'd just be a bother ta Carlene and the kids."

"No you wouldn't, they'd love to have you around, and you know what?" Ben waited until Old Percy asked, "What?"

"I'd love to have you too ... I mean it." He handed him the bottle.

Dodge could see that Bennie did mean it. He could see how much he loved his grandfather. It wasn't just because he was relieved that he'd found him alive, there was a true sense of love here. Dodge started to choke up. He wished that he had had this type of opportunity to express his love to his grandfather, and Gramma Emma; wished he had spent more time with them lately. But it was too late now.

"Are ya sure?"

"Yeah ... I'm sure."

A wide smile grew on Old Percy's face, "Well then," he raised the bottle, "let's drink ta it!" and they sat and passed the scotch all around.

Ben was talking about how he'd clear out the settee and set up a bed for him. Dodge said Percy could have one of the beds from the Maddison farmhouse and Percy was wondering if he could learn to use the computer Ben had set up in the den, "I hear they got porn stuff on that insta-net."

All of a sudden they were having a good time, just like the old times they used to share up here at the shack, laughing and drinking and carrying on. But there was something missing. Old Percy held up the bottle to the stars and said, "This one's for Jed," and took a long swig. The boys did the same, Ben getting the last drop. He said, "Come on, it's gettin' dark," and jumped up. He lasted only a second on his feet before he swayed heavily to his side, made an unsuccessful attempt to grab onto the tree and then fell hard on his ass back to the ground. Dodge and Percy roared in laughter.

Dodge got up and extended his hand to his friend, "Come on, let's try that again."

But before Ben could respond, Old Percy placed his hand on Dodge's leg and said, "Sit down a minute, would ya ... I got somethin' ta say." He'd spoken in a somber tone. He picked up the scotch bottle, empty, damn, tossed it aside and leaned back against the tree, "I made a promise ta Jed." Dodge sat down next to him and looked at Ben as if to ask what's this about, and Ben lifted his shoulders saying, I don't know.

The two grandsons waited quietly as Old Percy fidgeted, drawing one knee up to rest his arms on, not satisfied, lowering that leg and drawing the other one up and getting it to his liking. He looked long at Dodge Maddison, as if wondering if he should say anything or not. Ben was just about to ask Percy what the hell he had to say when the old man said directly to Dodge, "Twasn't Emma's heart that gave out."

# 24
## LAST WALTZ

*T* he bedroom was candlelit. Emma had set it that way herself, leaving the tall windows open to bring in the enchanting scents of the autumn evening, and the long lace curtains tied back to allow the hues of the setting sun to drift in and rest upon the high puffy bed, neatly made with her favorite white antique spread. She wanted everything to be perfect. It was a special evening.

The soft amber glow set a romantic mood and pulled out the creamy pastel colors of her hand-made pillows, scattered atop the four poster bed with the white cotton canopy and matching white ruffled skirt.

Too feeble this year to reap the harvest of her outside gardening, she'd sent Jedediah to the florist to pick up her order of fresh flowers and had had him help her place them to her liking about the room. She'd mixed the chrysanthemums in with the sunflowers and bittersweet and set a vase on top of each of their bureaus, taking a moment to reflect on the framed photographs that she had to gently move aside.

On her vanity stood a vase of long-stemmed red roses. Emma sat in front of her mirror brushing the length of her silver hair with the silver brush given her by her husband on their twenty-fifth wedding anniversary, thirty-something years ago. She was wearing a silk dress Dodge had given her for her eightieth birthday. It was a special one-of-a-kind, simple and subtle in its design and elegant in silhouette. It hung on her a little, even moreso than it had a month ago on one of those rare occasions when she had felt well enough to brave the confines of her bed and try some of her outfits on, wanting to find just the right one. But it fit well enough, the best of any of them now, and she hoped Jedediah wouldn't notice that it was a trifle loose. It was his favorite. The color a deep blue, and the silk embracing a subtle tone-on-tone floral print.

*There were tiny amethyst chips along the vee of the neckline that sprinkled onto the soft-padded shoulders like a bright constellation in the evening sky. Jedediah said the little sparkles on the shoulders complimented the sparkle in her eyes. He could be so charming.*

*Emma set her brush on the vanity top and reached into an ivory jewelry box, pulling out a gold chain with a small diamond pendant in the shape of a cross. She tilted her head back to allow her hair to be free of her neck, struggling with the clasp, her hands frail and shaking. Finally it caught and she lowered her head and looked at the image in the mirror. You never lie do you? She said to it, not even once. She pulled the cap off her lipstick and twisted the tube, applying it only to her bottom lip and then pressing her lips together and smearing from side to side in a perfected way.*

*In her mirror she saw a tall man approaching. He was dressed in a nice wool suit and wearing a white cotton button-down shirt with a familiar striped tie. His white hair was neatly groomed and he was sporting a wide captivating smile. He stood behind her and placed his long kind hands gently onto her shoulders and gave them a tender squeeze. Emma looked in the mirror at his pale blue eyes, dry and softly staring, and said, "You know Jedediah Maddison, you are one handsome man."*

*He held his smile to her, "And you are the most beautiful thing in my life."*

*Emma picked a rose out of the vase, snapped the stem close to the top, and stood and placed it into the breast pocket on her husband's suit, "There, now you're the perfect gentleman caller."*

*Jedediah embraced his wife, "I love you, you know."*

*Emma smiled to herself with her head upon his shoulder; it was nice to hear him say those sweet words to her.*

*"Come here," she said taking his hand in hers and leading him over to her bureau. She was quick on her feet, jubilant, almost walking on her tiptoes, and Jedediah marveled at how young and lithe she always seemed no matter how much pain and age tried to rob her of her youth. She was still his precious 'Em', the wonderful young girl who had captured his heart and filled it with love and life and special things that only she could put inside with her magic key.*

*"Do you remember this day?" she asked him of a picture propped against the fresh vase of flowers. It was their wedding picture, which had watched over them from its spot on Emma's bureau since she had placed it there the day they had returned from their honeymoon.*

*Jedeiah leaned close and squinted at it, "Like it was yesterday, and look, you haven't changed a bit."*

*"Oh, Jedediah, you always were a dreamer."*

*"No, look at those eyes," he held her close to him and lifted a hand mirror lying there and held it to her face, "see how they sparkle? They're still the same pretty eyes in that picture, except now they're even more beautiful, more sparkly."*

*Emma became misty-eyed, "And now you're making them teary." She went to her vanity and pulled up a tissue from inside an ornate wooden box and dabbed at her face, "I just put on this make-up, now don't make me have to start all over again."*

*Jedediah went to her side of the bed and pressed down on the top of the CD player he'd set up for her on a short table next to the nightstand. A silver disc slid out and he read the top of it. Frank Sinatra's greatest hits. He pushed the button again and the disc returned back inside and a moment later "Old Blue Eyes" came softly into the room.*

*There were two stemmed glasses next to a bottle of red wine. He lifted the bottle, pealed the foil top off, and twisted the corkscrew into the cork. Setting the metal lever onto the lip of the bottle, he lifted the handle upward and made the cork 'pop' out. He set the bottle down, untwisted the cork from the screw and placed it on its side on the table. Slowly he poured two glasses of the deep red cabernet, just above halfway, as Emma had shown him. She stood behind him watching the square of his shoulders moving strongly beneath the smooth lines of his suit and thought how lucky she had been to find such a wonderful man to spend her life with.*

*They clinked their glasses together and said simultaneously, as old lovers do sometimes, speaking the same words at the same times, "To us."*

*As the night fell, the room lightened and Emma glowed like a perfect sunset, radiant in her happiness and dancing in the arms of the man she loved. She had never before felt so comfortable, the music and Sinatra casting a spell over her, and her beloved Jedediah, on their final night together.*

*They danced and danced wrapped in each other's arms, waltzing with their memories as the evening stretched out its arms to them, time standing still.*

*"Whew," Emma said, fanning herself with her frail hand, "you always were a tireless dancer, Jedediah, always wearin' the girls out on the dance floor," she smiled up at him. "I've got to rest a moment,*

*dear." He didn't want to stop, didn't want to let her go, didn't want this to be the last time he danced with her, the last time he held her close.*

*She went over and sat on her edge of the bed. Jedediah noticed their glasses empty and went to refill them. He came over to her and held out the wineglass.*

*"Oh, no Jed, I only have one, jist one."*

*"But we forgot to toast in the sunset, Emma. I think we missed it."*

*"Oh, it's still out there, Jedediah, it's still out there."*

*She patted the bed. "Come, sit down next to me."*

*He placed the glasses onto the table and took a seat next to his wife on the bed. They spoke a few moments about certain matters, Jedediah nodding his head as Emma went through her mental checklist.*

*"And don't you forget your promise to me."*

*He was silent.*

*"I'm tired Jedediah, I need to lie down."*

*He fluffed her pillows for her and helped her to lay back and become comfortable.*

*"Sit there awhile," she said, "let me look at you."*

*They were that way for a time, silent, like in a sweet spell, silently passing memories to one another with a sweet endless love in their eyes. She in repose looking up at him, and he sitting by her side, holding her hand and trying his best not to break down, to keep his smile strong for her.*

*Finally Jed spoke.*

*"Em ... I ..." she touched a forefinger to his lips, quieting him. Slowly she spread open her hand and felt the full curve of his lips with her fingertips. She let her hand wander over his soft countenance, caressing his face, softly touching his eyes, drinking in the vision of the man she'd so gladly devoted herself to.*

*Tears began rolling down Jedediah's cheekbones and gathering on Emma's fingertips.*

*"You are the man of my dreams ... you have fulfilled my life ... you have made me happy."*

*She reached out her arms drawing him down next to her. Bringing him close to lie beside her, she smiled into his teary eyes, kissed him softly on his lips and whispered, "I love you."*

*Carefully she takes a pillow and places it on her breast between them. She motions for him to lie on top of her. He hesitates, but her will brings him there. They are close, face to face, intimate. A tear falls from his eye onto her cheek and she smiles. She places the pillow over her face and draws his chest onto it. Her embrace becomes strong as she holds him ever so dearly to her. He can feel her strength as he begins openly sobbing into the pillow. She feels his body trembling with his weeping and holds him closer to her. A long time seems to pass and she is drifting off into a bright yellow field with him, running through the tall grasses together, happy and young again.*

# 25

## *A MESSAGE*

"The cancer came on her quick; terminal, untreatable, twasn't nothin' they could do. She didn't want anyone ta know, so she stayed in the house doin' the best she could. Jed said it withered away at her, she couldn't eat right, fightin' a lot a pain. Wouldn't take much for it 'cuz she wanted to keep her senses alive. You know Emma, little woman as strong as an ox, God bless her."

Dodge sat quietly in the dark against the tree, the words of Old Percy's story sinking heavily upon him.

"I did see Jed every so often," Ben said, "but he never said anything about how sick she was, and when I asked about Emma, he said she was doin' fine, just staying inside out of the summer heat."

"Jed was keepin' ta her wishes," Percy said. "She always was a proud woman. Guess she didn't want anyone ta see how frail she was. Hell, I didn't even know 'til Jed told me the other day."

"But why wouldn't they tell me?" Dodge spoke. "She always seemed fine on the phone when I called her."

Ben and Old Percy sat quiet.

"Why'd they do that?"

Percy took a breath and said, "She said she was afraid you'd worry, maybe even want to leave your business in the city and come home and baby-sit her, she didn't want that."

"What?"

"Jed asked a favor of me. He had made a promise ta Emma. She made him promise not ta feel bad about what they were gonna do. Made him promise he'd stay and take care of you and tell you her feelings, sorta like a verbal letter. Said she'd tried ta write it all down, but near the end she was just too weak ta concentrate. So she wanted Jed ta tell you what they had done and why, and ta make you understand, that they had no remorse and you shouldn't feel any guilt 'bout it all, it was their decision they made together. She wanted Jed ta tell you how much she loved you. That she wanted you ta always have nothin' but the fondest memories of her, that she'd be watchin' over you and that you could talk ta her whenever you needed to."

"Why'd Jed ask you to do this?" Ben asked.

"Guess he knew he was gonna break his promise to her; couldn't face what he'd done, didn't want to go on without her, wanted ta be buried with his beloved Emma."

Ben said, "So you knew he was gonna kill himself?"

"Twasn't sure what he was gonna do."

"Why the hell didn't you tell me?! We could have done something! We could have stopped him!"

"Goddamn it! Don't you think I've thought about that a hundred times!"

"Geesus, didn't you try to talk him out of it?"

"I didn't know for sure what he was gonna do. All he told me about was Emma's wishes ta not go on any more. She couldn't handle the pain and she wanted ta go while she still had her mind and her memories. I didn't know he was gonna kill himself, least I didn't think he would."

"You're a damn fool, Percy!"

"Fuck you! Don't you think I feel bad enough without your comin' down on me!?"

"Hey! Hey, you guys." Dodge said, "Stop the quarreling. There wasn't a damn thing any of us could have done. You know that. You know Jed, once his mind is set, that's it." They got quiet. "Shit, there wasn't anything any of us could have done."

Dodge got up and paced a few yards off. He stood at the edge of the mountain with his back to them in the black copse of trees. Looking into the brightening constellations, he saw the splendor there, a luminous hope. "God, he must have loved her."

\* \* \*

There was a helicopter hovering in the valley, a white beam of light falling from it and moving in slow circular patterns illuminating the ground beneath. The wind had risen at his back so Dodge couldn't hear the rotors yet, but he watched it coming noiselessly towards the mountain, if it stayed on course it would find them and bring an end to the searching. He should tell the chief so they could signal it, but it would find them, the laser-like light would latch onto Ben's cruiser clutching the craggy side of Crow Hill and they would find them. The ordeal was over. At least now he knew. A sense of closure steadied him as he looked into the cool night. They had long ago made a pact to live their lives together, and now they would spend their eternity together. He couldn't help but smile into the heavens, *God bless you Gram and Gramp, I love you.*

\* \* \*

"Next mornin' Jed didn't come out ta the porch, I waited quite a time," Percy was telling Ben as Dodge rejoined them, "then I saw him. Jed came out the side door and came along the driveway, but he stopped just shy of the end. I could see his eyes, and even from across the street I could see they were red. He stood there awhile, guess debatin' whether ta come across or not, and then he lifted his hand. He just sorta held it there." Old Percy held his hand up, reliving the moment. He cleared his throat, "Then he turned. He walked down the length of the gravel way and went inta the barn." Percy stopped his story, fought to clear his throat again, and sat still, Ben next him, quiet, and Dodge standing beside the tree, hands in his pockets.

"So, I sat there awhile longer, then I went down ta the cemetery ta spend some time with my Cora," Percy's voice was low, he looked at his grandson, "then I walked over ta the station and waited for you on the steps." He stretched an arm and squeezed Dodge's leg. "I'm sorry, boy, I'm truly sorry, I should a…"

"No, don't say it Percy." Dodge squatted next to him, "You did what you did for your best friend, out of love and respect. Don't shoulder any guilt. I've been doing enough of that on my own the past few days. But you know what? It's time to move on. They did what they did, together, because they loved each other more than anything else. Jed and Emma wouldn't be pleased to have us wallowing in remorse and living the 'what ifs' for the rest of our lives. They'd want us to move on. Cherish the memories and dwell on the fun times we shared and to think of them as happy together, just as they always were. I feel like they've sent a message through you and I think I know what they're saying. Live your life and be happy with the time you've got, we'll all be together soon enough. So, what do you say, let's you and I stop feeling bad over it

175

and respect their wishes and get up and move on." Dodge stood and extended his hand to him, "Deal?"

Percy grabbed on and got to his feet. "Deal."And they hugged.

Ben wrapped a big arm around his grandfather's shoulders, "Come on you crankity old bastard, let's get you out of here and into your new home."

The three men started off through the trees, Dodge in the lead, then Old Percy followed by Ben.

"Maybe we should stay at the shack and wait for daylight," Percy said. "I think there's nuther bottle hidden in there somewhere."

"Oh no!" Ben said. "We're plenty shit-faced as it is. We'll probably fall on our asses and roll down this hill."

*Whoop ... whoop ... whoop ...*

"What the hell's that?" Old Percy said.

"Sounds like a chopper."

"Huh?"

Ben looked over the edge and saw the chopper, "Hey, the fuckin' Staties found us," he laughed. "We're rescued." The three of them stood together looking into the valley at the helicopter hovering below them, the searchlight scanning the cruiser and locating the narrow trail to the top. Ben, in the middle of his best friend and his grandfather, his big arms wrapped over their shoulders, took in a deep breath of the fresh night air and grinned, "What a beautiful fuckin' night this is!"

# 26

## HOME SWEET HOME

"We've got 'em!" the State Police Captain's voice came over the radio in Ben's Den. "All three of them; the Chief, Maddison, and the old man."

"Thank God," Carlene sighed, "where are they?"

"Top of Crow Hill."

"The shack ... why didn't we think of that before?" Carlene asked herself.

"We're bringing them down now. They all seem to be fine."

"Captain, please have the Chief call in as soon as he's clear."

"Will do."

"Oh God," tears flowed openly down Carlene's face, "I'm so glad they're alright."

The past three hours had been trying. They had had no contact with the men. Carlene had gone from concerned to pissed to frantic and then dead quiet; sitting at the command console chewing on her fingernails for nearly the past hour. Annison went through some changes of her own. Spawned by the worry exhibited by Carlene, new feelings swept over her. Brand new. Feelings she wasn't sure she had ever felt before. It wasn't just the anxiety of the ordeal, but something else, deeper. She wasn't necessarily as worried as Carlene, she thought Dodge and Ben were alright, that they'd surface sooner or later, but the time of not knowing seeped into her. While Carlene was glued to the radio, Annison found herself wandering freely about the house struggling to identify these feelings. She had stood in the kitchen making a cup of tea and felt oddly at ease, not only with being in this house, but also with her newfound concern. She felt comfortable in worrying about Dodge. Like it was natural for her to do so, as if she should be, like as if he was her ...

her what? Husband? Lover? It was weird, she'd only met this man a few days ago, had spent only a brief amount of time with him but she couldn't help but feeling that they'd been together much longer. As if there was a prior relationship between them, something that had been there a long time. She thought she must be crazy, but she couldn't ignore the fact that her heart leapt when she heard that they were all right and would be coming home. No, if she was to remain honest with herself, like she was supposed to be doing on this sabbatical, she had to admit there was an intrinsic mystery at work here.

\* \* \*

Perhaps it was this mystery that propelled her into his arms when Dodge arrived home with Ben and Percy. And oddly enough, he didn't seem to be taken aback by it. He held her close, intimately; there was a warmth between them as they held their embrace at the side of the cruiser.

"I'm glad you're okay," she said.

"Me too." He held his head back to look at her, his arms still around her waist. "I think I am, I think I am okay now."

Annison didn't know exactly what he meant; she wanted to believe that he meant he was okay now that he was in her arms, so she did. She allowed herself to believe that.

As for Dodge, he was feeling something too. He hadn't expected her embrace, but it was having an effect on him. On the one hand it seemed natural, almost as if they'd been in each other's arms many times before. On the other hand, her embrace was igniting him, sending a searing blaze throughout his whole being, not just passion, but deeper, more profound. There was something happening to him. Unmistakably.

"Well, ain't cha gonna introduce me to this pretty lady yur hangin' onta?" Percy had exited the back seat.

"Sure." Dodge said. "This is Annison, Annison Barrett."

Percy shook her hand. "Nice ta meet you, I'm Percy, Old Percy ta some."

"It's nice to meet you too," she held his hand, "I'm so glad you're alright."

"Awh, twasn't nothin' ta worry about."

"That's what you think, mister!" Carlene came around to their side of the SUV with her husband. She glared at the old man not knowing if she should kick him or hug him.

"Oh, oh," Percy said.

She decided to hug him.

Penny came bounding out of the house followed closely by her brother Brent, and they gave their great-grandfather a welcoming hug too. Everyone was glad to see him, glad the nerve-wracking ordeal had a happy ending.

"Come on, let's go inside, I'll fix something to eat, I'll bet we're all hungry." Carlene walked towards the house with Old Percy on one arm and Ben on the other. She sniffed at her husband's cheek, "What's that smell?"

"Huh? Nothing. What are you talking about?"

"Smells like gasoline or something. Is that on your breath?"

"Nope, must a got some on me when I filled up."

"Filled up alright!" Carlene made Percy snicker. "And what are you giggling at," she said to him.

"Said I couldn't wait to fill up on your food." Old Percy twisted his head around and gave Dodge a wink.

"Any of that casserole left?" Ben asked, quickly moving the topic of conversation along.

* * *

There was, and plenty of assorted leftovers too. Carlene could never be found for want of good food. Cooking was a favorite pastime, relaxing for her, and the fridge always held a trove of healthy dishes.

First on the menu however, had been a shower and change of clothes for Old Percy. The men were ushered off to the bathroom and Annison followed Carlene into the kitchen, helping her put together an impromptu array of cold chicken, vegetable/pasta casserole, butternut squash baked with maple syrup, fresh fruits, and a huge tossed salad.

The kids had already eaten, and Penny had excused herself to go to her panda-laden bedroom, ostensibly to prepare for school tomorrow (which meant she had to make some phone calls) and Brent went upstairs with the men and became instrumental with Old Percy's wardrobe. Ben's clothes were far too big, but Brent found a pair of sweatpants and a tee shirt that fit him okay.

"Oh for chrissakes!" Carlene said as the men entered the kitchen. Ben and Dodge were standing on either side of the new spiffed-up version of Old Percy; Brent behind them with a proud smirk on his face. Percy was wearing black sweatpants and a black over-sized tee shirt that said "*Daggerz*" in huge neon yellow letters. The *Z* had a huge dagger running through it dripping with bright red blood.

"We're goin' moshin'," Percy said.

"You don't even know what that means. Take that ridiculous thing off," Carlene said.

"Brent says I'm dressed fur the mosh pit, he says it's fun."

"Well *your* mosh pit is right there at the table. Take a seat, food's almost ready."

It was a hearty meal with warm feelings. Annison was amazed how at home she felt with this new group of people, and Dodge, sitting so comfortably next her, was in a great mood. He was telling them about the scarecrow incident and Old Percy almost choked on his food he was laughing so hard. They all seemed so happy together. She knew part of it was the elation of finding Old Percy alive and well, but there was something wholesome here, a true family spirit. The whole town had it. She'd been in the people business her entire life, but had never before sensed this type of camaraderie. She was thinking that she had never before felt so at ease, not even in Barrett's Bluff. Her family life revolved around the Inn with its own demanding personality. This town, these people, these feelings were all new to her. Each day she spent in Bryce Corner changed for the better; new, exciting, crisp, as if the beauty of the ever-changing foliage outside was also taking place inside of her. She could feel the slow, steady, irreversible metamorphosis of the colors changing, as if the fading chlorophyll in the leaves, causing the transformation from green to a brilliant array of colors, was coursing through her veins, bestowing upon her a fresh new look. She was becoming a different person, vaguely familiar, yet stronger, more self-assured. Something that was dormant inside her was now glowing upon the surface. And she liked it. She also liked the fact that Dodge Maddison was beside her. He didn't seem like a world famous fashion designer. He was at ease, a country boy, warm and charming. There was no arrogance about him like the other famous personalities she dealt with at the Inn, the ones wanting to be constantly pampered. No, he was different, not at all what she might have expected under different circumstances. She wondered why they had been thrust upon each other, if there was some grander force at work, the sly and wonderful hands of fate perhaps. She saw him beaming, laughing with his wide smile, and when he turned it to her she felt her insides begin to glow. Suddenly, she wanted to be alone with him.

The hour got late and everyone was exhausted from the long day, all except for Dodge Maddison. He seemed fresh, effervescent, as if he'd snuck in a nap somehow when they weren't looking. Carlene wanted to get Old Percy settled. She decided to have Brent sleep on the living room couch and Percy in the "mosh pit" of Brent's room. "You can look at all the posters and pretend you're at a concert," she told him, "but they'll probably give you nightmares."

He didn't care. He was thankful to be back in a real home again, away from the sterile atmosphere of the nursing home.

"Tomorrow," Ben said, "Dodge and I will get a bed from Jed and Emma's and get you all moved into the den. We'll stop by and pick up your stuff at the nursing home. In fact," he pushed his chair back to get up, "I'll leave Alice Shaw a message right now so they can get everything ready for us."

"Come on you old coot," Carlene helped Percy from his chair, "time to call it a night."

Annison and Dodge found themselves alone in the still of the dining room.

"Very interesting town you have here, Mr. Maddison."

"Oh, we have it all; damsels in distress, missing persons, you name it - never a dull moment in Bryce Corner."

"With so much excitement, I can see where one might get attached to it."

"Not hard to do. Is that what's happening to you?"

He was looking at her with those blue eyes again. Actually, not at her, but through her. Annison hesitated, she wondered if he could read her mind.

"You're hesitating," he said.

"No, I ... I was just ..." she was subconsciously running the middle finger of her right hand around the rim of her water glass. "I feel kind of different." How did he make it so easy for her to open up? "I mean, I can't quite explain it. It's as if ever since the other morning I've felt totally different, like something has awakened inside of me," she looked at him for help. "Go on." he said.

"It's like I'm seeing myself for the first time, but I know what I'm seeing, it's familiar in a renewed kind of way. Am I making any sense?"

"Yes." He turned towards her, giving her his attention.

"I don't know," she threw her hands up, "Maybe I'm crazy, maybe my brain lost too much oxygen with all of that smoke."

181

"No, I think I know how you feel."

"You do?" She turned in her seat to face him.

"You're going to think I'm crazy."

"We'd be even."

"I think I may be feeling somewhat the same way," Dodge said. "So much has happened to me in the past few days, so many changing feelings," he paused, "*renewed*, that's a good word."

"Ever since our conversation at the diner, which was only yesterday," Annison said, "but seems like a month ago, I feel wonderful. Even today, with all the trauma and anxiety, I felt good, really positive. I knew you were going to come back okay. I knew you'd find him and it would end all right," she paused, getting serious for a moment, "and throughout all that's happened I've had this feeling, this mysterious but strong feeling that we were …" she stopped. They looked at each other closely, a silence between them, with eager thoughts screaming to be spoken.

Dodge sensed what she was going to say next, so he said it first. "That we were meant to meet each other?"

Annison's lips curled into a broad smile. She placed her hands on his knees, "Yes, do you feel it too?"

He told her he did. He'd felt it since that morning he rescued her from the log cabin. He didn't recognize it then, everything had happened so quickly, but that was when it had begun. Something that day told him there was a reason. Fate with her felicitous foresight.

"And then after our lengthy conversation at the diner," he found himself saying with ease, "I couldn't stop thinking about you."

"Me either," she grabbed onto both his hands with hers. "I was thinking about you all day and I was delighted bumping into you at the general store." She sensed his demeanor as favorable and bravely continued, "Excited actually. I couldn't wait for the morning to come, I don't know what it was but I just needed to be with you again."

Dodge's heart was pounding inside his chest. She was saying all the words that had been hiding in his subconscious for the past few days. He'd tried to suppress them and thought he'd done a good job at it, but now he wanted to set them free. She was verbalizing his exact thoughts. There was definitely something at work here bigger than the both of them. He squeezed her hands in his and said, "It's almost like …"

"We're all set." Ben came back into the room, "I spoke with the nurse on…" he noticed their clasped hands "…duty and she'll have everything ready in the morning." He was taken aback by their behavior and began fumbling with the dishes.

Annison and Dodge realized at the same moment that they were once again caught with their hands together, as they had been at the diner the day before and they burst out laughing.

"What's so funny?" the chief asked.

"Nothing," Dodge answered. "You had to be there."

Annison got up and took the dishes from Ben, "You sit down, Chief, let me clear the table. Would you like coffee?" she asked them.

They shook their heads no and she piled a heap of dishes onto her arms and went into the kitchen.

"What the fuck are you doing?" Ben whispered to Dodge.

"What do you mean?"

"Holding hands? What the fuck is that all about?"

"We were just talking."

"Talking my ass! What's the matter with you? That Single Malt got you crazy? You don't even know this woman."

"I know her. There's something about her."

"Yeah, there's something about her alright and I can give it to you in one word … she's married."

"That's two words."

"Oh fuck you. You know what I'm sayin'. She's pissed off at her husband and she takes a vacation away from him to piss him off even more. Don't get yourself mixed up in that shit, Dodge."

"I'm not mixed up in any shit, Bennie, there's just something about her, that's all."

"Yeah, she's damn good lookin' and you think she's easy pickins. Christ, ain't you getting' enough from the model chick?"

Dodge didn't answer.

"And what the fuck is going on with you and Harlow anyhow?" he was above the whisper now. "Don't you realize …"

Annison returned and gathered more dishes. "Boy, you two are awfully quiet." She disappeared back through the doorway.

Ben sat staring at his friend trying to figure him out.

"Are you done yet?" Dodge asked.

"Yeah, I'm done," he leaned back in his chair and gave a big yawn. "And I'm damn tired too. My legs are killin' me."

"Well," Carlene returned, "I can see you two are busy."

"Yup, got just 'bout everything cleared off the table for ya," Ben grinned.

"Come on, let's get the rest of this into the kitchen," she said.

Annison was scraping the plates and lining them up into the dishwasher.

"I'll finish that, Hon, the boys are bringing the rest in. You sit, you're a guest."

"Oh please don't bother about that, I don't mind, really."

"This is the last of it, Sugarplum," Ben placed the remaining dishes onto the counter. Dodge was putting away the condiments.

"How about some coffee and dessert?" Carlene asked.

"Not for me thanks," Annison replied.

"Me either, I think it's time I got Annison home, we don't want to spoil her with too much Corner hospitality for one day do we?" Dodge said. "Can you give us a lift back to McGreevy's, Bennie?"

"Ab-sa-tootly."

Annison said good-bye to Carlene and thanked her for everything. Carlene in turn thanked Annison for being with her through the whole ordeal, "You were a comfort," and they parted as new friends. With all the excitement Carlene hadn't had the opportunity to fully complete her usual 'new person dossier' on Annison. She seemed nice enough, she thought, but no matter, she'd soon be gone back to her world in Connecticut and probably quite busy at her Inn. Maybe she'd be back next year at the lake and she could get to know her better then.

Dodge held the door for Annison and she slid into the middle of the front seat. He waved to Carlene as they backed out of the driveway and said through the open window, "I'll see you tomorrow."

Carlene waved back and stood and watched until the taillights had faded down the long tree-lined street. She turned back to her house, feeling composed and whole again in the cool of the night, and said a *Thank You* to the deep blue heavens hovering like a veil of reassurance above her delicate world. She decided to sit on the steps and wait for her husband to return, he'd only be a few minutes. She supposed Dodge would be returning to New York sometime this week after he completed his business here. He seemed to be doing okay, but sometimes people hide their true feelings. She wondered how Harlow was doing, how she was handling her feelings or if the conversation they'd had about Dodge had been just a lot of bull. Was she hiding her true feelings? She wanted to call her now and tell her all about the events of the day. She checked her watch and thought it too late.

Tomorrow was the first of October, foliage season would be peaking soon, lots of things to do in and around Bryce Corner. She wondered if she could get Dodge and Harlow away from the city and back here together again under more favorable conditions. Maybe a weekend getaway, the four of them could take a long drive through northern New England, maybe stay at a B&B in Vermont. Or at the very least Thanksgiving. That would be here before you knew it. She'd invite them both up for Thanksgiving! Good idea.

She was thinking of how many people she'd have and what size turkey to buy and *where the hell did I see that new stuffing recipe?* when Annison Barrett came back into her thoughts. There was something about her that gave Carlene a funny feeling. She couldn't identify it and it made her uneasy. She was still curious about the McGreevy cornfield thing, but dismissed it as a thankful woman paying off a debt, as Annison had alluded to.

Carlene hadn't witnessed the hand holding scene at the dinner table or she wouldn't have been dismissing Annison Barrett so casually.

# 27

## *BLUE MOON*

A full moon was up and glowing bright in the vast dark isolation of the McGreevy farm. The coupe sat in the moonshine next to the barn, the deep-red metallic shone like a star-studded galaxy as the headlights from Ben's SUV washed over it.

"Okay, Buddie," Ben said, "what time do you want to meet?" They had planned on getting a bed from the Maddison farmhouse in the morning.

Dodge stood outside holding the door open for Annison. She gave the chief a light kiss on his cheek and said, "Goodnight, I'm glad everything turned out alright."

"And I appreciate your staying with Carlene. Will we see you again?"

"Maybe, I'm not sure how much longer I'll be around. Sooner or later I'm going to have to get back to reality, I'm sure they miss me at the Inn."

"Well, if we don't see you again, it's been nice meeting you. You come back anytime."

Annison smiled and got out the passenger door. Dodge shut it and leaned against the window frame, "How about ten o'clock at the farmhouse?"

"Sounds good. See you then." Ben extended his hand to Dodge. "Thanks Pal, I appreciate all your help." He circled the Excursion around the McGreevy backyard and left them alone in the quiet night.

Annison was standing next to the coupe looking into the sky. The full moon was huge and brilliant, suspended over them like a giant flashlight illuminating the quiet scene. "It's beautiful."

"Yes."

"This is the harvest moon, right?"

"Yes," he stood beside her, the moonlight casting an enchanting shine upon her upturned face, drifting through her hair, accenting its natural luster.

"Actually," he said, "it's a blue moon."

"Like, *'once in a blue moon'*?"

"Yes, second full moon in the same month. Very rare."

"But it's so white, why do they call it a blue moon?"

He stepped behind her and placed his hands onto her shoulders, "Sometimes, when it's close to the horizon, either rising or setting, it has a bluish hue from dust particles in the atmosphere." She leaned her head back onto his chest. Two stargazers on a perfect moonlit night.

"But why blue?"

"Because the millions of tiny dust particles have a strange effect on the moonlight passing through them. They scatter the light in different directions. Red light is scattered more strongly than blue light and doesn't pass as easily through the dust particles. So, the moon has a blue tinge."

She turned around, keeping his hands on her shoulders and placing hers on his forearms. She squinted at him, "You're making that up."

"No, really. You're an artist, you know about color and hue, right? Did you ever see a red sun at sunrise or sunset?"

"Uh huh," she said slowly, letting him know she wasn't buying any of this.

"It's the opposite effect, the sunlight passing through the dust particles has the exact opposite effect as the moonlight and pulls out the red colors."

"Oh yeah?" she teased.

"Yeah," he laughed, "really."

Annison looking at him said, "And I suppose the light from the blue moon is what puts that blue sparkle in your eyes?"

"It's you that's putting the sparkle in my eyes."

"Hmm, an astronomer *and* a flatterer."

"Mostly flatterer," he smiled. Gently he brushed a loose strand of hair off her forehead and allowed his fingers to find the softness of her cheek. "You don't believe a word I've said do you?"

She almost didn't hear him. His fingers on her face were having an effect all over her body. She was slipping into a spell, carefree and wantonly. "Which part," she heard someone saying, "the blue moon or the twinkle in your eye?"

Her smile was captivating, irresistible. Dodge could feel the heat of the moonlight starting a slow burn deep within him. His hands traveled down the length of her back and found her waist. He pulled her closer. Annison couldn't take her eyes from his; she placed her hands on the sides of his neck and gently rubbed his strong cheekbones with her thumbs. Dodge saw her there, her mouth slightly open, her breath warm upon his face. He saw her lips glistening in the moonlight, invincibly beckoning him. They kissed, softly at first, stirring the desire, and then harder, more hungrily, tasting the dizzying sweetness of their passion. They were alone, there was nothing else in the world and the wings of the evening spread open for them and they were aloft, floating along the magical hues of the harvest blue moon.

The ride back to the log cabin was short. And mostly quiet. Annison was deep in thought, pondering their embrace and the kissing. She hadn't kissed another man in that way for a long time. She wondered if she should be feeling the guilt, but she felt warm and comfortable in the absence of it, with her head resting on his shoulder. Dormant desires that had surfaced only days ago and had been stirring every hour since were bubbling over inside of her. She liked that. She liked the moments they spent at the side of the car in the moonlight embracing, the way they held each other, exploring, reeling in the outer frills of newfound love, words gratuitous as their emotions carried on a dialogue of their own. And the quietness, the soft sounds of the stirrings within them, the simple way he said, shall we go? and the arousing implications that it brought.

Dodge was in his own world subconsciously driving the car, winding along Wickaboag Valley Road shifting through the gears, consciously resting his hand comfortably on Annison's thigh. The coupe on autopilot winding along the curvy road polished in silver by the moon, taking them to a place, an inevitable and familiar place. He felt a strong resonance of fresh new feelings, sexual, but not just sexual, deeper. Something different. Different than those he felt for his other women. Unidentifiable but unmistakably present. Rumblings like the wheels on the road or the sound of the twin exhaust system echoing the powerful feelings erupting within him. He wanted her. Wanted to be deep inside of her, wanted to give himself wholly to her, wanted to call out her name and have her hold him like he's never been held before.

The moon was waiting for them over the lake as they pulled into the gravel way next to the log cabin sitting tiny in the gray moon-shadows of the tall pines. Dodge let the coupe idle while he waited for something to be said. He heard the throaty idling, like incessant distant thunder, drifting over the calm waters of the lake, laying mirror still and quiet in the stillness of the full moon. The hour was late. He thought of the neighbors and turned the engine off.

"I should go," he said.

She didn't answer.

"It's late."

"No, I don't want you to go."

"I don't want to go."

"Don't."

"Are you sure?"

"Yes."

There was a bright shard of light coming off the water below the blue moon. It came with them, following them into the cabin through the open doorway and shining upon the wooden floor, finding a peaceful spot to nestle in the colors of the braided rug before the fireplace. She took a small wooden match from a small matchbox and lit it with the emery on the edge of the box. There was a glass candle jar on the mantle. Carefully she picked it up, tilted it to the side and lit the wick. She replaced the jar in its spot on the mantle and blew out the match. She stood with her back to him holding onto the burnt match. Dodge was near the front window at an easel she had set up there. It held a large sketchpad with a pen and ink drawing of the log cabin set against the backdrop of the lake.

"This is very good," he said.

She hadn't turned from the mantle. She was frozen. He saw her there and went to her carefully.

"Annison ... I can go if it would be better."

She liked how he said her name. "No, it would be better if you stayed." She turned to him, standing tall and handsome with the candle glow on his face, and looked into his eyes. "This isn't going to be easy for me, it's been a long time."

She brushed past him allowing her shoulder to linger a moment next to his. "There's whiskey on the shelf in the kitchen if you'd like, I'll only be a minute."

Annison went into the other room and Dodge went to the kitchen. He found the bottle of whiskey, filled a short glass with ice cubes and poured an ounce of the whiskey into it. The ice turned copper as he swirled the glass in his hand. What was it Bennie had said?... *one word, she's married.* He thought about that and took a sip. It hadn't really entered his mind before then. The whiskey stung the back of his throat. He'd never been with a married woman before. Why didn't she seem married to him? The second sip fell smoother over the numbness. He didn't want her to be. He didn't have the feeling that she was. He heard the shower starting. He wondered if what they were doing was right. He took his drink over to the doorway and stood there looking out at the lake.

*Oh my God, what am I doing?* She was letting the water flow cool over her nakedness. She was afraid. Afraid to let it happen and afraid to not let it happen. *Shit! I came here to get out of a relationship, not to get into one. Goddamn it Annison! Don't complicate your life any more than it already is.* Had she led him on? Didn't she see it coming? Hadn't she secretly wanted it all along? Is she trying to punish Jack? She could stop it. She could tell him it's not right. Or maybe he was having second thoughts. He could have left. She might walk out there to find him gone, not even a note. Or maybe a note that he'd call her in the morning. *Oh God, what am I doing?* The cool water felt good, she stuck her head under the spray and let it wet through her hair and down her back. "No," she said aloud, she wanted this; she wanted this night and whatever it would bring. *Go with it. Be selfish.* That's what Nina would say. *Don't forget you're a woman, act like one.* She turned to pick up the shampoo from the shelf above and the shower curtain opened. He was there, in front of her. He stepped naked into the shower and took her quickly into his arms. His mouth found hers and she could feel the hot wetness of his tongue. For the briefest of seconds she hesitated and then she gave in, voraciously, and with a passion so hot, so ablaze that not even the cool running water could quell it.

It had been easier than she'd thought.

# 28

## PICNIC

The morning opened with a new sky of light colors spreading across the horizon like a brushstroke into the mist. An early fisherman sat in his boat in the pensive quiet casting his line into the evaporating shadows of the shoreline. Pulling it back with the steady whirring motion of the reel, tiny droplets dripping from the taut silver line like falling diamonds in the yellow-gold sunlight, dropping into the still waters of the lake and making it ripple in small concentric circles beneath the fishing line.

In the rising colors of the dawn they made love; softly, slowly with lingering moments of feather tip touches and easy caresses, exploring their newfound bodies and pleasing one another with a new freedom. They drifted back to sleep and let the day begin around them.

Annison had risen first. The sun was over the lake and a mild wind stirred the bright foliage of the first day of October. She had freshened with a shower, and was in the small kitchen when Dodge came out of the bedroom and moved to her, coming from behind and wrapping his arms around her.

"Hmmm," she laid her head back onto his chest, the wetness of her hair cool and soothing to him.

"Good morning."

"Yes," she whispered. "Would you like some coffee?"

"Sure."

She poured him a cup and handed it to him standing naked in the open kitchen. He took the cup in one hand and pulled her close to him with his other. She could feel him wanting her again. "Hmmm," she said, pressing her lips to his chest and flirting with the soft hairs there.

"I think I need a shower," he said, "a cold one, or we'll never be able to leave this place."

"Would that be so bad?"

"No."

On the green lawn they sat in white wooden armchairs with colorful leaves spread around them, sipping their hot coffee and eating buttered cranberry bread, thick and toasted warm from the oven.

"It's beautiful."

"Yes."

"Let's do something today."

"What would you like to do?"

"Go somewhere."

"Where?"

"I don't know, anywhere. Maybe a picnic."

He laughed.

"What's so funny?"

"I feel like we're having a picnic now."

"No," she said, "you have to be on a blanket on the ground for it to be a picnic."

"Oh, I must have misunderstood the rules."

"I could get some cold cuts," she said, "and some fresh fruit at the farm stand and fresh rolls from the bake shop in town."

"And a bottle of wine?"

"Champagne."

"Champagne, yes, even better."

"Should we?"

"Sure."

"I'd like to go to Amherst. Nina says there's an art store there. I'd like to pick up some paints and some brushes and watercolor paper, I feel inspired all of a sudden."

He liked the way she talked. She was cheery and bubbly, childlike in her enthusiasm.

"Okay," he said, "we can picnic at Quabbin, it's on the way."

"Quabbin?"

"Quabbin Reservoir. It's beautiful there and I know a great spot where we can set the blanket down."

"Tell me about it."

"It's on the slope of the hill near the big dam. You can see most of the reservoir from there and way off into the hills on the northern side towards Petersham and then into the taller mountains of New Hampshire."

"I think I'd like that. It sounds peaceful."

"I used to go there to wax my car, when I wanted to relax and do something menial but pleasurable."

"You must be a type A personality."

"So I've been told."

"You should do that today."

"What?"

"Wax your car, I could help if you'd like."

"Wow, a picnic with a girl who wants to polish my car! What else could a man hope for?"

"Careful testosterone man, they'll be a price to be paid."

"Oh yeah?"

"Yeah."

"Like what?"

"Oh, I'm sure I can find some girly thing you could do for me."

"I thought I did that this morning."

"Yes you did. And very well I might add."

"Maybe that should be my price to pay."

"Maybe."

The wind picked up and brought a slight chill to fend with the sun, bright and persistent, hovering solo and proud in the cloudless fall sky. Today the sun would win the temperatures and chase whatever chills away and present them a glorious day to nurture their newfound emotions. It would be a great day for romance. The morning had already promised them that.

"Do you have a cooler?" he asked.

"I don't think so."

"I'll get one from the house when I ... oh shit!" he said. "I'm supposed to meet Bennie this morning. What time is it?"

"I don't know, but it was a little past ten when we came out here."

"I'm late," Dodge got up and tossed the remainder of his coffee out of his mug and onto the lawn. Annison gathered the napkins and empty plate and walked with him back towards the cabin.

"I'll only be about an hour. I've got to help him get a bed for Old Percy."

"Take your time, I'll go into town and get the picnic together. That'll probably take me at least an hour."

"Okay, I'll meet you back here then." He kissed her lightly on the lips, and then again, their lips wanted to stay together awhile, so they let them.

He turned from her and went to his car.

"Dodge," she said from the porch.

"Huh?"

*Nothing,* she shook her head and smiled, then went back into the cabin.

\* \* \*

Jedediah's pickup was backed up near the back door of the Maddison farmhouse. There was a mattress and box spring in the bed of it standing on their sides and sandwiching a tall oak headboard and matching footboard. A tie-down strap went from the forward stake-pocket near the cab on the driver's side, diagonally over the mattresses to the opposite side, winching at the rear stake-pocket near the tailgate. The tailgate was down and Chief Benson sat leaning against the mattresses when Dodge pulled his red coupe into the driveway.

"Come to give me a hand?" Ben asked with a disgruntled smirk.

"Shit, Bennie, I'm sorry I'm late," Dodge said walking to the rear of the truck, "I lost track of the time."

"Uh huh."

Absentmindedly Dodge pushed on the mattresses, testing the security. "You took the bed from my room?"

"Alright with you?"

"Yeah, sure." He hopped up on the tailgate next to his friend, "You could have waited you know."

"I did."

"Longer, I mean."

"Well," the chief reached into his shirt pocket and took out a stick of gum, unwrapped it, folded it over and popped it into his mouth. "I did wait a few minutes," he chewed for a bit, "but then I figured, seeings as though you hadn't been home last night, you may have had a previous engagement. Not knowing how long that might take, I decided I may as well load up the bed on my own." He paused for effect, "How is Mrs. Barrett anyway?"

"How did you deduce all that?" Dodge asked, not giving him the benefit of a reply to his sly question.

"I'm a cop, remember."

"Didn't know you went in for small town snooping."

"Hey, watch it smartass. I wasn't snoopin'. I stopped by the cottage to pick you up and you weren't there. Being the clever cop that I am, I noticed the place looked exactly the same as it had the morning before when I was down there. Didn't look like anyone'd been there overnight. So," he smirked, "I deduced, as you put it, you were probably otherwise occupied." He stretched out the last word giving it emphasis. *Occu-piiiied.*

"Don't start with me."

"Hey," the chief held up the palms of his hands, "you're a big kid now. You're on your own, pal. Just remember what I said." He got down from the tailgate and walked towards his cruiser. "Come on, let's get this over to the house, I gotta get back to the station, Monday's my paperwork day."

Ben drove out of the driveway in a hurry like he always did and Dodge got into his grandfather's truck. Jedediah had had this one for twenty years and it still had less than forty thousand miles on it. He started it up and dropped the shifter into drive. There was a faded picture of Jed and Emma on the dashboard stuck in where the speedometer and the other gauges were. They were younger, the way they were when he was growing up with them. Gramma Emma had on a white dress, cotton, short sleeved with big white buttons down the front. He remembered she had made it in springtime. It was one of his earliest designs and she had worn it to the annual Rights of Spring Bazaar on the common. They had gotten a few requests from it and they had replicated several in different pastel colors. But the white had been their favorite. She looked happy and healthy in it in the picture with her husband smiling next to her, his arm around her and the house in the background. They had been standing in the front yard, *look how small that maple tree is.*

"Hey, Dodge!" It was Eggman pulling up on the lawn next to him. His pickup had a load of lumber, roofing shingles, and tall, thin white boxes of replacement windows. "Got most of the stuff I'll need, gonna drop it off here now and I can probably get started on things tomorrow mornin'."

"Need a hand unloading?"

"Naw, my helper's right behind me, just had to stop at the hardware store for some nails."

"Okay then, I'll see you later."

"Gonna be at The Tavern later?"

"Oh, I don't know, maybe."

"You can buy me a beer."

"It's a deal."

"Then I'll buy you one, and so on and so on," he laughed. "Have a good one, Dodger."

*Dodger, that's what Gramps used to call me, my old townie name.*

\* \* \*

"How is he?" Annison asked when Dodge returned an hour later.

"Great, just great," he answered her. "By the time Bennie and I got there with the bed, Percy had been up since dawn and was outside fussing with Carlene's garden. She's thrilled."

"So, he's all set up then?"

"Yup, we cleared out half the stuff in the den and set the bed up for him on the wall opposite the window, said he wanted to be able to watch the stars at night."

"I'm glad he's there, he'll be much happier. Nursing homes are no place to be."

"He'll be fine. Knowing Old Percy, he'll be more of a help that a hindrance. They're going to have a health care nurse stop in and check on him a couple times a week."

Noticing the basket on the porch floor, Dodge said, "Are you ready?"

"Yes. Did you get the champagne?"

"Yup, two bottles on ice."

"Okay, I'm ready."

Dodge grabbed the picnic basket and said, "Let's go."

\* \* \*

The coupe purred along route 9 westward passing through the small New England towns settled along its way in the late sixteen hundreds when it came into existence as the Boston Post Road, the pilgrims pathway to the Mohawk Trail and onward into Albany, New York. There wasn't much traffic on this October Monday and the open road seemed to be theirs alone as they traveled into the rolling mountainous region of the Quabbin Reservoir. The foliage was brightening in the Indian Summer sunshine, beginning to peak as the reds and yellows of the maples and the oaks and the elms stood bright against the dark green of the pines and perennial evergreens. Annison had a picnic basket setting atop a Scotch-plaid blanket in the back seat. On the floor was a cooler with sandwiches and apples, bottled water, and the two bottles of Perrier-Jouet. She sat in her seat with the wind streaming in through her open window and blowing through her thick burnished hair. She felt wonderful, carefree and alive, with a new sense of cheerful abandon.

"Oh look! Look!... Stop the car," she pleaded.

"What?"

"Pull over," she was turned in her seat looking behind them. Dodge slowed to a stop on the side of the road.

"Back up, carefully."

"He put the shifter into reverse and slowly backed up in the shoulder of the road. "What are we doing?"

"A little more," she was sitting on her knees in her seat looking out the back window, "keep going, a little more."

"There!" she said, "see it?"

"See what?"

"It's a Wooly Bear caterpillar, come on," she got out of the car.

She was squatted at the edge of the road as Dodge approached.

"Hurry up, hurry up," she was saying to the caterpillar.

"Annison, be careful."

The caterpillar was thick and furry-like, almost two inches long. It was orange in the center of its length and black on either end. It tiptoed off the edge of the tarmac and onto the sandy gravel of the shoulder, apparently listening to Annison's coaxing. She petted it softly with her forefinger.

"Isn't she cute?"

"Just adorable," Dodge winced as a car came around the bend, luckily having plenty of time to see them huddled at the side of the road.

"See the black band? Depending on the length of it, you can foretell the severity of the upcoming winter."

"Oh really?"

"Really. I think it's the wider it is the longer the winter will be."

"This is a scientific fact?" he asked in an amused tone. "Or something you got from Martha Stewart?"

"Or maybe it's supposed to predict the amount of snow."

"Let's ask her."

"Ask who?"

"Martha, I'm sure she'll know."

She looked from the caterpillar to Dodge and said kiddingly, "How did you know her name was Martha?"

"Oh," he petted it, "I know all the Wooly Bear caterpillars around here."

"By first name too. Impressive."

"We go way back."

"Come on, Martha," she said to it, "you're safe now."

"Now that we've gotten her safely across the road, how about we get us off the highway, huh, nature girl?"

"Okay, okay … bye-bye Wooly Bear, you have a nice winter." Annison got up and entwined her arm in Dodge's and walked back to the car. "Boy, you fashion designers have no sense of adventure," she grinned.

"Oh, we have adventure all right; I'm just not sure it's on the side of the road."

"Oh no?" she stopped and put her arms around his neck and drew him to her, bringing his lips onto hers and kissing him strongly. He tasted the sweet flavor of her lipstick and felt the stirring passion of her tongue. He could devour her, right here, right now on the edge of the road.

*Whommp! Whommp!* An eighteen-wheeler drove by, the driver enthusiastically honking his appreciation. They broke apart laughing and waved to the passing truck, still pulling on the air-horns as it disappeared around the bend.

A short while later they turned from route 9 into the access road to Quabbin Reservoir; situated in the middle of the state of Massachusetts and spreading north and south almost touching each of the bordering states of New Hampshire and Connecticut. The posted speed limit was ten miles per hour and Dodge down-shifted to first gear and idled along the narrow roadway leading through the open fields spreading quietly and well-maintained on either side and drawing you tranquilly toward the waters. Quabbin is an Indian name meaning "land of many waters". It is one of the largest manmade reservoirs in the world. Its four hundred billion gallons supply the metropolitan Boston area and most of the towns along its sixty-five mile pipeline with fresh water. The reservoir itself covers forty square miles and encompasses sixty small islands and boasts one hundred and eighty miles of wild shoreline. The natural preserve covers thousands of acres of forest and field and provides sanctuary for untold species of bird and wildlife. It is very peaceful.

"The whole project took a dozen years to complete," Dodge was informing his captive audience of one, "somewhere back in the twenties and thirties." They were coming up to the brick visitor center at the beginning of Winsor dam, the larger of the two making up the reservoir. Before them lay the striking vista of the main lake, blue and crystal clear, spotted with the tiny islands carrying the eye as far as it could see to the distant wild shores and hovering mountains. "They actually flooded over three or four towns to make it. They're still there, below the lake, mostly intact; homes, farms, churches, stone walls, roads, everything. An incredible engineering feat."

Annison was enjoying his history lesson and the view she was taking in as they drove over the dam was truly breathtaking. "It's beautiful."

"Look," she pointed to an eagle soaring high above the waters, his stealthy wings, soft-feathered and silent in flight, spread wide and strong as he soared motionless in prey. It had gold-colored feathers at the nape of its neck, the designating characteristic of the Golden Eagle. He was doing his sky dance; hovering with tail fanned and talons dangling down.

"What happened to all the residents?" she asked.

"They got bought out and relocated."

"That's awful. It must have been so hard for them to leave their homes, their heritage and everything."

"I'm sure it wasn't easy. They made a great sacrifice."

They hadn't seen the eagle drop, fast and unheard, tucking his wings tight to his body, dropping unseen from a height of several hundred feet. In the blink of an eye, he had swooped within an inch of the water, thrust his razor sharp talons beneath the surface and extracted his kill with perfect precision and pure raw force. It was as he regained the surface that they saw him, beating his powerful wings and pushing off the water clenching a large fish in his talons. He quickly ascended to a dizzying height and became small and dark as he flew casually in perfect wing strokes to a nest far off and sitting high in the colorful distant tree line etched into a perfect blue sky.

At the end of the road over the dam there is a rotary where you can either go right along the grassy side of the dam where families would picnic and kids would fly their kites, or circle it fully and return along the roadway. Or, as Dodge did, you could take a left and ascend along the mountainside with the stream below you, just over the barren edge of the road, running swift and sure over the rocky bed, spilling ferociously into the reservoir. On this getaway weekday they were alone winding their way to the top, driving deeper into the lush foliage and deeper into the exciting unknown of a fresh, new relationship.

Maddison turned off the roadway and squeezed the car between two large boulders and onto an abandoned grassy pathway leading into thick woodland. He maneuvered through the woods until they approached a small clearing near the water. He parked beneath a large maple tree still full with its treasure trove of autumn leaves.

"Not many people know about this spot."

"It's perfect." Annison got out and walked to the water's edge. The Quabbin vista unfolded before her like someone was unrolling a large canvas. "Look at those colors, they're absolutely beautiful. God, I wish I could paint this."

"Think you could?"

"I'd love to try."

They spread the blanket on the ground in the shade beneath the tree. They ate sandwiches of thick chicken slices she'd cut from a whole chicken purchased at the market, still hot and turning on the rotisserie. The fresh bread from the bakery was generously slathered with honey-mustard sauce and layered with thin apple slices sprinkled lightly with cinnamon. They sipped champagne and talked of casual things, enjoying the easy day.

"So when do you think you'll be going back to the city?" she asked.

"I'm not sure. I'd only planned on staying 'til after the funeral, but that was before ..."

"Before?"

"Before I met you."

"Oh sure," she blushed and wondered if he meant it.

"But I've been bad. I haven't even called in to see how things are going."

"You must have confidence in your people."

"I do, Harlow's been with me since almost the beginning."

"Harlow?"

"Yes, she's ... my assistant."

"Oh?" Annison's intuition picked up on the slight hesitation.

"Yeah, she's the best. She holds the whole thing together. I don't know what I'd do without her." He wondered how she was doing and was angry with himself for what had happened between them. He hoped he hadn't blown it. But it was a two way street, right? Maybe it was inevitable. Maybe it had had to happen. "I hope she's doing alright." He hadn't meant to say this aloud, and didn't realize he had.

"What about you?" he asked, "what are your plans?"

"Oh," she fidgeted on the blanket, "I don't know. I'm in a quandary. I feel so good about myself that I find I'm fantasizing about staying here, living in Nina's cabin, catching up on my artwork, just taking the time for myself. That's on the one hand. On the other hand," she paused, "I feel guilty."

"Why?"

She lifted her champagne glass to her lips and held it there like she was going to say something, then didn't. She sipped slowly, the sparkling effervescence tingling her palate. "It's all I've ever done. It's a business. A well-established one with people counting on me to be there for them, to protect their livelihood. I'm sure they're nervous with Jack in charge. God knows how that's going. I'll bet a few of them have already quit. And I'm sure they're all wondering just what the hell is going on ... where is she?... when's she coming back?"

"Do you miss it?"

"No. That's what worries me. I mean, it's only been three weeks, but it seems like a lifetime ago. I find myself pacing around the cabin, talking to myself, and wondering if all that I've done has been only a dream. Like some novel I've just finished reading and I enjoyed the main character and I'm glad she's gotten on with her life and I'm anxious to read the sequel to see what she does next."

"What will she do next?"

"Well, she's kept to her plan of secluded introspection, faced her demons, and she's pretty much figured out her options. But," she looked at him coyly, "she's not stupid, and she realizes there's a new kink in the armor."

"A kink? Would that be me?"

"Could be you."

"Are you calling me a kink?" He laughed and grabbed at her sides to tickle her. Annison jumped up quickly, trying not to spill her champagne, "Whoa, don't do that," she giggled, "I'm way too ticklish."

"You are, are you?" and Dodge was up chasing her down the length of the field toward the water. She ran in circles just out of his reach, tossing her champagne at him to fend him off, but he kept on until he caught her and tackled her to the ground. They rolled together, laughing playfully in mirth. He wrestled his way on top of her, sitting carefully astride her, holding her hands against the ground. "A kink, huh?" He laughed and bent his head down to kiss her. She twisted her head to one side avoiding his kiss. He pressed his face closer, seeking her lips, and she laughed and twisted her head to the other side, again avoiding his playful advance. He faked the next one and when she turned her head he caught her and their lips pressed together. Her arms became free and wrapped around his neck as she gave in to him. He slid his legs down and lay gently on top of her. They caressed each other with the passion growing quickly between them. Impetuously she rolled him over and took command, reversing their positions; she, now straddled atop him holding his arms to the ground.

"Do you see," she said, "see what I mean?"

Hypnotized, he looked into her crystal green eyes, "Yes."

"Do you give in?"

"Yes, I give."

"Good boy." She released her grip from his wrists and he immediately went for her and they again were rolling over and over along the ground laughing hysterically. Finally they came to rest just shy of the water's edge near a group of large rocks. There was a tuft of flowers there, orange and yellow and a deep red.

"Mums," he said. "These are my favorite flowers. He sat up and leaned into them inhaling deeply. "I love their smell. Gram always had these planted around the house each fall. They're so hearty and strong, enduring many frosts and lasting long throughout the season. Sometimes well into winter. They're the final survivors."

Annison picked one of the crimson ones and held it to her nose. "Yes, they're beautiful. They have the perfect autumn colors." She handed it to him, "Here, my peace offering, I surrender."

He took it in his hand. "I humbly accept, and only as your servant," he bowed his head.

"Agreed," she smiled.

They were walking arm in arm back to the blanket when he said seriously, "I don't want to be a kink for you. I don't want to get in the way of your resolves."

"I'm not implying that you are. But if it's anything I've learned these past few weeks, it's how to identify and address my feelings, and I'd be foolish not to recognize the fact that I have this new feeling that has swept over me." She looked at him walking next to her, attentive, holding onto his flower, twisting it in his hands.

"But you need to know I can handle it. I'm a big girl and I'm not going to impose upon you. I am in no way attempting to corral Fashion Maddison," she teased.

"Fashion Maddison?"

"That's what Nina calls you."

"Can't wait to meet her."

"You'd love her." Annison smirked at the thought of it.

"At any rate," she continued, "what's happened between us, or whatever is happening between us, is something I'm doing willfully, with no strings attached. I don't want you to feel pressured." They walked a bit in silence, Dodge weighing her words and giving her the time to finish her thoughts.

"Besides," she said, "it may all be moot, one-sided."

He stopped. "No, it's not one-sided. You're being open and honest with me, so I will be with you. I'm not sure what's happening between us, but I do know there's something happening with me. You may not want to hear this, but I am very much enjoying us. I feel as if our meeting last week wasn't a chance one. And at the risk of sounding presumptuous, I would very much like to spend more time with you."

She had no response. "Am I scaring you?" he asked.

"No ... yes ... I mean ... am I scaring you?"

"No," he answered emphatically.

"Then I'm not scared either."

"Good! So, how about this? How about we not be so deeply philosophical, and just go with it. See where it takes us and not drive ourselves crazy?"

"I will if you will."

"I will."

"Okay then."

"Okay."

They had reached the blanket and Annison busied herself with picking up and putting away. Dodge had gone over to the car and was rummaging through the trunk. He took out a spray bottle of wax and a small terry cloth towel. He sprayed a section of the coupe and then rubbed it with the rag. Annison was thinking about their conversation. She wasn't exactly sure what they had accomplished by it, but she knew they had accomplished something and she felt good. In fact she felt great and she wore a bright smile upon her face as she packed everything back into the picnic basket and tidied up the blanket.

"Where do I come in?" she asked.

"Anywhere you'd like."

"How about I spray, you polish."

"Sounds good to me," he handed her the spray bottle, gave her a soft kiss on her cheek, and went to the trunk to retrieve another cloth.

She liked the little kiss.

# 29

## *AMHERST*

"So, when do I get to drive this old girl?"

"Can you drive a standard?"

"Are you kidding me?" Annison placed the picnic basket into the open trunk and went to the driver's side and got in. She pulled the seat up an inch or so, getting it just right and then adjusted the rear-view mirror. She noticed he'd placed the crimson mum on the dashboard and she smiled. She turned the key and the coupe fired up. She revved it a couple times, making the dual exhaust system rumble like thunder.

Dodge lowered the trunk lid and got in the passenger side. "I haven't ridden on this side for a long time."

"Fasten your seat belt, cowboy, we're goin' for a ride." Annison put the clutch in and pulled the floor-shifter toward her, resting it momentarily on her right thigh, and then pushing it upward into reverse. She gave the accelerator pedal a short tap with her foot and eased up on the clutch. She backed the coupe up several yards, skillfully spun the wheel in the opposite direction, and quickly put it into first gear maneuvering through the field, between the tight boulders and onto the roadway. With her eye on the tachometer, she brought the engine up to three thousand rpm, shifted smoothly into second, and settled the coupe into a steady pace down the mountainside; her hand on the shifter knob, and using the low gear of the transmission as a brake on the downgrade. Dodge couldn't help but snicker as he watched her sitting cool and casual-like with one hand on the wheel and one on the gearshift cruising down the road with the glass-packs purring and popping behind them.

"Where'd you learn to drive like this?"

"My brother. He's been a hot-rodder since day one. Still is. A real gear head. I grew up with the smell of engine oil and the sound of big blocks redlining out in the garage. He was always tearing engines down and rebuilding them with bigger bores, better cams, headers, blowers, you name it. Anything to make his cars sound louder and go faster. He's the one who taught me how to drive," she laughed. "I think the only reason he did was so I could be his test driver. He would have me take his latest creation up and down the road in front of our house, screaming through the gears as fast as I could, and he'd just stand there listening and cheering me on. Then he'd take it back into the garage, fiddle around with the engine some more, and have me do it again until it sounded just right. *Second gear!* he'd shout and I'd start the car off about a hundred yards away, stretch first gear as long as I could and then slam it into second just as I was going by him; burning as much rubber as possible. He'd get such a kick out of that."

"I can't believe it."

"What?"

"You keep surprising me."

"I'm just a simple country girl."

"Right." Dodge got comfy in his unaccustomed seat. "Is he still into it?"

"Very much so. He's got a half dozen rods now, I can't keep up with him. He's got his own car club, The 5 Card Bluff Hot Rod Club. They do a cruise night on Tuesdays at the Inn, and they're involved in quite a few shows for charity each year.

"Do you have one?"

"A hot-rod? No," she smiled at him, "I'm just a test driver, remember."

Annison made her way down the hill, over the dam, past the brick visitor center, and out to the main road. She stopped, looking for traffic, "Anyone around?"

Dodge looked both ways, "Looks all clear to me."

She revved the engine and let out on the clutch carefully engaging first gear. She headed onto the smooth tarmac of route 9 West, bringing the coupe gradually up in rpm's. Dodge could see her concentration as she held tight onto the wheel with her left hand keeping the car laser straight while watching the tachometer. When it hit four thousand rpm, she checked the rearview mirror and floored the accelerator. Dodge was pushed back into his seat as the Holley four barrel carburetor kicked in. Behind him the dual glass-packs opened up and screamed in a deep sonorous staccato like an orchestra awakened by its feisty conductor. Annison watched the tach needle climb rapidly to sixty-five hundred and then quickly, without backing off of the accelerator, pumped the clutch and slammed into second gear. The coupe, adeptly responsive to its new maestro, spun the posi-traction rear tires making them screech and burn, wafting the smell of hot burning rubber into the cab.

"Whoo-Rah!" Dodge yelled.

They were doing over seventy miles per hour. Annison skipped third, shifting directly from second into fourth, and settled it down. "I've been dying to do that! This car kicks ass!"

"You and Bennie," he laughed. "You guys drive this car harder than I do."

They cruised into town a half-hour later and Annison took the short cut Dodge had shown her that brought them past Emily Dickinson's house. The stately Victorian home sat quiet and graceful on its unmarked side street, unaware of the changing times, just the way Emily would have wanted it. The rest of Amherst however, was alive and bustling with the fresh energy and sassy exuberance of a popular college town. UMass students were everywhere; on campus, on the athletic fields, on the front lawns of their frat and sorority houses, and in town on the common, on the active sidewalks, and in the many busy shops and restaurants. The New England colors of autumn were dull in comparison to the bright eccentric fashions exhibited by the students wearing their own carefree ensembles, rebellious of the "in vogue" standards set by distant, out of touch, commercialized designers.

"I love college towns, you can get great ideas here," the designer said as they rolled slowly along in the thick line of traffic. "Look at that," he pointed to a trio of co-eds standing on a corner, their apparel a fascinating blend of avant-garde consignment store and auntie's attic. "Phenomenal color coordination. No one on Fashion Avenue would dare to put a collection like that together, but see how well it flows, how well it expresses their individuality."

"Phhrrittt phhrreww!" A wolf-whistle came from a group of boys crossing the street in front of them, "Nice car," one of them said.

"Nice driver!" said another.

"You have admirers, my love," Dodge smiled.

"Jealous?"

Annison gave them a loud rev and they cheered.

"I love you, Milf," one yelled.

"Milf?" she looked at Dodge who had a wide grin on his face.

"M.I.L.F."

"What's that mean?"

"You don't want to know, Mom."

The wolf whistler gave Dodge a thumbs-up and he nodded back.

"Mom?"

"Don't worry about it. It's definitely a compliment."

"Well then, I'll take it, whatever it is. Compliments are good."

Annison saw a car parked at the curb waiting to pull out into the traffic. She stopped, motioning for it to do so, then pulled up next to the forward car and maneuvered in reverse into the parking space parallel to the curb.

"Good job, Hot Rod Annie."

"Why thank you, Mr. Maddison. This is fun. I love this car."

They walked along the sidewalks arm in arm stopping occasionally to peruse the shop windows, Annison enamored with the various jewelry shops and boutiques, and Dodge checking out the fashions passing them by. They were looking at an array of custom-made jewelry in the window of Amherst Silverscapes, when they noticed a group of co-eds giggling behind them.

"Go on," the first one said.

"No, you."

"You come with me."

"Ohh no!"

"Yes, come on, all of us together."

Bravely they approached the couple at the window. They got almost to them and stopped and began their giggling again. Annison turned to see what the giggling was about and the first one said, "Hi."

Dodge turned around and they all said in unison, "Oh, My, God."

"Hi," he said.

"Dodge." The first one said matter-of-factly.

"Yes."

"I love your designs," she said, suddenly sounding composed and mature, the schoolgirl giggles a thing of the past. "I saw your latest premiere from Paris last week."

"Yeah," the second one said, "we watched it in our fashion design class, our professor taped it and brought it in. It was really cool."

"Thanks, I'm glad you liked it. Are you all taking design courses?"

"We are," the second one said pointing to the first one, "but Meghan's taking Archaeology."

"That's sounds interesting," he said to Meghan.

"Yeah, someday I'll be digging up the fashions of the Pharaohs." They all laughed.

"Well let me know when you do, I could probably get some great ideas from them."

"It's very nice to meet you," the first one said.

"And it's nice meeting you, too," he shook their hands. "Maybe I'll see you at your own premiere someday," and to Meghan, "and please let me know if you unearth some fabulous garments I could knock off."

They laughed, said good-bye and went on their way, the schoolgirl giggles back in full force.

"Popular guy," Annison teased. "Does this happen often?"

"Only when I'm walking with a pretty lady."

"Ouuu, good answer."

They found Amherst Art in the basement of the bookshop located in the center of an antiquated block building that also housed an art studio, framing shop, lawyer's office, and a bank on the corner. You entered the doorway of the bookstore and then immediately took the wide creaky stairs down a dozen steps to the basement. The ceiling was low, fine for Annison, but Dodge had to watch his head and duck clear of the water pipes and electrical conduit running from side to side. The merchant had somehow managed to inundate the small space with every conceivable art supply one might need. Squeezing through the narrow aisles, Annison eventually found what she had come for. She stood before a well-stocked rack of watercolor paints and began lifting the small tubes, one by one, from their rows. Vermilion Red, Permanent Orange, Gamboge Yellow…

"Oh, Alizarin Crimson, this looks nice," she said, gathering the little tubes in the palm of her hand.

Cadmium Hue Orange, Rose Madder, Yellow Ocre, Cerulean Blue, and Prussian Blue.

Her hand quickly became full, and Dodge cupped his hands so she could dump the paints into them.

"Thanks," she said and continued shopping, "Let's see, definitely Van Dyke Brown, hmmm, Burnt Sienna would be good, Raw Umber…and…I guess that's it!"

Dodge turned and took a step towards the front of the aisle towards the counter, "Oh," she grabbed his arm, "whites, I'll need some whites." She picked out two tubes each of Titanium White and Chinese White and dropped them into his hands.

"What else?" he chuckled.

"Brushes."

"Of course!"

She perused the watercolor brushes standing on end in their rack next to the paints. "I'll need a wash brush, a ¾", a ½", and maybe a ½" stroke," and she continued to pick out some rounds, a variety from size zero up to size sixteen and plopped them into his overcrowded hands.

"Are you planning on painting the entire cabin?"

"Hey, you can never have enough paints and brushes. This is fun, I'm getting excited."

"What else?"

"Ummm, paper."

They located the papers on the far wall where a clerk was restocking the shelves from a shopping cart she had blocking the aisle. Her hair was jet black, a butch-cut with the front brushed straight up. Her lips were glossed black to match the gelled black of her hair and she had a large silver hoop nose ring. She was chewing gum and blowing bubbles. Dodge watched her while Annison shopped the assortment of watercolor pads. He was waiting for a bubble to pop and get stuck in the nose ring.

"There's a special on all Strathmore pads this week," she said, and began a new bubble.

"I'm looking for watercolor paper," Annison said. "I'm just getting back into it and I'm not sure which type of paper I should get."

"Do you want a cold press or hot press?"

"I'm not sure."

"The best idea might be this assortment pad," the clerk took one out of her cart. "It's got both cold and hot press and some rough also. It's on sale."

"Great."

"Are you using an easel?"

"Yes."

"This 20" by 30" should be good."

"Thank you," Annison took the pad from her.

"Hey," the girl said to Dodge, "don't I know you? You're on TV, right? Like an actor or something?"

"Yes, I'm on a soap," he said kiddingly.

"Oh, I don't watch that crap," and she blew another huge bubble and popped it loudly just before it reached her nose ring.

They brought everything to the sales counter. There was a short pile of books sitting there, the top one opened and upright atop the pile; *Emily Dickinson's Favorite Poems*. Annison added one of these to her purchases. She handed her credit card to a girl who could have been a twin to the other one, except she had orange hair. Bright orange with of course the matching lip-gloss.

Outside, they returned to the car and put in the large paper bag of supplies.

"Let's walk around," she said, "I'd like to see more of the town."

They strolled in the late afternoon, up one side of Main Street and down the other, casually, taking their time, chatting about idle things. At Legal Grounds they bought coffees and took them over to the common and found a bench to sit on. They sat there in the cooling shadows of the tall trees sipping their coffee and watching the sun set behind The Lord Jeffery Amherst Inn. With the sunset came a slight chill. "Are you cold?" he asked her.

"A little bit." He nestled her closer to him.

They were that way until dark. The streetlights had come on and the foot traffic had thinned. The common was still and quiet. The waning full moon wasn't visible yet, but they could see the glow of it coming above the old Amherst architecture.

"Hungry?"

"No, not really," she said. "You?"

"Hmmm, something sweet."

"Sweet?"

"Like dessert."

"Dessert?" She said with interest.

"Judies has *THE* best dessert."

"That sounds delightful! Let's go."

Judies Restaurant is in the center of town near where Pleasant Street crosses Main. It's small, always crowded, has great food, and a scrumptious dessert menu. The hostess sat them at one of the petite tables at the front window. It was hand-painted in that erratic, multi-colored hippie style. Lots of colors, lots of squiggly lines and tiny dots covering every square inch, like someone had gotten high and spent a whole afternoon dabbing away with an array of paint jars and soft-bristled brushes and then had said, *Wow, man, look at this!* There are probably still some of those artists out there, Dodge thought, intrinsically happy, doing one small thing at a time; into it, without a care in the world.

Their table had a peaceful feeling to it. From it they could see the trees lining the street. They had strings of little white lights wrapped around their trunks and running out onto the branches. A waitress came over and dropped off a menu. Her nametag said Marissa and below it, Chicago.

Annison was perusing the desserts. "These are wonderful, there are two whole pages! I've got to steal one of these menus for my pastry chef at the Inn."

A petite woman with straight white hair, wearing a purple muumuu dress, with big white daisies, approached their table. She was wearing earth sandals. Her toenails were polished in purple, matching the dress, and each big toe had a painted daisy on it. She had an attractive face with no make-up and a wide, Cheshire cat grin.

"Hello," she said. "I'm Judie, welcome to my restaurant."

"Hi, Annison Barrett," she responded, accepting Judie's offered hand.

"And Dodge Maddison ..." Judie said a little too loudly as she took his hand in both hers. "I'm so pleased to meet you."

"Likewise. You have a nice place here, with quite a reputation."

"Oh, thank you. Are you dining this evening?"

"We're going to try some of your famous desserts."

"Oh, lovely, lovely. I'll make up a special sampler of my favorites for you, a little taste of each one."

"You don't have to bother."

"No, no, I insist. You'll love it, trust me."

Marissa came up beside her holding a camera.

Judie asked, "Would you mind if I got a picture of us?"

Dodge obliged, standing next to Judie with the interior of the restaurant as a background.

"Thank you, thank you. I'll be right back with your sampler," and she bounded off towards the kitchen.

Marissa shyly extended a menu with a pen to Dodge. "May I get your autograph, Mr. Maddison?"

"Sure."

"Thanks." She turned away and then remembered, "I'm sorry, I almost forgot, can I get you a drink?"

"I'd love a cappuccino," Annison said.

"That sounds great, I'll have one too."

"Great, be right back."

"This must happen to you all the time, huh?" Annison said.

"Pretty much. They say you get used to it, but I never have. I always think they're talking to someone else. Do you see why I enjoy the anonymity of Bryce Corner?"

"Yes, I'm beginning to."

It seemed like only seconds later that Judie was back. She placed a lazy Susan tray filled with an assortment of her fresh desserts onto the center of the small table. It took up the whole table.

"Okay," Judie said, pointing with her index finger, "this is the Derby Pie; warmed caramel with chocolate chips, coconut, and pecans. This one is the Fudge Lava Cake; dark chocolate cake/brownie combo in a cylindrical form slightly warmed for a lava-flow center, it's incredible. And this one is the Vanilla Bean Cream Brulee Cheese Cake, yummm," she was hovering over them explaining each one with such enthusiasm that Dodge thought she might pick up one of the treats and pop it into her mouth.

"The Key Lime Pie speaks for itself and this is the Bananas Foster; caramelized bananas with a brown sugar butter rum sauce, I couldn't fit the vanilla ice cream onto the tray so I squeezed some fresh-whipped cream on top. These are Toasted Almond Tiramisu Cream Cakes; layered ladyfingers with a thick Italian almond cream topped with crushed Amaratti cookies, my fave! And these little jewels here are Godiva chocolates filled with a variety of different pleasures ... to kill for!"

Marissa appeared and put down two frothy cappuccinos, and both she and Judie said at the same time, "Bon appetite!" and left them with their tray of delicacies.

"Wow," Annison said, munching on one of the ladyfingers, "this is unbelievable."

They sat in silence awhile, sampling and moaning ohhhs and ahhhs.

"Mmmm, try this one," she said, cutting a bite size of the Fudge Lava Cake with her fork and holding it up to his mouth.

"Mmm, delicious. Here, try this."

"Mmm."

The desserts were exceptional, and the casual, subliminally sexual way they were feeding each other was very pleasing.

"You're not making it easy, you know," she said.

"What? Dessert won't kill you."

"I'm not talking about dessert."

Dodge was silent.

"I'm really having a good time and I don't want it to end. But I know it must."

"Why?"

"Because sooner or later we'll both be going back to our different worlds."

Dodge fidgeted in his seat. "Maybe ... I don't know. How much longer are you planning on staying at the lake?"

"What do you mean 'you don't know'?"

He thought for a moment, sitting forward, his arms on the small table, "I've been thinking about what you're doing, your self-imposed sabbatical as you call it, and I guess I've been doing a lot of introspection too. I obviously didn't plan on it, but the circumstances thrust upon me really jarred me, took me by surprise. Both my grandparents at once and then almost losing Old Percy. Even the harrowing morning when I pulled you out of the cabin. All these things have forced me to take a hard look at myself; who I am, what I'm doing, where I'm going."

He sat back in his chair and gave out a heavy sigh. "All my life I've struggled to be an achiever, proving to myself and everyone else how independent I was. How this poor little kid, from a quiet little town in Massachusetts who lost his parents when he was only five, didn't need anybody, could go on, could be something, didn't need anyone's sympathy or pity. He was so strong and self-assured that nothing could touch him - no amount of tragedy, no obstacle too high. I'll show 'em, I'll show 'em all."

Annison put her fork down and picked up her cappuccino. She blew lightly across the top and took a sip.

"And where has it really gotten me? What do I have to show for it? I've got plenty of material things and a lifestyle that people dream of, but who do I pass it onto?"

"Maybe you're being too hard on yourself."

"I don't know. I feel like maybe I've been too wrapped up in myself. Just like wrapping my models in my fashions, I've wrapped myself up in my business; too tightly perhaps. That's how I lost my marriage - too pre-occupied with the fashion world, with making a success of myself and keeping it going. 'Arrogant,' she called me, 'can't see beyond your fucking drawing table to see what's waiting right in front of you.' Maybe she was right."

"Why did you let her go?"

He paused, took a bite of the Key Lime Pie, thinking. "The fear of settling down, maybe afraid I was going to die early."

"You're not dead yet, I mean there's still plenty of time for you to start a family, if that's what you want, don't you think? What about Dana?"

This question struck him. What about Dana? Wasn't he just setting himself up for a repeat performance? His ex had been a model who, somewhere in their relationship, had grown up and wanted to settle down and start a family with him. But he had balked at it, ran away from it. Was it his way of hiding? To keep some young fashion model on his arm and in his bed to divert the focus from his own mortality? Maybe Bennie was right, *stop playing Hugh Hefner with those fucking teeny-boppers.*

"I don't know. We haven't really talked seriously. Hell, I've had deeper conversations with you the past few days than I've ever had with Dana. Maybe that relationship is just superficial; Bennie thinks so. Funny huh? Our best friends can see us better than we can."

*Superficial.* Why did that comment make her feel good?

"Well, I know Nina has a good sense of who I am, she's been a tremendous supporter and ego booster for me. I'd probably be in an asylum by now if it weren't for her. I pushed myself too hard for too long, very near the breaking point. It took me getting away from it all to realize who I am again, and how much I like that person. Is that where you are? Do you feel lost?"

"I hadn't until I got back home. Maybe it's taken me getting back to my roots to realize how unhappy I am."

"You have gone through quite a lot lately, maybe it's all part of grieving."

He twisted his cappuccino mug around in a slow circle. "Even in Paris I felt detached. I was surrounded by a thousand people, all there because of me, yet I remember having this sense of loneliness. I almost wasn't surprised when I got the call from Old Percy. It's like I knew somehow, subconsciously, that something was changing inside of me. Maybe it's been brewing for a while now."

"What?"

"Mid-life crisis?" he laughed.

"Could be," she looked straight at him, "or it could be you're burnt out. I know you globe-trot a lot, but when's the last time you took a vacation, a real lay-back-and-relax type, not a working one?"

"I have no idea."

"That's not good, you know."

They were quiet for a while, he picking away at the desserts they'd never be able to finish and she deep in thought.

"If this were a conversation Nina and I were having, this is where she'd ask something like, 'What's your fantasy?'."

"What do you mean?"

"If you could do anything you wanted to do right now, what would it be?"

Dodge pondered this while he finished his cappuccino, looking at the abstract artwork peeking out from beneath the dessert tray. He followed a fluorescent pink zig-zaggy line to where it ended at the edge of a blue circle filled with lots of tiny white dots. Impulsively he started counting the dots, realized what he was doing, and placed his coffee mug over the circle. Maybe she had a point. Maybe he was wound up too tight. "A fantasy?"

"Yes, anything. What would you do right now, at this point in your life, if you could do anything you wanted?"

"Run away with you."

"No really, come on, what?"

"Run away with you."

"Dodge!"

"Hey, you said anything."

"Anything serious, it has to be something serious."

"What if it is?" He had said it half-kiddingly, but was surprised he'd said it at all.

"You don't even know me."

"Oh … I know you."

She could sense a gravity in his deep blue eyes. It should have made her feel uneasy, but it didn't.

"Are all designer's this impetuous?" she smiled at him.

"I'm not all designers."

"Don't tempt me Mister Maddison," she said, "I'm at that point in my life where I *am* doing crazy things, you know."

Annison picked up her fork and began turning the lazy Susan, slowly making the selections revolve round and round. She wasn't paying them any attention. "Where would we go?"

"Anywhere. Europe, South America, Canada, Amherst, it wouldn't matter to me. We could hide away and spend all our time in bed eating Judie's desserts."

"We'd get fat."

"No, we'd work off the calories with long walks and wild sex."

"Or just the wild sex." She blushed, "I can't believe I just said that."

He laughed.

215

They settled into a comfortable silence again, each in their own thoughts. The thoughts were similar. "It was really nice this morning," he said.

"Yes, it was."

"I …"

"What?"

"I …" he wanted to say never made love like that before, but said, "I can't believe how easy it is to talk with you, to be with you."

"You make it easy for me too. I've told you, it feels like I've known you from before."

"Like we've been together before."

"Yes."

"It's weird isn't it?"

"No, I don't think so. I think it's more than that."

"So do I. I can't pinpoint it."

"Dodge," she said cautiously so the other patrons wouldn't hear her, "I've never done that before."

"What do you mean?"

"Gone with my feelings like that, let myself be so free."

"Are you sorry?"

"On the contrary," she looked steadily into his lovely eyes. "I feel wonderful. I don't want it to end."

"Let's not let it."

\* \* \*

Judie wouldn't allow Dodge to pay, saying that the photograph she was going to add to her celebrity wall would cover the tab. He left Marrisa a worthy tip and stood at the entrance waiting while Judie chatted with Annison about recipes. She had heard of The Inn at Barrett's Bluff and was thrilled to give her one of her dessert menus and promised to visit Annison there next time she traveled away from Amherst.

On the ride back home they were silent. He drove along the dark autumn road deep in thought. She was beside him, close, resting her head on his shoulder watching the stars high above and far away on the other side of the windshield. Occasionally she would see a shooting star and keep it to herself, making her own silent wish. For a while he thought she was asleep, she was so still. He drove along in the flickering darkness, passing Quabbin and seeing the moonlight spill out of the slow-drifting night clouds and pour into the dark rippling waters, seeking the ghost towns buried below. She stirred and asked him if he was okay. Yes he had answered. But his mind was full. Thoughts racing around helter-skelter. Questions.

"What about your marriage? Your husband?"

She didn't stir. She sat still, with her head snuggled into his shoulder, her hands in her lap and her legs curled up on the seat. She had kicked her shoes off earlier and rode comfortable in the twilight with him. She reached over and picked the crimson chrysanthemum from the dashboard and held it to her nose, inhaling its clean, strong scent.

"I've never had feelings like those I felt with you last night, and this morning."

The road wound through the bright trees, now black with the night.

"You have awakened something inside of me that I didn't know existed."

She contemplated, watching the headlights wash the curves with their white light.

He admired her openness, her undaunted honesty.

"Annison ... I feel so close to you I'm almost afraid. There is this burning inside of me, deep and intense, like I get when a new design comes out of me. I can't stop it. It comes out on its own. I just put it down on paper, but it has a life of its own. It's like it's been hidden inside of me swelling up and then it breaks the dam and gushes out of me and I have this incredible excitement consume me. I feel phenomenal and I know I've got something sure and great in front of me. I can't wait to cut some fabric and sew it together. Then when it's finished I stand in awe of it, as if someone else had just brought in this marvelous design and I'm seeing it for the first time, jealous of it and wondering how anyone could have thought of something so beautiful. I can't wait to get it into production before I lose it; before I wake up and find it was only a dream, too beautiful to be a part of real life." He paused letting the thoughts gather on their own time. "Whatever this is happening between us, has got me in awe, frightened even, but I don't want to lose it."

She could feel it too. Not just the raw excitement of a new affair, but the wonder of discovering something new, bestowed upon you by forces out of your control. Like when you wake up that fateful morning and discover you have breasts. That exhilaration mixed with the fear. That excitement, that precise moment that changes you forever. When you stand in front of your mirror and realize you're going to be a woman and a whole new world of adventure and dreams opens right before your eyes. That feverish intoxicating thrill of finding something sought.

"I think they're gone," she almost whispered, "whatever feelings I had for him are long gone. We've been together for such a long time that I guess he'll always be a part of me, but I need to move on with my life. Jack will always be Jack. He's like the little kid that never grew up. Or a cute, lovable puppy, naughty at times, but still endearing, you just can't hate him. I guess I'll always love him in a childish kind of way, but I've long since outgrown him. I love him, but I'm not in love with him."

"So, what are your plans?"

"I need to confront him. I'm sure that at this point he's gotten beyond the anger and the hurt of me disappearing on him, and on everyone else. Funny, I feel more guilt about abandoning my staff and the Inn than I do my husband. But I need to talk with him and let him know how I feel - to be honest. To let him know he has to get on with his life, and I with mine."

"When are you going to do this?"

"Soon. I was thinking of going down to the City this week to visit Nina and bounce the whole thing off her, she's a great sounding board and she's kind of my therapist at the moment. But now I don't know."

"Why?"

"You."

"Me?"

She brushed the mum faintly, like a whisper, along the length of his cheek, "I don't want to lose it either, Dodge."

The coupe followed the nocturnal country roads back to Bryce Corner, to Lake Wickaboag and down the narrow gravel way to the Maddison cottage. They spent the night together there, and the next. It became a habit.

# 30

## *B & B*

They spent time together alone in the solitude of Camp Nyla, further isolating them from the world, playing hooky from reality and enjoying the serenity of the lake. Dodge had called his office in New York and spoken to Harlow, telling her he had some things to take care of and that he was going to take that long overdue vacation time. She sounded concerned but didn't voice it, she thought it a good idea, things were okay there, and told him not to worry. He thought he detected something in her tone, but dismissed it as his own imagination. To buy solo time without Ben's big-brother-meddling he had told him he was going to the City and would be back in a few days.

Annison contacted Nina, fabricating that she was venturing off to Vermont to find a quaint Bed & Breakfast to nestle in and enjoy the foliage. She'd be gone a few days and didn't want her to call the cabin and get no response and worry about her. She was doing fine and would call her when she got back. Nina had rattled off a dozen B&B's for her to consider and told her she sounded pleasantly different, the retreat must be doing her wonders. Dodge and Annison had cleared their slates and made it possible to devote their time to each other.

The relationship grew quickly, fast and furious and vibrant, like the rapidly changing foliage all around them. She was easy to fall in love with, her emerald eyes and soft skin and her easy smile. She and everything about her fascinated him. He was captivated by her cheerfulness, enamored with her playful demeanor, and enchanted by the way she made love to him, eager and warm and true. She was experiencing that wonderful feeling of giving wholly of oneself, that exuberant freedom of letting go and allowing your passions to rule your every moment, unafraid of consequence, and graciously reaping the reciprocal gift of appreciation.

He too was easy to fall in love with, handsome and funny, gentle and sweet. He had a good ear and listened to her well, no matter how silly the topic. And she liked the way he held her in his arms. They thirsted for each other the way lovers, separated by a long time and great distance do. Hungrily making up for lost time, each moment packed with the emotions of an hour, and each hour filled with the wantonness of lost days and weeks and years. They grew upon each other, lovers from another time, rekindling their misplaced spirit, fusing their newfound emotions, and stoking the kiln fires of new love until their separate hearts melted into one, and they were cast in love.

For the most part they didn't stray far from the cottage. Post summer Lake Wickaboag was quiet and presented them a rhapsodic refuge allowing them free reign for canoeing and long country walks or just hanging out on the banks of Camp Nyla and watching the lake. Time passed, but they were unaware of it. Two happy children on vacation, oblivious to the world, inventing things to occupy their secret time together.

They did, however, venture up to Vermont. They had been sitting in the rowboat one morning, drifting in a calm southern wind, the lake their own private paradise; Annison was saying how she'd have to invent some Bed and Breakfast story to tell a sure-to-be-inquisitive Nina, and Dodge had said *let's go find one*. So, on a whim, they threw a few things into their bags and headed to Vermont.

At Annison's suggestion, they took her car; she'd said Dodge attracted enough attention on his own and didn't want to further add to it with the bright red hot rod. So, in her less conspicuous white Lexus they left Bryce Corner, traveled west on route 9, and met up with interstate 91 North. Just after crossing the border into Vermont, Dodge took the exit ramp for the visitor center. The roadway twisted through a large open farm field leading to a huge red barn. The field was dotted with rusted antique farm equipment scattered randomly about. The barn was newly renovated and upgraded to house the welcoming center whilst keeping with, and expressing, the authenticity and flavor of the picturesque Green Mountain State.

Inside, Annison gathered an armload of pamphlets and magazines as Dodge marveled at the interesting displays and historical exhibits. The kind gentleman at the info counter offered to call a few B&B's for availability, but Annison had said no thanks, they weren't sure where they were going yet, and had rejoined Dodge back in the car. With their fresh hospitality coffees and volumes of brochures, they proceeded along the interstate.

The further north into the high mountains, the more spectacular the foliage became and Vermont's autumnal vista spread out before them like a multi-colored quilt. While Dodge drove, Annison perused the brochures and read him the ones she found interesting.

"Here's one," she said, "Woodstock, Vermont. I've always wanted to go there." *The Village of Woodstock, she read him, is nestled in the foothills of the Green Mountains in the crook of the Quechee River in a picturesque valley free of giant industry and corporate malls. The Shire Town, early home to the Windsor County Seat, was spawned in the late 1700's by successful, rich, business and professional people who surrounded the Village Green and quaint nearby streets with stately and amply-built Federal houses, Greek revivals, and Georgian Mansions. Today, tourists from all over enjoy it's Currier & Ives charm, augmented with whimsical shops, gourmet restaurants, a two hundred year old General Store, jewelers, potters, tinsmiths, bakers, cabinet makers, art studios, and several hospitable Bed & Breakfasts. Last but not least, it is home to the world-renowned Woodstock Inn & Resort.*

"I've heard of The Woodstock Inn and have always wanted to see how it compared to The Inn at Barrett's Bluff." Annison seemed excited. "Let's drive through the town and see what it's like, and I could check out the Inn."

Dodge wondered why the interest in the Inn at all, if she was indeed thinking of leaving Barrett's Bluff, but he kept silent and steered onto route 89 at White River Junction and took the exit marked "Route 4, Woodstock."

Once in the village, Annison found the Victorian architecture, grand homes, tree-lined common, stone walls, covered bridge and narrow shop-filled streets, picturesque and enchanting, and wanted to stay and explore it all. They spent an hour combing the B&B's in the Village, only to find them full. Their options were to continue driving deeper into Vermont, or give up their cozy B&B idea and go to the big and elaborate Woodstock Inn; they had more than a hundred rooms there, and there'd certainly be availability. But of course, with foliage peaking, they found even the Woodstock Inn was booked.

However, the manager, a Mr. Seth Hapgood, standing at the front desk, had recognized Dodge Maddison, the designer, and offered to make a personal phone call to Eleanor Grey. Eleanor Grey was a local widow who had retired from operating her quaint B&B a few years ago upon the death of her husband, Senator Graham Grey. Occasionally though, she was known to open it by happenstance during the peak season. The phone call was initially unsuccessful, the Grey B&B was indeed closed, but the call became fruitful when Seth Hapgood boastfully mentioned that it was Dodge Maddison looking for a room. Eleanor thence insisted that Mr. Hapgood send them right over. She had a lovely room available in her charming turn of the century Victorian; she would love to have the famous fashion designer as her guest. The manager walked with them to the front door, and in conversation with Annison, remarked that he had actually stayed at her Inn at Barrett's Bluff just last year. He would be honored to personnally give her a tour of The Woodstock Inn. Annison graciously accepted and promised Seth Hapgood she'd return tomorrow for his tour.

They pulled away from the main entrance to the Inn, waving to Mr. Hapgood standing proudly on the front steps, and took a left onto High Street; a narrow side street perched on the side of a hill that wound along the Keedron Brook. This returned them into the center of the Village where they again drove past the myriad of shops adorning Central Street, halfway along The Village Green, then bore right over the covered bridge and onto Mountain Avenue. They easily found Eleanor Grey's B&B by the description given them from Mr. Hapgood; a cute yellow house on the corner with a white picket fence.

Eleanor Grey was standing on her porch amidst a fancy array of pumpkins, gourds, and cornstalks adorned with little orange lights that spread out along the gingerbread railing. She was a refined, well-dressed lady in a healthy small frame, still attractive and spry in her seventies. She was excited to have the company and welcomed them with open arms.

"Whenever Mr. Hapgood told me who 'twas," she said in her homespun Vermont accent, "I said, Seth Hapgood, you send them right t'over, and don't you take no for an answer!" Eleanor had grabbed Annison's bag out of her hand and was leading them into the house. "I usually like to open a room or two each season, mostly for the company (she pronounced it cump-nee), but I didn't this year 'cuz I took in a couple of borders. Awfully lonely here without my Senator, that's him over the fireplace," she pointed to the portrait with her free hand as they ascended the wide staircase, "handsome as hell, he 'twas."

Annison smiled at Dodge and squeezed his arm and whispered, "She's *so* cute, I love her."

"Why thank you young lady," Eleanor Grey laughed, "Didn't think my ears were still in tune, did ya?"

She led them down the hallway past several rooms, each with a brass plaque on the door inscribed with the name of a different Vermont county. Theirs was *The Windsor*, at the far end of the house. It had windows on three sides offering spectacular views of the Quechee River, the covered bridge, and a lovely panorama of the Village, now sporting its evening lighting as twilight casually crept in. To the back, a sprawling lawn ran half an acre to the base of Mt. Tom, an environmental preserve offering roughhewn hiking trails and incredible views, donated by the Rockefellers, one of the Village's early settling families from New York.

"The boys live upstairs, but they're very quiet," Eleanor explained as she dropped Annison's bag onto the loveseat at the foot of the high bed and went about tying back the window curtains and pointing out each of the views. "They're my borders, Kenneth and Robert, a lovely couple. Kenneth is a waiter at Bentley's Restaurant in the center of the Village, and Robert is the head of maintenance at Killington Ski Resort. Do you ski?" Not giving them time to answer she continued, "Don't think they're making snow just yet, but soon they twill be. We do a brisk business here in Woodstock during ski season. Did you know this is a four-season resort town? I'm thinking of opening up this ski season now that I've got Kenneth and Robert. They're a big help to me." She was fluffing the pillows, "We worked out a sweet deal," she winked at Annison, "I give them a nice break on their rent and they help me keep up the place. Kenneth is wonderful at cleaning and decorating, all those pumpkins and such on the front porch were his doing. And all the interior flower arrangements he does himself. Aren't they wonderful? He's the one who's pushing me to re-open. I do enjoy it so! I just might.

"The bathroom's in here; fresh towels, soaps, shampoo, everything you'll need. There's books downstairs in the Senator's library and the kitchen is well stocked and open twenty-four hours, so feel free to help yourselves to whatever you like. There are lovely restaurants right in town - I'd suggest either Bentley's or The Prince & The Pauper. I'll have Kenneth make us a hearty breakfast in the morning – he loves making breakfast! But, enough about all that, I'll leave you be. Enjoy your stay, I'm thrilled to have you as my guests," she squeezed Dodge Maddison's arm and then said quietly to Annison, in a whisper, "I'm going to go put on a pot of tea, dear, and I'd love to hear about your Inn. Seth Hapgood tells me you own the one in Barrett's Bluff. I've always wondered what it t'would be like to run a grand Inn like that. Please do come down and join me in a cup, won't you?" and she disappeared down the hallway.

"She's absolutely adorable!" Annison said. "And I love her home. Let's go check out the rest of the rooms." They did; Annison marveling at the interesting way Eleanor Grey had them impeccably decorated in traditional subtle Vermont themes.

"I would love to do this," Annison Barrett said, "so much easier to handle, and you could do it on your own, you wouldn't need an elaborate staff with their elaborate problems and incessant whining." She was almost talking to herself as they passed from one guest room to another. Dodge was absentmindedly perusing the different wallpapers and subconsciously gathering design patterns in his head. At one point they were actually in different rooms and Annison was still talking to him, unaware that he was not behind her. "Look at how she did the colors in here, Dodge," she said to herself, "marvelous."

Back in the *Windsor Room*, Annison unpacked her things and placed them into the bureau. Dodge asked in a British accent, "Are you going to join her for a cup of tea, dear?"

"Yes, I'd love to hear how she manages her Bed and Breakfast. I wonder how long she's had it. Are you coming along?"

"No, I think I'm going to take a quick catnap, then I'll shower and we can go out to dinner."

"Okay," she went to him and kissed him lightly on his lips, "maybe I'll join you in the shower."

"Mmmm, that's a nice idea."

"Yes," she kissed him, "it is."

\* \* \*

In the catnap he had a dream. He was in his apartment, in his building in New York. He was in bed. Old Percy was on the roof looking through a telescope. He could hear him calling to him, *Come on! Quick, you're gonna miss it. See it? See it? Here it comes!* He imagined a huge fireball, like a glowing pulsar, forming huge in the lens of the telescope. Beneath him, the building was empty. Everyone was gone, the studio was empty, the workers' machines had been stripped of their patterns and all the heavy yards of fabric had been thrown out the windows and lay in a huge pile in the middle of the street. The shop on the first floor was closed and lay empty except for the bright red coupe sitting in the center. Grampa

Jedediah was behind the wheel, revving the engine loudly so that Dodge could hear it. Jedediah put the coupe into first gear and floored it, burning rubber as he drove it across the empty sales floor and up the stairway to the second level. The tires were screeching and peeling from the chrome rims like ribbons of black satin, wet and shiny, spitting out from beneath the tires and covering the empty display racks and chasing after the bare mannequins running towards the door with their heavy pedestals in their fake hands. There was someone in his bed lying next to him, raising her smooth leg up and down against his naked thigh, arousing him. Jed was on the third floor and had crashed the coupe into one of the pattern tables, crushing the fenders and scraping the paint off of one side; it dripped like fresh red blood onto the glossy floor. He backed up hurriedly and smashed the rear of the coupe into one of the large cutting machines, red smoke billowed from the exhaust system, ripped wide open and roaring louder than ever. Her hand had found his hardness and was stroking him softly with her silken fingers. *Hurry up! You're gonna miss it!* Old Percy yelled from the roof. Harlow was standing in the middle of the room, she was wearing the dress she had on in the rowboat, she was motioning for him to come to her. He saw her there and wanted to reach for her but couldn't move his arms, they were locked around the woman in his bed. She was atop him, gliding him into her. He tried to brush the hair from her face, but he couldn't. He heard the coupe racing through the gears and could see it in his mind, dented and destroyed like a demolition derby car, tearing along the work floor, bashing into table after table, sending the delicate sewing machinery into fireballs against the walls as it sped toward the freight elevator standing open at the end. Ben was there on the manufacturing floor, holding his revolver and shooting at shadows. He chased after Jedediah, gaining on him and jumped onto the running board, shooting away like Elliot Ness as they raced down an endless runway. Dodge was sweating, hot and feverish, swooning in the throes of ecstasy as the faceless woman above him rocked back and forth holding his hands tight to her waist and shaking her hair wildly, her long dark curls flailing from side to side. He became dizzy, trying desperately to open his eyes, but they remained clamped shut. Old Percy jumped through a hole in the roof screaming *It's too late! It's too late!* The telescope was in his hands but it had turned into an umbrella. He opened it above him and ran to the far end of the room, grabbing Harlow as he whisked by her. The freight elevator door opened and Jedediah and Bennie were standing there. Jedediah stood holding onto the steering wheel in one hand by his side. Bennie had one of the coupe's dripping red doors, holding it open for Dodge. They were leaving him, he wanted to go with them, but Annison was soothing him. Yes, it was Annison, he could almost see her now, her beautiful long hair swaying across his face. Annison, slowly, sexually, riding him, faster and faster. The room became brighter, illuminated by a stark white light, like he was inside a huge white cloud and someone was turning a rheostat, brighter and brighter. He tried to tell her they should go, but he couldn't speak. She became wilder, domineering in her reckless abandon, easily controlling him and making him want her more than anything else. The room was white hot and getting brighter. He tried to slow her down, but she was writhing uncontrollably, gasping and shrieking in her passionate delirium. He reached for her face. She was twisting her head wildly and his hands got caught in her hair, and then it was in his hands, her wig was in his hands and he saw Dana's short cropped blonde hair and she laughed. She held a devilish smirk on her face and she was laughing at him. He was stunned and confused. What was going on? He tried to stop her but she kept on, laughing and teasing him with her perfect naked body, glistening with sweat as she writhed wildly above him, selfishly and successfully making him want her beyond anything else. The others were leaving; the elevator door was closing. He was torn, wanting to push her off him and make a dash for the elevator, or to give in to his primal passions and just enjoy it and let it happen. He wanted to come fast and then join them in the elevator, but she wouldn't let him. She was being cruel in her seduction, bringing him to the threshold of a climax, only to stop abruptly, driving him crazy, and then slowly starting all over again. At one moment, he wanted to throw her off him and run, and the next, to roll her over and take her savagely and hard, knowing they might leave without him, but not caring, caught in the hunger of his own selfish lust. *Stop,* he said weakly, *we've got to go.* She was tormenting him, playing with his primal emotions, testing his willpower. *Stop it Bitch!* he yelled at her, *we've got to get out of here!* She snickered and continued her overpowering entrapment. The elevator door was almost shut. Harlow took the umbrella from Old Percy, closed it, and threw it out the door. It tumbled and slid along the floor, transforming into a noose and snaking along the floor toward him. It reached his foot and began slithering up his leg. The elevator door slammed shut, making a loud ominous industrial sound that reverberated across the empty room and pounded into his eardrums like a rumbling wave crashing onto a quiet seashore. He would fuck her hard, the bitch, give it to her like she's never had it before, then he would jump off her and take the stairs, quickly, he still had time, he could meet them at the bottom. The rope tightened around his leg. The light in the room became red and explosive, *Dana, you Bitch! This is what you want isn't it!* He became rough. Madly, in a powerful movement that despised gentleness, he grabbed onto her and threw her to the mattress. *You like it like this don't you, Dana!* He straddled her, towering strong and forcefully above her, holding her arms tightly to the mattress on either side of her head, and then, with a lustful savage anger, raped her beneath him.

*  *  *

Annison was biting her lip hard, her face turned deep into the pillow, trying desperately to muffle her painful moaning, to keep her cries from the sharp ears of Eleanor Grey.   Dodge was atop her, raging uncontrollably, hurting her. She was unable to stop him. He had been so calm, sleeping so innocently when she had first sneaked into the bed, caressing him, softly making love to him while he slept, but now he was brutal. He was calling her Dana and she didn't like that.

The cloud was clearing and the bright red light was dissipating, they were turning the rheostat down. Dodge was waking up and gradually becoming aware of his surroundings. He was in a guestroom, at a Bed and Breakfast, in Vermont, the lighting was dim, he was in bed, he was making love. He slowed his frantic pace and looked through blurry eyes to the woman he was making love to. She was obscured by a white veil. He struggled to recognize her, but her face was harmonious, the countenance of a universal lover. Dana? Harlow? Annison? The veil lifted and he began to see her clearly. Annison. *Oh, Annie*, he spoke. He rolled off her and lay on his side holding her tenderly to him. She embraced him and stroked his head like a child's and he fell back to sleep. Annison listened to his breathing become calm and peaceful, his head on her breast as he slept. There was a painful throbbing between her thighs. Outside, the wind was swirling. Brittle branches brushed against the wooden clapboards, making an ominous squeaking sound. Through the window with the curtains tied back she could see the swaying shadows of the night. She lay still, watching the night fall.

After a while he awoke, and with the waking, the dream faded, tucked away in his subconscious. He saw Annison at his side and he was happy. He smiled at her.

"Did I sleep long?"

"A while."

"Must have been tired from the drive. What time is it?"

"Nine."

"Wow. Are you hungry?"

"Sure."

"Shall we go out?"

"No, I think we can find something in the kitchen."

"Great," he jumped up, "give me two seconds for a quick shower."

She looked at him.

"What?"

"Nothing. I'll go downstairs and see what I can rustle up."

"Great, I'll be down in a minute."

A second later Annison heard him start the shower and she got out of bed, reached for one of the Grey B&B robes that Eleanor had on hooks behind the door, tied it around her, and left the room.

# 31

## *HOVERING*

"**L**ook," he said.

Annison lifted her head off his chest, "Oh, it's beautiful!"

A bright colored hot air balloon was hovering on an early morning thermal just above the mountain right outside their window.

Dodge was sitting up with his back against the headboard, stroking her hair as she lay with her head settled comfortably upon his chest. She raised herself a little higher in the bed, fluffing her pillows and sitting up next him. The balloon loomed large and still, its bright rainbow colors framed perfectly in the window. They could see tiny figures in the brown wicker basket suspended below the balloon and bright orange plums of fire sporadically shooting up into the center of it. They watched as it slowly moved against the morning horizon. As it drifted from view, she got up and went to the window to watch it and he lay there gazing at her, enjoying her nakedness in a pale silhouette against the window. He could see the tip of the balloon, luminous like a sunset, dropping over her soft white shoulder, sinking below the edge of the mountaintop, seeking a soft landing spot in the adjacent valley.

At breakfast they met Kenneth and Robert who both hailed from Charleston, South Carolina and loved to ski. Last year on their winter ski vacation, they had found, and fallen in love with, Woodstock, Vermont. They had chosen it not only for its proximity to Killington and other nearby ski resorts, but also because Robert's father had served in the Senate with Graham Grey, and thus knew of Eleanor and her Bed and Breakfast. She had been pleased to offer the upstairs rooms to them, and when they again contacted her the following spring and told her of their plans to move to Woodstock, the current arrangement materialized.

Robert had transferred his skills as director of maintenance for The Charleston Country Club to a similar position with Vermont Seasons Resorts, Inc. which owns and operates the nearby Killington Ski Resort and the adjacent golf course and private club. He was content with his job, absolutely loved Vermont, and was thinking of purchasing a house with Kenneth in nearby Pomfret.

Kenneth was biding his time as a waiter at Bentley's Restaurant in the center of the Village not only to get acquainted with the local business owners but more importantly to get a pulse on the demographics and needs of the year-round tourist industry. He was hoping to realize his ambition for a catering business.

This morning Kenneth had prepared his Sunrise Omelet; whisked eggs with red and green peppers, a medley of cheeses, onions, Tabasco sauce, a half cup of orange juice and, drawn on top at the last moment, a swirl of grenadine in the form of a rising sun. Annison and Dodge, sitting at the breakfast table with 'the boys' and Eleanor, were duly impressed. They sat comfortably throughout breakfast bantering about recipes and fashion, Charleston, New York, favorite travel spots and such. Breakfast done, Robert and Kenneth excused themselves to go to work, then Dodge left to go to the Senator's library, leaving Annison alone with Eleanor Grey.

"Did you folks go out to dinner?"

"No, we decided to stay in. We raided your fridge."

"Oh? Did you find enough to eat I hope?"

"Yes, plenty, thank you. We weren't all that hungry. We had cheese and crackers, and I cut up some fruit."

"Good cheese?"

"Yes, delicious."

"Vermont cheddah, t'ain't no beddah," Eleanor sang. "My Senator loved Vermont cheddar cheese. Used to cut up thick little pieces and place 'em on oyster crackers. He'd line up a whole row of 'em and then sit here at the table and eat 'em one by one."

"He sounds like a nice man."

"Yes," Mrs. Grey reflected, "he 'twas."

Annison began gathering the breakfast dishes and Eleanor said, "So, whatch'ya up to for taday?"

She told her of Mr. Hapgood's invite to tour the Woodstock Inn, and said she'd like to walk the town, "It seems so lovely and charming and the houses are adorable."

"It's a beautiful mornin' for a walk. The Inn, tain't far at all," Eleanor said. "You just go out the front door and walk down the street across the covered bridge, and then walk straight across The Green to the other side and that'll put you smack in front of The Woodstock Inn. If my legs weren't so damn old, I'd go with you."

\* \* \*

He was standing in the library in front of a wall of books with his back to the doorway. Annison came up from behind and wrapped her arms around him, laying her head into the small of his back, "It's so nice here, I'm glad we came."

Dodge reached up and returned the book he was holding back into its vacant spot on the long shelf. He drew the one next it off the shelf and opened it in his hands, flipping the pages in an animated way.

"Are you ready, darling?" she asked him.

"For...?"

"Our tour of the Inn."

He held onto the book in one hand and drew another off the shelf. "I don't think I'm as excited about that as you are. I think I'll just stay here for a while, the Senator kept a fascinating library. Okay?"

"Well, you're going to gravely disappoint Mr. Hapgood," she smiled, "but I'll send him your apologies."

"Please do."

She kept her arms around him and her head nestled on his back. Was it tension she felt between his shoulders?

"Did you sleep alright?"

"Yes, fine." The question made him wonder if he had. "Why?"

"You seem a little tense." She brought her hands around and kneaded his shoulders. He stood in the same position, perusing the new book. Annison thought of what had happened last night, he had scared her, but he hadn't said anything about it. They'd gone downstairs to the kitchen afterward and everything seemed to be okay, as if it had never happened. She wondered if he remembered it, he'd so quickly fallen back to sleep. Obviously he'd been dreaming. She wanted to ask him about it, but wasn't sure she wanted to hear his answer. *Does he miss Dana?* He hadn't really talked about her and their relationship. *Is he in love with her?* She realized then that she hadn't thought about that. Not really. She'd been too enthralled with this new romance. *Romance.* She wondered if he was having second thoughts about them. *About us*. The tension, stretched tightly across his back, was creeping into her, making her feel uneasy. She was having such a great time, carefree for once and really enjoying it. But was he? She didn't want anything to spoil it, to puncture the balloon ride she was on. Maybe she needed a little solo time.

"I guess I'll go then. Okay?"

"Okay."

"I'll be back in a couple hours."

"I'll be here."

"Okay. Bye."

"Bye."

Annison walked out the front door and stood on the porch. She could see the covered bridge from there and watched a pair of joggers enter it. She heard their footsteps thumping faintly inside the old wooden structure and then listened to them disappear as the joggers emerged at the other end and ran along the quieter grass on the edge of The Green. The morning was cooler than she'd expected; Vermont was colder than Massachusetts. She returned inside to put on a sweater. She passed the door to the library and saw Dodge still at the far wall perusing the books.

Upstairs, in their room, she opened the bureau drawer and took out an off-white fisherman's sweater. She removed her blouse and then her bra and donned a tight fitting tank top, tucking it into her jeans. Over that she pulled the sweater, taking a moment at the mirror to adjust the thick turtleneck. She sensed that something was bothering him. Maybe she should ask him again if he'd like to join her. They wouldn't have to go to the Inn, they could walk the Village, maybe stop somewhere for a coffee and talk. Perhaps they needed to talk. She took her black wool blazer from the closet and went back along the corridor past the doors with the engraved brass plaques and down the staircase. She got to the bottom and stopped a moment to finger-comb her hair over the shoulders of the blazer and then entered the library. He wasn't there. The books he had held in his hands were back in their place on the shelf. She went outside, but the porch was vacant. She stood there a minute thinking of what she should do and then decided to keep to her original plan and walk over to the Inn. Maybe she was reading too much into it. Things were probably fine. It was a gorgeous morning for a walk.

Dodge had gone out the back door and was standing on the flagstone walkway in the rear courtyard. Eleanor Grey was at the white picket fence on the side of the house that ran along River Street. She was standing at one of her flower boxes perched along the length of the fence, dead-heading her chrysanthemums. From her vantage point she could simultaneously see Annison walking over the covered bridge and Dodge Maddison standing in her garden. He was staring at the mountain that began at the end of the Grey property, looking up to where the balloon had been earlier.

Meticulously she wove her tiny fingers through the close-bunched flowers, pinching the dead mums and tossing them over the fence into the yard. They fell like droplets of faded paint onto the green ground and took their place with yesterday's pruning, withered and brown and mulching into the cool soil at the base of the white fence.

"Not going to the Inn?" she asked, already surmising his response.

He hadn't seen her there and he walked over to her. "No, I thought I might go for a walk. Your flowers are beautiful."

"You like them?"

"Yes, mums are my favorite."

"That so."

"What's the name of that mountain?"

"Mount Tom, but most folks call it Star Mountain because of the large star on top. It's illuminated every night. Did you see it last night?"

"Yes, through the back window."

"Woodstock's version of the Hollywood sign," she snickered. "There's a nice hiking trail clear to the top. Takes 'bout an hour. Wonderful view of the Village. You can see the Quechee River run through the valley and most all the way to New Hampshire."

"Hmm," he thought. "I think I'm going to walk around the town for a bit."

Eleanor Grey looked at him standing there with the three buttons on his sportcoat buttoned and the collar feebly turned up against the morning cold, his hands thrust into his front jean pockets. She smiled to herself, *flatlander.*

"Come here a minute," she came through the gate and led him back to the house. In the mudroom she picked an old coat off a wooden peg on the wall. "Put this on, belonged to my husband, should fit you. Carhartt, nice and warm." She took his sportcoat from him and placed it on the hook and stood watching him get into the coat that held warm memories for her.

"Thanks, Eleanor, fits fine, very comfortable."

"The senator loved this coat, t'wouldn't go outside without it." She zipped it up for him like a mother sending her son off to school. "There," she said, "now you look just like one of the locals. You blend," she ribbed him, "You'll be incognito." She brushed the shoulders and let her hand rest there a moment, enjoying a private memory. "Well," she said softly, "that ought to do you for the morning. Probably be too warm after an hour or so, 'spose to be a nice day. They said it might reach seventy by early afternoon, but I don't think 'twill get out of the sixties."

"Thank you," he walked off the porch and to the gate. As he was lifting the latch, she said to him, "That's a nice lady you've got there." He turned to acknowledge her, but she'd already disappeared inside.

He closed the gate and noticed her handiwork on the mums standing colorful in their thick bunches in the flower boxes. She had them arranged in threes; orange on the left, yellow to the right, and the red crimson in the center. He lowered his head and took a sniff of these and his thoughts sped back to Quabbin, to the wild mums on the shoreline, to the one Annison had picked for him, the one lying on the dashboard of his coupe. A souvenir, a reminder of that day, keepsake of those feelings they had shared. He had been happy that day, and every day since, ecstatically so. *So what's bothering you now, Dodger?*

He walked along River Street in the cool fresh air of the morning. It was quiet. The wind was still and the trees on the mountain to his left were still, silently dropping their leaves one by one in the windless air. He walked along the center of the narrow roadway passing the occasional houses on his left and keeping in pace with the casual flow of the Quechee River just down the bank to his right. There were autumn leaves on the top of the water, miniature kayaks floating in the calm current. *I don't know.*

*Come on! You can't say I don't know!*

He was on the quiet backside of the village. Across the river, through the thinning trees, he saw the backs of the old buildings lining Elm Street. The shops would be opening now and the leaf-peeking tourists would be walking along Elm and Central Streets, shopping and buying mementos to take back home to remind them of this sunny fall day they had spent in this quaint Vermont town.

He was glad they'd come here. It had been an impromptu decision that had turned into a pleasant adventure. Everything they did together was pleasing to him. He'd probably never felt this way before. No, not probably, he'd *never* had these feelings before. There was something intrinsically special about her. Alluring. She made him feel alive.

*I think you're in love with her, man!*

*Is that possible? To fall in love with someone in such a short time?*

*Hey, people fall in love at first sight ... it still happens.*

Maybe that was what was bothering him. Love can be scary at times. Especially when it blindsides you, coming out of nowhere when you least expect it.

*Is that it? You feel caught off guard? Annison Barrett wasn't on your 'to do' list? She didn't fit into your busy, compulsive schedule?*

This was the first time they'd been apart since the day they had picnicked at Quabbin and then had gone on to Amherst, and that was well over a week ago and they had spent every waking moment together since. *And non-waking don't forget!*

*Maybe you need this solo time to get your head out of la-la land. What the hell are you doing, Dodge? You can't just put your world on hold 'cuz you get infatuated with some new woman in your life. You're stronger than that! Right?*

He thought he was. He'd always thought he was. All of his relationships had been at his discretion, fitting appropriately into his schedule, not interfering with his ambitious life-style, but rather enhancing it, being worn for attention like one of his flattering designs. But this one was different, way too different. He wasn't prepared for this one. Not prepared for the inner feelings this relationship ignited in him. Maybe he was at a weak moment in his life, the death of Emma and Jedediah weighing too heavily upon him.

*Or maybe it's because of that.*

*What do you mean?*

*Maybe I'm addressing my own mortality. I feel so fucking alone now.*

*Maybe you're just afraid.*

*Afraid of what?*

*Of being alone. Maybe you're just grabbing onto her because she became available to you. You're using her.*

*No! I didn't need her in my life, I've got Dana.*

*There is no Dana. Dana's just a dream. Someone you keep around to remind you of Dodge Maddison the designer. She keeps up your appearance, just as the others have. She satisfies the image you have of yourself, or perhaps the image you think others have of you. But now this Annison comes in and shakes everything up, throws you off balance, makes you unsure, has you questioning your mortality. Maybe you are using her, just as you've used all your women. All except for one, Dodge.*

*One?*

*Harlow. She's the only one you've never used. She's the best thing in your life, don't you think?*

"Fuck!" he said out loud. Too loud. He looked about to see if anyone had heard him.

*Confusing isn't it? Thought your life was all hunky-dorey, eh?*

He walked along the road trying to keep his thoughts quiet. He needed a refuge, if only for a minute, from his own mind. He'd successfully hidden not only from his business in New York, but also from himself. Allowing himself to get caught up in Annison's own retreat, letting her newfound freedom rub off on him. Admiring her for her bravery of being able to walk away from her daily life and selfishly pamper herself, something he'd never been able to allow himself to do. Maybe that was too hard an assessment. He was being cruel to her for no reason. He knew that what she was doing was hard, difficult for her to be doing, necessary, but still emotionally wrought. It was unfair to blame her for his own apprehension. She was doing what she had to do and maybe touring the Inn was part of that.

*Ahh, that's it isn't it! It's the Inn thing. You're pissed that she's even thinking about an Inn. You don't understand it. Why would she be interested in touring The Woodstock Inn if she was truly thinking of leaving Barrett's Bluff? If she holds similar feelings towards you like she claims to? You think she's deceptive? Playing you? Heaven forbid you might be used for once!*

Dodge was tired of listening to himself. He walked along the quiet roadway, undisturbed and alone, fighting to suppress his contemplation and just enjoy the beautiful morning. But he couldn't. His thoughts swelled over him just like the waters rumbling beside him washed interminably over the boulders in the riverbed.

"I've got to get back to the city," he said aloud, "I've got to get back to the studio and catch up on my business, get back to reality."

*That's what she's going to do, right? Why else would she be at The Woodstock Inn right now? Obviously she misses her business. She's not really thinking of leaving it. She'll be going back to it soon and you'll be back in New York, just like that. It'll be nothing but a memory. After all, she's married, remember?*

*Yeah, you're probably right.* Dodge found himself leaning against a stone wall gazing empty-eyed at the day.

A white Jeep with U.S. Postal Service lettering was making its way toward him. The lady behind the wheel on the right side was stopping at each mailbox and delivering the mail. He watched her gradually getting closer. She'd pull up to the mailbox and pull down the little door with her right hand. Then she'd reach over to her left, retrieve the occupant's mail and pass it through her window into the box and then close the mailbox door and crawl up to the next one. Between the houses she had her head down gathering the mail for the next one and it looked like she wasn't even watching the road, the truck well-accustomed to the route and rolling on auto-pilot. When she passed by him she waved. She had the radio cranked up. Jimmy Buffet was wasted away again in Margaritaville still searchin' for his lost shaker of salt.

*Searchin' ... I know how you feel.*

* * *

Eleanor Grey had been right, the morning was warming up and the Senator's jacket was heating with the sun and the walking. Dodge walked along River Street and made his way down to Elm Street, still keeping the river to his right, then crossing over it on the black metal suspension bridge that hovered above the clear running waters. The houses were huge now, some with massive pillars and elaborate frontal work, each with a sizable piece of land around it. Although as he got closer to the center of the village, the lot sizes shrunk in scale with the houses as they clustered nearer one another then finally gave way to the antiquated block buildings making up the heart of the commercial center.

It was busy in town, the tourists hustling and bustling about, keeping the local entrepreneurs happy. He wandered in the open door of one of the art galleries on Pleasant Street and absent-mindedly perused the colorful collections adorning the white walls. He thought of his paintings he had done early on, before he got too preoccupied with Dodge Maddison the designer, and wondered where they were. Gramma Emma probably had them stored in the attic, he'd have to dig them out when he got back. He tried to remember them but could only envision a few. It had been years since he'd seen them. He wondered if he could paint again like he did so furiously in London while he was attending the Royal Academy of Fashion Design twenty years ago. *Wow, time's flying by.*

He decided to have a heart to heart with Annison to see where her head was at. He needed to know. He had to get control of himself and place his world back in order. He wanted her. Deeply. But how could it work? Could there be a future for them? Could she fit into his world and he into hers? Was she truly leaving her husband? Her life at the Inn on Barrett's Bluff?

The morning passed onto noontime and Dodge had made a loop throughout the village and back to the Grey B&B. He entered the front door, searched the library, living room, and kitchen, and then ascended the staircase, returning to their room. Eleanor was there, setting a vase of her chrysanthemums onto the bureau.

"Nice walk?"

"Ah, yes, it was. Have you seen Annison?"

"Nope, she hasn't returned yet."

Dodge looked at his watch. He thought for sure she'd have been back before him. He became perplexed again. Those ugly thoughts he'd wrestled with during his walk reared their head again and furrowed his brow.

Eleanor noticed it, "Everything alright?"

"Huh? Yes," he paced. "I think I'll go back to town, maybe to Bentley's. When she comes back would you let her know?"

"Sure." She pronounced it with two syllables, *shoe ahh.*

"Tell her I'll wait lunch for her there."

# 32

## *BENTLEY'S*

Bentley's was crowded with local business people and tourists. Dodge found a seat at the bar. Inside, away from the high sun, it was dark. The dark walls and the high polish on the wood floors lent a posh backdrop to the antique furnishings and the elegant artwork in ornate gold frames. Large frosted-glass globes suspended from the tin ceiling lit the white linen tablecloths with a soft light and reminded him of a restaurant he frequented in Paris, on Rue Boiteau. He'd love to take Annison there. Kenneth came up to the server's side of the bar to pick up an order of drinks and said something to the bartender. Kenneth waved to Dodge and the bartender came over. "Hi," he said, "what can I get you?"

"Absolut Bloody Mary please, extra spicy if you could."

"Coming right up."

The noontime luncheon banter was soothing to him, giving him room to get lost in his thoughts as he sat comfortably in the warmth of the fellow patrons.

"Here you go, can I get you a menu?"

"No thanks, I'm waiting for someone."

"Will you be joining us for lunch?"

"Yes."

"I'll let the hostess know to reserve you a nice table."

"Thank you."

"Enjoy."

Dodge was on his second Bloody Mary when a group of people approached the other end of the bar. He didn't notice the two couples dressed in a New York yuppie kind of way, starched L.L.Bean way overdone. One of the gentlemen ordered drinks for all of them. The ladies sat and the men stood behind them. One of the women saw him and said aloud, "Well as I live and breathe ..." She walked over to Dodge, coming up behind him and placing her hand on his shoulder, "Hello, stranger," she said.

He turned around on his stool, "Gail!" he said surprised. "How are you?" He got up and gave her a formal hug. "What are you doing here?"

"The real question, dahling, is what are *you* doing here?"

"Maddison! How the hell are you?" The gentleman who had ordered the drinks grabbed onto Dodge's arm and shook his hand.

"Fine, Leon, how are you? Hello Blythe, Camden, how are you?" The foursome had now joined him. "What are you all doing here?"

"Leaf peeking," Leon said, "our annual sojourn from the City to the wilds of autumnal Vermont. Gail and I come every year and reside at The Woodstock Inn for a few days; this year we appropriated Camden and Blythe. What are you up to? We heard you'd disappeared."

"Decided to take a little time for myself after settling things with my grandparents."

"Yes, sorry to hear about that, our condolences."

"Thank you."

"How did you cull Woodstock?" Gail asked with her unrelenting, inquisitive manner. Gail Skalberg-Vaughn was an editor for *Scene Around*, a New York based tabloid that specialized in prying into the privacy of the rich and famous. She was good at her job and didn't necessarily care if her information was either accurate or endearing, she thrived on scandal, and Dodge wasn't exactly thrilled that he'd bumped into her. He knew her husband Leon Vaughn as the president of Citi-Bank, having done business with him on several occasions, and they liked and respected each other. But Gail was a wild card. She usually treated him politely, but there had been one or two issues that had portrayed him in a less than favorable light, *a sly playboy, a crafty heartbreaker* she had written. *Fashion's most eligible bachelor chasing middle-age with a youthful treasure trove of lithesome models.* A few juicy photos had accompanied the last article, and had in fact elicited an angry phone call from Dana. Gail had been secretly pleased with her fervor. Dana wasn't so much angered by the unflattering portrayal of her new beau as she was by the fact that there were no pictures of her in the article. As the world's highest paid fashion model, annd Dodge Maddison's supposed only love interest, she was furious that she'd been left out. Gail Skalberg-Vaugn was of course aware of it, but nevertheless apologized for the "oversight" and appeased her by promising to do a special feature on Dana in an upcoming issue. Dodge knew he had to be careful with Gail, especially with Annison around.

"By happenstance actually," he answered her, "we decided to drive to Vermont for the foliage and discovered Woodstock."

"We?"

"I'm with a friend."

"A friend?"

"Gail!" her husband Leon cautioned.

"Well, I know it's not Dana," Gail Skalberg-Vaughn said. "Our photography crew is in the Cayman Islands as we speak covering the Victoria's Secret shoot, and I know Dana's there, but," she said coyly to Dodge, "I'm sure you're aware of that."

Camden Beaumont broke into the conversation and changed the subject, "We've already gotten receivings of your new collection Dodge and they're blowing off the racks. It's a great line. It's going to be a killer."

Camden Beaumont was the CEO of Bloomingdales and had shared a ripe and profitable relationship with the designer ever since Maddison's earliest years when Bloomies had been the first uptown store to feature the young hot designer from down in SoHo.

Camden's wife Blythe was a socialite who had reared their three children. She was happy that they were all grown and out of the house so that she could devote one hundred percent of her time socializing with the "in" crowd. She had never worked and never intended to, there was simply just too much to do. She was fidgeting with an absolutely wicked piece of thread that she had discovered protruding from the seam of the pocket on her pressed plaid blouse. She had turned from the others so that she could extract it before (heaven forbid) the others noticed it. She made a mental note to call the L.L. Bean people as soon as she returned to their Trump Tower condominium.

"Thanks Camden, I hope it does well for you."

"Oh hell," Camden Beaumont said, "everything you design does well for us. You could design a dress from a potato sack and it would sell."

"Not a bad idea," Leon said. "You'd buy a couple of those dresses wouldn't you Blythe?"

"Huh?" She turned around realizing she'd been neglecting the conversation. She had successfully extracted the random thread and surreptitiously rolled it between her right forefinger and thumb and let it drop to the floor. No one noticed.

"Won't you and your friend join us for lunch?" Gail asked.

"Well, I ..."

"Sure you will," Leon Vaughn took charge. "I'll let the hostess know we're now a party of six," and before Dodge could respond, Leon was talking to the girl at the front podium.

Gail smiled at Dodge and leaned into his ear, "So, tell me, it's a woman friend isn't it?"

"Ut! Ut!" Leon grabbed her elbow, "I know what you're up to Gail, and you need to cease. We are here on a mini vacation. We're all trying to forget about our work, remember?"

"Of course, dahling. How rude of me Mister Maddison, I do apologize."

Dodge and Gail smirked at one another, they both knew she didn't mean it.

It wasn't long before the formalities of their chance meeting were exhausted and the foursome stood at the crowded bar, circled around Dodge, competitively engrossed in conversation about themselves. Dodge kept an eye on the door for Annison. She appeared several minutes later and stood in the entranceway next to the hostess stand and scanned the restaurant through the etched-glass partition behind the podium. She found him sitting at the bar and saw the group of people around him. They were laughing and obviously having a good time. Apparently it was people he knew. She watched for a minute debating whether or not to go in. She had gotten the message from Eleanor Grey and was looking forward to a quiet lunch, just the two of them. She wasn't sure if she wanted to share him. Maybe it would be better if she left them alone; she could wait for him back at Eleanor's.

He spotted her just as she was turning, quickly excused himself from the others and made his way to her.

"Annison," he caught her at the door. She turned to him, "Hi," she had hoped to sneak out without being noticed.

"I've bumped into some friends from the City, or rather, they bumped into me. They've invited us to lunch with them and I couldn't say no."

She looked pensively at him, "I was hoping to be alone with you."

"Ditto, but it's one of my bankers and his wife and the Beaumonts, he's the CEO of Bloomies, and a good friend."

"Blythe Beaumont?"

"Yes, do you know her?"

"She sponsors an annual fund-raiser at the Inn, for Zonta, the women's group."

"Great, she'll be thrilled to see you, I'm sure."

"Who are the others?" He told her.

"The editor of *Scene Around?* Wonderful!" Annison could see them watching them and talking amongst themselves. "What am I doing here with you?"

"Having fun, I hope."

"I am, but you know what I mean."

"Would you rather hide?"

"No."

"Don't worry, Gail's okay, I'll keep her in check."

She had her doubts.

"Everything's going to be okay," he told her with his charming boyish grin.

"Okay," she entwined her arm in his, "then let's do lunch." They walked bravely into the bar area.

Everything did seem to be okay. Lunch was fine, the conversation was light and lively, and the time passed amicably. Afterwards, Leon picked up the check and the three ladies adjourned to the ladies room. Leon mentioned that he and Camden had scheduled an afternoon tee time to get in a round of golf and asked if Dodge would like to join them. The ladies were going to do some shopping and Annison could accompany them, and then they could all get back together and have dinner at the Woodstock Inn. It would be a grand time Leon assured him. Dodge graciously declined.

"Suit yourself, old boy," Leon said, "I think I have an idea of what you'd rather do," he winked. "She's hot!"

"She seems very nice, Dodge. Is this something serious?" Camden Beaumont asked.

"Well ..." he hesitated.

"Never mind, I didn't mean to pry."

"Camden," Leon said, "don't be ridiculous, of course it's a serious relationship, eh Dodge?" he wiggled his eyebrows.

The women returned and the men stood and prepared to leave. They walked single file through the tables making their way to the door. Dodge hung back purposefully and pulled Gail aside.

"Gail, you know I love you babe, so let's not upset the apple cart."

"Why what on earth do you mean?"

"You know what I mean."

"Don't worry Dodge dahling, I'll behave, *this* time, but only because she's such a nice lady. *And*, I must say, it *is* rather refreshing to see you with someone more your own age." She touched the inside of her forefinger to her pursed lips and then placed it onto his. "Mums the word," and she trailed off after the others.

They said pleasant good-byes on the sidewalk and Dodge and Annison watched the foursome blend into the tourists walking the village in the sunny Vermont afternoon.

"What would you like to do now?" he asked her.

She slid her arms inside his open coat, embracing him, "Just be with you."

He returned the embrace, "I think we got through that okay, don't you?"

"Yes, our first little test with the real world. I think we did fine."

The sun was high and the temperatures had reached their peak for the day. Eleanor Grey had been right, they wouldn't get out of the sixties, it was sixty-eight degrees. Across the street, above the picture postcard town, Star Mountain loomed in the refreshing day.

"Hey, I've got an idea."

"What?" she asked.

"You feel like walking off that wholesome lunch?"

"Sure."

"Come on."

# 33

## STAR MOUNTAIN

The trail up the mountain was well marked in some places and not so well marked in others. It was good to go with another person and share in the fun of discovering which way the trail went. It was narrowing, extremely so at times, and covered with a thick blanket of fallen leaves. Whatever markers had originally been set along the way were in dire need of refurbishing. Some were hardly discernable, others had fallen from the trees they had been nailed to and were lost in the thick ground foliage, and some were missing altogether, taken as souvenirs over the years. In addition to the mystery of its turns, the trail unfurled many elements; it was winding, steep, slippery, treacherous and smooth, but mostly it was intriguing and challenging. There was a large flat boulder at the halfway mark where you could stand isolated from the world with the trees wrapped in a semi-circle behind you. You could hear the quiet pace of the day below and see the village, tiny, with the river running around it.

To ascend the top you had to climb a steep rock ledge that had footholds chipped into it. Annison was glad to have Dodge's helping hand there for her and glad to finally claim the summit. The star was a huge wooden structure perched precariously but solidly on the edge of the mountaintop. It was made out of thick wooden beams crisscrossing from point to point. There were hundreds of large light bulbs on it spaced every twelve inches, and an access ladder built onto the backside that went up about ten feet to a narrow platform stretching between the top two star points. Then another ladder, even narrower, rising to the tip. Dodge helped Annison up the first ladder and they stood on the high platform resting their arms on the cross beam, their heads protruding through the star center and hovering high above the peaceful valley.

There were initials carved into the wooden beams, faded gray with the passing of time.

"Spectacular!" Annison said.

He put his arm around her shoulder and she turned to him. They kissed.

"It's so quiet up here," she said.

"Are you tired?"

"No, more like exhilarated. You?"

"I can feel it in the back of my legs."

"How far did you walk this morning?"

"All around the village, couple miles I guess."

"It's a beautiful little town."

He got silent for a while. They stood side by side overlooking the valley.

"Are you all right?" she asked him.

"Yeah, why?"

"You seem pre-occupied. Thinking about your friends?"

"No." He wanted to say *thinking about you,* but remained silent.

"Dodge … just say it. I know something's bothering you, you've been acting strangely ever since last night."

"I'm thinking about us."

"So am I."

"A lot."

"Me too."

"But I'm going to be honest with you, I'm a little bit confused."

"About?"

"You, I guess. Your feelings. I mean I know all this has happened quite suddenly between us, but I'm not sure where it's headed."

A chord was touched inside her, a disharmonious chord. "I think you know how I feel about you, don't you?" she asked with a tone of incredulity.

"Maybe I'm not sure."

Annison's eyes began to water. "I thought I was making my feelings very clear, we've talked about this, Dodge. I don't just hop into bed with anyone. Do you think I'm on some sort of joy ride or something?"

"I'm not saying that Annison, I …"

She turned her back to him so he couldn't see the tears starting to roll down her cheeks. The very idea that he had even an ounce of misdoubt cut her like a knife. She suddenly felt impure, like she had been violated, her innocent honesty trampled on like the untainted leaves on the trail. She flashed back to last night when he was on top of her, reeling in his delirium. Where did this doubt come from? "I'm just trying to be me," she said trying to hold back the tone of anger rising in her voice, "for once, just being me. I'm sorry if I'm not living up to your standards."

"Hey," he tried to turn her around but she remained steadfast. She wiped the tops of her cheeks with her fingertips and then crossed her arms in front of her and stood looking away from the view. She stared at the treetops stretching out endlessly below her like a prickly carpet, willing her stubborn tears to go away.

"I'm not saying anything about standards," he said, "whatever the hell that means, and I certainly don't believe you're just hopping into my bed. I'm not questioning your feelings, Annison ..."

"You just said you were!" She spun around and faced him, showing him the redness in her eyes like a wound that he had given her. "You said you're not sure of my feelings! Right?" She was challenging him, unafraid, with her anger beside her as a bodyguard. She gave up on restraining her tears, she didn't care anymore. Let him see them, let him see what he was doing to her. Damn him! How dare he question her! "How can you question me?! Don't you think what I've shown you, given you, of myself is sincere? I'm not some starry-eyed teeny-bopper, Mr. Maddison! Don't you dare cheapen me! Don't make me out to be another one of your fucking fashion model groupies!"

Annison went to the ladder and took a step down. Dodge caught her and drew her back up to him, forcibly bringing her into his arms. She was wrestling like a filly, pounding her fists into his chest.

He squeezed her tight to him, "Hey, hey, take it easy ... take it easy." He gained control of her tempestuousness and held onto her strongly. He felt her tension subsiding as she gave into his resolve, finally resting her head calmly upon his chest until the anger subsided.

"I'm sorry, Annie, I didn't mean to hurt you."

"For once in my life," she said softly into his chest, "I feel good about what I'm doing. For once in my life I'm following my own true feelings, without anyone else's input, no one else's opinions, just mine," Annison lifted her head and stood tall, looking Dodge straight in the eye, "and I'm not going to back down. You say you're confused about my feelings for you? Then I'll try to make them as clear as I can." She took a breath and let it out slowly, "I'm in love with you."

His lips parted as if he was going to say something, but he didn't.

"Deeply," she said, "like I've never been before."

He embraced her, "And I with you. I am so much in love with you that I'm not sure this is even happening. I've never had such feelings before, so overwhelmingly consuming me." He gazed into her wet hazel eyes, "Is this what real love feels like?"

"I hope so," she said. "That might explain why it scares me so."

"Scares you?"

"I've gone through a lot in the past month, a lot of changes, for the better I think. But what we're sharing scares me. It's not that I'm afraid of it, I'm thrilled by it, alive again. What scares me is the thought of losing it, losing you."

"You're not going to lose me."

"But do I have you?"

"What do you mean? Now you're doubting me?"

"What about Dana?"

Dodge broke away from her and retook his position on the crossbeam of the star looking out into the day. "On my walk this morning I came to a resolve, a couple actually, but one of them involves Dana." He turned and leaned his back on the wooden structure so he could address her face to face. "I realize I'm just kidding myself with her. She's a great kid and I do admire her, but I'm not in love with her. I don't think I ever was. But it took me falling in love with you to realize it. I need to get back to the City, to break it off with her. It wouldn't be fair of me not to, now that I have these feelings for you."

"Are you sure?"

"I'm sure about that, but ... now don't get pissed off again ..." he raised his palms, "I'm not sure about where your feelings are headed."

"Dodge!"

"Wait, hear me out. I guess I'm a little confused about your enthusiasm for the Inn. I mean, on the one hand you say you want to leave Barrett's Bluff, but then on the other, you're so enthralled with visiting The Woodstock Inn. It makes me think that maybe you're fooling yourself, maybe you really miss Barrett's Bluff, maybe what we're doing is all a fantasy, and maybe ..."

"Wait! You don't need to go any further. Do you know why I wanted to go to The Woodstock Inn so badly? To take a tour with Mr. Hapgood? It was because I wanted to find out how I'd feel. How I'd feel about the Inn, my Inn. I wanted to get inside of it, a surrogate of course, but with much the same feel. I needed to know how I'd react. And you know what? I don't miss it. I'm rather relieved actually. Now I think I can face it again. I made a resolve this morning also. I'm going to go back to Barrett's Bluff and repair the damage that I've done by walking out on everyone. Put things back in order so that I can leave it once and for all free and clear, and not have to worry about carrying any guilt around with me for the rest of my life."

"And your husband?"

"Ditto. And it has nothing to do with you. I want you to understand that. Jack and I had our problems long before I met you. A divorce is inevitable, and I truly believe the best thing for him also. It's time to stop playing the charade."

"Then what would you do?"

"I don't know, but I'm much less worried about that than I am about losing us. Life is too short and I realize that now is the time for me. Now is the time for me to stand up for myself and my wants and my needs. And if somehow that means us, then I'll be happy. But, I too have misgivings," her eyes began to water again, "I'm not sure if I fit into your world."

"What are you talking about?"

"I'm not like you. I live in a very small circle. My world is the Inn. It always has been. My roots have always been at Barrett's Bluff; my family, my staff, my friends, and hell, even my guests. And your world is, well, your world is the world. You're recognized everywhere you go. People stop you on the street, ask for your picture in restaurants, and even open up their homes to you. Everywhere you go there's someone you know. Like today, I mean, the CEO of Bloomingdales? That doesn't happen to just anyone every day. You're famous and I'm just a quiet, homespun little country girl."

Dodge laughed.

"What's so funny?"

"Come on, smile, let me see the straw sticking out of your teeth."

"Ouu!" she pinched his sides. "You can be so condescending at times. Have you heard a word I've said?"

"Yes," he was still laughing, "I've heard all of them, and you're certainly not a quiet little homespun country girl."

"Then what am I?"

"I think you're more of a repressed hot-rodder that loves to burn rubber and tear up the asphalt."

This got a smile out of her.

"Maybe you should enter the Grand Prix. Hot Rod Annie. Watch out! Here she comes!"

"Very funny."

"Then after winning a few races, you'd become famous. Your picture would be on the cover of *Hot Rod* magazine. You'd appear on ESPN as the fastest woman alive, and I could get jealous of all the young studs around the fast-track spinning their tires, trying to catch you and get into your pants."

"They'd never catch me."

"I'll bet I could."

"You already have."

He took her into his arms and they kissed. The afternoon shining high on them and making them warm.

"You know," Dodge said, "I'm not sure I fit into my world either."

Annison's eyes said *what do you mean?*

"I've been in a spotlight for so long that I'm not sure if I've seen myself lately. Fame makes you invisible. It's not all that it's cracked up to be. Sometimes it's downright hard to deal with. You miss out."

"Miss out?"

"On things, normal things like love and family."

Annison sensed his disillusionment. "Has it been that bad for you?"

"I too have been doing a lot of soul searching lately and I'm wondering if I'm doing the right thing. I feel like home is calling out to me. I see Bryce Corner in a whole new light, the outpouring of concern and support from everyone has really touched me. It feels so genuine, like family. And Bennie and Carlene and the kids seem so happy, and the way they took in Old Percy ... I don't know, maybe it's time to slow the pace down a little, less travel, less spotlight." He looked into her sweet green eyes, "And the time with you, at the lake, here, anywhere, it's like a dream, a wonderful dream. I'm in love with you too, Annison."

"Oh, Dodge." She hugged him. "Let's follow it, let's follow the dream and see where it takes us."

\* \* \*

They spent the next few days in Woodstock, at Eleanor Grey's B&B, dreaming. They pampered themselves with wild abandon - dreamland has no boundaries. They talked of being together and planned how to make it work, how to blend their separate worlds together; or not. Perhaps to just start a new one on their own; brand new and exciting like what they were experiencing now. Run away and hide forever or settle down and get married and have a child, yes, they'd even talked about that. Annison could give him the family that he longed for, she'd said *I'm not too old for that yet, y'know!* They would be happy and blessed and everything would work out. A new life was opening up for them. Happiness was theirs for the taking. There were endless possibilities; all they had to do was make the commitment; to be sure of their feelings for each other and to make a commitment. Their enthusiasm was challenging them and their hearts gave in willingly, blissfully succumbing to the luring euphoria. They would return to reality and do what had to be done to follow their dream.

# 34

## BRYCE CORNER

The cooler temperatures of Vermont followed them back to Maddison's cottage on the lake in Bryce Corner. It was that time of year when the shortening days were warm and the longer nights cool. Nearing sunset, Dodge busied himself outside at the woodpile chopping wood while Annison unpacked and settled things inside. He started a fire in the wood stove that would warm quickly and take the chill out. That night they made love in the sleeping loft in the comfort of their new resolve. They fell asleep to the rhythmic cackling of ducks sounding like laughter as they bobbed in the untroubled waters of Lake Wickaboag, resting there for the night, an autumn stopover on their journey south.

In the mid-morning sunlight they drove into town to breakfast at Dot's Diner. As they neared the center they noticed hundreds of cars parked on both sides of Main Street and along the adjacent lanes. When they had maneuvered through them to the common, they found it abuzz with the annual Apple Fest Bazaar.

"Wow, I'd forgotten about this," Dodge said.

"What is it?"

"Apple Fest, Bryce Corner's version of October Fest. People come from all over. The weekend will be busy with the festivities; music, dancing, food, crafts, artwork, clowns – the whole shebang. Lots of apples, of course, and beer and wine from the local vineyards and breweries."

"This looks lovely. Let's park and walk around."

They circled the common in the slow moving traffic and found a spot behind the church to park. They made their way over to the myriad of white tent tops and walked about enjoying the festivities and hob-knobbing with the locals and the many craftspeople. Chief Ben was walking around the common making sure everyone was having a good time and that no one got out of hand. Carlene was stationed at the Vet Tent, handing out literature to current and would-be pet owners regarding all types of animals and birds. They had a mini kennel set up in the shade of the tent full of dogs and cats for adoption. Penny was helping her mom by bringing the animals to and from the fence so the kids could pet them. Children tugged at their parent's sleeves begging for a new pet, quite a few were successful and the veterinary clinic was doing a brisk business.

Later at home, Carlene would remark to her husband about Annison still being in town and her blatant walking around arm in arm with Dodge. She didn't understand, nor coddle well to the whole idea, she thought she'd gone back to Connecticut. What the hell was she doing still here? The word gold-digger may have even been mentioned. Ben hadn't said much. He'd known Annison was still around, and that she was with Dodge. He hadn't been fooled by Dodge's *"I'll be in New York for a couple days"*. He knew Dodge too well, knew when he was fibbin'; but, he'd let it slide. Ben told Carlene about none of this. If Dodge wanted his business kept secret, he'd abide by that; what are best friends for? He just hoped he knew what he was doing.

They stopped at Katelyn Van Ness' booth. She was advertising classes for her new dance studio. Annison expressed a desire to join but said she didn't know how long she'd be in town. Katelyn gave her a flyer and jotted her name down on her sign-up sheet, "Just in case," she smiled.

Eggman was manning the beer tent with Lindsey from The Tavern. They were pulling cold beer from a keg and had quite a crowd around them even though it was hardly noon. Eggman said he'd finished the work at the Maddison farmhouse and Dodge said he was anxious to check it out and would probably do so later that afternoon. He declined Eggman's offer of a cold beer and was surprised when he offered one to Annison by name and she accepted.

"Do you know, Eggman?" he asked her.

"Oh yeah, we go way back," she replied teasingly.

Dodge looked from one to the other, perplexed, until they both broke out laughing.

"He fixed my chimney after the mishap with the flue."

"Oh, well, then as long as we're all such close friends, maybe I will have a beer." He laughed.

"Here ya go, handsome," Lindsey had already pulled a draft for him. "We should all get together and shoot some pool sometime."

"I'd like that," Annison said.

Sounds like a plan," Eggman added.

Dodge and Annison said they'd be back for a refill and took their beers to meander about.

Cregan Realty had a tent set up and Dodge went over to talk with Jack Cregan about listing the farmhouse. Annison drifted off into the crowd.

"Nice ta see a happy lady ta day."

"Oh ... hi," she turned, "you snuck up on me!"

"Well, I do that sometimes. How ya doin'?"

"Fine, and how are you doing?"

"Fair ta middlin', I guess. You two gittin' along?"

She had a feeling he already knew the answer, so she just gave him a wide smile.

"Calm this mornin'," he said. "The wind is down." His head was tilted backward, his eyes scanning the silent treetops. "But she'll pick up."

"Ya know," he leaned into her shoulder and spoke softly into her ear, "some things happen fur a reason," and then patted her twice on the back and drifted off into the crowd.

"Here, try this," Dodge appeared and held a huge pretzel to her mouth. Annison took a bite, "Mmm, it's good ... apple cinnamon?"

"Un huh." He took a big bite and passed it off to her, wiped his mouth with a napkin and took a big gulp of beer. "What a beautiful day!" he said, "I feel great."

"I just saw Old Percy."

"Yeah? Where is he?"

"I don't know, he kind of appeared and then disappeared, like a magician."

"That's him. Part wizard, I swear."

\* \* \*

In the afternoon they went to the farmhouse. It was the first time Annison had been there. She was immediately struck by it. Dodge walked around the outside looking at the roof and the windows and then went to the front to inspect the new floorboards on the veranda. She found the back door unlocked and showed herself in. It was adorable; every room proudly exhibiting its own charm to her as she toured the first floor then ascended the staircase to the second. It was absolutely lovely, the ambience and décor reminding her of Eleanor Grey's B&B in Vermont. There was a feeling here. She thought someone was watching her, but in a good way. Hundreds of ideas were popping into her mind like the tiny bubbles blown through the wand from a bubble jar and she went from room to room dreaming and decorating and gathering thoughts. *It really wouldn't take much.* She went back downstairs into the kitchen and was standing in the center with her hands on her hips when Dodge entered the backdoor.

"How daring are you?" she asked.

"What?"

"How *daring* are you?"

"What are you talking about?"

"Come here," she grabbed his hand and ran up the staircase to the second floor.

"What does this remind you of?"

"My old house."

"I know, but besides that?" She spun around, twirling down the hallway presenting each room like Vanna White turning letters on Jeopardy.

Dodge leaned against the stairway railing. He could see what she was talking about.

"Annnd," she said, opening a door and running up to the attic, "there's plenty of room up here," he heard her voice echoing, "to have two more rooms with maybe a shared bath," she came back down. "We could take this wall down and expose the attic stairway and carpet it with the same pattern as here." She looked at the carpet again and had second thoughts, "Or maybe replace it and do a lighter theme all the way from the front parlor, up here along the hallway, and to the upstairs." She was excited. Design ideas were pouring out of her and she drifted from room to room, sometimes talking to him and sometimes just standing there and thinking to herself.

It was easy to get caught up in her enthusiasm. Dodge joined her in the master bedroom, Emma and Jed's room, where she was deep in thought, her arms folded before her and her tongue moving back and forth across her top lip.

"This could work you know," she told him.

"A bed and breakfast?"

"We could have … how many, four? five? rooms up here, and probably two downstairs? Convert the living room with the fireplace into a master suite encompassing the downstairs bathroom, and the parlor is big enough to be the reception area, that would give us the opportunity to re-do the dining room into another guestroom, and the kitchen, ohmygod, the kitchen is huge! We could have breakfast set up in there; it'd be so cozy, especially with that beautiful old gas stove and the bead-board all around. And we could even put a deck right off of it and set up alfresco during the warmer months." She looked at him and he was smiling.

"A bed and breakfast," he said matter-of-factly, slowly nodding his head, "hmmm." Then he laughed.

"What?"

"Emma would get such a kick out of it."

Annison sat on the edge of the bed, "So … what do you think? Stop me if you think I'm crazy."

"I'm not going to stop you, I don't care if you're crazy. I think you're wonderful!"

She took his hand and got up. "You could set up your office in your old room, or maybe the attic. Or we could keep that for our own little apartment and live up there."

"No, I think I'd set up the office at the cottage," it was the first sign that he was joining in her fantasy. "We could live here and have the lake as a retreat. I could use it as my design studio and you could use it for your painting."

"I could get up and make breakfast for our guests, you could go down to the cottage to work and I could join you later in the day. We could do our business things half the day, you with your communication with New York and the rest of the world, and I with the B&B, and then I'd bring a lunch over and we'd spend the afternoons together relaxing and doing creative things. I could paint while you sketch."

He looked into her hazel eyes, sparkling in the excitement of her enthusiasm, "I love you, y'know."

Annison hugged him tightly. "Oh Dodge, I'm *crazy* in love with you! I feel like a new woman! A whole new person!"

"Will you marry me?"

Her breath stopped, and maybe her heart also. She was stunned. In an instant a million things raced through her mind. She wanted to ask him if he was serious but saw the calm look in his eyes, the gentle smile spreading across his face. He was serious.

"Yes," her fluttering heart pushed the soft whisper through her lips.

They stood there in each other's arms in the room where Emma and Jedediah had created life, and had also ended it, not speaking any further to one another; rather letting their hearts beat wildly in deafening tones like primal drums playing a rhythmic love dance to each other. A tear squeezed through Annison's closed eyelids and rolled across her cheek into the soft fabric of Dodge's shirt. She had never before felt as happy as at this moment. She wanted it to last forever.

\* \* \*

"WHAT?!" Big Ben had his coffee cup halfway to his lips before he slammed it onto the counter.

"She's the one, Bennie. I can feel it in my heart."

"You can feel it in your dick!" The chief was up and pacing back and forth in the middle of Dot's Diner.

It was now Sunday morning. They were alone; everyone was either in church or at the Apple Fest. That's where Dot was, at her booth selling hot coffee and fresh pastry. John had opened the diner as usual even though they never did any business during the Fest. He liked the time alone and was seated at the end of the counter reading his Sunday paper. He had looked up at the two men when the chief had shouted, and then calmly gone back to his paper.

"Geesus Christ Dodge! What the fuck is the matter with you?!"

"Sit down Bennie." The chief took up his seat on the stool at the counter.

"You've asked her to *marry* you?!" he shook his head. "Old buddie I'm torn between getting you into therapy or pulling my gun right now, right here and shootin' you. That'd probably knock some sense into you!"

"I had a feeling you'd react this way."

"Well how da fuck did you think I'd react?! Am I the only one here who knows that she's *already* married?!" The chief got up and went to the other side of the counter to get the coffeepot. "Man, she must give great head," he muttered. He refilled his mug and poured a little into Dodge's, replaced the pot on its burner, then placed his big hands onto the counter in front of his friend. He leaned over him like a football coach talking to his wayward quarterback. "You've only known this woman for what? Two, three weeks? A month? It hasn't even been a month has it? In all seriousness, pal, do you know what you're saying to me?"

"Yes, I do, and I know it's sudden, and I know we've got some things to work through ..."

"*That's* an understatement!"

"...but I'm telling you Bennie, she's the one. I can feel it. I'm sure about this."

Big Ben came around the counter and reclaimed his stool. They sat in silence, Dodge giving him time to let it sink in. He knew Bennie, he just needed time with things like this.

"What are you gonna do about the husband?"

"She's getting a divorce as soon as possible. We've already contacted my attorney. I called him last night. We're going to meet with him in the City tomorrow morning. The husband's not going to be surprised; it hasn't been a good marriage from the start. And besides, he's got a lengthy history of running around."

"What about Harlow? And the sex kitten?"

"Dana's young. She'll throw a fit, then be over it and move on." Dodge turned his mug around in a circle using his fingertips. "Harlow? I don't know, I think she'll understand." Something came over him as he said this, but he pretended he didn't notice it. "I think she'll be alright with it. We had a heart to heart before she left after the funeral and we're on the same page. Our relationship has always been platonic..."

"Yeah, right!"

"...and we understand that the business part is the more important."

"Love is blind."

"Come on!" he slapped the chief's big shoulder, "You're supposed to be happy for me. I need you to be my best man!"

"Ohhh no! I don't want anything to do with this."

"You don't mean that, Bennie, come on."

"You are one crazy son of a bitch, do you know that?"

"Yeah, I do, but I can't help it with Annison. She's truly an angel sent from above and I'm not going to let her get away from me."

"Whew. You got it bad."

"Helplessly."

"Goddamn Red Sox!" John folded up his newspaper and slapped it onto the counter. "You guys gonna be here for a few?" Not waiting for an answer he continued, "I'm gonna go check on Dot over to the common, see if she needs anything. If anyone comes in just give 'em a cup a joe and tell 'em I'll be back in a little bit. Place is yours," and he exited by the front door.

The two men sat quietly, consumed in their respective thoughts.

Dodge broke the silence. "Do you think true love exists, Bennie?"

The chief bristled and gave the diner a quick perusal. Thank God it was empty. "Excuse me?"

"Maybe I've been too involved with my business, too consumed, not realizing what's truly important in life. I mean what really counts?" Dodge swiveled his stool around so he could face his friend, "Love, right? Aren't you in love? Aren't you totally in love with Carlene?"

"Well, I..."

"I don't think I've ever been in love before, not like this anyway. Maybe before it's just been sex. I think everyone gets so focused on having a relationship that we fool ourselves. We think we're in love because we don't want to admit that we're not. It's all superficial. We hide in our relationship by turning our attentions elsewhere. Like into more primal endeavors. We excel in stuff we can control, like a business or a career, because we don't want to feel like a failure. We give up too easily on love and become complacent, even phony. Afraid to remember that what really counts in your life *is* a relationship, *is* love." Dodge paused for a brief second, "But true love, true love only happens once, once in your lifetime. Like what you and 'Lene have and what Emma and Jed had. Pure and true and undying. Lasting forever regardless of the constraints of time. Don't you think? Don't you have that feeling?"

"I guess," Ben said slowly, he wasn't used to deep conversations like this. "I don't know about anyone else, all I know about is 'Lene and I. She's all I ever wanted, since the first damn day I saw her."

"See! Love at first sight."

"I just looked at her and said to myself, *wow, that's what an angel must look like.* And when she ever smiled back, phew! That was it. Something fluttered inside a me, I mean I felt an actual fluttering," the chief wiggled his big open hands for effect, "and you know what? I still feel it. Simple things, like the way she brushes her hair, or how she can never make up her mind on what to wear. Or like catchin' a secret glance at her when she doesn't know it, and just watchin' her, smilin' to myself. So if that's the kinda true love you're talkin' about, I guess I got it. Damn lucky too."

"I can see it with you two, your happiness, the completeness of having a family. You're as much in love as Jed and Emma were."

"I don't know about that, Buddie. They had something special for a long time. I think of what they did at the end and I marvel at how much courage that took; how much love for each other they had. I tell you Dodge, that whole thing scares me, the way they planned it and kept it to themselves, and the way they did it. I know there are some folks who don't like it, and I sure as hell hope it doesn't come to that with 'Lene and I, cuz I know I couldn't do something like that. But they sure had an unbelievable kind a love for one another, and I'd be willing to bet that somehow they're together now continuing along with each other. That's love." Chief Big Ben thought for a moment and then shook his head, "I can't believe you've got me talkin' about this shit."

"Why? Are you afraid to talk about love?"

"With *you* I am!"

* * *

They spent a couple more refills talking about Dodge's plans. He was going to keep the farmhouse and they were going to convert it into a Bed & Breakfast. Annison would bring her expertise into that, and she was actually there now, meeting with Eggman and going over their remodeling ideas. They'd live either at the farmhouse or at the cottage, they weren't sure yet. He was going to cut back on his traveling, relocate his office/studio from New York and work out of Bryce Corner. If at all possible they'd like to have the B&B conversion done by Christmastime, they're hoping for a holiday grand opening. As soon as Annison's divorce was final they were going to get married; a small, quiet service at the house. Neither one of them were keen on honeymoons. They'd honeymoon by working their bed and breakfast together. He was anxious to be back in Bryce Corner again and looking forward to changing his life-style and putting some real meaning into his life. He didn't tell him about their plans for a child, one shock at a time.

Ben was letting it all sink in. "I'm gonna wait 'til you get your shit together before I mention any of this to Carlene, I'm not looking forward to *that* conversation."

"Why not?"

"Are you shittin' me? You know how she feels about you and Harlow. This is going to hit her like a load a bricks."

"Naw, I don't think so Bennie. I think she knows just how Harlow feels, she's her own woman, always has been. She's an integral part of *Maddison Designs,* my only other best friend besides you, and I know Harlow's going to be happy for me, so why shouldn't Carlene be?"

"Y'know, for such a smart guy, you've got a lot to learn about women."

Dodge laughed. "Aw, don't be such an old stick in the mud! It's all going to work out, you'll see. I'm happy Bennie, at least appreciate that."

"Wellll, I guess I can do that for my best buddie," the chief extended his hand. "I guess congratulations are in order then. Congrats pal, I wish you the best. Really. If you two end up half as happy as Carlene and I, you'll be blessed."

"Thanks Bennie, I knew I could count on you."

"Count on me for what?"

"For just being you and being there for me."

"Oh I'm *there* for ya, pal ... I just don't know where *there's* at."

# 35

## *SPIRALS*

Roberto had just opened the door of the white stretch limo when he noticed Dodge's unmistakable red Ford coupe sitting at the stoplight on the opposite corner from the *Maddison Designs* building. He held the door wide as two ladies from New York's Upper West Side emerged, claimed the sidewalk and sauntered with him along the fuchsia colored carpet leading to the boutique. Roberto, tall and thin, was wearing his customary black tux; a handsome man with an ageless countenance defying the fact that he was an immodest grandfather of four. The ladies, walking arm in arm on either side, shared a humorous moment with him and then entered the boutique through the automatic revolving door. He shut the door of the limo and rapped on the roof twice alerting the driver to move on.

A wide grin spread across his bronzed, Central-American face as he stepped from the curb and waved his hands high. The coupe flashed its headlights acknowledging him and making his smile even wider. He was happy to see his boss back at the building again. He'd missed the camaraderie and casual banter they shared in the mornings when Dodge helped him roll out the carpet and open the door for business. Whenever schedule permitted, the designer liked to open the shop and would stand with Roberto greeting his customers. Maddison liked to keep in touch with the reasons he was in business and his clients were always thrilled to find him there and loved to chat with him on the sidewalk. Roberto felt privileged and enjoyed his mornings, it made getting up and going to work a pleasure for him. Dodge Maddison made him feel a proud part of it all, *you're the first one they see Roberto*, he told him, *it's your friendly smile that brings the ladies in.*

The coupe pulled up to the curb and Roberto opened the passenger door. A new lady swung her legs out and accepted his offered hand. She was elegant in her movements and rose gracefully like a cat, a jaguar or a leopard, calm and sure and unafraid in the serene wilds of the vast environment surrounding her.

"Good morning, Miss," he beamed. "Welcome to *Maddison Designs*."

"Good morning, Roberto," she called him warmly by name. He immediately liked her. Her hands were soft and her demeanor alluring. "I'm Annison. I've heard so much about you."

"Why that's nice, I expect Mr. Maddison's been weaving his tales again then."

"Hello, Mr. President," Dodge stepped onto the carpeted sidewalk and greeted Roberto with his good-natured moniker, he always called him that, he said it was due to his tux and his staunch professionalism. They shook hands and Maddison officially introduced Annison and Roberto and then said, "Keys are in her." Roberto knew what this meant. He was the only one Dodge allowed to drive his precious car and Roberto would take it down to the private parking garage beneath the building and tuck it into its special spot. Later, after his duties at the front door were complete, he would change into more casual attire and spend his own time washing and detailing it. Not because he was asked to, but because it was a labor of love.

Roberto admired Dodge Maddison. He had been good to him ever since he had hired him away from *Tiffany's* uptown doorway over a decade ago. They had become good friends during the years of their morning ritual and Roberto's loyalty was unwavering, even more so since an uninsured errant delivery truck had jumped the curb and pinned him against the hard wall of the building four years ago. Roberto had been hospitalized for six months and then spent another six in PT and rehab. Dodge had paid all the hospital bills and continued Roberto's paychecks uninterrupted so that his family didn't have to worry. Upon his return to work he'd tried to get the stubborn man to accept a position inside in the office or on the sales floor, but Roberto wished to remain at the door. He said he liked greeting the *Lady Maddison's* and seeing them leave happy with their bundles. Loyalty like that cannot be made nor bought, it can only be given.

It was lunchtime and the shop was busy. Well-dressed women of all ages were perusing the racks and the walls and the freestanding gondolas in the theme sections set throughout the boutique's open floor plan where grand eye-catching displays teased you with ideas for your varying life-style; haute couture, cocktail, office, travel, etc. Two young Wall Street gentlemen were in the lingerie section feeling awkward choosing a lacy outfit for a new girlfriend. The lucky guy was a little nervous, explaining to the sales associate, Amber that they'd only been dating for two months. She said to wait a few more months before getting the merry widow with the garters that his accomplice was favoring and presented a silk teddy with an attractive neckline and matching silk robe. They nodded sheepishly together and Amber took the outfit to her side of the lingerie counter to ring it up and wrap it in a lovely gift box. Men were so easy, she was thinking, they just need a little direction.

She was the first to notice Dodge walking through the aisles and gave him an enchanting smile and lip-synced, *welcome back*. Maddison waved to her and smiled. Amber wondered who the attractive lady on his arm was and immediately scanned the boutique for Harlow. This should be interesting. They all knew Harlow was jealous of Dana (who wasn't) but *who was this one* strolling so self-assuredly with their designer? Amber hurried her wrapping. She didn't want to miss the fireworks.

Dodge proudly escorted Annison throughout his store and up the wide spiral staircase leading to level two. They stopped a moment at the top and he could be seen gesturing to the sales floor below, pointing out the different departments to her and returning waves to his department managers and sales associates as word quickly spread amongst them that Dodge was back. They entered *Café Mad* and Dodge chose a table for them at the railing overlooking the boutique. He excused himself and went into the kitchen and spoke with his chef, Pietro. They exchanged ideas for a special luncheon plate for his special guest. He said she owned The Inn at Barrett's Bluff and he'd have to be pretty creative to impress her. "Don' worry abou' it," Pietro grinned, "I make som'zing spezial like she's neever had b'fore. Eat t'will keeep her coming back, eh meester M?" he winked.

Annison was up and walking around the tiny café perusing the framed sketches adorning the walls. She leaned down to read the dates on the tiny plaques at the bottom of each of them and marveled at how talented Dodge Maddison was. Even the earliest ones clearly showed incredible talent and she saw another spellbinding side to him. She progressed around the room from the pencil sketches done in his childhood, to the later pen and inks, to the vibrant watercolors of his most recent collection. She was in awe and felt inadequate in her own rekindled artwork. She came full circle and took her seat. She watched the salesgirls below, now grouping in small clusters of twos and threes and caught them glimpsing up at her. She turned, slightly embarrassed by all the attention, and watched Dodge's profile through the circular window of the kitchen door. She could see a full view of him standing with the chef as the waitresses breezed in and out of the swinging door. *God, they're all so beautiful,* she thought, *you must have to be a model to work here.* She was suddenly feeling ugly and self-consciously flicked her hair on the sides of her forehead. She saw the sign for the rest rooms and decided to freshen up. Why did she feel like she was competing all of a sudden?

A few minutes later, Annison returned, her face freshened and ready to dazzle the competition. Passing the kitchen, the door swung open and she saw Dodge with his arms wrapped around a very attractive woman. She had bright red hair like Bonnie Raitt and was dressed in a tight cotton dress, black and extremely complimentary. She wore gray silk stockings and stood on her tiptoes in heels of charcoal suede. A sheer scarf lay fashionably across her shoulders. It was almond and gray in color with a thin red line running through it that seemed as if it had to have been dyed to match her hair, it accented her color so perfectly. In the next glimpse offered by the swinging door she saw them kissing. He was kissing her. Annison quickly hastened her step to the table and had just gotten seated when they emerged together from the kitchen and made their way toward her.

"Annison, I'd like you to meet my right arm ... this is Harlow. Harlow, Annison."

"Hi, Dodge has told me so much about you."

"I'm so glad to meet you," Harlow replied and then smiled into Dodge's eyes, "now I know why you've been staying in New England so long." And then she said to Annison, "You're very beautiful."

"Why thank you, coming from you that's quite a compliment."

The two women smiled to one another in that female way that appeared cordial but was really not. Thank god Carlene had kept Harlow informed on the "goings on" in Bryce Corner - at least she had been prepared for this moment. There was no way she could have acted so cool, calm and collected at this inevitable meeting had it not been for Carlene's persistent phone calls. Harlow had had the time to shore up her defenses and to closet away her contradicting emotions. Yes, she had told Dodge that she wanted their relationship to remain as it always had been, that their night of passion had been inevitable, a wonderful page of need and desire and circumstance turned gently in the book of Fate. And yes, it was she who stressed the need to keep that time as a cherished memory and to move on professionally as always, that she was strong and complete and wanted her world to continue turning uninterrupted. But since then, in the din maze of her day and the hushed solace of her nights, Harlow had wondered. Wondered if she had been right or just scared, afraid of her true feelings, afraid to face them, face to face, and now it was all too late. Dodge was lost to her, pushed away by her own hand, standing next to her, gazing into the eyes of an unforeseen rival, oblivious of her heartfelt cravings. She had been a fool to not listen to her heart, to retreat back to New York so quickly, to think that immersing herself into their business would sustain his admiration and win his delicate heart. She had thought of their lovemaking and little else since she'd left Bryce Corner that day after the funeral. Something had awakened in her. She eagerly awaited his return with a renewed sense of poise, fantasizing about a conversation wherein she would pour her heart out, devil-be-damned, and throw her emotions onto the table and let him see them exposed like a myriad of vivid and colorful sketches boldly strewn across his drawing table.

But then the days had slugged along and smeared into weeks and then she had heard of the reason why and she had gathered all of her unleashed dreams and stuffed them into a deep pocket locked somewhere in the depths of her psyche. Harlow arose from it all unblemished, her façade intact, and returned to her prominent vocation at the helm of *Maddison Designs* with no one the wiser. Well, except for Carlene, she'd probably been right all along, but certainly not Dodge. He was a man, and he had taken her at her word and moved on with his life, allowing his fragile state, open and vulnerable, to be broached by the wiles of another woman.

But she wasn't being fair. She knew little to nothing of this Annison, this Annison Barrett who she now quietly envied and secretly despised. It was wrong to see her as the pariah that Carlene presented; for in his eyes, you could clearly see that Dodge Maddison was in love and Harlow would try her best to listen to her own ill-wrought words and move on with her life, forever cherishing their private memory. She loved him and wanted him to be happy. It was her own fault if she had grabbed the brass ring and then so hastily, for whatever reasons, tossed it aside. She would not let him see the despair in her eyes. She would remain steadfast and resolute and bite her pride no matter how painful.

She could do all this, but for right now she could not. Mustering every ounce of composure she had, she excused herself from this man that she was in love with, standing beside the woman he was in love with, and walked away quickly before her tears gave her away.

"But aren't you having lunch with us, Harlow?" a naive Dodge asked.

"No, I've got to make these calls before London closes," she lied over her retreating shoulder. "Nice to have met you, Annison."

Women are strange. For as much as they think they can deceive each other, they cannot. They share that sixth sense together like a private silent language, an angel at times and a devil at others. Annison had witnessed the kitchen embrace and the kiss. And no matter what Dodge had told her about the professional relationship he shared with Harlow and how it was only "platonic", she had seen how easy the two of them were together. Even the way Harlow stood next to him exhibited more than just a business stance. There was a posture of possession, an admiration, and an evident love. Yes, there was a love there. She had glimpsed the agony hiding behind the mask of Harlow's cheerful countenance and felt her pain and even in her own stomach felt a slight twinge.

* * *

Annison and Dodge had left Bryce Corner early in the morning and had driven straight through to Maddison's attorney's office in mid-town. They had skipped breakfast and now, seated in *Café Mad*, they found themselves famished and eagerly attacked the special plate Pietro had made for them. They sat silent during lunch, each deep in their own thoughts. Dodge happy that his attorney was moving forward with Annison's divorce papers, they would be ready this week. He would wait to serve them 'til after Annison had gone to Barrett's Bluff to speak with her husband; her request. Eggman was back in Bryce Corner drawing up plans and costs to convert the Maddison farmhouse into a Bed & Breakfast. Harlow had stressed a need to go over some pressing business issues with Dodge asap. He'd do that with her tomorrow. Today, he wanted to show off his business to Annison and complete the tour of his building. He was proud and anxious to have her see the manufacturing floors, his Studio on Level 5 and of course the penthouse suite.

They made love in an animated way that evening and Dodge fell quickly to sleep, pleasant dreams were awaiting him. He was happy and filled with the peace of a new contentment. Annison lay awake a long time. The sounds and shadows of New York City intermittently, yet consistently, waving in through the high windows of the loft penthouse stoking her troubled mind, emblazing it with doubt and confusion as only the shadowy nocturne does so well. Everything in her life suddenly seemed magnified and out of proportion, things were happening so fast; her life that she had thought to be all figured out, became blurry and out of focus. She thought of the sure-to-be dilemmas awaiting her back at Barrett's Bluff. How would Jack respond? How would she handle telling the kids? The rapidness of the B&B idea, Dodge's enthusiasm, his beautiful shop here and the building - could he be happy leaving it? And Harlow, what was really happening there? And where the hell was Dana in all of this? Why were there so many women in his life? She would see Nina tomorrow. She needed that, her soul sister. She wanted her to meet Dodge and they had planned on dinner. She was anxious over how Nina would react. She'd probably be thrilled - anything to get her away from Jack Barrett. And Fashion Maddison ... yowzah! Annison giggled to herself envisioning the look on Nina's face when she told her of his proposal. She looked over at Dodge and placed her hand on his chest and flirted with his shadowy chest hairs as they rose and fell with his breathing. She snuggled next to him layering her leg over his and nestling her cheek upon his chest and fell softly to sleep listening to the heartbeat of the man she was in love with.

* * *

Distant voices rose and fell in wavering tones, breaking into her sleepiness like a muffled radio on scan. Annison's cloudy consciousness struggled to hear them. They were low, then louder, fluctuating. Were they tones of anger, straining to be quiet?

A sleepy arm reached over for Dodge, but he wasn't there. She awoke and rolled onto her back and stretched her legs, wiggling her toes at the end of the mattress where they hung beyond the confines of the sheets. She sat up and stretched her arms high above her. She yawned and brought her arms down to rest on her drawn up knees. She rested her head on top of them and smiled, thinking of him. *There it is again, voices from downstairs.* Annison donned a shirt from Dodge's wardrobe and went to the spiral staircase at the edge of the loft. She was above them now and could almost make out their conversation wafting upwards from the Studio. She could see Dodge sitting at the large drawing table with a coffee cup encircled in his hands. Harlow was walking behind him, pacing, speaking to him softly. She stopped and rested her hand on his shoulder. Dodge turned to face her and as he did so, caught sight of Annison.

"Oh … good morning. Did we wake you?" He got up and went to the staircase.

"No, no," she lied, "I just smelled the coffee."

"Come on down and have a cup." He held his hand out to her.

"No, I'm not dressed."

"You're fine, please join us. It's only Harlow and I."

*Only Harlow*, Harlow said to herself *that about sums it up!* She walked to the other side of the large table and shuffled some papers that had been lying there, extracted earlier from her leather valise, now lying open in the center.

Annison descended the spiral stairs in her bare feet, buttoning Dodge's thankfully long shirt as she did.

She offered a "good morning" to Harlow and received an almost amiable return.

"Coffee's in the kitchen," Harlow said.

Annison went to the kitchenette and stood on a woolen half-moon rug before a short granite countertop fixing her coffee. Harlow had taken up a stool opposite Dodge and the two of them were going over paperwork, talking calmly in a professional manner unlike the earlier tones that had stirred Annison from her sleep. She joined them at the large table and took a seat on the stool at the end. They had suddenly become engrossed in a business conversation, something about piece goods and gray goods and yarn dyes; she didn't recognize the nomenclature they were so well-versed in. Feeling like an outsider she rose and ventured about the studio.

It was open, as all the floors were, adhering to the original loft design of the building. There were dual offices set along the street sides of the corner building, one for Dodge and the other Harlow, with high windows overlooking the bustling streets of New York's SoHo district. Upon the refurbished wooden flooring, elegant furniture stood on elaborate sectional rugs and the open-air offices seemed to gravitate toward one another and met in the spacious corner at a grand round table clustered with padded leather chairs. Annison pictured Dodge, King Arthur and his Knights of the Round Table, holding meetings there with his design team, ohhing and ahhing over their design ideas as the fashion world spun around them outside the tinted glass of the tall windows.

The opposite corner had the kitchenette, also open, with chrome shaded lighting suspended from the high ceiling by thin black cords. Scattered throughout the vast floor plan were easels holding sketches of future lines in various stages of completion. The center of the room, on what everyone called Level 5, was where the tall, massive drawing table stood, offering workable access from all sides.

Harlow was poised on the edge of the table, one knee over the other, revealing a sculpted thigh. She was pointing to a color chart spread on a sketch before them. Dodge had risen from his seat and stood next to her with both palms on the table. He was nodding his head in agreement with her choices and then reached into a tray at one end of the table and extracted some pencils and began making hurried revisions and notations. Harlow went quickly across the room to her office area, her heels clicking in loud echoes on the spaces where the wood was bare. She returned with a handful of swatches. They spent a few minutes arranging and rearranging the swatches upon the sketch until they both seemed to agree, standing back and visualizing whatever creation they were working on. Dodge looked at his watch and said something to Harlow and she gathered all the paraphernalia and took it over to her office area and immediately got on the phone. She hadn't looked at Annison any of the three times she had passed by her, standing quietly with her coffee, feeling small in the big room.

"So," he startled her, "what do you say to some breakfast?"

"Huh? Umm, no thanks, I'm not hungry." She was feeling insecure in the New York world of Dodge Maddison and needed familiar ground to stand on. She felt an impulsive urge to be with Nina.

"I think I'll take a shower and go visit Nina. Do you mind?"

"Well, actually that might be better." They had planned on spending the day together taking in some of the sights of the City. "I didn't realize there was so much to catch up on. Harlow's handling a mini crisis right now and depending on how that goes, I might have to get involved."

"Is something wrong?"

"Yes, but in a good way. The line is selling extremely well and we've already exhausted the run on some of our fabrics. We desperately need to find material to honor our commitments for Holiday."

"So ... perfect then." She was relieved. "You handle your business here and I'll round up Nina for brunch."

"Great. Then I'll see you back here sometime this afternoon?"

Without hesitation Annison replied, "It would be silly for me to come all the way back here just to get ready to go out to dinner, right? We are still planning on dining with Nina aren't we?" Annison had set up the dinner date prior to driving into the City.

"Absolutely. I can't wait to meet her."

"Okay then." She returned to the kitchen and placed her cup on the counter and headed to the spiral staircase.

"Hey," he gently grabbed her arm and turned her to him, "are you alright?"

"Yes, I'm fine." She placed her hands on his chest and gave him a peck on the cheek. "Really. Do your business here and I'll wait for you at Nina's. We've got eight o'clock reservations at GreenTrees. It's on Christopher, just around the block from her brownstone. So why don't you plan on meeting us at seven-ish and we can have a cocktail at her place before we walk over to the restaurant. You've got her address on Grove Street, right?"

"Yes."

"Good," another quick cheek kiss. "I'll see you there tonight then," and she jaunted up the spiral steps.

"Anni...."

"Dodge!" Harlow called loudly from across the room, "I've got Milan on the line, Giovanni needs to speak with you."

He watched Annison hurriedly disappear into the apartment above and stood a moment with his hand on the railing, wondering if he should go after her, but instead went over to Harlow's office and retrieved the phone from her. "Ciao, Giovanni. Buongiorno!"

# 36

## *To Even the Wind*

Sanderson Realty Specialists was in mid-town, on the corner of Seventh Avenue and Thirty-First Street. Nina had purchased the twenty-one story building years ago for an amount she had called *An irresistible price to pay to be surrounded by furs.* It was in the heart of New York's fur district. Numerous manufacturers' houses abound in the few tight blocks from Twenty-Ninth Street to Thirty-First between Fashion Avenue and Eighth Avenue. In the fur district, vast and various (and sometimes controversial) wares are assembled in numbers unequaled anywhere else on earth. And whenever Annison called on Nina there, she was amazed at the racks of exquisite, expensive furs constantly being wheeled along the streets and sidewalks by seemingly non-caring union workers; as if they were delivering inconsequential castoffs from the Salvation Army store. At any time during the day it seemed there were at least a dozen racks rolling by at racetrack speeds. She always wondered if any of the multitudes of people scurrying along the walkways had ever had the guts to just grab one off the rack and run like hell. She'd never heard of it and Nina had said she was pretty sure those carriers had guns on them. They sure were beautiful, if you liked furs, which she didn't, being supportive of animal rights. But she caught herself admiring a passing array of Sable furs as she exited her taxi and waited for an overstuffed rack to whiz by.

Annison crossed the sidewalk and entered the former Holmes Building, sitting stately across from Madison Square Garden, and took the elevator to the top floor. The doors entered into Nina's reception area where a young, athletic looking secretary sat behind a wide glass-top desk. Luminous on the wall behind her was a large pewter "*SRS*" logo. Below that were double smoked-glass doors, elegantly rimmed in thick pewter framework. The secretary, who preferred the title of Administrative Assistant, wore a tight black boat-neck tee shirt with "ME" in grand white letters across the front. The letters did not stand for the state of Maine. Through the glass desktop Annison saw black slacks with short black boots with big silver eyelets. The silver was picked up again on a large belt buckle worn on the outside of her identity top. She had an earphone in her left ear with a short thin wire microphone extending along her high cheekbone. She wore absolutely no makeup and her hair was cropped and gelled so perfectly that it looked like it belonged on a ceramic figurine. She was exhibiting a curt attitude to someone on the phone and was much too busy to acknowledge Annison, pacing nervously on the carpet between the twin couches facing each other in the center of the room. She had brought with her a huge carry bag and dropped it heavily onto one of the couches and stood impatiently in front of the girl. Finally the Administrative Assistant clicked off the phone and asked, curtly, "May I help you?"

Annison told her who she was and asked if Nina was in.

"Do you have an appointment, Mizzz Barrett?" she asked her sarcastically, knowing that she didn't. She was the palace guard who kept track of the precious appointment book. Absolutely no one was going to just walk in and get by her without paying the proper chattel.

"No, I don't, Missy!" Annison wasn't having the best of days and was in no mood for prissy little games.

"Missy?!" the secretary stood as if she was going to do battle; crossing her arms in front of her and flexing her biceps as if to say, *careful, can't you see I pump iron?*

Annison closed her eyes and said to herself, *Oh my God, I don't need this right now!* "Listen," her eyes opened and stabbed into the receptionist, "do us both a favor and drop the Schwarzenegger act. Place one of those little muscle-toned fingers of yours onto the intercom and tell Nina that Annison is here. Please." Her tone was commanding and the look in her eye penetrating. The girl did as she was told and a second later the glass doors behind her opened wide and Nina Sanderson came bounding through them screeching, "Annison! Darling!" reaching her arms out for her as she came around the receptionist's desk and giving her a great big hug.

"Oh my God!" Nina exclaimed standing back from her, "You look absolutely fabulous!" They hadn't seen each other since that hot summer day in August when they had lunched at GreenTrees on Christopher in the Village and had brainstormed Annison's Retreat.

"Wonderful! You look wonderful." She hugged her again and stood back smiling widely at her, proud of what they had accomplished together, the retreat obviously having a sublime effect on Annison.

Nina's expression suddenly changed, "What's the matter?" Tears were forming in her girlfriend's eyes. "Oh my God! Get in here," she ushered Annison into her office.

"Hold all my calls, Priscilla, and don't let anyone in!"

"Yes, Nina." Priscilla closed the office doors. She was pleased to have seen the tears welling in her adversary's eyes. *Straight women! So weak and emotional.*

"Tell me all about it," Nina said in a motherly voice as she sat Annison down on her fluffy office couch, took a seat next to her and placed a consoling arm around her shoulders.

"Oh Nina," she began, and for the next hour, in a fascinating story that kept Nina spellbound, Annison went through the events of her life over the past month, openly confiding in her best friend and therapeutically releasing her pent-up anxieties and emotions - both the good and the troublesome. Nina listened well, leaving Annison's side only once to pour sherry into two pony glasses. This had been at the point when Annison recounted Dodge's marriage proposal.

"I thought everything was going so well for us, but I don't know anymore. He was supposed to be here to break off with Dana and now there's this Harlow. And his store is filled with beautiful women, I mean, Christ, drop-dead-gorgeous women are all around him."

"Are you jealous?"

"Yes ... No ... Oh, I don't know!"

"That's his world, Honey. After all, he is a good looking, successful, famous man who's immersed in the glamorous world of fashion. You've got to expect that. It's part of the territory. You've got to be able to handle that."

"I'm not sure I fit into his world."

Nina reached over to the square glass table in front of them and procured a tabloid from atop a stack of magazines, flipped it open to a dog-eared page and put it on Annison's lap and said, "Oh, you're in his world Sweetie."

It was *Scene Around.* There in living color, in the middle of a collage of pictures of Dodge Maddison in a myriad of exotic settings with a myriad of various women, was a picture of her and Dodge seated at the table in Bentley's Restaurant in Woodstock, Vermont.

"Oh my God!"

The byline read, Is *Fashion's Bachelor Playboy Changing His Designs On Women*? In the short paragraph wrapping throughout the snapshots Gail Skalberg-Vaugn presented, in her slanderously trademark way, an expose of the designer as a *Casanova who changes his women as often as he changes his designs.*

The article went on to say that *his latest creation, seen most recently adorning his table at a clandestine rendezvous spot deep in the autumnal hollows of Vermont, might present a real challenge to D.M.'s bachelorhood. She's a lovely woman (not a teenager for once!) who matches his caliber, not only in posture, good looks and professionalism (she's a successful businesswoman who owns and runs a famous Inn on the Connecticut coastline – can you guess which one?) but also in the ability to make ones heart throb. And Mr. Maddison's heart is pounding loudly!*

"Shit!" Annison said, holding the journal before her in both hands, "Dodge isn't going to be happy." and wondered, "how'd she get the shot? When did this come out?"

"Today."

"I've got to get to Sarah before she sees this."

"What about J.J. and Jack and the Inn?"

"Jack doesn't read this stuff, nor J.J. and I don't subscribe to it at the Inn."

"One of the girls might bring it in."

"Let them, he's going to know anyway, whether I get to him first or this does. I don't care. It's over between us one way or the other. I don't think he'll be surprised."

"Oh, he'll be surprised alright."

"I'm more worried how Dodge will respond. She specifically told him she wouldn't do this."

"She's a snake. It's her schtick, she lives for opportunities like that. She'd expose her own mother having an affair, if she ever had a mother."

Annison threw the magazine back onto the table.

"She does have a point, you know," Nina said. "He does have a reputation for running with quite a few different women. *Changing his women like he changes his designs* isn't far from the truth."

"Now it's you?"

"I just don't want you to get hurt darling, don't want you to become just another one of his discarded dresses."

275

"I don't feel that way. He's really not like that, that portrayal is just sensationalism. Besides, we've talked about it. He says he's in love with me and I believe him."

"Are you sure?"

"Yes, I'm sure."

"Then why all the concern about his assistant and the model chick?" Nina raised her eyebrows at her.

"I'm being contradictive aren't I?"

"A little, but perhaps cautiously so."

Annison was thinking of Gail Skalberg-Vaugn's unnecessary article. She'd seemed so pleasant that lovely day in Vermont and she thought she was a friend to Dodge. This was exactly the type of thing he said he wanted to get away from.

"Our whole dream is to get away from the limelight and settle into a quieter life with our Bed and Breakfast in Bryce Corner."

"Did he say that's what he wants?"

"Yes."

"Well then, give him a chance, I'm sure he's not distancing you, he's probably got a lot on his plate; like business to catch up on and take care of - you can appreciate that." Nina placed her hand on Annison's knee and gave it a consoling squeeze. "You'll fit in if you want to, if this is what you truly want. Is it?"

"Yes," she answered with her bright smile returning, "more than anything. Do you think I'm crazy, Nina?"

"Of course I do," she smiled, "but as long as you're happy, who cares. I've never before seen this glow about you. You truly are in love aren't you?"

"Yes, oh yes, he's wonderful. I'm happy, really happy."

"And I'm happy for you. You deserve it. You've sacrificed long and hard your whole life, I think it's great! When are you going to tell Jack? I want to be there!" They laughed. "Better yet, let me tell him." They laughed even harder.

Nina rose to replenish their pony glasses with the deep red sherry. "So, you haven't told the kids yet?"

"No, I wanted to have the conversation with Jack first. Hopefully he'll be civil about it."

"Right."

"What do you think?"

"I think he'll try to talk you into coming back. Not because he's madly in love with you and can't bear the thought of you being with another man, hell he's probably been with a different waitress every night, but I'm sure he's fucked up the business enough by now and will be begging you to come back."

"It's too late. He can have it, have it all. I'm over it. I'm not looking for a thing from him or his family. The kids are on their own now, and neither of them wants nor need the Inn. It's the past for me and life is too short to not be happy."

"Good for you girl!"

They chatted awhile longer over their sherry, Nina full of a hundred questions and Annison feeling stronger as she expounded happily about her new love and their plans of a quiet marital ceremony - Nina would be thrilled to stand up for her. She rambled on about the designs for the conversion of the Maddison farmhouse into a Bed & Breakfast. Telling her how they were going to fashion it after Eleanor Grey's B&B in Vermont; about utilizing the lake house for their creative retreat; and that they had actually discussed the possibility of having a child.

"Wow! You don't mess around do you? I've heard he's charming, but honestly Annie, isn't that a little premature?"

"I feel like I'm reborn. Like something has directed me towards Dodge, towards this relationship. Ever since that night at your cabin when I almost died, and then him being there, and then what happened between us, falling in love; I mean it's ethereal. Call it providence or fate or whatever but it's real and I'd be a fool to let it pass me by. I need this, Nina, want it with all my heart and soul. I've never been so consumed, so happily filled with new emotions. Something is giving me a sign and nothing else matters, not Jack, not the Inn, and to a degree not even the children. They'll be fine with it, I hope, but regardless, it's time for me to be me and I've never felt so sure about anything ever before. And I owe a big part of it to you, for your support," she put her sherry glass down on the corner of the table, "and your love." Annison wrapped her arms around Nina and they hugged each other.

"I'm so happy for you," Nina said, "you're going to make me cry."

The double glass doors opened slightly and Priscilla peeked in, "Excuse me, Nina, I'm going ..." she noticed them embracing and felt embarrassed "... to lunch now and I, I wondered if I, if I could bring you back anything. I ... I'm sorry, Nina," and she quietly closed the doors.

The two ladies looked at each other and burst out laughing. "I'll bet that freaked her out!" Annison said.

"Oh God," Nina was laughing, "that was perfect! She's been trying to get into my slacks ever since I hired her six months ago. I'll bet she's heartbroken!"

"I'm sure she didn't expect me to be a dyke when I first came in."

"Sweetie, you'll never be a dyke," Nina was wiping the laughing tears from her eyes, "but if you ever decide to try it …" she teased Annison.

"You'll be my first, honey, I promise," Annison said, and they began laughing all over again.

\* \* \*

Feeling refreshed and enlightened, the ladies decided to step uptown for lunch and a spree of shopping. Annison wanted a new outfit to wear for Dodge this evening and Nina was always up for new clothes. She was feeling more feminine today and hadn't shopped uptown for a while, generally preferring the eclectic boutiques of the Village. They had a wonderful afternoon. New York was bright in the Fall sunshine and the temperatures were pleasantly cool. Nina decided to skip returning to her office and, with their bundles of new packages, they took a cab directly to her brownstone on Grove Street in Greenwich Village. Nina called Priscilla at the office and told her she could leave an hour earlier in exchange for dropping off Annison's bag that she'd left behind in the reception area. Priscilla grumbled something inaudible into the phone but would do as instructed. The girls laughed at what she must be thinking and when Priscilla arrived a short while later, they invited her in for a glass of wine and told her of their best-friend relationship and their childhood beginnings in Barrett's Bluff. Priscilla left in better spirits, feeling relieved that Nina was still potentially available to her.

Nina's home was pleasant and comfortable; stylish in its contemporary furnishings and warm with its subtle antique accents and original mid-eighteen hundreds wood-trimmings around the doorways, along the bright polished flooring and up into the high vaulted ceiling. A grand living room spread out before you as you entered from a long shotgun hallway, past the small guestroom, the downstairs bath and the cozy kitchen tucked beneath the loft. Straight ahead, through the wall of glass opening onto the balcony overlooking the courtyard appeared the set of Hitchcock's *Rear Window*. To the right, behind a lovely pastel sectional, peach-colored beveled mirror rose from floor to high ceiling, lending a cheery glow to the room and reflecting the long, rich mahogany staircase diagonally climbing the exposed brick wall opposite. The staircase brought you up into the master bedroom and bath. The bedroom looked as if Greta Garbo herself had fashioned it, wallpaper and fabrics light and welcoming and the room soft and alluring complete with a high bed canopied with white lace. Tucked neatly and unobtrusively to one side against the railing overlooking the grand room, Nina kept a tiny desk and low bookcase, her home office for those days when she preferred to handle her business in the comfort of her slippers and robe.

By seven o'clock that evening the ladies had already napped, showered and freshened themselves and were standing on the outside balcony admiring their new outfits.

"I don't remember the last time I saw your legs," Annison said. Nina, always exclusively adorned in slacks, had bought a dress, short and sassy, perfectly accenting her athletic body.

"What do you think?" she pirouetted.

"You look hot! Too hot maybe. I'm jealous, you're going to get all of his attention."

"Don't worry, Darling, I'm sure his eyes will be all over you." Annison was wearing a black leather mini-skirt with a white silk blouse unbuttoned just enough to reveal the lace on her camisole. "You look positively radiant," Nina said, "and sexy as hell!"

The intercom buzzed and Nina walked down the hallway to the box on the wall, "Yes?"

"Dodge Maddison."

"Please, come up."

"Your Prince is on his way," Nina said to Annison as she reentered the living room. "You let him in. I'll fill the ice bucket," and she disappeared into the kitchen. "Or should we have wine? Does he like wine?"

Annison was checking herself in the wall of beveled mirror. "Um, how about martinis?"

"Oh, wonderful idea! I've got a chilled bottle of Grey Goose."

"Perfect."

"I'll add just a touch of Chambord," Nina said to herself, "raspberry martinis, yum."

Annison was standing in front of the peach-tinted mirrors, giving her hair a fluff and checking her lipstick when a light knock came to the door. She went to answer it. She opened the door and saw him standing there in a double-breasted charcoal suit. It had thin, light gray chalk-stripes that accented his heather gray crewneck sweater. He wore no shirt beneath it and Annison thought the look handsome and casually elegant. He held a cashmere topcoat folded over his left arm and a bouquet of flowers in his right. "For our hostess."

"Oh, how thoughtful, she'll love them."

He kissed her lightly on the lips. She took his topcoat and led him down the hallway, stopping at the guestroom to place his coat on the bed. He noticed her travel bag there amidst some shopping bags from uptown. "Did you go shopping today?"

"Yes, the girls went on an outing," she stood back from him, "what do you think?"

He admired her, "Verrry nice." The top was playful in its design, the silk lace resting in her cleavage sexy, and the leather skirt young and provocative. "You're tempting me."

"That's the idea," she fingered the peaks on his lapels and reached up on her tiptoes and planted a firm kiss on his mouth. His arms went to surround her but she turned and pulled on his suit coat, leading him away, "Come on, let's meet Nina."

She was just coming out of the kitchen, a martini in each hand, "Hi," she said and walked into the great room and placed the stemmed glasses onto the low table. Turning, she held her hand out to him, "I'm Nina, so nice to meet you."

Dodge shook her hand and offered the flowers.

"Oh my! I don't think I've received flowers from a man since ..." she looked at Annison, "... my high school prom?"

"You didn't go to the prom, remember? You thought it too ritualistic."

"Oh, that's right. Then this is a first. Thank you." She accepted the flowers in both hands, "they're lovely."

"Not as lovely as the lady they're for," he was admiring her dress in a nonchalant, professional manner.

"Well thank you, Mr. Maddison," she smiled at Annison. "Flowers annnd a compliment."

"And I'm sure it's not a first, an attractive lady like you must be showered with gifts from men all the time."

"Gifts yes, men no," she laughed, winking to Annison and went into the kitchen.

"She's nice," Dodge said, "does she live here alone?"

Annison had told him all about her best friend; almost all. Nina preferred to keep her sexual preferences quiet. She competed in a business largely occupied by conservative, right wing men who admired her good looks and sharp business acumen, both of which she was not above utilizing to her advantage. But she had clawed her way to success and didn't want to jeopardize it by scandal. She had never felt compelled to come out publicly; she'd leave that for the insecure movie stars and talk show queens. She was quite comfortable with her life and Annison admired and respected her for that. "Yes," she said to him, "at the moment she's between lovers."

"Speaking of lovers," Nina said as she brushed past them, placing the flowers in the center of her coffee table, "I hear congratulations are in order." She raised her martini glass in a toast. "To my best friend and her new love, may you keep your happiness forever." They clinked glasses.

"Sounds like the cat's out of the bag," Dodge laughed.

"Sisters can't keep secrets," Nina said, "I think it's great. I've never seen Annie so vibrant. You've stolen her heart Mr. Maddison."

"Please, call me Dodge, and I'm afraid it's more like Annison has stolen mine," he placed an arm around her waist, "and I'm a happy captive."

Nina saw the smile on her friend's face, "I can see you're both captured and I think it's wonderful. Let's sit, shall we?"

The conversation was light and jovial, filled with questions and brief dissertations of each of their three quite different businesses. Everyone enjoyed Nina's raspberry martinis so much that they decided to have another before they ventured out to dinner.

\* \* \*

At their dinner table at GreenTrees on Christopher, Nina sat looking at them. She was pleased to see the happiness in their eyes and enjoyed the respectful way they spoke of each other. She was truly happy for her lifelong friend. She'd been with her through all of her life changes; from childhood days to teenage; her pregnancies and child-rearing; from faulty marriage with her steadfastness to maintain it; her success as a business woman; her recent breakdown; *The Retreat*; and now this newfound love and happiness. Through all of these times, Nina had always been there for Annison whenever she needed her, and vice-versa. They were true sisters.

"Are you coming?" Annison asked her again.

"Where?" Nina realized she'd been lost in her own thoughts.

"To the ladies room."

"Umm, no. I think I'll stay here with your fiancée."

"Don't get any ideas." Annison reached her pocketbook from off the floor next her chair. Dodge, the gentleman, stood and pulled her chair back for her. She brushed his cheek with her hand and smiled and made her way through the cluster of dining tables.

"She's gone through a lot lately," Nina said.

Dodge sat replacing the napkin on his lap. He didn't know how to respond to her comment. "I know," he said.

"Do you?" Her eyes stared at him, unblinking, challenging him.

"Nina, I know you're Annison's best friend and I know how close you two are and I imagine this all must seem rather sudden to you, perhaps somewhat unbelievable..."

"*Unbelievable's* an operative word."

"But I assure you, it's real. I've been blessed with finding her."

Nina went on, "Annison is one of the strongest, most stubborn and steadfast women I've ever known and I've known her forever. She's also the most fragile. She's like a little bird perched on her branch singing away in the sunshine. She loves the sunshine and is at her best in it, but when it rains she gets wet and retreats to her cozy little nest. Now her nest is empty and she's vulnerable."

"To hovering hawks?"

"To even the wind."

"You think my intentions are false?"

"Habitual maybe."

"Meaning?"

"Let me ask you, Mr. Maddison ..."

"Dodge."

"...Dodge, do you really know what your intentions are?"

"You don't beat around the bush do you?"

"No. Your reputation precedes you."

They were sparring.

"They're exactly as I've stated them. I'm in love with her. Madly. And I want to marry her and make a life together." Nina's gaze was unwavering. He had thought she'd have a clever remark to this but she sat unstirred. "Is there something I'm not aware of?" Her silence made him uneasy. "Is it her marriage? Do you think I'm breaking up her marriage?"

This got a laugh out of Nina, "Oh God no. That's been broken for years."

"Then what is it Nina, what's bothering you? The suddenness?"

"No, not the suddenness, I can tell just by looking at her that she's in love, and I am genuinely thrilled to see her so. The reputation, I guess. The Fashion Maddison that keeps popping up in the rags like the *Scene Around* article." He had seen it earlier in the day when it had arrived at his office. He had immediately called Gail Skalberg-Vaughn to chastise her. Something he was convinced she thrived on.

"Has she seen it?"

"Yes."

"Damn it! I didn't mean for that to happen."

"It's not the article. Annison is a big girl. She's aware of what she's gotten herself into and is prepared to handle it. But for me, there lies the question of your intentions. I don't know you, Dodge. All I know of you is what I've heard and read, and of how Annie speaks about you, which seems to be quite different. I'm certainly prepared to give you the benefit of the doubt and welcome her version of you, but I will be frank with you, Annison is very special to me and I don't want to see her get hurt. So if this is just another one of your flings…"

"It's not a fling. I can understand how you may feel about me, and you are right in one thing, you don't know me." He was sitting back in his chair, his hands on the table and his look stern in concentration. "She's very special to me too, more than that actually, but I'm not so smitten that I don't realize how sudden this has come upon us," he looked directly at Nina and smiled, "well, I guess I *am* smitten, you know," the charm of his smile took her by surprise; not in a startling way nor an offensive one, but in the way that it touched her; authentic and warm, with a touch of boyhood innocence. "How about you give me a chance? I'm sure I'll grow on you."

"And if you don't?"

He looked directly into her stubborn eyes and grinned, "Annison said you were tough. I can see how you've become so successful." She returned the grin. "I assure you, Nina, my intentions are true. I've never before felt so filled with …" he stopped a moment searching for the right word, "… warmth. There's something about her that reaches into me and touches emotions I've never felt before."

She could see why Annison was attracted to him, consumed by his persona. He exhibited an air of sincerity, an honesty, that touched her. She'd give him the chance. "Okay, you've impressed me."

"So, do I get the official Sanderson stamp of approval?"

"Yes, but don't blow it!"

"I *knew* there'd be a but."

They smiled to each other, both genuinely liking the other.

"She's lucky to have a friend like you," he said raising his glass in a toasting motion.

"I know," she touched her glass to his and they sipped.

"Well," Annison was taking her seat back at the table, "what have you two been talking about?"

"Oh, just the birds," Nina said.

"And the bees," Dodge added with a chuckle.

"I hope no one got stung," Annison said.

\* \* \*

The three of them were walking along Christopher Street in the coolness of the night, glad they had worn their coats, Dodge in the middle with the ladies on either side of him, Annison's arm entwined in his. It was a Tuesday night so foot traffic wasn't too bad. Occasionally they had to maneuver toward the curb to allow room for others to pass by, but they quickly reformed their stance, the three of them walking together, laughing and chatting away.

The plan after dinner, Annison had thought, was to return to Nina's, get her travel bag, and cab down to his place in SoHo. That was until Dodge mentioned he was going to Europe tomorrow. He and Harlow.

"We've got to substitute some fabrications in the line and our vendor in Milan has got some piece goods that I'm hoping will suffice, but I've got to see them, feel them, make sure the hand is right."

"Tomorrow morning?" Annison asked. "For how long?"

"Probably most of the week, depending on how much goods he's able to provide. I'm hoping we can get enough from Milan to cover the balance of the orders. Otherwise, I'll have to get them from the Orient, but that'll take longer. Holiday season is upon us and we've got to get the goods to the building and onto the cutting tables as soon as possible."

A quietness settled over them all and Nina could feel an awkwardness passing between the two of them.

"Why don't you come along," he asked her enthusiastically. "You'd love Italy, we'd have a great time. Maybe spend a few extra days and visit Florence and Rome (he pronounced them Firenze and Roma, rolling the R's). I'd love to show you around."

"No, I'd only be in the way," she said, "and besides, I've really got to get back home and settle things there." It was the first time she'd called it home.

"Are you sure?"

"Yes. I want to confront Jack before the papers are served and I need to have the conversation with Sarah and J.J. They need to hear it from me first. I may even take the train down to D.C. to meet with Sarah, I'm not sure yet."

They turned onto Bleecker and were met with a fierce blast of wind.

"Brrrr, where did this come from?" Nina said as they quickly grabbed at their wraps, clenching them tight to their necks in unison as if a choreographer had suddenly given them a cue. "I hate this time of year," she felt she was talking to herself. "Warm days and cold nights, you never know what to wear. Whatever happened to Indian Summer?"

They walked the short distance along Bleecker Street, silently, pushing into the fall wind. Rounding the corner onto Grove Street, the lee side of the wind allowed their shoulders to relax. But Nina could sense the slight tension remaining in the air along the night sidewalk. No one had spoken and when they got to the stoop at her brownstone, Nina, feeling a need to give them some time alone, bounded up the stairs ahead of them and entered her security code onto the keypad. Annison had stopped on the sidewalk and held onto Dodge's hand. "I think I'll stay here for the night," she said to him.

He exhibited a bewildered look.

"You've got an early flight to catch," she continued, "and I'd like to get an early start too. Besides, all my stuff is here anyway."

"Hey," he said softly to her, "what's the matter?"

"Nothing. Really. It's just that I'm a little tired and I don't feel like packing up now and then again in the morning. It would be easier to just stay here. When will you be back?"

He stood facing her, holding onto both her hands, sensing something was bothering her; Harlow. "Saturday, Saturday evening. I think the flight gets into JFK around seven-thirty."

"Well then, that gives me a few days to handle my situation and then I can meet you back here in the City Saturday night."

"That may not be a good idea, I've got a return flight scheduled for that night but you never know. I've experienced some horrendous delays on that return flight, and I'm not really sure if we'll, if I'll, be back on Saturday. If Milan can't handle the orders, I'll have to go to Hong Kong."

A hush fell upon their conversation.

"How about I call you once I get there and let you know how things are going?" he said.

"No, it would be better for me to handle my confrontations without worrying about that. I don't want to be there any longer than a few days anyway, so let's plan on Saturday night and just give me a call if you can't make it. I'll stay with Nina."

"You don't have to stay at Nina's, y'know."

"I know, but I'll probably want to stop by to see her anyway, maybe we'll go out to dinner if you're not going to be back on time. Then I could go on to your place Sunday and wait for you there. Okay?"

He was still holding onto her hands but she had loosened her grip, he could feel the weight of her arms.

"It's business, Annie."

"I know."

"Do you?"

"Yes," she squeezed his hands, "I do, and I'll miss you."

"I'll miss you too. It's only for a few days."

"Are you two coming in for a nightcap?" Nina called out.

Dodge kept his eyes on Annison in a hopeful manner. "No," she answered, "you go on in, we'll only be a minute."

"Okay then," and Nina left them alone in the night.

"So," she said, "let's play it by ear. Call me if there's a change in your schedule. Otherwise, I guess, just give me a call when you land."

"Okay."

They had settled that, but there seemed to be something unsettling remaining in the air.

"Annie," Dodge said, "I love you, you know."

She closed her eyes, holding onto his hands and the moment tightly, "I know, Dodge, I do." She embraced him, burying her face into the soft cashmere of his topcoat, squeezing her eyelids to hold back her tears. "You go do what you need to get done and I'll do what I have to do, okay?"

He held her tight. And she held him back. And then, in an instant, she was gone from his arms and ascending the stairway, keeping her back to him and fighting to keep the tears at bay. At the top, in the safety of the dark doorway, she turned and waved, "Good-night," and vanished into the dim foyer, the heavy door closing slowly behind her.

Dodge stood in the cold air, his feet shuffling on the sidewalk. Above him the sky was dark. Clouds were thickening in the quiet safety of the darkness, silently covering the distant stars. Nature's puffy comforter tucking in the sleepy night.

He didn't remember walking away, but Annison saw him turn and go along the fading sidewalk, out towards Seventh Avenue. She opened the heavy door and stood with her back against it in the doorway watching his figure shorten in the distance. She was biting her lip, tears slowly seeping from her eyes, warm, almost scalding as they ran over her cheeks and dripped one by one onto the cold flooring beneath the archway. Emotional. She wondered why she was so emotional. Why were those old insecurities rearing their head again? Her moist eyes trailed behind his heavy footsteps imprinting behind him on the moisture of the cool sidewalk. He hailed a cab at the curb on Seventh, his soft gray figure disappearing into the yellow cab and streaking out into the vastness of the New York night. The door weighed heavy on her back and eventually she would give into it and allow it to close. But for a moment, just a few more moments, she would lean on it with her eyes closed and keep the image of him standing at the bottom of the steps with her. "Annie, I love you, you know," he was saying.

"Say it again."

*Annie, I love you, you know.*

# 37

## *LITTLE RIVERS STREAMING*

Annison had a pretty good idea of what to expect upon her return to Barrett's Bluff. She'd been secretly regretting the return not only because she knew there'd be a thousand problems awaiting her - lost sales, cancelled functions, kitchen dilemmas, and general disarray - but mainly because she just didn't want to deal with it anymore. Her biggest fear, even outweighing the upcoming conversation with her husband Jack, was staffing. She expected to find half the staff missing and had prepared herself for a day of pleading phone calls to get them back. She wanted to leave the Inn, maybe forever, but as a matter of professionalism and staunch pride, she needed to make her official departure on a high note. She wanted all those years of hard work and sacrifice to not be all for naught. She wanted to hold her head high and leave respectfully. She planned on cleaning up the mess Jack had made of things, settle any and all pending issues, re-establish business harmony, and then walk away knowing she'd left things as cohesive as possible. She'd do her part one last time and then The Inn at Barrett's Bluff would be on its own.

Also, she needed to cleanse herself of the guilty feeling she harbored due to the manner in which she had so hastily left a month ago. She needed her children and close friends to understand her decision and to duly respect her, not only for all that she had done, but also for what she needed to do. It wasn't a matter of owing it to them as much as it was a matter of personal self-esteem. She didn't want any lingering feelings of doubt or betrayal following her into her new life.

On the train ride up, she laid out the itinerary in her mind. The first day, Wednesday, she'd tackle the inevitable rounds of questions, quickly take hold of the business, establish its revitalization and set the game plan for the future without her. Then contact the children, and set a time that evening to have the heart to heart with Jack. Thursday she'd travel to D.C. to comfort Sarah, if need be. If not, if Sarah was okay with everything, she'd remain at the Inn concentrating on the business. (Although, she would love to see her daughter. They were close and she missed her) Annison wondered how her new marriage was going, and, with her eyes closed as the Amtrak Express whizzed along the Connecticut shoreline, wished hard that Sarah would be happy forever. Hoped that she felt as much in love with her new husband as she did with her new love, Dodge Maddison; the mention of his name in the hallowed privacy of her inner thoughts brought a smile to her countenance, she was missing him already. The awkwardness of last night troubled her, especially how it ended. She hadn't wanted to be without him and was sorry she'd acted as coolly as she had. She had wanted to call out to him, to call him back to her. But she watched silently his diminishing figure fade along the evening sidewalk of The Village, feeling somewhere inside of her that it would be better to be alone that night to sort out the demons swirling around her. Too stressed, too much going on in both their lives. But soon it would be right again and they'd be together and happy forever and ever. She loved him so.

Friday she would go through her personal things and box whatever she needed to forward to Bryce Corner and set up a UPS pickup. She didn't want to take much, preferring to make a fresh start and leave the old memories and mementos behind. But there were some personal things she'd like to bring with her to the new Maddison B&B. Then, Friday night, figuring Jack would be beyond the initial shock of her divorce request (and probably relieved by it) she'd have a quiet dinner with him and they would talk civilly about everything. She didn't want the divorce to be complicated and didn't think it would be, but there were some things they needed to agree on to make life easier for the two of them and of course the children. She and Jack had known each other a long time. They'd been friends, then lovers, then spouses, and perhaps they could be friends again. She harbored no grudges against him. What they had done, they'd done, and they'd gotten two wonderful children out of it. But now it was simply time to move on, for both of them. She knew he'd felt maneuvered into the marriage and had always regretted it and this would be a good time for him to do the things he'd always wanted to do. Maybe he should get out of Barrett's Bluff too. Let his family take the Inn back, or sell it off to that group of investors that was periodically pestering them to sell. It might be good for him. She'd suggest that to him.

Saturday she'd reserve for herself. With the business dealings and the talk with Jack behind her, she'd rent a car and take a final drive around Barrett's Bluff. As an owner of the town's historic Inn and a stalwart in the business community, Annison had many friends - acquaintances really, for Nina was her only true friend. But there were a couple people she wanted to say good-bye to and a few of her private places and secret spots she wished to visit. Then, after one last solo cruise around Barrett's Bluff, she'd drive into the City and meet Dodge Saturday evening.

She had it all thought out. She'd planned on everything. Everything, of course, but the inevitable surprises:

like, how well the Inn was functioning, how Jack had taken charge of things and how smoothly everything was going; no exodus of disgruntled staff; no cancellations of functions; no interruptions in sales and marketing; no disarray in accounting; and not even a single problem in the always chaotic kitchen;

like, how impressed she was, she hated to admit it, but she was actually impressed. She didn't think he had it in him;

like, the warm and heartfelt reception she received not only from her staff, but also from the regulars, the locals who dined once or twice a week, and the members of the Barrett's Bluff business community who'd quickly heard of her return and had called happily welcoming her back;

like, Jack pulling an emergency family meeting on her and having the kids fly in on Thursday morning - a surprise intervention to confront her with her madness and to shake her back into reality. J.J. had gotten a half-day leave from his commanding officer and would only be able to stay a few hours. Sarah stayed the night. Long enough to tell them she was pregnant.

The cards were sliding across the table in Jack's favor. An unexpected ace - Annison was going to be a grandmother. Her heartstrings were being pulled.

Jack, the perennial conniver, had called the family meeting an emergency. It really wasn't, but in his mind it was. He wanted, needed, to get Annison back; not so much as a matter of undying love, but simply a matter of having things his way. He'd turned his initial anger of Annison's walking out on him into an attack on the business. He couldn't find her to have the big argument with, so he released his tensions in a way that he thought would really piss her off. He decided to show her up.

Show her that he was capable of maintaining the business without her. That would be his way of getting even with her. So, he laid on the charm, sweet-talking everyone into pulling together and keeping Annison's precious Inn alive and well and prosperously functional whilst she recuperated from a slight breakdown at a retreat he'd secreted her away to. He promised them she'd be back soon and gained their support in his quest. With the entire staff on his side, all Jack had to do was emulate Annison's business acumen and let things continue on. He'd never lost at anything before and he wouldn't now. Not even to this designer fellow she was supposedly attached to. One of Jack's castaway mistresses had been only too happy to run to the Inn and rub the issue of *Scene Around* into his face. But he was undeterred. Confident that his performance on the business end, combined with the kids' appearance, would prevail. The pregnancy of their daughter had been unexpected, but nicely enhanced his plan. He would win another victory and keep his life on an even keel.

For Annison, already emotionally teetering on the shaky ground of the overwhelming world of *Maddison Designs,* the return to the Inn was bringing a return of her old demons. The insecurities she'd felt before were once again lying in wait for her in the antiquated rooms, the low-ceilinged, twisty hallways, and the brick walkways curling through the leaf-covered grounds. The newfound strength she'd garnered at her retreat was no match for the inherent subliminal pressures, floating all about her at every turn, invisible as ghosts, but as strong as the ancient stone foundation and hardened beams of the old Inn itself. Sarah's revelation had had a powerful effect on her. Maybe there was something to work for. Maybe her grandchild would be the next heir to the Inn at Barrett's Bluff. Her family ethics began to get the better of her. Suddenly, she missed her family, even the damn Inn. Shit! She was going crazy again. Who was she kidding? Dodge Maddison, Bryce Corner, the lake house, a new marriage, a Bed & Breakfast, a chance at a new and wonderful second life. She *was* crazy. She didn't belong in his world. He'd never settle down. He'd already gone away from her hadn't he? With just one visit back to the city, to his world, his building. That's all it had taken, and zoom, he's off to Europe with Harlow. She didn't have a chance. What a fool she'd been to fall for him. *Oh Annison, what an idiot you are! Living in a fairytale illusion. Can't you see? The Inn is what you are, always will be. This is where you belong.*

It is always easier to fall back to old habits than to leave them behind. An old pair of jeans perhaps. Easier to climb into than to buy a new pair and go through the time and agony of breaking them in. Isn't life about comfort? And isn't comfort easy to get used to? Every once in a while we get a glimpse of what life could be if we broke out of our molds. Usually it's from a movie or a good book or a lazy afternoon of daydreaming in the warm sunshine. But occasionally we're given an actual situation, an affair that tempts our primal spirit. Takes all those everyday yearnings for the good life, and plops them into your lap. Then what do you do? You run with it of course. That's only natural. And it's exciting to live someone else's life for a while, but sooner or later, we always retreat to the comfy world we've made for ourselves. For better or for worse. Right? You can take a city girl away from the city, but you can't take a country girl out of the country. *What does that mean? What does anything mean?*

New England has a way of fooling you. Just as you get comfortable with one season, wham, another one appears out of nowhere. Summer, for instance, seems to magically appear and then lazily lollygag along with its warm days and pleasant nights (except for the obligatory HHH week from hell) and then slowly transition into fall with its brilliant colors, cooler temperatures and promises of an October warmer than usual and without the future of another bleak winter ever setting in. In autumn you become accustomed to the subtle daily changes in foliage, the colors changing, the leaves dropping, almost to the point where you don't even notice them. It's easy to become cozy with the season. Then one day you wake up and the leaves are gone, the trees are bare, and you're rummaging around the house looking for a warm jacket.

New York City is cushioned from the visual changes seen in its sister New England states simply because granite and cement don't change colors and skyscrapers have no leaves to lose.

As Annison traveled along the Amtrak rails returning to the City early Saturday morning, she realized how much even a few days had changed the appearance of her Connecticut coastline. The window was gray, smudged, and out of focus. She wiped it with her sleeve. Nothing. Outside in the cold morning air water vapor was clinging in a thin veil, spreading horizontally across the warm window - little rivers streaming across her window in the wind of the rolling train. The sun was up but the day was gray. The vibrant colors of autumn were withering on the lawns of the passing homes and dying in the gutters of the bleak roadways. Barren branches of passing trees stretched dark into the cold gray sky. The first hint of winter was already in the air.

She had left Barrett's Bluff earlier than originally planned. Her head filled with old dilemmas and her heart being tested in a new way. She stayed as long as she could, wrestling with the old ghosts. Now she needed to talk with Nina again, to sort out the revelations of the past few days. And to see Dodge. To see him and run into his arms. He'd make her feel whole again, help put the scattered pieces of Annison together again. She couldn't lose all that she had gained. *God, don't let that happen.* A month away from her old life and she had made so much progress. Just a few days back at the Inn and she had the feeling that she'd never left.

*Confusion, so much confusion.*

Sarah had told her mother to do whatever she had to in order to be happy. She wasn't exactly thrilled with a tepid romance between her mother and the designer Dodge Maddison, but she knew her mom wasn't happy with her dad, and hadn't been for a long time. She had suggested that maybe she'd gotten sidetracked up at the lake. Maybe the time alone was good, but the involvement with Dodge Maddison was a mistake. Even J.J. had said to chalk up the affair as a fun time and to get back to her real life. *Yeah, Dad's a womanizer, we all know that, but isn't Maddison just the same? Maybe you and Dad are even now. I think he's tried hard to make things work. You two have so much history together it would be a shame to throw it all away. I think you should give it one last try.*

Even? What did he know about even? How many affairs had his father had? How many that she knew about, never mind those she didn't. No, they were far from even, but it wasn't a contest. What she shared with Dodge wasn't an affair. She had fallen in love. They were deeply in love with each other. Weren't they?

Like extinguishing the lone light bulb in a small room, snapping it into darkness, the train became suddenly dark the instant it entered the tunnel nearing its destination at Penn Station. A second later the interior lights lining the floor fluttered and then stayed on. The conductor's voice crackled through the intercom announcing their approach to track number nine, right on time at nine thirty-six a.m. Transfer to track number eight for Baltimore and Washington D.C. and track number two for the Montreal Express leaving at ten oh five.

Annison walked animatedly up the long stretch of stairs from the train platform to the vast open waiting room. You could see the pew-style seats rimming the perimeter of the circular room, half the size of a football field. Usually they were full and hidden by the masses of people hurrying to and fro. Saturday morning at Penn Station was much quieter than the weekdays. She placed her travel bag onto one of the seats and dug into her pocketbook extracting a Scrunchy and twirling it randomly around her hair. The bag was lighter than when she'd left the City earlier in the week. She had decided to shop. Get new things; a prescription for her melancholy. She walked past the ticket booths, around the flashy three-sided advertising pillars and into the underground walkway marked Seventh Avenue / 32$^{nd}$ Street. Save for the newsstand and the coffee shop, the mall stores in the wide walkway were closed. Ten o'clock was their opening time. Just as well, she didn't want to shop there anyway, underground shopping was too tacky. She needed the bristling air and the flashy doorways of Fifth Avenue. She bought a coffee at Gyros and ascended the vacant stairway to the street and took a seat on one of the crescent shaped cement stools in the small piazza fronting Seventh Avenue. The air was cold, but the day looked to be brightening. Rays of struggling sunshine came through the corridors of the east-west city streets running from the East River over to the Hudson. A flock of pigeons flew off the rooftop of Madison Square Garden behind her, landing all around her and cooing for food. When they realized she only had a cup of coffee, they flew off in search of another target. The cement seat was cold and she took the folded *Hartford Courant* sticking out of the side pocket of her bag and used it as a cushion. She'd bought it from one of those boxes on the platform at the station in Barrett's Bluff. She hadn't read it.

Nina's office building was on her right, on the corner of 7$^{th}$ and 31$^{st}$, a brownish gray twenty-one story edifice amongst a myriad of blue-gray skyscrapers. She knew she wouldn't be there. She never went to the office on the weekends. Not because she enjoyed weekends off, she should, but didn't. She always had showings on the weekends. Nina was a workaholic.

Annison sipped her coffee. She had the lid off. It cooled faster that way and she was never adept at the little flip-top thingy. She could never get it to stay down as it should and whenever she attempted to tear it off she'd get splashed with scalding hot coffee. And the tops with the ridges that you pushed down with your lip as you sipped? Those were a nightmare! She always burnt her lip on those bastards. So she always took the lid off. These were the mundane things she was thinking about as she sat alone on her bench on a chilly, Saturday morning at the end of October in New York City. Stupid, meaningless things that took her mind away from her problems.

*Oh Annison, what to do? What to do.*

Yesterday morning she'd taken Sarah to the railroad station and hugged her on the platform. *You're going to make a wonderful mother*, she'd said, and Sarah had replied, *And you're going to make a wonderful grandmother.*

At the southern end of Barrett's Bluff there's a cove accessible from an overgrown, hidden walkway at the dead end of Daylily Lane - a narrow way with only four cottages off the shore road. Annison had gone there after dropping her daughter off. She parked her car at the very end (Jack's Mercedes actually, for her car was still at the lake in Massachusetts) nestling it close to a hedgerow stretching across the dead end of the lane. It was heavily overgrown with bittersweet, little red beads popping out of their little yellow shells. She had to lift up a dangly branch of them and duck into the hidden pathway leading to the rocky shoreline. It was private here, one of her quiet spots. She sat on one of the big rocks and watched the sun struggle through the high clouds, sending its periodic beams across the rolling ocean and onto the high bluff to her left on the eastern point. Standing atop the point in all its grandeur was The Inn at Barrett's Bluff; her home for the past twenty-plus years. Her life really. All she'd ever known. All she'd ever wanted to get away from. Looking at it, it was beautiful, in its grand innocent way. The huge Victorian Inn sitting large on its sprawling estate on the cliffs of the Connecticut shoreline was envied by many. A historical manor with lots of history, lots of income, but also lots of hard work, and, for her, considerable heartache. *Good times and bad times, like anywhere else, I guess.*

She hadn't slept with Jack, though not for the lack of his trying. He'd pleaded with her with his puppy-dog eyes. All would be forgiven. He'd forgive her if she'd forgive him and give him another chance. Promises to be better, the need to be a family again; especially now that they were going to be grandparents. Blah blah blah, promises, promises.

Although, she *had* thought about it, having sex with Jack. In their sex life, she'd always felt too submissive. He'd even told her once that she was uninspiring and needed to get more creative. That had been early on in their marriage, just past their teens and into their twenties. But she had children to raise and an Inn to run. Many demands on her time. She liked sex and Jack was a good partner, but their sex life had quickly become routine and had remained so for the balance of their marriage. To a degree Annison blamed herself for her husband's wanderings from her bed. Maybe if she had been more nymph-like things would have been different. But now, with this rejuvenation, this sexual explosion she experienced with Dodge, she felt quite different. More self-assured and sexy. Confident in her sexual self. She certainly was creative with Dodge, she blushed. She'd thought of having sex with Jack and fucking his sox off, showing him what she had learned, what he was missing, that she wasn't the prude he thought her to be. She was a real woman, powerful in her emotion, comfortable in her physical expression and uncontrollably wild when she wanted to be.

No, she hadn't had sex with Jack. She was in love with Dodge. She'd stayed in one of the guest-suites, away from her husband's pseudo-romantic advances. She felt funny in a room alone, but welcomed the solitude. It had a warm feel to it. Cozy on the top floor, with a lovely view of the ocean. *Maybe I could move in here. It might work better if we had separate rooms.* A Freudian slip. *Bastard!*

"Ma'am?" A tall man with a two-day-old beard and a gentle smile stood before her holding her coffee cup lid. It had blown off the bench, unnoticed in a short gust of wind. He had been exiting the train station and saw the lady sitting alone in her thoughts. *Pretty*, he'd said to himself as he passed by her. That was when the wind had gusted and the cup lid had rolled in front of his lanky gait.

"Oh," she said awkwardly, accepting the proffered lid, "thank you."

"You're very welcome." He tipped his head to her and went on his way.

\* \* \*

She thought of Dodge Maddison. She was anxious to see him, to be with him. She hadn't heard from him all week so she assumed he was on schedule and would be back this evening. She couldn't wait to see him. She had decided to go to his place after all. The first thing she was going to do was make love to him. She'd be waiting for him in his apartment; in a seductive pose on the couch. Maybe she would pick up some sexy lingerie this morning. Yes, definitely. Black. She could have the tub filled with bubbles and lit with tiny candles all around the edge. They'd make passionate love on the couch, on the floor, she didn't care, and then she'd lead him to the bath and they could ease into the warm water and rub each other softly with thick sponges. She envisioned her sponge reaching into the suds and finding him, making him rise again, and sliding him into her beneath the slippery sudsy water. And they'd do it again. She'd lean back in the claw-foot tub with her arms spread wide, her fingers biting into the rolled top edge and her head back, giving in to him as he lusted into her, wildly splashing the sudsy water in rhythmic waves onto the wooden floor. She would scream as he made her come, wrapping her arms around him and clawing at his strong back crushing onto her swollen breasts.

"Ma'am?" The man was back. "Are you alright?"

"Ah, y-yes," she stuttered, coming out of her daydream. "Why?"

"You were moaning."

"No, no," she said, trying to hide her embarrassment, "I'm alright."

"Listen, I've got a cab hailed here," he pointed to the curb, "can I drop you someplace?"

"No, thank you, I'm fine."

"Sure?"

"Yes, thank you though."

"Well then, have a nice day." He entered the yellow cab and shut the door.

Maybe she should get a cab and go to Dodge's building and drop her stuff off before going shopping. *Nina, I've got to talk with Nina first.* She'd cab down Seventh to the Village. *She might not be home.* Annison dug into her pocketbook and found her cell-phone. She pressed the talk button and said, *Nina,* and the phone magically called her.

"Hello?"

"Nina."

"Hey, Annie B'nannie," Nina yawned.

"Are you still in bed?"

"Uh huh."

Annison heard a soft cough and a rustle of bedding, sounding like it was coming from next to Nina. "Oh," she said coyly, "you're still *in bed.*"

"Mm hmm," Nina paused, "Say hello to Annison."

A sugary voice came on the line, "Hello, Annison."

"You see?" Nina had the phone back.

"She sounds young."

"Adorably so."

"You nasty old woman you."

"Absolutely." Nina muffled something to her consort and Annison could hear her getting out of bed. Nina fluffed the pillows behind her and sat up against the headboard, "Where are you?"

"In the City, at Penn Station."

"Back so soon?"

"Yeah."

"Why?"

"Well, it's kind of a long story."

"Oh Oh!"

"I was thinking of going shopping and thought you might want to come along."

"What happened?" Nina knew her friend well.

"Nothing, I just thought you might ..."

"Annnnison." Nina said.

"I, I've got a lot to tell you."

"Tell me."

"I thought we might meet for breakfast?"

"Tell me now," Nina, the no-nonsense businesswoman.

"I can't, it's too complicated."

"Yes you can, just open your mouth and speak to me."

Silence.

Nina said, "It's fucking Jack, right?! He got to you!"

Annison was sitting on the cement bench, on her ineffective newspaper cushion, almost in a fetal position, with her shoulders hunched, the cell phone pressed to one ear and her free hand absentmindedly twisting her coffee cup round and round on the cool bench.

"Sarah's pregnant."

"Well," a pause, "congratulations." Another pause. "You don't sound too thrilled though. Is she alright?"

"Yes, she's fine, they're doing fine, and they're both very excited."

"And the Grandma to be?"

"I'm happy for her."

"So where's your enthusiasm?"

A woman in a long coat took a seat on the crescent-shaped bench across the piazza from where Annison sat. She had on one of those bandana scarves pulled over her head and tied beneath her chin. She looked old but may not have been, her lack of make-up giving her a worn, grayish countenance. She opened her coat and removed a plastic bag, a bread bag. She was immediately welcomed by the barrage of pigeons. They pecked at the breadcrumbs she parceled out sparingly to them; taking her time, making the morning last. A smile came onto her face, removing the gray. She spoke to the birds and seemed to be happy.

"I have enthusiasm, it's just ..."

"Just what?"

"I hope she's going to be happy."

"Don't you think she is?"

"Yes, I do. I just don't want her to end up like me."

"And how are you?"

"Confused and lost at middle age."

"Hey, you're hardly middle-aged. If you're middle-aged then that would make me middle-aged too, and I'm not. So cut out that crap. Besides, Sarah didn't have to get married remember? She took her time and found the right guy, not like her mother. So you see, she's not like you, she's smarter."

"Very funny."

"It's not funny, Dahling, it's just the facts. You were never in love with Jack."

"I wouldn't say that. We were in love once, at least in the beginning, maybe still."

"What?! What did you just say?!"

"Not like that. I mean, you know, in a family kind of way."

"No, I don't know. What the hell are you saying?"

"We'll always be a family, I can't lose that, especially now. I wouldn't want my grandchild coming into the world into a broken family."

"Annison, what are you saying, not into a broken family? What does that mean? You didn't reconcile with that bastard did you?!"

"No, I wouldn't say that exactly, but you wouldn't believe the job he's done at the Inn." She went on to tell her of the unexpected good things she'd encountered on her return to Barrett's Bluff. She told Nina of how Jack had gotten the children to the Inn and how surprised and excited they all had been at Sarah's news.

"That's low. That's below the belt. That inconsiderate, self-centered son of a bitch!" Nina was heated. "Family crisis! Bullshit! Jack's *ass* crisis is more like it. I can't believe how low that prick will stoop. You didn't actually fall for that crap did you?"

"What crap?"

"Oh Annie, pleeease tell me you're kidding. Don't you see? All he wants is you back with him so he can continue being the major fuck-off that he is. I'm sure he finagled some way of dazzling everyone, of keeping the Inn running smoothly. Hell, that's a testimonial to your influence. It's *your* blood and sweat that's influencing business, keeping it going while you were away, not Jack. He's just a lucky conniving bastard and always will be. What happened to you up there? You're not falling backwards are you?"

"No, I'm not!" Annison shot back at her sharply.

"Then *what* are you saying to me?"

"I didn't expect things to be the way they were, that's all. Everything running so smoothly. Maybe my little sabbatical was good for everyone, you know, even snapped Jack into shape. He's so excited about being a grand dad."

"Uhhh." Nina sighed heavily.

"And me too, I mean, *wow*, a grandmother."

"I don't like the sound of this."

"Of what? Me being a grandmother?"

"No, of you talking so highly of Jack. Tell me you're not thinking of going back there."

"Why do you ask that?"

"Your tone of voice, what you're saying to me and how you're saying it."

Silence.

"What about Maddison? Huh? Do you remember telling me just a few days ago that you were in love? Engaged for chrissakes!"

"Of course I do, and I am."

"You were so happy. Don't let fucking Jack talk you …"

"I'm not!" Annison sounded angry. "Dammit! It's not about Jack." The solo guest suite flashed through her mind. "It's about Sarah and her baby and J.J. and being a family, being there for them, being a family."

Nina was upset, "I don't get it Annison, you go away for …"

"Of course you don't get it! You don't have a family," her voice was raised, "you have no idea what it's like, what it takes to be a mother. No idea!"

"Nice, very nice. Thank you so much."

"So don't try to lecture me about who I am or what I'm doing or not doing!"

"Don't get pissy with me Dahling."

"And don't *Dahling* me! You can be so condescending at times."

Annison was up and pacing on the flat bricks of the piazza. Her quick movements startled the pigeons and they jumped into the air and settled a few feet away. The lady feeding them looked at her forlornly then threw her breadcrumbs over to where the birds had lighted.

"You're taking it out on me."

"What?"

"Your anger with yourself, with your indecision."

"Bullshit."

"Bullshit? You go away for a month, seclude yourself to do some soul-searching, fall in love, design this whole new utopian life-style for yourself, make incredible personal advancement, and then what? Allow yourself to go back to the shitty life you're trying to run away from? Allow yourself to be manipulated once again? And you don't think you're indecisive?"

"I know what I'm doing."

"Yeah? What are you doing?"

"I'm going to have a talk with Dodge. Tell him what's going on with me and find out what's going on with him."

"Are you having doubts about your relationship with Dodge now?"

"No, I know how I feel about him. That I'm sure about. I just need to discuss some things with him, that's all."

"Like?"

"Like maybe we're moving too fast. Maybe he's moving too fast."

"Oh Christ. Little Miss Insecure again."

"Oh, fuck you, Nina!"

"There you go. Now you're getting it out."

"Stop it!" she shouted. "Stop it!" The pigeons were really alarmed now. First by the hasty pacing, which they'd just learned to deal with, and now the shouting. It was too much. They flew off high in a tight pack, back to the safety of their lofty roost. The woman with the breadcrumbs got disgusted and flew off too.

"You aren't holier than thou," Annison yelled into the cell phone, "your life isn't better than everyone else's."

"I never said it was. But at least I know who I am and what I want, and I deal with it. Something you seem to be having a problem with."

Annison was biting her lower lip trying to control her rising anger. She didn't want to say something to Nina that she'd later regret.

Nina said, "Sweetie, I didn't think this possible, but I think you may be more fucked-up now than you were before you retreated to the lake."

"You don't get it do you? You just don't get it. I can't explain it to you, Nina. Your world is so removed from mine. I have obligations."

"Christ, you called me to wallow in self-pity again? Don't get melancholy on me."

"I'm not." Annison sat down hard on the bench. "I shouldn't have called you, I'm sorry I did. This is my problem. I can't expect you to understand. Go back to your little plaything and your damn carefree I-don't-give-a-shit lifestyle."

"Hey!"

"No, fuck it, Nina," Annison was shaking, her whole body trembling, "forget I called, I should have known better. How could I expect a lesbian to have any understanding of what I'm going through?"

"Oh, that's nice! Very smooth. And I thought you had finally grown up, but I guess timid little girls who like to play house never really come into their own. Especially those who have everything handed to them. All they have to do is whore themselves to men with family money or famous fashion designers. Poor, poor Annie, has everything she needs but can't find herself."

"Oh fuck you Nina!" she punched off the call so violently that her cell phone fell from her hands and slid across the piazza like a flat stone skimming atop the water.

"You little shit!" Nina yelled into her phone.

"Me, Nina?" Nina's young friend said innocently, reentering the bedroom carrying a tray of coffees and buttered muffins.

"No honey, not you," she replaced the phone on its cradle. "Come here," she patted the bed mattress, "sit next to me."

Annison sat on her bench feeling small, crying with her head in her hands. It was a long cry. The walkway surrounding her got busier with the advancing morning. No one noticed her. People scurried to and fro on their own missions with their own thoughts. They had their own lives to deal with. The sun sneaked around the buildings and washed onto the high windows making them glare with hot blinding flashes of fire. The day would be bright, easily conquering the gloom of human emotion. Nature could do that.

# 38

## *SPEECHLESS CONFRONTATION*

Saturday morning business at *Lady Maddison* was usually brisk and today was no exception. The inevitable cool weather of Fall had arrived and it was time for the ladies to address their winter wardrobes. Roberto stood at his post in the corner doorway of the *Maddison Designs* building wearing his impeccably tailored black woolen topcoat and his trademark white gloves. He was as friendly and courteous as ever receiving his morning customers in their taxis and limos, one by one rounding the corner into SoHo, pulling to the curb and alighting onto the bright fuchsia carpeting. Roberto was greeting the Winston's from Park Avenue, Carolyn and her daughter Hilary, when he took notice of the yellow checker cab pulling close behind the Winston's car. It looked as if it would be next in line but the cab only hesitated and swung around advancing to the side of the building. Roberto escorted the ladies to the door of the boutique then returned to the curb - it was only three or four steps with his long stride. The Winston's driver had already moved away. Roberto watched the checker pull tight to the curb at the far end of the building near Dodge's private entrance. A moment later the trunk popped open and the cabbie got out and retrieved a leather carry bag and placed it on the sidewalk. He shut the trunk, opened the rear door and leaned in procuring a pink shopping bag with white straw handles and set that next to the other bag. Roberto recognized the *Victoria's Secret* logo. He also recognized the lady exiting the cab. It was Annison. He smiled and gave her a wave but she didn't see him. From the distance he watched her pick up her belongings and cross the sidewalk to the discreet unmarked doorway that was Dodge's private street-side entrance, accessing the elevator that took you directly to his penthouse loft. He watched her entering the security code onto the keypad at the doorjamb and gritted his teeth. He knew what awaited her up there, but it was none of his business. A car horn moaned behind him, he hadn't realized he'd taken a few steps away from the carpet. He felt a need to call out to her, to distract her from the doorway, from the penthouse. None of his business. But upon meeting her the other day he had taken an immediate liking to her. He decided to warn her. Roberto turned and motioned *just-a-minute* to the white town-car behind him and then turned back around calling out to her. It was too late. She'd already disappeared into the building. *Well*, he shook his head sadly, *I sure hope he knows what he's doing. I like that lady.*

The retired freight elevator made its way slowly up the dark shaft at the rear corner of the old Silverman & Sons building that Dodge had begun his career in so long ago. Old and rickety, it was no longer used for freight and now had only three stops on it; Garage, Boutique, and Penthouse. Dodge had had a larger, code adherent freight elevator installed at the back of the building accessible from the alley.

The private lift bypassed the boutique, the manufacturing floors and the Level 5 Studio, and brought Annison directly into the far end of the penthouse loft. She slid the black antique elevator gate to the side and entered upon the wide-plank flooring. The sunlight that had been snarling around the taller buildings in mid-town had a more formidable presence on the lower rooftops in SoHo and streamed generously through the oversized skylights of Dodge Maddison's expansive apartment. The sun-enriched colors of the wood floor spread before her like a calm golden sea as Annison walked across the ocean into the open living area. She dropped her bag on the couch and placed the *Victoria's Secret* parcel carefully next to it on the floor.

Annison unbuttoned her coat and was loosening the silk scarf tied around her neck when she heard the music. It was coming from the bedroom. Unmistakedly. Not loud, but heavily rhythmic. Contemporary; hip-hop, like what they played in the nouveau uptown clubs at night. She smiled. He was here. He must have taken an earlier flight home, to be with her sooner she wistfully surmised. Eagerly her steps took her into the bedroom. And that's where she saw her, Dana, standing naked at the dresser, with her back to her.

Annison stopped dead in her tracks. She heard the shower running in the master bath and looked instinctively towards it, her eyes scanning the unmade bed. The pillows were tussled and the bed sheets lay in a heap at the foot. There was a champagne bottle, upside down, in a silver bucket on the floor next to the bed. A long-stemmed champagne glass laid on its side next it. Another sat atop the nightstand next to a petite silver cell phone. Her heart rose to a lump in her throat.

With the music, Dana had not heard Annison's approach. Now, as she straightened and pushed the drawer closed with the front of her thighs, she saw her in the mirror. Dana turned and the two women faced each other. Annison in her jeans and sweater with her unbuttoned coat and Dana, unashamed, wearing her nakedness like a freshly donned design.

"Well," Dana said in a long sigh, "hello."

Introductions didn't need to be made, each woman instantly recognized the other. Dana was a renowned fashion model who graced the covers of magazines and lauded various cosmetics on TV; and Annison was Dodge's newest love interest, the rumors and the tabloids hadn't bypassed Dana, she knew all too well who this Annison Barrett was.

Frozen in the doorway, Annison locked her eyes onto Dana's and stared. Peripherally she saw her naked body, tanned, perfectly tanned, with not a tan line to be found. Dana was showing it off in a self-assured manner. Cocky even, as she leaned her tightened buttocks against the bureau and casually placed one ankle across the other, undaunted, brazenly exhibiting her ultra-thin, ultra-toned model's body. She rested her hands on the bureau top on either side of her. A pair of lace panties dangled from one hand. She let Annison absorb the scene, wanting her to be embarrassed by her wares.

She was. Annison saw before her the uncompromising elements of Dodge Maddison's world.

Her gaze cast off the model's dramatic temperament and landed on the bathroom doorway.

Dana smirked, "Are you looking for Dodge?"

Annison had no response. She had nothing.

Steam poured thick from the doorway like a rolling fog wafting into the bedroom on the waves of the beating music.

"He's *unavailable* at the moment," the vixen continued, "but I *may* be able to get a message to him later," she paused for effect and ended, "*if* you'd like."

Annison's heart bled.

She wanted to feel anger.

But instead, she felt nothing.

And without a word, she left.

Dana triumphantly sauntered behind Annison's retreating footsteps, scorching the wide-plank flooring as she stormed through the loft and entered the lift. Dana stood next to the couch and watched the elevator gate close and a moment later her rival was lowered away from her world.

"Well," she said aloud, "that was *too* easy."

Dana noticed the package on the floor. Annison had grabbed her bag on her way through, but had left the *Vicky's* bag. Dana opened it and pulled away the pink tissue paper and held up the lacey lingerie.

"Oh my. Size small? That would just *hang* off me." She laughed and took the lingerie and the bag over to the kitchen and tossed them into the trash.

In classic runway style, Dana strutted across the loft, re-entered the bedroom, gave the volume control knob a healthy twist and danced toward the shower.

# 39

## *The Swells At Sea*

"Y'know," Harlow said, "even with all the exhausting business we conducted in the past few days, I had a good time."

They were standing outside the terminal at JFK Airport awaiting the shuttle that would take her to the long-term parking area.

"So did I," Dodge responded.

He stood in the midst of their luggage on the sidewalk. He was going to take a cab into the City and Harlow would drive back home tonight to her house on Long Island.

She started laughing.

"What?"

"I was just thinking of Giovanni's reaction when you said you wanted the piece goods dyed and shipped in forty-eight hours."

"I know," Dodge laughed. "He jumped up and started racing around the table yakking away in Italian. It was like Ricky Riccardo when he gets all flustered with Lucy and jabbers away in Cuban."

"He was so funny, like Danny DiVito going around in circles saying *No, No, cannot do, impossible, cannot do.*"

"And then when he left the room, I had no idea what to think."

"You were fine a minute later when he came back with that gigantic bottle of wine though."

"Hey, I didn't see you refusing."

"How big was that anyway?"

"Must have been a gallon."

"He was so funny, pouring himself the first glass and guzzling it down like a shot. And only then did he fill our glasses."

"That's Giovanni. That's how he conducts business. You always know he's serious when he brings the vino out."

Harlow dropped her head softly onto his shoulder. "That was very nice of him to offer his home to us. I love staying there. It's such a beautiful house and Milan is such a beautiful city."

"And let's not forget about Maria's cooking."

"Oh my God, she's sensational."

"Giovanni is a lucky man to have her, she's a wonderful woman."

Dodge rested his arm atop Harlow's shoulders. Their bodies were back in New York but their minds and spirits were still swimming in the charms of Italy.

"So, what time is your flight tomorrow?" he asked her.

"Twelve fifteen, which is good 'cuz I'll have the morning to pack and water the plants and clean up a little before I have to come back here." Harlow was on vacation next week. She was flying to California. She owned a bungalow right on Malibu Beach with her two best friends Michele and Kristin. They all lived and careered in different parts of the country now, but kept their little beach house for vacations and impromptu get-togethers. The first few years after they had bought, they had rented it out seasonally to help with the mortgage. But after experiencing a horror story with the "tenants from hell" (which had necessitated some extensive remodeling) they decided it more prudent to keep it just for themselves. Besides, by then their careers were blossoming and they could afford to. Michele lived the closest to their bungalow, three hundred miles south in San Diego and was thus the designated caretaker, trying to check on it once a month or so. Kristin was six hours away in Phoenix and Harlow a flight away in New York.

This rendezvous was a planned vacation for the three of them, an R&R away from the job stress. Harlow had been working hard, especially while Dodge had been away from the office on his little sabbatical, and she was looking forward to California. A lot had happened emotionally to her during that time and she needed to get away and just be with the girls.

"I can't wait," she said with a false enthusiasm, suppressing her habitual fantasy of being at the California beach house alone with Dodge. But she knew he was going back to Annison and she needed to learn to live with that. She was hoping that getting away from New York for a while would help.

"I hope you have a great time," Dodge said. "You've earned it. Say hello to Michele and Kristin for me."

Different colored shuttle buses with various rental agency logos drifted past them. Eventually the parking lot shuttle came and Harlow got on. Dodge handed in her luggage and the driver put it in the rack behind his seat. The bus pulled away and she waved to him from her seat at the window. He waved back to her and then signaled a taxi.

"SoHo," he said and the cabbie headed for the bright lights of the City.

\* \* \*

Annison's name hadn't been mentioned. Not once during their business trip. But now in the solitude of the taxicab, Dodge smiled. *Annison.* Her name hadn't been on his lips, but she had been in his mind. Always. Prevalently. He was aching to be with her. He had missed her. He wondered if she had gone to the apartment or was still at Nina's. He called her from the cab. They could go out to dinner. No, he was too tired from the flight and the jet lag. They'd order in. Chinese maybe. Whatever she liked. There was no answer. He knew she'd asked him to call her when he returned and that she was probably out to dinner with Nina, but he wishfully speculated that she was at his place, in the shower maybe. That's why she didn't answer. He left her a message telling her he had landed and was on his way home, *give me a call when you pick up this message*, and pushed end on his cell phone. He hoped things had gone okay at Barrett's Bluff. Hoped there hadn't been any problems with her husband, hoped the kids had been understanding. They had a lot to talk about. A lot to catch up on. A lot to plan for. He wondered how the farmhouse was coming along. Maybe they could drive up tomorrow and check progress. Have dinner with Ben and Carlene. He'd done well in Milan, handled the crisis. They'd meet all their shipping obligations for holiday. He could afford to spend some time back in Bryce Corner. Harlow could handle everything in the City. *Harlow.*

It was past eight o'clock when Dodge paid his fare and entered the doorway to his private elevator. Riding up, his heart began to flutter. She hadn't returned his call yet, but he was excited and couldn't wait to see her. If she was out to dinner with Nina, maybe he could grab a quick shower and meet them at the restaurant.

He reached the top floor and entered the loft apartment. The lighting was dim. The dining table was set with two chairs placed next each other on the corners. Tall white candles burned in their brass holders. Soft jazz hummed in surround-sound. Romantic. She was here.

She hadn't answered his call because she wanted to surprise him. He smiled. He was pleased.

He dropped his things on the couch and eagerly ventured to the far end and entered the bedroom. She was lounging on the bed, sitting Indian-style in front of the pillows propped against the headboard. She was wearing a pair of his silk boxers and one of his white broadcloth dress shirts, unbuttoned, the white accenting the tanned copper of her chest. The sleeves were bunched up on her forearms and she held her silver cell phone to one ear. She saw him and spoke *gotta go* into it and threw the phone onto the bed. In a mili-second she sprang off the mattress and jumped onto him feet first. Dodge grabbed onto her to prevent the both of them from falling over. With her long legs wrapped around him she showered his head with kisses and squeaked into his ear, "Baby, Baby, Baby! I'm soooo glad to see you! Mmmm," she smacked a kiss on his cheek with her puffy lips.

He hadn't expected her. He really hadn't expected her.

"Dana," he said, "what are you doing here?"

"I'm kissing you, you silly man. Surprised to see me?"

"Dana, we've got to talk."

He made a motion to set her down but her arms and legs were wrapped tightly around him. "Ohhh! You feel so good!" she screeched.

"Dana," he struggled to release her hold on him, "please. Get down. We need to talk."

"Not now, Baby," she arched her back and dropped her head over backwards almost to the floor like a figure skater with her legs scissored around her partner. The white shirt, trailing on the floor, hung open, displaying her petite breasts, her tiny pink nipples erect.

"Put me down on the bed," she said seductively, "let's talk later."

"No Dana, now," his voice serious and commanding.

She tightened her leg grip and pulled herself up, sitting on his waist with her hands dangling to the sides. She puffed her lower lip out and pouted. "Why are you so mean to me?"

"I'm not trying to be mean to you."

"You've been avoiding me."

"I've been extremely busy."

"So I've heard."

"Dana, listen ..."

She reached a hand behind her and felt for him beneath her buttocks.

"Dana, don't."

She giggled and reached her other hand in front of her between her legs and grabbed onto his belt buckle. "Come on lover, take me to bed."

He reached forward to grab onto her hands but she lunged her body backward, knocking him off balance and forcing their entwined bodies to fall onto the bed. Wiry and strong for her size, Dana manipulated Dodge into the center of the mattress and climbed on top of him pulling at his clothes.

"You've been a naughty boy, Mister Maddison. Not returning my calls ... having an affair behind my back ..." she tore open his shirt and pulled on his belt, "I think you need to be punished."

Dodge lay on the bed, his arms at his sides. Almost inaudibly he said, "We can't do this."

Dana had his belt unbuckled. She unzipped him. She slid both her hands onto him, pleased to feel his swelling in her palms.

"We can't?" she snickered.

"No!" he sat up, grabbing her forearms and forcing her hands away from him. "We can't." He held her tightly until she calmed. "I need to have a conversation with you, but not now." Gently he placed his hands on her waist and moved her off him. Her fight was gone. He got off the bed and stood with his back to her readjusting his pants. "You can't be here now."

"Dodge, I *am* here."

"We need to set a time to talk, maybe next week sometime, I'll..."

"Why not now?"

He turned, tucking his shirt into his waistband. She was leaning her back against the pillows, the blouse open and her legs drawn up so that her feet were heel to heel. She was exercising her legs in a butterfly motion.

"Because," he said as an answer.

"Are you expecting someone?"

He looked her straight in the eye and said, "Yes."

Dodge sat on his bed next to her. When her legs butterflyed into the up position he placed his hands on her knees and stopped them.

"I know all about her Dodge. I may be blonde but I'm not stupid."

"I wanted to talk with you. I really wasn't avoiding you."

"Right!"

"Things were hectic and I was busy."

"Busy with what?"

He took a deep breath and released it slowly out his nostrils, "Falling in love, I guess."

"Oh God," Dana rolled her eyes.

"So much has happened. Ever since the funeral I ..."

"Which you didn't want me to attend!"

"I know, I admit that. But it wasn't for the reasons that you think. I just needed that time alone."

"Alone? Like alone with Harlow?"

"I don't want to argue with you, Dana. It's not a good time. I've just come in from Europe, I'm tired and ..."

"And you're expecting *her*."

"Yes."

"Who is she, Dodge?"

"I think you already know."

"Say her name."

"Dana ..."

"Say it!"

"Annison Barrett."

"The one you were in Vermont with? And *here* from what I've been told!"

Dodge liked her still. He saw her there in front of him, hurt and fighting for her place in his life. But he saw her differently. Still young and so beautiful. He could look at her now and think of Annison. Without any guilt. He was sorry if he'd hurt her. They'd shared some wonderful times together. But he knew she'd rebound. She'd be fine. Probably sooner than later.

"I, I'm sorry if I hurt you Dana, I truly didn't mean to. But I must be honest with you, I've fallen in love."

"Oh fuck you! Fuck you Dodge Maddison!" She leaped from the bed and ran to the bathroom.

\* \* \*

Ten minutes later, Dana walked out of the bedroom. She was dressed in jeans and a turtleneck sweater and wore a short black leather jacket. She was composed; the consummate model. Her face painted with a bright smile. She carried a flowered overnight bag over her shoulder.

He was standing in the kitchen holding a cup of coffee. He'd made a pot while she was gathering her things. He went from feeling bad to feeling alright about it to feeling bad again. He hadn't wanted it to end this way. He was methodical and organized in every aspect of his life, except his women. His relationships somehow never seemed to fit snugly

312

into his scheme of things. They had an uncontrollable mind of their own. And he hated this part. He was never good at this part of it.

She came to him across the darkness of the room. He hadn't turned any lights on. The candles still glowed on the table. The flames sauntered back and forth in the wake of Dana's passing stride and lent a surreal presence to the shadows of the large room making it teeter and totter like a ship bobbing in the swells at sea.

He didn't know what to expect and he didn't know what to say. She stood a moment before him, not sad, but something. And then she smiled and kissed him gently on the cheek, letting the kiss linger.

"If you ever change your mind," she said softly, "find me."

He didn't watch her leave. He heard her footsteps go to the lift. He heard the hum of the elevator. He listened to the silence arrive with the light jazz behind it. He put the coffee cup down on the counter and took a bottle of white wine from the fridge and a glass from the rack over the sink and walked across the room.

# 40

## *AGAIN THE MACHINE*

"Hi, it's Dodge ... anyone there? ... It's about ten-thirty, I got in a couple of hours ago, and ... hey, you two go out to dinner without me?" he laughed. "Okay, I guess you're not there. Give me a call, Annie, when you get in."

He had told her his flight itinerary, saying he'd probably be back in the city by eight o'clock, but you never knew about delays. He wanted to have dinner together and she had said she wasn't sure what time she'd be back either, but if it was early, she'd probably have dinner with Nina. He wondered for a second if she'd come while Dana was here, but dismissed it being certain that Dana would have said something.

He sat in the dim apartment listening for the sound of the elevator being activated. He'd showered and was wearing casual drawstring pants and a long sleeved cotton pullover. The sleeves were bunched up on his forearms. He sat on the couch watching the candles shorten. At midnight he tried her cell phone again, and again got no response. He left another message at Nina's. Overtired and mellowed by two glasses of wine, he fell asleep.

He didn't wake until nine-thirty the next morning. He rose from the couch and stretched. The candles had extinguished themselves and the room was now lit with a bright day. The satellite music was still playing soft jazz, but he changed it to light classical and made a pot of coffee. He tried her cell phone again, and then Nina's house - both to no avail. Now he was concerned. He thought they might have gone out together, maybe even to a club and gotten in too late to return his calls, but what? They'd had too much fun and were still asleep? Maybe. He chuckled to himself. Nina probably took her out on the town. They'd probably had a great time. Maybe things had gone well for Annison back in Connecticut and they'd gone out to celebrate. *Those two*, he laughed. Dodge took his coffee into the bedroom, picked out some clothes for the day, and then took a fresh shower.

A half-hour later he was downstairs wandering around the shop. It was Sunday and *Lady Maddison* didn't open 'til noon. The staff wouldn't arrive until eleven and he liked the quiet time alone to peruse his shop, to be with his baby and see how she was doing. He hadn't done this since the Paris premiere, just before his grandparents died. The store looked fresh and inviting. He had a great manager and you could see she took pride in her work. The shop was immaculately clean, the displays were perfect and the storefront windows spotless and displayed with attractively adorned mannequins. He checked the sales receipts from yesterday and was pleased with the week-ending figures. The retail end of the business was only a fraction of the whole, the manufacturing and wholesale being far superior, but he liked the boutique. He was proud of it. You could buy his wares uptown in the department stores and across the country in the fancier malls, but the shop was a special place. There was part of him here. And he admired the women who made the special effort to shop here. And it was they who were on his mind when he sat at his drawing table sketching new designs. Something he needed to do again soon. He realized he'd been away from it too long and the next line needed to be put to bed soon.

He went to the Studio on Level 5 and walked around checking the design boards of his young designers. Fletcher Ross, his design-team leader, had a vast assortment of new sketches. Dodge leafed through them and saw some interesting things. He'd been working hard in his absence, they all had. He made a mental note to have a design meeting Monday. They'd been doing a great job and he wanted to commend them. And judging by what he saw, he felt confident that he could handle the design end of the business from Bryce Corner. Maybe one-day-a-week trips into the City to keep everyone on track and the business cohesive. He thought of the lake house and the idea of it as his design studio and of running his business from a distance and all that that would entail. He thought of the farmhouse as a Bed & Breakfast and of Annison running that and how happy she'd be, how happy they'd be together. It could work. It would work. He checked his watch. It was almost eleven o'clock, *they must be up by now.* He ascended the spiral staircase to his loft apartment and called Nina's. Again the machine.

"Good morning sleepy-heads. It's time to get up and smell the coffee." He waited for someone to pick up the phone. "Hey, come on, you guys can't still be in bed. It's almost noontime," he exaggerated.

When it actually became noontime he left the building and took a cab to the Village. He pushed the intercom at Nina's doorway and spoke into it. He still didn't get anywhere. He was sitting on the stoop when Nina walked up to him. She had an attractive girl on her arm.

"Hi," Nina said.

"Good morning," he rose, "or good afternoon, actually."

"This is Lavender," Nina introduced her companion, "and this is Dodge Maddison."

"Hi," Lavender smiled, keeping both her arms intimately wrapped around Nina's right arm.

"Hello."

"Doesn't she have a beautiful name?" Nina offered.

"Yes, very."

"Sweetie," Nina said to Lavender, "how about you go on in. I'd like to talk to Mr. Maddison for a minute."

"Sure," Lavender kissed her on the cheek and went up the stairs.

"Girlfriend," Nina said and Lavender turned to look at her, "The access code. It's g-i-r-l-f-r-i-e-n-d."

She punched it in and disappeared into the house.

"I got your message late last night. Messages I should say. But it was very late by the time we got home."

By 'we', Dodge knew she meant Lavender.

Nina sat on the stoop and he did the same. The day was sunny and the sun had warmed the stone steps. It was cool, but they were warm in the sun.

"I'm afraid I don't know where she is, Dodge."

"What do you mean?"

"We had a fight."

"A fight?"

"Just a girly fight. It'll blow over."

"When?"

"Yesterday, yesterday morning. She called me from Penn Station around ten o'clock."

"She was back in the City yesterday morning?" he was confused.

"Yes."

"Did things go alright for her back home?"

"Well, there were some good things and some bad." Nina told him of their conversation; how things had gone at Barrett's Bluff, the surprises she had encountered, Sarah's pregnancy.

"That must have made her happy."

"Yes, that part did, but it may be a double-edged sword."

"How so?"

"Dodge, I'm going to level with you. Annison is my closest friend and I love her without reservation. I would do anything for her. But there are things she has to do herself. When she came to me last summer and poured her heart out, we came up with the idea for her self-imposed rehab at the lake in Massachusetts. I was so proud of her when she actually did it. That was a big step for her. And it did wonders for her. But, meeting you and falling in love with you wasn't on the agenda. That said, I think it was the best thing that's ever happened to her and I believe without hesitation that she is deeply in love with you. Hey, even I like you," she laughed trying to lighten his mood. But he sat quiet on the step next to her. She could tell he was bewildered, a million things racing through his mind.

"I like you and Annison," she continued, "there's something classically romantic about the two of you; the way you met, the point in your lives that you're at, what you've done together, the decisions you've made, and all in such a short period of time. Very romantic."

"What happened, Nina? Where is she?"

"Well, that's the bad news. On the one hand, she is her own person; vibrant and alive, fun, a joy to be around. But, of course you know all that. What you don't know, I suspect, is the Annison Barrett tied to the Inn, to Barrett's Bluff, to the security of her family. She has this," she thought for a moment, "this uncanny habit of spreading her wings and taking flight, a beautiful soaring flight, and then, this, this character flaw comes into play and she thinks she doesn't deserve her wings, and she tumbles back to the sanctity of her earthbound life."

"I don't have a clue what you're saying, Nina. All I want to know is what happened and where she is. I've got to see her."

"What happened is that she went back there and fell into her old habits again, buffered by the ploys of her fucking-selfish-conniving-bastard husband."

"But, I don't understand. She wants to get away from that whole scene. She's so thrilled with the Bed and Breakfast idea. It must be more than that."

"It's the shell-shock too."

"What?"

"You've got to realize that only a few weeks ago she was deep in her own personal therapy, cleansing her soul and becoming a new woman. That's when the two of you met. She was ripe for a new relationship. And wonderfully so. But reality has a hard edge to it and I don't think she's quite rounded it yet."

"Where does the shell-shock come in?"

"Part of it is Sarah's news. That jolted her back into her motherly responsibility thing. She's always carried the weight of the family on her shoulders. She's the only one who ever did. Maybe she feels she has to compensate for her shit-ass husband, I don't know, but she's very protective of Sarah and wants desperately for her marriage to work."

"That I understand. What's the other part?"

"You, your world. She's having a hard time allowing herself to fit in. It's not that she doesn't want to or that she can't, I think it's just that she's been so overwhelmed in such a short time. She said she thinks you may be moving too fast."

"She said that to you?"

"Yes, it came up in our brief conversation. She wanted to talk with you about it."

"Do you think she's sorry?" Nina knew he meant about their relationship.

"No. I think she's truly in love with you. But it might take some time for her head to catch up with her heart."

"I don't know, Nina. I realize you've known her much longer than I, but I just don't see the weaker side of her that you're portraying. She seems so sure and steadfast to me. We've had some deep talks and made some challenging decisions together, I just don't ..." Dodge lifted his shoulders and held them there, shaking his head slowly back and forth, chewing on his bottom lip. Nina sat quiet while he struggled with the pieces. Finally he said, "We've talked about our worlds, a lot. I think she's comfortable with who we are and who we want to become," he looked over at her, "don't you?"

Nina raised her eyebrows with an expression of sarcasm that said, *what do you think?* She said, "You're in a big world Dodge, much bigger than hers, with many more people, especially women."

"Do you think she's jealous?" he asked as if the only answer was no.

"Do you?"

"No, of course not."

"And what about Dana?"

"There's nothing there. She knows that. We've talked about it. I've had my conversation with Dana and it's over. It never really began."

"And Harlow?"

"She knows about our relationship, it's purely business." Why did he feel so defensive?

"Apparently it may not always present itself in a purely business manner."

Maybe Annison had told Nina more than he knew about.

Dodge went on, "Harlow and I are close friends that have known each other a long time. The passion we share is for the business, nothing else." He felt an irony as he said this. An irony or dishonesty? He'd never told Annison about what had happened between him and Harlow. It didn't matter really. They'd shared a moment and had moved on from it; without regrets, without guilt and without obligation. And besides, that had been before he had fallen in love with Annison.

"She's never said she was jealous." Dodge got contemplative.

Nina said, "Women are always jealous. Even when they say they're not, they are."

A minute passed.

"You didn't see her at all yesterday?"

"No."

"And she didn't stay with you last night?"

"No."

"Where do you think she is?"

Nina took in a deep breath and exhaled it slowly through her puckered lips. "If she didn't go to you, then I have this sick feeling that she's returned to Barrett's Bluff."

Her words fell on him with an unpleasant weight.

"But I don't understand. That doesn't make sense."

"Not to you maybe. Dodge, understand, Annison's always had a cushy life, not totally happy perhaps, but she's always been able to control everything around her. You come along at just the precise moment in her life when she's metamorphosing and sweep her off the ground and she flutters off to fairy tale land. A wonderful, exciting place with a handsome prince. Happily ever after. Then her world beckons to her again and she can't say no. Back she goes. Regressing to the comfort of false security."

"I cannot believe that." He was up and pacing in small circles, "She disappears on me, won't answer my calls, tosses away everything we are, just like that?" he snapped his fingers. "I will not accept that."

"It's her M.O. She's done it numerous times in her past."

"But we've shared too much, given so much of ourselves to one another. We're in love."

"Sucks doesn't it?"

Dodge glared at her. Nina rose and placed her hands on his forearms, making him stand still. He was amazed by her strength. Her hold was strong.

"Give her time," Nina said, "she'll be back. Let her sort it out on her own. Let her come back to you. Better for her to expunge the demons from her system once and for all, than for you to go fetch her away from them. It'd only start over at some other time in your future together." She could tell from the way his arms were tensed that he wasn't listening to her. He was upset. His testosterone wanted him to lash out and strike at something. Ride on his armored horse into the castle at Barrett's Bluff, slay his enemy Jack and steal away with the fair damsel.

And that was exactly what he was thinking.

"Don't do it, Dodge," she knew his thoughts. "Give her the room. Let her come to you."

# 41

## *CLUES*

Dodge walked away from Nina Sanderson and her advice. He didn't believe in her assessment, nor did he view Annison Barrett in the same vein that she did. True, he had known her only a fraction of the time Nina had, but he felt that he knew her better. They had shared something intrinsic. Deep. Soul touching.

He walked across Bleecker and along the next block of Grove Street until he stood on the corner of Seventh Avenue South trying to make sense of it all, struggling with the overtones of Nina's conversation. An eclectic mix of people grew around him waiting on the light. Traffic on the one-way avenue whisked by. When the 'walk' sign appeared Dodge blended with the pedestrians, moving with them, helplessly drawn into their wake, across the street and down along West 4th Street deeper into Greenwich Village.

Why hadn't she returned his calls? What was she afraid of? Was she angry with him? Why? What had he missed? He needed to speak with her, desperately. He was angry with himself that he had forgotten to bring his cell phone. He wanted to call her now. He needed to get through to her.

He continued along West 4th with its diverse offerings of small shops and impromptu eating establishments. Celestial Café; The Erotic Bakery; Sue Me Shushi; Rick's Comix. Clues. *There had to be clues.* Bitchen Kitchen Supply; The Lacy Victorian; Own Lee Books; West 4th Pizzeria.

In Vermont he had had misgivings about her, about the Woodstock Inn thing, but they had resolved that. Bumping into the Beaumont's and the Vaughn's. Neither one of them enjoyed that, but they did well. Except for Gail. Maybe the Scene Around article bothered Annison. He was used to things like that, part of the territory. Maybe Annison just didn't …

Dodge played over and over in his mind different scenarios that might justify her behavior. He kept coming up blank. Barrow Street, Jones Street, Cornelia Street, none of them gave him a helping thought as he drifted past them and walked across MacDougal Street and into Washington Square Park. Maybe there was more to her marriage than she'd let on. Maybe it wasn't irretrievable. Had returning to Barrett's Bluff rekindled it? He didn't believe that. Didn't want to believe that. She'd shown him her heart. He hadn't been looking for it, nor had she been looking for him. Circumstances had put them in Bryce Corner at the same time. The chimney fire; being in the boat so early that morning. Fate had brought them together. So what the fuck was Fate doing to them now?

Aimlessly he wandered the small park. On Star Mountain she had said she was "scared by our love". But so was he - the suddenness and the power of it. They had talked about blending their two worlds together – starting a new one of their own. The Bed & Breakfast idea. She had seemed so sure of herself, of them. He didn't see where Nina saw the insecurity. But where did this strange behavior come from? How could she turn so cold on him so quickly? On the sidewalk after dinner the other night he knew she was upset. The impromptu trip to Milan. With Harlow. But he'd asked her to go and she didn't want to. She couldn't be jealous of her could she? He's explained his feelings to her about Harlow, more than once. She'd said she understood. Business. Only business. But there had been more. Once. Just once though. Hell, now Dodge was getting confused.

He stood at the corner of Washington Square where the chess players were. He had never learned the game. He knew he possessed the intellect and diligence for it, but not the patience. But these guys - they had a command of the game, and they were fast. They moved the pieces with such flurry that the pieces were still wobbling within their checkered squares as the player slammed his hand down hard onto the top of the timing clock. Hardly a second passed without their hands and the chess pieces flourishing about as if caught in a never-ending whirlwind. And then, when there was a momentary lull, the player scratching his chin, hand poised a molecule above the clock, the observers stood in awe, mustering their collective brainpower, contemplating what move would be next. Then it would hit and the flurry picked up its pace again, some observers nodding their heads in agreement with the move, others slowly shaking theirs from side to side, not sure the move was prudent. Dodge got mesmerized in the game. His consciousness taking a well needed break from the stress of its newest overpowering dilemma. He marveled at them, not only at their skill, but also at the fact that at any of the several, always occupied tables, it wasn't unusual to see one opponent dressed in his meticulous Brook's Brother's suit facing an advisory looking remarkably like Jethro Tull's *Aqualung*. It was all about the brain power; looks, job title, stock market portfolios (or lack thereof) didn't matter one iota. Here on the small cement tables with the worn out paint-chipped black and white squares, the playing field was indiscriminately even - and ruthlessly unbiased.

At one of the lulls Dodge heard some music. It came from across the square. He looked to see a crowd standing around the Arch and absentmindedly got drawn over to it. Two longhair musicians sat on the ground in the center of the Arch between the pillars, the heavy stone Arch hovering above them, bathing them in sun shadow. They were picking away on their acoustic guitars. The crowd surrounded them nodding their heads and tapping their feet to the music. He recognized the music but he couldn't place it. It was familiar yet strange to him. A placard set beside the musicians identified them as *LasRever*. The crowd was a diverse one, smiling and happy. They seemed to understand the music and were pleased with it. Beatles. They were playing a medley of the Beatles songs but they sounded weird, off key or something. They were into it, the two guys, playing steady and humming in harmony, but the harmony was weird too. Then he got it. They were playing the songs backwards. Dodge stood with the others, akin to their appreciation and joining in their foot tapping. They were good, very good. Amazing actually. How did they do that? How long had they practiced it? Backwards. Searching for hidden clues. One of them had on a black sweatshirt with the word SELTAEB spread above a white piano and DAOR YEBBA beneath it. Beatles, Abbey Road. The other musician's sweatshirt had the familiar graphic of The Beatles crossing Abbey Road. Except that John was at the back in his white suit. Dodge was pretty sure John had been at the front and then who? Paul? No, Paul was last, right? No George was last dressed in denim. (Dodge the designer remembered things best by outfits) and Ringo and Paul wore dark suits. Paul; Paul had been barefoot sparking the rumor that he was dead. Somewhere, supposedly, in the lyrics of one of their songs, if it was played backwards, you could hear The Beatles say ominously, *Paul Is Dead*. Dodge had never figured out a way to play a song backwards, but obviously *LasRever* had. He stared at the sweatshirt. George in the lead then Paul, Ringo, and John. Paul now wore shoes and the three others didn't. Everything was reversed. Dodge looked at the placard, *LasRever*, he got it; reversal in reverse.

Suddenly Annison returned to his thoughts. Maybe there was some hidden clue in their short relationship. He thought backwards through the events of last Tuesday night's dinner, cocktails at Nina's, back through all their conversations, their love-making. The spawning of the B&B idea at the farmhouse, Vermont, Amherst, Quabbin, their time alone at the lake, the cornfield, Dot's Diner, all of it. Even to the beginning of it, that early morning when he'd rescued her and knew nothing about her. Nothing. He couldn't for the life of him come up with any solid reason or thing that would have alerted him to her behavior. But it was there. Obviously something was there. Everything was fine 'til she had gone back to Barrett's Bluff. *Damn it!* It must be there.

Maybe if he told the *LasRever* musicians his story, gave them all the specifics, maybe they could figure it out. Put a melody to the last few weeks of his life and pick it on their acoustic guitars, find the harmony that had run off, fix the discord in his life. Dodge became anxious again. Neither the chess tournaments nor the music offered lasting reprieve. He tossed a few dollars into the open guitar case and moved on.

"Dodge Maddison?" a voice said behind him.

Dodge turned and found two young men addressing him. They smiled to one another, their recognition had been correct.

"Yes," he said matter-of-factly.

"We, we thought that was you." They were admirers. They were fashionably dressed in a manner that bespoke not only their individuality, but also their intimate life-style.

"I'm Joseph," the first one extended his hand. Dodge could not help but notice Joseph's soft handshake. "And this is my partner, Francois." Same handshake.

Dodge greeted them both. Joseph mentioned his admiration for the designer and talked briefly about fashion. He was very knowledgeable and explained that he had a desire to become a designer. He had a knack for making clothes and had in fact made the outfits that he and his partner were wearing. Dodge was kind and said the outfits were very nice.

"I was wondering though," Joseph continued, "do you have any plans to design a men's line?"

Dodge had been asked this question many times and he gave his standard reply with a broad grin, "I'm afraid the women keep me too busy."

As Joseph went on about his perception of a need for a great men's line in the contemporary world of fashion, Francois stood a pace behind him talking excitedly into his cell phone. Dodge could make out parts of the conversation, "I swear to God ... no, really ... Joseph's talking to him right now ... Washington Square ... he's as handsome as hell ... believe me, I'd love to honey ..."

"Well," Dodge said to Joseph, "maybe that'll be your calling to design a new line for men." But you'd better firm up your handshake, he thought.

"May I impose upon you for an autograph? I know how silly that must seem to you, but I'd love one if you wouldn't mind."

"Sure."

Joseph turned to Francois and made him get off the phone. They fumbled through a shoulder bag to find a pen and something to write on. That done, Francois dropped the phone into the purse.

"I'll make you a deal," the designer said as he accepted the material to sign on, "one autograph for one quick phone call." They both looked at him dumbfound.

"May I use your cell phone?"

"Oh my God, yes," it registered and Francois extracted the cell phone and handed it to Dodge.

Maddison dialed Annison's cell. As it rang he was saying over and over in his mind, *pick up Annie, please pick up.* To no avail. He got her phone-mail again. He left her another message. He was certain she would hear the desperation in his voice. *Please*, with emphasis *call me.*

He gave the phone back to Francois and said cordial good-byes. The boys left huddled together marveling at the designer's autograph. Dodge turned and walked sullenly toward the south end of the park.

# 42

## PRINCE STREET PUB

Dodge Maddison was walking down Lower Broadway in suspended animation. The sunny New York afternoon was having difficulty maintaining its shine as high gray clouds thickened above Manhattan Island. He crossed Houston and entered SoHo. He hadn't walked along this end of Broadway for many years. He thought of that distant day when he had transgressed this sidewalk in search of Silverman & Sons Mfg. The day he had met his mentor, Stanley Silverman. The day that had begun his new life. He wondered how Stanley was doing, or even if he was still alive. After his son had died and the Silverman's had left New York, the two had lost touch. Stanley too deep in his grief. When Stanley's wife died, Dodge had gone to the funeral in Boca Raton. And he had driven up one time from South Beach when he'd been there on a photo shoot. Dodge's new wife had accompanied him and he wanted Stanley to meet her. But by then Stanley was truly a broken man. Dodge wasn't sure Stanley had even recognized him. They hadn't communicated since then. It was sad. Life was ironic. Such a powerful relationship the two men had shared and then it was gone. Just as his marriage, that too was gone. And now Annison. Such a sudden romance, so powerful a love, and now what? It was gone?

He wandered off Lower Broadway onto Prince Street. His life was a series of losses. First his parents when he was only five; the drifting away of Stanley Silverman; his wife leaving him to go on to another man who wanted to give her the family she dreamed of, and that Dodge had had no time for. He'd lost his grandparents, that had finally sunken in, and now Annison. Could it be possible? Was she leaving him too? Fuck it. He'd been a survivor all his life and he still was. He'd move on just as he always did.

But Dodge was unsure. Unsure of Annison's behavior. Unsure that he had the fight left in him to go on from one more heartache. He'd done some heavy soul-searching lately and had been looking forward to re-aligning his life, taking more time to enjoy what things he had and would have with Annison; the Bed & Breakfast, Bryce Corner. Maybe it just wasn't in the cards for him to have a life like Bennie and Carlene. Could he even expect that? He felt lost again. And then angry. Had he been just a fool?

Overhanging the sidewalk at the corner of Mercer Street was a neon sign for The Prince Street Pub. Dodge went in and took a seat at the bar. He ordered a draft beer.

And then another. The first one went down fast. He rationalized that due to his long walk and his mounting anxiety. He'd go slower on the second beer. Dodge was familiar with the bar, it not being too far from his building, and he knew the pub still had a working public phone. *Part of the ambiance* the owner had told him once. It was in the narrow hallway where the restrooms were. He pushed open the saloon type shutters. Someone was on the phone. He went into the men's room. It was vacant. The lighting was dim. He stood at the sink and splashed water onto his face. In the mirror he saw droplets of water dripping off his face. He hadn't shaved this morning, nor last night, nor even yesterday morning at Giovanni's house in Milan. He had a European look going on. Dark, two-day stubble like what the male models wore or guys like George Clooney and Pierce Brosnan. He thought about growing his beard. He hadn't had a beard since back in his college days in London. He stared at the eyes staring back at him. *Blue eyes for a guy who's feelin' blue*, he laughed. Maybe he had the beginning lyrics for a country song.

Behind him the door swung open. Dodge pumped the lever on the paper towel dispenser and dried his face. The phone was free. He dialed directory assistance. When the electronic operator answered he said, "Connecticut," then, "Barrett's Bluff," then, "The Inn at Barrett's Bluff." He pushed one to have the number automatically dialed. The computer voice asked him to enter one for coin deposit, two for calling card. He pushed two and entered his calling card number.

"Good afternoon, you've reached The Inn at Barrett's Bluff, how may I help you?"

"Annison Barrett, please."

"One moment, I'll connect you."

His heart beat in his ears as the connection went through. Four rings later an answering machine answered, "Hi, you've reached Annison Barrett. I'm unavailable at the moment but if you leave your name and number I'll be happy to return your call as soon as I'm free." Beep.

The sound of her voice stopped his breath. Dodge hung up and then went through the motions to reach the Inn again.

"Good afternoon, you've reached..."

"Yes, hello again. I just called for Annison Barrett but I got her answering machine. Could you connect me to her personally?"

"May I ask who's calling?"

He hesitated a moment trying to think of another name to use but blurted out, "Maddison. Tell her it's Mister Maddison returning her call." He hoped that would work.

"One moment please."

He listened to Muzak for two long minutes and then, "I'm sorry, she's not answering her page, may I take a message?"

"Could you tell me please if she is in?"

"Ummm, hang on." Dodge heard her put the phone down on a counter. There was noise in the background and people talking. Front desk. He heard her talking to someone and placed a finger in his free ear, straining to pick up on the conversation. "Kathy, do you know where Annison is?" *They're not here.* "When will she be back?" *I don't know, they've gone off somewhere together. Who is it?* "Some guy, I think he said Patterson." *Just take a message.*

"I'm sorry sir, she's not in, may I take a message?"

"No, thank you, no message." He placed the phone in its cradle and leaned his forehead onto it. His eyes were closed and he gave a heavy sigh. He hadn't liked the background conversation. *They've gone off somewhere together.* He was thinking of what Nina had said. He didn't like that either.

Dodge returned to the bar and asked the bartender what she had for single malt scotches.

"We've got Cragganmore, Dalwhinnie, Lagavulin, Oban ..."

"Oban, neat please."

After the second scotch (or it may have been the third) Dodge took a finger pinch of bar snacks from the glass bowl the bartender had set in front of him. The taste didn't go well with his scotch. He pushed the bowl an arm length away. He contemplated asking for a menu, but ordered another drink instead. "On the rocks this time," he said, as if that would make any difference.

He passed by the telephone two more times during runs to the men's room. Each time he thought of calling again. But where? Her cell phone? The Inn again? Try to get her home phone number from the front desk? They wouldn't give it to him, and Annison hadn't. There hadn't been any need to. But call for what? To leave another message that wouldn't be returned?

He ordered another drink.

"Um," the bartender placed her elbows on the bar and leaned into him speaking quietly, "I really think you should have something to eat, Dodge."

He got her message. He should eat, but didn't have an appetite.

"That's okay," he said forlornly, "I'll just have the check."

"It's right here." The folded check sat in a tall thin glass in front of him. The bartender had replaced it with a new one each time he had gotten another drink. He hadn't even noticed.

She accepted his credit card, ran it through the register terminal and presented it to him in a small black portfolio with a pen clipped on the outside.

"Are you going to be alright?" she asked softly.

"Yes, I'm fine. Thank you." He wondered what she meant.

"Sure?"

Yes, he nodded.

"Okay, take care. Hope to see you again." She was an attractive girl, in her twenties. Dodge noticed for the first time. Healthy breasts tucked beneath a white sleeveless sweater. She turned back to her business and he saw her from behind. Also attractively tucked in. But it didn't affect him. All he could picture was Annison, the way she fit into her jeans.

"Dammit!" he said and left the bar.

# 43

## *No Stirrings Inside*

Outside the sky had surrendered its light to the dusk. The evening clouds were open, releasing cold raindrops in a steady sheet of rain into the cold air. The streets were almost deserted save for the brave few who walked briskly along the sidewalks beneath their umbrellas. The building wasn't far and the rain didn't bother him. He felt warm with the scotch, and happily comfortable with the light-headedness. He wondered what time it was but instantly didn't care.

By the time he got two blocks down and stood on the corner across the street from his building, Dodge Maddison was wet. His jacket was drenched and his hair had flattened from the rain. Little rivulets streamed down his forehead. He brushed his forehead with his sleeve. *Lady Maddison* shone through the dark, dreary night in pink neon. Bright pink against the dark edifice's gray. The shop windows were well-lighted and attractive with their displays. The big glass revolving door was shut and locked tight for the night.

> *"So is there?"*
> *"Is there what?"*
> *"Is there a Lady Maddison?"*

She had never let him down, *Lady Maddison*. Through all the years of toil and sweat and romances and heartaches, she had always been there. Steady. Constant. Loyal. Unwavering in her affection and commitment to him. He'd never questioned her. He'd given her everything she ever asked for and had in return received her undying gratitude and admiration. This lady he admired.

Annison Barrett had come at him from out of the blue. And he had fallen for her easily and quickly, casting his inherent sensibilities aside and giving in to the delirious allure of good fortune. He allowed himself to believe he was in love with her. That had been in New England. It was somehow different here in New York. Her aloofness, her unknown whereabouts, her refusal to return his calls, all baffled him. Standing in the incessant rain, he couldn't for the life of him figure it out. He doubted his feelings now. Partly because he was pissed off at everything and partly because he was angry with himself for letting his guard down, not foreseeing it. But mostly because he was drunk and tired. The scotch and the rain ganged up on him and Dodge moved against the fleeting traffic, in the rain, across the street, to his building.

Upstairs he stripped his wet clothing, toweled down, and stood naked in front of the bathroom mirror. He looked like shit. He donned a bathrobe from the door and went into the kitchen and microwaved a bowl of soup. He sat at the counter in the silence of the loft slurping it cautiously, impatient for it to cool. He thought of having another scotch but knew by the ringing in his ears that he had had enough. Dodge Maddison was exhausted; mentally and physically. His mind had been on overload ever since this morning's conversation with Nina. He finished half a bowl of soup and went to bed.

\* \* \*

The night tossed and turned him in a troubled half sleep and he was awakened early by a massive hangover. He thought about going to the gym but decided to take a short run instead. A half-hour later Dodge was in the shower remarking how out of shape he was. He hadn't adhered to his exercise routine lately. Weakened by love. Wasn't that a song? It should be. Coffee. Coffee would help. He set a pot to percolate while he shaved. The mirror was kinder this morning. All was forgiven; but it sternly admonished him to *get your shit together, Maddison!*

At a little before eight o'clock he called Bennie at the police station in Bryce Corner.

"Hell-low."

"I need you to do me a favor - without a million questions."

"Yeah," Big Ben said, "good-morning to you too."

"Drive over to the Sanderson cabin and tell me what you see."

"What's up?"

"I'm looking for Annison and I think she might be there."

Chief Ben took a moment to contemplate what that meant. "You want a description of the wallpaper or would you like me to play peeping-tom and give you an erotic overview?"

"Just give me your professional observations."

"What the fuck is *this* all about?"

"I knew you'd have a million questions."

"That's only one."

"I'm not sure."

"Sure you are."

"Could you just do me the favor?"

"Have a little tiff with your new girlfriend?"

"That's two."

"And only nine-hundred-ninety-nine-thousand-nine-hundred and ninety-eight to go."

"New math?"

"Old math gleaned from the same place you got it; B.C. Elementary."

"Gleaned?"

"I learned English there too. Where are you?"

"In the City, at the building."

"Alone I take it."

"Yes." He hadn't wanted to but Dodge re-capped the events for him. He suddenly felt an urge to confide in his old friend. It made him feel better.

Big Ben took it all in in his professional analytic way. "So you think she may be back in town?"

"Maybe."

"With the husband?"

"That's what I'd like to know."

Ben wanted to say something like, *Boy you sure can pick 'em,* but instead said, "Give me a few minutes to get this report finished and faxed off, and I'll take a casual drive over there and scope it out."

"Thanks, Bennie."

"No problem. I'll call you in a few." He hung up shaking his head. *I told him she was married! Goddamn fool.*

Dodge clicked off his phone and for a second thought of calling her cell again. *No. I'm tired of doing all the chasing.* Nina's words came to him, *Let her come to you.*

But when would that be?

He was nervous and edgy, pacing the loft waiting for Bennie's call. He thought of going downstairs into the comfort of the boutique to get his mind off it but wanted to stay close to his phone. His apartment phone was a private number that only a few people had. Bennie would call him back on that.

It took an hour, but the phone finally rang.

"Nada."

"Nada what?"

"Nobody here."

"Are you there?"

"Yup, standing on the porch lookin' at the lake. I can make your place out from here. Nothing going on over there either. I checked there first before I drove over here."

"Is it closed up?"

"Yeah the door's locked and the windows are down."

"No, I mean does it look like it's closed up for the season?"

"Shit no. Her car's still here."

"Her car is still there?"

`Bennie didn't answer him.

"Describe it to me."

"Well, it's a white Lexus with ..."

"I know all that. I mean does it look like it's been driven?"

"Ever?"

"Don't fuck with me Bennie, I'm not in a good mood."

"All right, all right. No it hasn't been moved lately. I can see the spots in the gravel where the rain dripped off the car and there are no tread marks in the driveway. And there would have been if she'd driven it since the rain a couple nights ago. So I'd say it's been in the same spot it was left in when you two left it last."

"You don't think she might be out for a walk?"

"Naw, she ain't here, pal. There's leaves at both the front and back door. Still brittle. No one's walked in or out of the house for a while. I walked around peepin' in the windows and everything looks hunky-dunky inside."

There was a long pause in the conversation. Bennie could almost hear Dodge thinking, "What are you gonna do?" he asked.

"I don't know. I'm frustrated. I'd like to talk to her but ..."

Big Ben stood with his tiny cell phone pressed to his ear. He didn't like it. Too small. He couldn't understand how it could possibly work with the phone so small and the microphone (which was only a tiny hole) so far away from your mouth. Besides the whole thing was too girly for him. He liked a real phone; big and obnoxious with a regular earpiece and mouthpiece and a handle to it. Like the one he had in the cruiser. He'd of used that one, except calls from the cruiser were considered official business and routinely recorded. He figured this conversation should be private.

"Bennie?"

"Yeah?"

"Can you keep an eye on it for me and ..."

"... And let you know if she shows up? Yeah, will do."

"Thanks. Call me anytime, day or night."

"Hey ..."

"What ..."

Ben took in a deep breath and let it out through his nose. It made a sound like the wind blowing across the cell phone, "She'll come back."

"I hope so."

"Try to relax, you know how women are. Can't figure 'em out sometimes, that's all."

"I've never been good at that. This time was different. I thought I knew her."

"Stay busy, that'll help."

"Yessah boss, whatever you's says."

"Fuck you, pal."

"Likewise."

"I'll be in touch."

"Thanks."

"Oh! Do me a favor," Ben said. "If she shows up, give me a call so I can stop playing Dick Tracy. Don't want to be chasin' around lookin' for her if she's back in the sack with you."

* * *

Dodge decided to take the Chief's advice, staying busy might get his mind off things. He checked his watch and decided to go down and help Roberto roll out the carpet.

"Mornin', Mr. M." Roberto had already rolled the carpet onto the sidewalk and was brooming the entranceway, cleaning up the aftermath of last night's rain.

"How are you Roberto?"

"Fine, just fine. Little chilly this morning isn't it?"

Dodge Maddison stood with his hands in his pockets. Roberto could tell he was preoccupied.

"How did things go in Europe?" he offered.

"Good," the designer bent down and tugged at the corner of the fuchsia carpet. Roberto knew there wasn't anything wrong with it, but he didn't say anything.

That's how the morning progressed, Dodge nit-picking at little things. The window displays weren't quite to his liking; the floor racks and gondolas needed freshening up; none of the departments throughout the boutique were set right. Upstairs on the manufacturing floors he found fault with the production and lost his temper on one of the pattern makers who wasn't at her machine. "I was only getting a coffee," she'd said when he found her in the break room. On the Level 5 Studio he made his way to his desk stopping at each of the drawing boards where his teams of designers were working. He was vocally unhappy with their work he had admired to himself just yesterday. He sat at his desk making numerous business calls - all within earshot of the young designers in the open loft studio, and all harsh-sounding and coarse. *He's in a mood*, Fletcher Ross whispered. He was making everybody nervous. They wished he'd go back to Milan or New England, anywhere, just leave them alone. "What's the matter with him anyway?" was the question of the day.

By late morning he couldn't stand it anymore. He went back up to his apartment (much to the delight of the design team) and called Barrett's Bluff.

"No, I'm sorry sir, she's not in."

"Do you know when she will be?"

"I'm sorry, I don't. But I'd be happy to put you into her phone mail if you'd ..."

"Is Jack Barrett in?" He didn't know why this came out but he was desperate. He'd ask him what was going on. He needed some answers.

"No, I'm afraid he's not in either. Would you like me to put you into ..."

Dodge hung up. He dialed downstairs. "Have Roberto bring my car up to the front, I'll be down in two minutes," he hung up without waiting for a response.

Dodge was already at the back corner of the building when Roberto pulled the coupe out of the alleyway, stopping just before the sidewalk.

"You need gas," Roberto said from the driver's window, "would you like me to …"

"I'll get gas," Dodge yanked the door open and a moment later Roberto watched him peel-off in front of an oncoming taxi, the cab driver standing on the brakes and laying angrily on his horn.

"Drive careful, Mr. M," Roberto said to the coupe as it rounded the corner against the light and escaped his view. He could hear the exhaust pipes echoing loud off the buildings of the adjacent avenue.

\* \* \*

Dodge drove to Connecticut, acquiring a speeding ticket on interstate 95, which he threw onto the floor, and resumed his haste towards The Inn at Barrett's Bluff.

When he got there, he ignored the signs at the entranceway for parking all vehicles and taking the carriage to the Inn, and drove into the way marked "delivery in the rear only". He cut across the side of the Inn on a narrow cobblestone way and pulled in front at the reception area right behind a horse drawn carriage. The driver, dressed in the garb of the 1700's, complete with a tall black top hat, was unloading luggage from the rear of the carriage. He said, "I'm sorry sir, you can't park your …" but Dodge was already out of his car. Guests were alighting from the carriage and walking towards the wide double-door entrance. Dodge got to the door before them. The in-going guests thought he was going to hold the door for them, but he didn't. He swung the door open and walked briskly into the Inn. He asked for her at the front desk. The two ladies behind the high counter reiterated the unknown whereabouts of both the Barrett's.

He glared at them wanting to shout out *Liars!* but saw that they either had no idea of where Annison was or had been told to give out no information. He wasn't going to get any further here. Standing with his hands spread in front of him on the counter, he looked to either side of the front desk, taking in the perimeter of the large reception area. To the right near a wide-open doorway was a small sign atop a pedestal designating the way to the dining rooms. To the left was a small group of signs pointing the way to various room numbers. At the bottom of them was a sign with an arrow pointing up the stairway behind the front desk. It said *Offices*. Dodge took the stairs two at a time. The front desk girls stared in awe at each other.

"Oh my God! Is that who I think it is?" the first one said.

"I can't believe it," the second one responded as she grabbed the front desk phone to spread the news.

"It must be true then ... she *is* with him. Oh... My... God!"

The Inn was very old and the upstairs hallways were low and narrow and crooked. The wallpaper was authentic for the period and provided neutral tones for the collection of old paintings and paraphernalia hung throughout. Dodge didn't take notice. He walked quickly past the various rooms. Most were guestrooms, but there were a couple of rooms set up meeting-style with long tables and high-back chairs. One of them that he stuck his head into was filled with smartly dressed business people watching their speaker exhibiting his adroitness with Power Point. Just past that was another room designated as *Sales and Marketing*. Walking in he was greeted by a gang of people all standing in the center of the room staring at him. They had obviously been alerted by the front desk and stood motionless and stupefied in the recognition of him. Annison wasn't amongst them and before they had a chance to speak, Dodge had exited, continuing his quest along the squeaky hallway.

The doors and woodwork were painted an antique white, or more of an eggshell he thought, or light khaki. British Khaki, like the color of the long pleated cotton skirt he was formulating as a design for his Spring line. The wood floors held several coats of a deep red, or burgundy, or even like the color of a light Merlot if you held a glass of it in front of a candle. A striking color that was picked up again in the wallpaper. It sparked an image of his model on the runway. He would have her in the floor-length khaki skirt with a light carefree top in the maroon coloring, sateen maybe with sheer accents. His mind was on overload. Random clear-pictured thoughts were mixing with the fragmented fireworks of his anxieties. Suddenly the softness of the colors surrounding him and the way they bespoke a richness and an allure seemed to wrap around him in the narrow hallway and he could feel her presence. He flashed back to the ambience of his apartment that he'd walked into Saturday night. And how he had wished Annison was there. Her face appeared before him. She was smiling, giggling in her own whimsical manner. He wanted to find her. To hold her tight and never let her go.

He found another taupe-toned door with *Innkeeper's Office* painted on it in the same maroon as the woodwork. He knocked and gave the knob a turn. It was locked. He knocked again, waiting for someone to come to the door. It was quiet. He put his ear to the door. Quiet, no stirrings inside.

"Dere e's no whon dere, sir," a small woman with a nametag identifying her as a housekeeper said. She squeezed by him in the narrow hallway with an armload of fresh white towels.

"Do you know where Mrs. Barrett might be?" he asked.

"No, I tink she e's back, but she e's gone agin," she responded with her back to him as she made her way down the hall intent on her business. "I tink dey go away on holly day," her trailing voice said to him, "or sumzing," and she disappeared.

He made his way back; past the Sales and Marketing team cloistered in their doorway; past the business meeting; around the maid allowing herself into a guestroom with her pass key (still holding the armload of towels) down the staircase; past the front desk girls; through the doors and into his car. Then he sat there wondering what to do next. The carriage driver came out of the Inn and resumed his seat atop the coach. The carriage moved on. Dodge watched the twin horses pull the antique coach with The Inn at Barrett's Bluff logo in gold leaf on the black side doors. The horses worked well together on their accustomed route around the circular way fronting the Inn, the driver holding the reins loosely in his left hand.

Dodge Maddison moved on too, driving his red coupe at a snail's pace alongside the golden grounds of the Inn, spacious and vast and seemingly threaded together by ribbons of long white fencing stitched throughout the open fields.

# 44

## *THE CRIMSON ROBIN*

At the end of the property, or the beginning, depending on which way you were coming from, Dodge Maddison, the famous fashion designer, sat alone in his car wondering which way to turn. On his right was the open parking lot where the Inn's guests would park their vehicles and board the horse-drawn carriage to travel in authenticity along the picturesque way to their accommodations at the Inn - to spend their night or weekend or holiday snuggled in the simplicity of the eighteenth century. To his left was an antique stagecoach, perfectly preserved on an attractive patch of landscaping, with an elaborate hand-carved gilded sign next it sporting the Inn's logo and a grand arrow with the letters *please park all vehicles here* spread across the center of it. The arrow pointed to the vast lot on his right. Directly in front of Dodge Maddison, at the "T" in the road, was a small white road sign with the familiar red interstate route badge with the number 1 centered within it. Below that was an "N" pointing right and an "S" pointing left. Route 1, stretching from Fort Kent, Maine all the way along the eastern seaboard to Key West, Florida. He thought about flipping a coin and driving to the end of whichever way won out.

His cell phone rang - the startling ring of it jarring the emptiness of his thoughts. By languid impulse he retrieved it from the seat next him and spoke. He was met with silence at the other end. Probably out of range he thought. He said hello again.

"Can you talk?" she said softly.

It was Annison. The sound of her voice poured over him, like thick honey from an upturned vat, soothingly coating all his problems with the sweet taste of her voice.

"Annie," his voice whispered, "where are you?"

"I'm at the Inn."

"No … you're not." She was lying to him.

"No, I'm not."

"I'm there."

"At the Inn?" She was surprised.

"Yes. I want to see you."

"I called the loft, to leave you a message, but I couldn't bring myself to. I hung up … several times."

"I've been worried sick about you. I went to Nina's."

"I know, we've spoken."

"Annie, what's the matter? I don't understand. I need to …"

"Dodge," her voice carried a slightly heavier tone, "I know you must be confused, and I owe you some sort of an explanation. That's why I'm calling." He heard her take in a deep breath.

A loud horn sounded behind him. A delivery truck loomed in his rear view mirror. Dodge pulled over to the grassy shoulder and the truck pulled up next to him so the driver could see either way. It pulled out turning left. It was loud and smoky with diesel fumes. There was another one coming.

"Annison, hang on a minute, I'm sort of in the middle of the road, give me a second to move out of the way. Okay?" he waited for her answer.

"Yes."

Dodge put the cell phone in his lap, pulled the shifter downward, out of first gear and slid it to his knee in neutral, then up into reverse. He turned, resting his right hand on the passenger seat and backed into the parking lot. He went way over to the far end against a weathered fence running along a copse of trees. He turned the ignition off and put the phone to his ear. The bright cherry-red coupe sitting quietly in the sandy corner of the gravel lot, on a quilt of multi-colored autumn leaves.

"Okay … you still there?"

"Yes."

"Tell me, Baby, what's going on?" There was no mistaking the pleading tone in his voice.

Annison had practiced her conversation a million times during the past three days and nights. Long, sleepless, heart-wrenching nights spent tossing and turning in her guestroom at the Inn, seeking solace and advice from the poems of Emily Dickinson. She'd even made a mental outline, a step by step guideline to whiz her through this conversation she felt so anxious about. But now, at the moment, she didn't know how to begin. She wanted it to be short and fast. She'd half thought about not contacting him at all, except that Nina had convinced her that she should. They'd shared some wonderful times together and no matter the outcome, there were cherished memories. And then her heart. Then too her heart. Still fluttering at its own pace, defiant of reality's boundary and pang.

*I had a crimson robin / Who sang full many a day / But when the woods were painted / He, too, did fly away.*

"Dodge," she began, "I need to say something, and I need to say it without interruption."

"I'm listening, Annie."

"Since September, a whole lot has happened in my life. I've had some ups and downs, but for the most part it's been a pleasant, eye-opening journey. I reaped fortitude from my self-imposed solitude. I re-learned how to appreciate myself again, and I like me. I feel a strength and confidence like I haven't felt for many years. All in all I accomplished much more than I set out to, and I'm not going to lose that."

She paused and Dodge sat with his eyes closed waiting for the shoe to drop.

"And I fell in love. That part was unexpected, and it too awakened dormant feelings within me, good feelings, an excitement long forgotten but pleasantly surprising me. I've been blatantly honest with myself about us. I wasn't looking for another relationship in my life right now, but what happened between us was special. Unexpected, profound and truly wonderful. You helped me to become me again and everything I said and did with you was true, coming from my heart. I'm alive when I'm with you."

"Then be with me now."

"I can't."

She may as well have thrust a knife into his stomach, these two words hurt him so.

"I can't take you away from your world, and, I guess you can't take me away from mine."

"I thought we were going to make our own world, Annie. Don't you remember?"

"Yes. Yes, I remember."

"Then what is it? I don't understand. Help me."

Annison couldn't respond. The lump in her throat was too severe. She took a moment to wipe tears from her cheeks.

"Is it Jack?" He hated to even voice this question. "Is it about your marriage?"

"No."

"Are you with him now?"

"No."

"Are you still in love with him?"

"I'm in love with you."

"Then meet me."

No response.

"Tell me where you are and I'll drive there now. Meet me, Annie. Let's talk this out."

"I need to keep my focus, Dodge, on myself."

"Tell me where you are."

"Maybe you need to focus on you, too."

"I want to focus on us."

"Do you?"

"Don't you know I do?"

She didn't want to get into it. Not now. Not this way. Not on the phone. But she didn't want to meet with him either. She couldn't trust her own emotions. She wasn't sure where her anger would fit in – or her love. She'd resolved herself to letting go. She'd conquered her angst over the past couple of nights. She'd been strong enough to face the woman in the mirror at the cabin on the lake and she could do it again. She was getting good at introspection and victory over emotional torment. She would rise beyond this setback and be who she had to be; Annison. What the future held was what the future held. And whatever it was, she'd meet it with her head high.

"Dodge, you're a wonderful man. Be who you are and let the future unfold as it will."

Inside him he could feel the hollowness. He had felt it before and it was revisiting him again. He had never been able to conquer it. Sometimes he wondered if he even had a heart, maybe it was taken away from him when he was five and all his life since then was just a shell living around a void. By learned instinct he would move on, the stubborn turtle with the unrelenting legs carrying his big empty shell to nowhere.

"Will I see you again?" he asked slowly. He wanted to see her. He was desperate not to lose her. One time, just one time he needed to triumph over this damned hollowness. It had to be with Annison. It was her or nothing.

"Let's give it awhile, shall we?"

He couldn't answer her.

"I, I've got to go now, Dodge."

"Annison, don't. Don't leave me hanging out here like this. Let's get together and talk it out."

"Good-bye Dodge … please take care of yourself."

The line went dead. Annison's hands were shaking. She clasped them together to steady them but her whole body was shaking and in a moment she gave in to the tremors and sobbed openly, burying her face in her hands and letting the tears overflow her wall of agony and bring it crashing down all around her.

\* \* \*

Dodge Maddison listened to the hum of his cell phone for a long time before he finally dropped it on the seat beside him. He started the coupe and pulled out of the parking lot, the tires spitting plumes of gravel behind. At the stop sign on Shore Road, he took a left onto Route 1 and drove the mile south to the main road; took a right and headed to the entrance of the interstate. He drove north on Route 95. He could be in Bryce Corner in two hours.

# 45

## *ROWING*

When he cruised into Bryce Corner late that afternoon and pulled up to Route 9 fronting Lake Wickaboag, Dodge took a left, bypassing the town, and drove around the far end of the lake going directly to Nina Sanderson's cabin. Annison's car was there just as Ben had described it, unmoved. Maddison walked up to the cabin and peered in. It was neat and tidy, just as they had left it a week ago. There were no signs that Annison had been here. Discouraged, he walked around the cabin, then about the property, then down to the lake. He stood gazing at the opposite shoreline. The trees had lost more of their color and the gray-brown of bare limbs was becoming the new shade on the horizon. She wasn't here, she wasn't at the Inn, she probably wasn't back in the City with Nina, so where was she? He didn't know where else to look. A week ago tonight they had been together, the two of them cuddled together in his bed, in his building, happy. The next night, with Nina, the three of them had gone out to dinner in The Village. Six days and nights since he'd seen her last.

The Maddison cottage, Camp Nyla, sat across the lake looking at him. *Maybe.* He turned and strode quickly back to the coupe. This time he took the road going into town. He'd drive past the farmhouse. She knew where the key was hidden; it was a hopeful idea. But when he came upon it, Dodge saw only Eggman's truck in the driveway. He thought about pulling in and checking on the re-modeling, but why? Where did that idea stand now? No, he'd drive right down to his cottage. If she were anywhere in this town, it would be there. Right? And how would she have gotten here? She could have rented a car, but then how would she drive two cars back. Someone would have to come with her. Someone from the Inn?

Nina? Annison had said they were speaking again. Did Nina have a car? God damn it! He was getting angry. *Where is she?!*

She wasn't at Camp Nyla, and by the looks of it, she hadn't been. *So, she's not in Bryce Corner. Well if she's trying to avoid me, she's doing damn well at it.* Dodge looked at his watch. It would take him most of four hours to return to the City. It would be dark soon. He'd stay here tonight, drive back in the morning. Maybe he'd call Bennie and get together. Naw, there'd be too many questions, especially if Carlene got involved. Maybe he'd go to The Tavern, have a few drinks, shoot some pool with Lindsey, just relax for the evening, try to forget her. *Easier said than done.*

He retrieved his cell phone from the car. No new messages. This was his private cell, only a few people had the number; Annison of course (although by now he was adjusting to the fact that she wasn't going to call) and Harlow, Ben and Carlene, his grandparents ... Dodge thought of them. So much had happened since their deaths. First, he'd felt so alone, then warmed by the genuine outpouring of emotions of Bryce Corner, then so alive again with Annison, with such hopes and dreams for the future, and now, so alone again. Dodge felt the melancholy seeping in again and stubbornly pushed it away. *No! I'm not going that route again. Fuck it! I'll survive this too.* He went into the cottage, he was pretty sure there was beer in the fridge.

Later he sat on the dock with a cold one. The sun had just set behind a row of fading white cumulous clouds, and was slowly turning them into a wandering mass of crimson puffballs. It was early, he thought, his watch showing not even six p.m. yet. When did the clocks go back? Was it this weekend or next? Pretty soon sunset would be four o'clock again. He disliked this time of year in New England. In the City you lost track of sunsets. Primarily because you had to go out of your way to find them, but more so because there was always too much going on to even notice. He liked being busy. And he liked the lights of the big city. How could he ever feel comfortable in the quiet seclusion of the country? Who was he kidding? It had all been her. She'd rubbed off on him. She was the one who came up with the B&B idea, he'd just gone along because... why? Why had he gone along with that? Was he so mesmerized by her that he'd have done anything with her? His mind immediately answered yes, and he knew it was true. Dodge missed Annison. He looked over again at the Sanderson cabin, across the lake beneath the pink clouds. In the twilight, with the lake being so still, he thought he could just reach over and touch it, turn the light on and make her come back to him.

Behind him he heard a scuffling on the porch. Footsteps. His heart leapt. Dodge jumped to his feet and turned around facing the cottage. There was a phantom shadow in the dusk. It was Willie, the cocker spaniel. He barked and then scrambled down the stairs to the dock and sniffed Dodge. "Hello, Willie," Dodge said and stooped to pet him, but he didn't want to be petted, he wanted a treat. Willie went along the dock and sniffed the rowboat tied there. He jumped into it, walked across the bench seat, peered into the water, then ran back again and jumped out. He scooted past Dodge, ran up the stairs, spun around, sat on his hind end and barked. The rowboat swayed and rocked against the rubber bumpers tied to the pilings. Dodge noticed the water in it. "I should probably bilge this out before it sinks, eh?" he asked the dog. Willie woofed his support and Dodge went up to the shed to get the battery operated bilge-pump. He set it into the boat at the stern, flipped it on, stood a minute to make sure the water was exiting through the hose properly, and then said, "Okay Pal, let's go get a treat."

Another beer later, Dodge stood at the front sliders watching the lake disappear into the darkening night. It was now late October and most all of the docks on the lake had been taken in for the winter season. Dodge thought that he should stay tomorrow and take his dock in. Get a hold of Bennie to give him a hand taking the boat out. He knew he couldn't get him to go into the water, *too cold* he'd say, but it would be nice to spend a little time with him.

Willie had gotten his treat, two actually, and had dashed off in the direction of his home. Dodge was hungry but didn't feel like eating. He knew he should. He could go into town, The Tavern had a light fare menu, but now he didn't feel like that either. A pizza, he could order a pizza and have it delivered. He went to retrieve the menu held onto the fridge by a magnet and remembered the bilge-pump.

He went outside to the dock to turn it off. It had done its job, the rowboat was empty. He lifted the pump out of the boat and by habit looked over to the little log cabin across the lake. There was a light on. He squinted to make out the light. Yes, it was coming from Nina's cabin and before he knew it he was in the boat and rowing strongly toward the light. Dodge's heart was racing, more so from excitement than the rowing. He could finally speak to her face to face. Find out once and for all just what the hell was going on. Nearing the shoreline, he put his back into it and rowed faster, sliding the bow onto the lawn at the water's edge. He yanked the oars in and jumped over the bow and walked briskly toward the cabin along the dark lawn, wet with the heavy dew of the cool air.

The curtains were pulled but he could make out her figure in the silhouette against the glow of the cabin light. She moved from one side to the other and was passed by another figure. There were two figures. Dodge stopped halfway up the lawn and stood watching the movement of the figures. They were moving too quickly past the two front windows and he couldn't make them out well enough to know which one was Annison - and he had no idea who the other silhouette belonged to. Closer, but then they were gone from the windows, standing in the space behind the front door, or maybe somewhere else in the confines of the cabin. He was at the driveway. Annison's car sitting still on the gravel as it had been earlier. Next it was another vehicle. In the shadows of the evening Dodge went around Annison's Lexus and found a Mercedes SL. It was black, perfectly polished and detailed, custom wheels, the gilded-trim package and the special order tan convertible top. It was flashy, even in the night, exuding its ostentation like an exuberant ego. He looked at the rear license plate. It was a Connecticut tag, a vanity plate. It read "BLUFF". He knew immediately who the car belonged to.

# 46

## *INERTIA*

Dodge Maddison was hurt. And angry. Angry at himself. Angry at Annison. She'd lied to him. Again. She said she wasn't with him, that the reason she needed time had nothing to do with her marriage. Bullshit! So why was she here with him now?

He'd been a fool. Had he been all along? Had he been too starry-eyed to see the real Annison Barrett?

He rowed powerfully across the lake, the oars slicing into the water with a vengeance. *Here's a guy who thinks he understands women so well,* he thought, *I can design anything out of any fabric and they love it – because I know what they want! But I can't keep a fucking relationship to save my ass!*

Self-pity was now mixing in with the anger. *Fuck it! Fuck women! Maybe those kids in Washington Square Park are right – I should design a men's line. Get away from females all together!*

"God DAMN It, Annison!" he yelled loudly into the vastness, hoping she could hear him.

With the rowing, his back was toward his cottage and he faced her cabin, unable to take his eyes from it. The fast rowing decreased the size of the cabin as it seeped into the dark shroud of the western horizon. The light-glow through the windows also diminished, yet the amber tint of it seemed to grow redder and redder, fueling his rage as he stared fixedly at the tiny cabin, wishing he'd never been out on the lake that morning when he'd seen the smoke.

*Fate? Bullshit! More like diversion. Why'd I ever get involved with her? Damn it, Bennie, you were right. I can't believe I ...*

The boat hit the dock hard. The force of the collision stopped the boat dead in the water and sent Dodge into the air, somersaulting backwards over the bow, like a wayward gymnast. He barely cleared the dock and fell heavy into the cold water. He sat stunned in the shallow water of the shoreline, his arms braced behind him, water streaming from his hair and dripping off the end of his nose. He stood up, running his hands through his hair, wiping his face, shaking his arms. *Well there's a wake-up call for you, Dodger!* He laughed as Grampa Jed's voice rang in his ears.

Dodge walked deeper into the water until he was neck deep. He lunged for one of the oars, freed from the impact and floating just beyond his reach, but he missed it and had to swim out a few feet further to retrieve it. Two minutes later he had climbed out of the water and had the boat secured. He was shivering and bounded up the dock stairs two at a time, entering the cottage and stripping off his wet clothes and jumping into a warm shower. He hadn't looked back to the cabin.

* * *

Dodge couldn't stay at the Maddison cottage on Lake Wickaboag in Bryce Corner, Massachusetts. Not now, not with her at the lake, with him. He dressed quickly, turned off the lights and locked the door behind him. His prized red coupe rambled along the dirt road, up the hill and onto the smooth, dark tarmac of Wickaboag Valley Road.

Dodge opened it up, stretching through the gears, watching for oncoming headlights and taking the curves wide. His burning anger had cooled a bit with the trip into the lake, but he was still irritated. He again thought of going to The Tavern, but knew he'd have a couple and end up too drunk to drive and he just wanted to get out of town, back to the City to regroup. To shake it all off as he had the cold waters of the lake and move on with his life. *That's what I should have done in the beginning, before it all got started.*

The coupe roared along the deserted roadway and approached the curve at the McGreevy farm. Dodge downshifted to third and took the curve tight on the inside of the road, the tires dancing on the very edge of the shoulder. His right hand was on the floor-shifter and his left was holding tightly onto the steering wheel, fighting the centrifugal force of the sharp curve. As he passed the halfway point in the curve he punched the accelerator, the coupe lurching toward the upcoming straightaway. In physics, inertia is the tendency of matter to remain at rest unless affected by some outside force, in this case, centrifugal force. Small, frail, items are affected first, and as Dodge floored the accelerator, the back two butterfly valves on the Quadra-jet carburetor opened-up, forcing double the volume of gasoline into the combustible chambers of the engine, pushing the tachometer towards red-line, and forcing the weight of the vehicle (and its inert contents) to distribute quickly to the left side.

The chrysanthemum from their picnic at Quabbin, now petrified by the autumnal sunlight and clinging to a different beauty, was snapped free from its sentimental spot in the center of the dashboard and slid with the forces of nature across the dashboard into the extreme left corner. Dodge released his foot from the accelerator, shifted into fourth gear, replaced his foot heavily back onto the gas pedal and roared into the straightaway. He placed his right hand onto the steering wheel and rolled down his window with the left. He picked up the flower, twirled it by its brittle stem between his thumb and forefinger then tossed it out the open window. He rested his elbow on the sill and drove off in the night, the black cold air ostensibly fresh and revitalizing.

# 47

## *A New Day*

"This is Dodge..."
   "Hey Dodge, it's Ben."
"How ya doin', Chief?"
"You sound pretty chipper today."
"Yeah, and I'm feeling pretty good too, it's a new day." And it was. The past few days had been traumatic and emotionally stressful for the world's foremost fashion designer. It was time for him to cast off last season's designs, get back to work and move onto the next line. "I had a long drive last night and did some hard-core thinking."
"Scary thought."
"Actually, some of them were, but I got past them."
"You were in town," Big Ben said this matter-of-factly.
"How'd you know?"
"Someone said they saw the coupe. Why didn't you call me?"
"I wouldn't have been good company."
"You never are. That wouldn't have mattered."
"I was looking for her."
"Find her?"
"Yeah, I did."
"Talk to her?"
"No. No I didn't."
"Why not?"
"You were right Bennie, all along."
"'Bout what?"
"She went back to the husband."
"How do you know?"

351

Dodge told his friend about Annison's car in the driveway, the light that came on later in the early evening and how he'd rowed over and seen the two figures in the front windows. "Then I saw his car sitting there."

"BLUFF vanity plate."

"Yeah, how'd you know?"

"I drove by early this morning, saw the Mercedes, ran a check on the tag. Jackson J. Barrett, Shore Road, Barrett's Bluff, Connecticut."

"Did you see her?"

"No, it was too early, the sun was barely up, I decided to give it awhile and go back later. I was going to knock on the door and say howdy and check things out…"

"But?…"

"By the time I got back, both cars were gone."

"And the cabin?"

"Locked up, shades are drawn, looks like whoever was there is gone."

"*Whoever* was there. What's that? Cop talk?"

"Used to have this instructor at the police academy who drilled into us, *Never Assume!* - you know, makes an ass outta "u" and "me" – anyways all I saw were two cars, I didn't see any people. So for all I know it could have been Ben & Jerry who drove the vehicles away. And for that matter, you don't know much more either. You saw two figures, but couldn't positively identify them, right?"

"It was her, Bennie."

"And the other one?"

"Had to have been her husband, who else?!"

"This instructor, Captain O'Malley it was, had another saying, *If it walks like a duck and talks like a duck, it still ain't a duck until you're SURE it's a duck.*"

"And this means?…"

"Without making a positive I.D. the other figure could have been anyone – an employee from the Inn giving her a ride up to pick up her car – could have been her daughter, or her son driving daddy's car – we just don't know."

"It was her, Chief. Annison and her husband."

"Okay, okay, I'm not going to argue with you, just giving you my professional take on it."

"And I appreciate it, but it doesn't matter now anyway."

"How so?"

"Time for ol' Dodger to move on, get beyond her. I can't sit around and wait on a dream."

"Move on, or stick your head in the sand?"

"Get back to work, things I can handle, things that'll make me forget. Going to take a trip, go back to Europe for a while. Immerse myself in next season's line, concentrate on the fashion business, let the present become the past."

"So you're gonna run away from it all by runnin' away from it all."

"And you've got a better idea?"

"Find her. Settle it. Put your mind at ease. You go off now and it may be too late to retrieve the relationship."

"I think it already is. For chrissakes, Bennie, I've been trying to find her. It's obvious she doesn't want to meet with me. She said so. It's me that's been hanging onto the dream, not her."

"Well ... I don't know. I'm not sure running away is the answer. It's not going to heal you like you think it will."

"Some of it might be running I guess, but a lot of it is really business. I've been away from it for too long. Harlow and Fletcher and the design team have been doing a great job filling in for me but now I've got to put my time back into it. The spring line is coming fast upon us and I've got a lot of catching up to do." Dodge paused here a moment and then added, "And I don't know what else to do." His stubbornness waned and his heart started to come through his ego, "I was close, Bennie, so close. I thought I had a new life. I was feeling good. I wanted to be as happy as you and Carlene, as Jed and Gramma Emma. I really thought returning to Bryce Corner was my destiny, to settle in, have a good wife, a solid marriage, maybe even a family. Still have my work, but not at such a rat-race pace. Tone it down a bit, let my younger designers take more responsibility, maybe eventually sell out and focus on the Bed and Breakfast idea, concentrate on my artwork again. But I guess it's not in the cards for me."

"Could still be in the cards, if that's what you really want. Maybe the fling – relationship – with Annison was good after all, made you take a hard look at what you're doing, where you're at and what you want. Look at it that way. Maybe the cards are still in your favor - just need to place your bets safer. Stay with the hand you're most familiar with, the one that's been the most steadfast. Maybe your queen of hearts has been right in front of you all along. Might be time to play it."

Dodge knew he meant Harlow and wanted to come back with some smart retort like, *"Wow, Dr. Ben, not only a cop but a love therapist too!"* But he was quiet. He felt the sincerity in Bennie's remarks. Maybe he was right. Again! Dodge laughed.

"What? What's so funny?"

"Nothing, Chief. Just funny hearing you as a philosopher, mixing with metaphors and such."

"Mull-tie talented, I am."

Dodge loved him for his simplicity, his easy way of looking at life. Ben exemplified the small town New-Englander, just as his grandfather Jedediah had. Keep life simple, love your family, cherish your friends, and live each day as best as you can. It was these austere standards that had been calling him lately, ever since he'd returned to Bryce Corner in September. Dodge had to admit, they were powerful.

"Anyroad," Chief Ben said, "do what'cha gotta do, but think about what I'm tellin' ya. Life's too short, Pal, to not have the things you want."

"Thanks for the counseling, Bennie, but I'm okay. Things are going to work out for me, I can feel it. Some unforeseen things have happened to me and have had a startling influence on me. First, Jed and Emma passing on, and then the relationship with Annison. I've gone through a lot of soul searching, trolling the waters of my deep inner-self. And I came out on top, still afloat. I know what I need to do now. And hey, thanks for being there for me, for being you. You and Carlene are the best. I'm fortunate having friends like you in my life."

"Damn right you are," Big Ben laughed, "and listen, Carlene's still got her heart set on you two coming up for Thanksgiving. You know who I mean?"

"Yeah, well, I'm not sure how that's going to work out. That's one of the things I'll have to figure out in Europe, I guess."

"When you going?"

"Either late tonight or first thing in the morning, I need to contact Giovanni in Milan."

"That where you're heading?"

"Probably. I need to check on his progress on some commitments we laid out last week. And he's a good friend, I always enjoy being there with him and his wife, Maria. They're like the Italian version of you and Carlene; they always make me feel welcome in their home and their beautiful city of Milan. So, yeah, if it's okay with them, I'll go there first and then just play it by ear."

"What about the cottage? Want me and Brent to close it up for you? Pull the boat in, winterize the place?"

Dodge thought a moment, "Naw, I don't plan on being gone too long, ten to fourteen days at the most, and I've still got to decide what to do with the farmhouse. So, I'll have to get back to the Corner right after my trip. Leave it as is and I'll take a rain check later."

"You got it."

They hung up and Dodge checked his watch to figure out what time it was in Milan. He placed a call to Giovanni.

# 48

## QUEEN OF HEARTS

Giovanni was happy to welcome Dodge Maddison back to Milan, but saddened that he hadn't brought Harlow with him this time.

"I like that lady," he said, "she's good for you, no?"

Yes, she was good for him, and had been all along. Dodge could feel this now - stronger than before. Bennie had made the point, play the queen of hearts.

Before he'd solidified his travel plans to Europe, he'd thought of flying out to California and dropping in on her unexpectedly. The thought had actually crossed his mind. But he didn't know what he'd say to her, didn't know where she stood. Wasn't quite sure where he stood on the issue either. The issue being he and Harlow.

Dodge spent five days in Milan. He spent time at Giovanni's facilities working on expediting the rushed Holiday orders and laying out production quantities for the upcoming spring line. They worked hard and long into the first two nights. It was good for Dodge to be working again. But, by the third morning, Giovanni, sensing a need to entertain his American guest with things other than business, insisted on showing off his beloved city.

"You have never seen her as I do. Come, we take the day off and play hockey, yes?"

Dodge laughed, "You mean hooky."

"Okay then, hockey," Giovanni trying in vain to get the pronunciation correct.

They spent the day playing tourists, Giovanni bursting with pride. He took him to the Duomo Cathedral with its spectacular adornment of over three thousand statues. He pointed to the top, to the highest spire, showing Dodge Perego's Madonnina, keeping her vigil over Milan since 1744. They entered the cathedral and walked up the lengthy stairs to the roof terraces where they stood taking in the breath-taking panorama of Milan. Today was clear and they could see far to the snow-topped ridge of the Bergamo Alps.

To appreciate true Renaissance Milan, Giovanni took his designer to Castello Sforzesco with its many museums and collections and then to Pinacoteca Ambrosiana, built as an art gallery and library at the dawn of the 17th century. Then to the church of St. Maria Delle Grazie – where Da Vinci's fresco 'The Cenacolo' (The Last Supper) graces the far wall. Dodge was truly impressed. He thought of being here in this beauty with Annison, but quickly dismissed it, quietly chastising himself for allowing the thought to come through. He wondered why he'd never done this before on any of the business visits he and Harlow had made to Milan. *She* would certainly appreciate it.

Would it be rebounding? Wouldn't she think of it as that? He goes from a whirlwind affair with Annison and then comes crawling back to good ole Harlow? How dare he! How cruel! *What do you think I am!? Another one of your playthings? Well go fuck yourself, Dodge Maddison! I quit!* Isn't that what she'd say?

What else could he hope for? *Do you really think Harlow's the one? Had she always been?* Had he suppressed his true feelings about her? Been too caught up in Dana's youthful aura and then the Annison thing? Too mesmerized to see her standing right before him, at the end of his nose? Could they work together? *I mean not like work, work. But as a couple. Work as a couple together.* And how would he even go about presenting the idea to her? He needed to think things through, to be hard on himself. And to be honest, he *had* thought of their night in the parking lot at The Salem Cross Inn. More than once.

That evening, with Giovanni's wife, Maria, they attended an opera at Teatro Alla Scala, "The most famous opera house in the world!" Giovanni exclaimed.

"And see," he had said, "there, in the ruins of the old church of Santa Maria della Scala? The monument of Leonardo da Vinci himself."

The next day they again set out to explore. Dodge thought Giovanni was having more fun than he was; he was jubilant and excited playing the role of tour guide. They went to the heart of Milan's business district, Piazza Cordusio - Milan's Wall Street - and then to Via Monte Napoleone, the most exclusive shopping area in Milan. An elegant home for all the top names in fashion and design. Except for Dodge Maddison.

"When, *WHEN* are you going to open your *Lady Maddison* shop here, my friend?" Giovanni pleaded. "You are the only one not here."

"Only if you can find time to run it for me, Giovanni," Dodge laughed.

Giovanni walked along, shaking his head. This was an old conversation. "It would be so nice."

"I know, I know, but it's all about time, Giovanni. You can only do so much with your time." Dodge was surprised at what he had said. He thought it quite an appropriate comment. Perhaps he should listen to himself.

They walked into the shops: Valentino, Gucci, Chanel, Hugo Boss, Fendi, Louis Vitton, Gianfranco Ferre, Hermes, Lanvin, Missoni, Prada, Balenciaga, and the just-opened Stella McCartney. They shopped the competition, talking openly about the designs of his peers; Calvin Klein, Versace, Armani, Perry Ellis, Cardin, Lagerfeld. All the while, Giovanni the manufacturer, the weaver of cloth, touching the garments for their 'hand', the tell-tale feel of the fabrics.

They lunched at a busy restaurant in Pinacoteca di Brera, perhaps the most beautiful area of the city. After lunch they spent the rest of the afternoon, walking the cobble-stoned streets of the artistic district the locals called simply, Brera. Here were the Pinacoteca Art Gallery, Braidense National Library, and the Accademia di Belle Arti in the beautiful Palazzo Brera, where you were greeted by Antonio Canova's bronze statue of Napoleon Bonaparte.

Giovanni had overwhelmed him. Dodge was fascinated with his city. He didn't want to leave, and on his last day, promised to return soon for a longer stay.

He rented a car in Milan, a silver Citreon, and drove to Paris. He took his time along the A4 out of Milano, through Torino, enjoying the fabulous scenery of Northern Italy and the breathtaking experience of the Alps. He crossed the border into France at Tunnel de Frejus, staying on A43 to Chambery with the intriguing old-world allure of France outside his window in the passing recurrence of little towns, vast open fields, and hidden forests. Dodge liked to drive. It was therapeutic for him, better than medicine or lengthy chats on leather couches. This impromptu European tour would cleanse his palate. *I wish I had the coupe. I'd love to drive it on these fabulous old roads.*

At Lyon, where he stayed a night, he picked up the A6 and drove at a leisurely pace to Paris. He arrived late afternoon, refreshed and feeling renewed.

He spent three days in Paris. Not contacting any of his business acquaintances in the fashion world, but rather, keeping a low profile.

Wandering alone along Avenue des Champs Elysees, standing humbled beneath the beautiful Arc de Triomphe, ascending the Eiffel Tower for the spectacular view of the city that had been so kind to him over the years. He visited the Musee du Louvre, taking his time, exploring the magnificent artwork exhibited throughout all three wings. And then the Musee Picasso, and the Musee d'Orsay with the masterpieces of France's leading Impressionist painters; marveling at the artwork of the masters, feeling them stir his own creative juices and giving him an eagerness to paint again.

He didn't stay in the center of Paris where he usually did. This time he found a quaint pensione on a narrow alleyway just off Boulevard de la Magenta, in the Montmartre area - famed for its nightlife and its nightclubs, ala Moulin Rouge. Dodge was pleased taking long evening walks unnoticed into the quiet corners of Montmartre, still retaining its picturesque atmosphere of the area's early days as an artist's quarter.

\* \* \*

Harlow was back from her California vacation and active again at the New York office. She'd had a great time. Really enjoyed being with the girls and just doing nothing. Didn't realize how much she had needed the rest and relaxation and the time away from the demands of the business and the hectic pace of New York City. She'd even mentioned how relaxed she'd felt living at a quieter, slower pace when Dodge had called her one night from Paris to say hello and ostensibly talk about business things.

It was good to hear his voice again and she couldn't help but feel relieved that they were again a team. *And what was that new tone in his voice?* Their phone calls became more frequent. They talked for hours about nothing and everything, never once mentioning *Lady Maddison* or *Maddison Designs*. It was good to laugh together, good to be sharing their special relationship again and they carried on like teenagers chatting happily away into the wee hours of the night.

After Paris, Dodge went to London. He took the ultra-modern Eurostar train that whisked him right into London's Waterloo International Station in just three hours. He stayed in Hyde Park at Gloucester Mansions Hotel on Gloucester Road in London's SW7 district, just down the street from R.A.F.D. – the Royal Academy of Fashion Design - the academy he'd attended so long ago. He visited the National Gallery of Art on the north side of Trafalgar Square the first day, and the Victoria & Albert Museum the next. He thought of going to the Tower of London,

Parliament, Big Ben, Windsor Castle, etc., but instead found himself taking the Tube to Chelsea and Knightsbridge and South Kensington, revisiting the old haunts and pubs from his college days.

In the early afternoon sunshine of a perfect fall day in London, the designer sat on a bench in Hyde Park, relaxed and taking in the sights of the world walking around him. He was ready. Ready to go back home. Pick up his life where it had been before that ominous phone call he'd received from Old Percy at the Paris premiere. He'd buried his grandparents, the last vestige of his family, and in the past ten days had made progress in burying the relationship with Annison. Some progress - for he suspected the piece of his heart that had broken off would probably never heal. But he had to move on. Had to do what he had to do to make the balance of his life worthwhile. He believed now that Harlow would play a part in that, a much more integral part than before. If she wanted to. He was nervous about facing her, unsure of how she'd react to his new plan for them. Unsure of where her heart was, yet he believed he knew. He had to get to her, to see her face, feel her in his arms and see if the undertones of their recent long conversations were what he thought they were. He called her and told her he was coming back home. He heard an excitement in her voice and could visualize the happy smile on her lips.

He called Heathrow Airport from his cell phone and booked a flight. When the agent read the flight info back to him Dodge said, "Boston?"

"Yes, sir. You said one way to Logan International, correct?"

"No, I'm sorry," he realized his error, "I meant to say New York, JFK."

*Logan? A Freudian slip?*

The agent said, "That's no problem, I can redo your ticket for JFK, just a moment ..."

"No, no, that's okay," he found himself saying, "Logan is fine, the ticket's fine just as is. Thank you."

Just as well. He could rent a car at the airport, drive to Bryce Corner, close up the cottage, finalize things with Jack Cregan Realty on the farmhouse, and then drive down to the City. Better idea.

His flight was the next morning. He had time to kill. Dodge decided to take a cab (a taxi the Brits adamantly called it) downtown to Harrods. They had a *Lady Maddison* section and this would be a good opportunity for him to see how Harrods was doing with the line.

\* \* \*

He was perusing the visual displays in Ladies Wear when she tip-toed up behind him. She covered his eyes with her hands and said, "Guess who?"

He knew instantly who it was and turned around.

"Dana," he said, surprise in his voice, "what a surprise."

"Ditto," she kissed him lightly on the cheek. "How are you?"

"Fine, and you?" She looked as lovely as ever. She wore skin-tight red jeans, a white angora sweater and a bright red beret.

"You look smashing," Dodge said in his best Sean Connery accent.

"This is Santiago," she introduced the young man standing beside her. He was dressed all in black - jeans, shirt, leather jacket - and had jet-black hair pulled into a tight ponytail. "Santiago … Dodge Maddison."

They shook hands.

"Very pleased to meet you, sir." He sounded like Antonio Banderas.

"He's one of our videographers, isn't he cute?" she squeaked and squeezed his arm.

"Very," Dodge smiled at him. "Are you in London on business or pleasure?" he asked her.

"Business for me, but pleasssure for Santiago," Dana kissed Antonio Banderas on the lips, "right Sweetie?"

He just grinned.

"Could you give Mister Maddison and I a private moment, Sweetie?"

Santiago dutifully excused himself and wandered across the aisle into the Polo section.

"He seems nice."

"Yes, he's a doll. He's been along on all of our shoots for the past six months but I never noticed him … I only had eyes for you," she teased, jovially.

"Uh huh," Dodge smirked, glad to see no animosity coming from her. "You look happy."

"I'm doing okay, and you?"

"Fine, I'm fine."

Dana fidgeted on her feet, shuffling her red high heels on the light beige carpet. "Dodge, I have a confession to make to you. I wasn't exactly honest with you that last night in your apartment."

She told him everything. How she'd let herself in, how she waited in his bed for him to come home, Annison's unexpected appearance, how she lied to her, intentionally giving her the impression that he was there with her, how she had been running the shower and allowed Annison to think he was there, and even how pleased she was when Annison stormed off.

"I was glad that she'd shown up. Thrilled to stick it to her like she'd done to me. I thought I could win you back, keep you all to myself. But I was wrong. Wrong with all of it. I'm sorry, truly sorry."

Dodge didn't say anything, letting the scene play in his mind, connecting the dots.

"That was Saturday? Saturday morning?"

"Yes. And then when you arrived later that night and we had our fight, I wanted to tell you, to stuff it in your face, to hurt you. But I couldn't. All I could do was leave."

Things were beginning to make sense to him.

"But then, I felt like a shit! And after a couple days, after I got the courage up, I called her."

"You called her? When?"

"I don't know, a few days later. Hasn't she told you?"

There was no response and Dana could see the empty mystery in his eyes.

"Oh God, I'm sorry, Dodge. I never meant to screw things up for you. Well, I did, but I really didn't."

"So, that was what? Over a week ago that you spoke with her?"

"Yes, I called and apologized and told her the truth. I told her you weren't there. I told her how angry you were when you got home to find me there. That you were waiting for her. I told her what you said to me, that you had fallen in love, in love with her."

"What did she say?"

"Nothing actually. She was real quiet and then she said, 'Thank you for calling' and hung up."

Dodge had the picture clear in his mind now. He fast-forwarded through the events of the days following that Saturday morning, plugging in her feelings, her anger, her disillusion, her reactions. Wondering how it had all played out in her mind. Seeing what made her do the things she had done. It was all tangible to him now. His next thought was of calling her. Then he wondered why she hadn't called him.

"A week ago, you said?"

"Yes."

Well, he thought, I guess it doesn't matter anymore, does it?

"Dodge, I'm so sorry, I …"

"Don't be," he held her shoulders, "don't be sorry. It's all right. Everything's fine." In a weird twist-of-Fate way she had done him a favor. Opened his eyes without him knowing it. He kissed her cheek.

"Take care of yourself, Dana. I'm glad I bumped into you."

"You take care too. I wish you all the happiness in the world."

"Thanks, but I don't need all the world's, just a little corner of it. I think I know right where my happiness lies."

Dana said, "I guess I'll see you in December then, for the catalogue shoot. Florida, right?"

"Yes, Sarasota."

"Well, goodbye."

"Goodbye." He gave her a hug and they parted.

Dana felt relieved. He seemed to be in good spirits, *I guess he's forgiven me.*

"Santiago!?" she called out, "where are you, Sweetie?" Dana saw his hand waving to her from Tommy Hilfiger and danced her way around the racks of clothing to meet him.

# 49

## *TWINE*

It was the beginning of November. A beginning. He knew what he needed to do now. High above the Atlantic Ocean in the sun of midday, Dodge sat in the airliner gazing out of his porthole window. As he passed indiscernibly from time zone to time zone, the ocean remained constant in its deep dark blue, little white lines rolling thin atop the crests of the swells like fine angel hair glistening in the sunlight, streaming in the wind against a new blue sky.

From his seat he called his office in New York and spoke with Fletcher Ross. He told him he'd seen some new ideas in Europe and England. Fresh, new ideas that they could translate into fabric. He'd been inspired by the artwork, the cathedrals, the statues, the museums, the culture of the lands and the people of the streets. And too, his own creativity was jarred from his doldrums and was flowing again. The trip had done him well.

"I've got the sketches in my mind and can't wait to get to the drawing boards with you. You're going to love them, and I'm counting on you to help translate them into a new line." He was thinking forward too. He wanted to get Fletcher more involved. This time he'd lay out the ideas and give Fletcher a free hand to design a line by himself - see what he was made of. He knew he was talented and why not give him more responsibility? He'd soon lose him to another design house if he couldn't keep him inspired. Maybe it was time to take him on a tour with him, show him the things he had experienced this time in Europe. Dodge had never done that with a designer before. Not only because he liked doing it all on his own, but perhaps also because he was afraid of losing one of his top designers. He'd worked hard to become who he was and didn't want to just hand off the guts of the fashion world to anyone else. Let them earn it like he had. But he'd had help from Stanley Silverman, hadn't he? Yes, it was a new beginning. Time for new ideas to take their own wings and fly where they may. Besides, how could he hope to move into his future if not by loosening the reins, delegating the responsibilities? Fletcher could play an important role in that. Dodge just needed to take him under his wing and groom him for the ride.

He said to Fletcher, "How'd you like to design a few Fletcher Ross pieces for the spring line?"

"Are you serious?"

"Maybe a dozen or so of your own creations, a small tasteful collection. We could highlight them at the trade shows and see what response we get. We'll present it as, *The Fletcher Ross Collection for Lady Maddison*. We can design a logo together and get your name on the label, get your name out there, see if any of my tutoring has paid off," he laughed.

"Oh my God! Are you kidding me?!" Fletcher couldn't possibly withhold his excitement; this was the opportunity he'd been waiting for.

Eventually, he thought, after Fletcher's name was more renowned, I could sell out to him and focus on my painting. *I'd love to do that!* He didn't know of any fashion designer that had made the successful transition from designer to artist. There had been rumors that Gianni Versace was painting, relinquishing his designing workload to his sister, and secluding himself in a secret studio in South Beach. But the world would never know. His untimely death rocked the fashion world and closed forever a brilliant colorful page in couture, and perhaps the art world as well.

But Dodge didn't need to break it all off at once. He could tone down one world and kindle the next. Harlow could still handle the day to day business as they got started on *their* new transition. Give him the time to bring it all together. He thought of her being in Milan with him. How had he not seen her there, waiting for him? He smiled at the image of her in the rowboat that day at the lake, in her black dress with the colors of sunset playing in her auburn hair. He'd been warmed by the conversations they'd shared while he was in Paris and London. They had always worked so well together. Why wouldn't it make perfect sense to bring it to the next level? He was anxious to see her, to see how she'd react to him. This time he'd pay more attention. He had a goal. They'd go over the business and then he'd take her out to dinner. Lay it all out to her. Let her lay it all out to him. God he hoped his hunch was right.

Hoped he hadn't been too much of a fool. Hoped he hadn't lost her with his blind stupidity.

"I can't wait!" Fletcher said with enthusiasm. "Are you coming straight to the building?"

Dodge had forgotten he was on the phone, his mind was in overdrive. "No, I've got to close off some things back home, but that'll only take me a day or two at the most. What day is this anyway?"

"Friday."

"All right, let's get together first thing Monday morning, just you and I. Does that give you enough time to put some story boards together?"

"I'll work straight through the weekend if I have to."

"You've got talent, Fletch, time to let it fly."

"Thanks Dodge. I'll design a kick-ass collection, believe me, I won't let you down. You'll love it!"

Dodge was thinking he could meet Harlow on Sunday. Meet outside of the office. That'd give him Saturday to close up the cottage, see what state the farmhouse was in, the farmhouse. He placed a call to Jack Cregan.

"Cregan Realty."

"Jack Cregan, please."

"This is he."

"Jack, its Dodge Maddison."

"Hi Dodge, how are you?"

"Great, and you?"

"Can't complain, nobody'd listen."

"Jack, I'd like to list the Maddison farmhouse."

"Sure. We can do that for ya."

"I'm actually on my way to Bryce Corner now, any chance we could do the paperwork later this afternoon?"

"No problem. I'll get it into M.L.S. today if you want, weekend's a good time to cast a line out, see what kinda fish are biting."

They talked about price, commission, Title Five requirements, etc. "That's a beautiful piece of property there and I know the house is solid as a rock," Jack said, "I'm certain it won't take long to sell."

"Great."

"I noticed you're having some work done on it."

Dodge told him of his initial hope to pass it onto another farmer, but that the Bed & Breakfast idea had materialized. "And I'm not sure just how far the transition has gotten, but I can let you know as soon as I get into town."

"No need, I was in there yesterday. Saw Eggman's truck and decided I'd be nosy. Came out beautiful. And I think you may get a better deal selling it as a potential B&B, and I may even have a client for you."

"Fantastic. I should be in town in about," he checked his watch, another hour of flight, and an hour's drive, "about two, two and a half hours. I'll come right to your office if you'd like."

"How about I meet you at the farmhouse? I'll get the work-up done. Walk the property, the barn, the house, take some measurements, and shoot some pictures for the internet listing. And I'd like to get my sign up this afternoon as well."

"Fine, see you there."

* * *

As the plane descended into Boston, Dodge saw the tip of Cape Cod: the blue waves of the Atlantic rolling onto the tan shoreline; the dunes from Truro to Provincetown baking white in the sun. And then, getting closer to the airport, the landscape of the South Shore, browner and more barren looking in the New England November.

The flight landed on time, the rent-a-car was ready and the Friday afternoon traffic west on the Mass. Turnpike flowed at a steady pace. He arrived in Bryce Corner on schedule. The farmhouse had come out splendid. It was weird walking from room to room and seeing them in their new décor. The interior work had been mostly cosmetics, paint and wallpaper, but Eggman and his crew had done a great job and Jack Cregan felt comfortable listing it as a single family residence with B&B potential. The sign was up and Dodge signed the contract on the kitchen table. He left the driveway at the same time as the realtor, not wanting to be alone in the house. With its new adornment, it reminded him of Annison, of their dream. He needed to get past that.

Dodge stopped by the police station to visit Ben. He passed on the beer at the Tavern idea, but promised to stop by the chief's house for dinner – Carlene was making her famous pot roast.

Dodge drove the rental car slowly, within the speed limit, along the curves of Wickaboag Valley Road and turned into the narrow dirt road bringing him to the Maddison cottage. The foliage had lost its luster and the fall leaves lay withered and worn on the gravel way. He walked up the knoll to the bank of the lake; green acorns lay fallen on the brittle lawn. He stood on the side of the cottage looking at the opposite shoreline, gray with its barren trees, hovering in the silver water against the fading skyline. The rowboat swayed quietly against the dock, calling to him to pull it onto dry land; the season was over and it was anxious to be set in its winter place on the sawhorses against the south side of the shed. The meteorologists were predicting a sunny weekend with temperature's mild and on average for this time of year, but tonight held a chill to it. It was quiet. Dodge stood alone in the peaceful quietude. The summer people were long gone and the lake was calmer, already adjusting to the tranquility of quieter seasons.

He hadn't looked over to the northwestern shoreline. He was consciously working on that. He stepped onto the porch and walked to the back door, the familiar squeak of the screen door welcoming him back home. A package leaned against the inside door. It was thin, wrapped in brown paper and tied with twine. It just fit in the doorway, the height of it just below the door handle and the width nearly as wide as the door itself. He grasped the top of it and leaned it towards him, looking behind it for a label or a card or a note as to its purpose there. The backside was as blank as the front. Dodge took it inside with him and set it on the floor next to the couch. It was dark enough to turn some lights on; the night was falling faster now. He wanted to open the front sliders, but it would be too cold. He thought he might even need to start a fire in the wood stove tonight. He turned the round dial on the front of the thermostat on the wall in the kitchen and heard the hum of the electric furnace begin beneath the floorboards. The chill would be gone in a few minutes. He went outside to retrieve his bags from the car. In a few minutes he was settled in. He turned on the satellite audio system, setting it on a light jazz station from Boston. He went to the refrigerator and took out a bottle of beer, opening it on the old Coke bottle opener attached to the side of the counter. He sat on the couch, in the softness of the surround sound, holding onto the bottle of beer. He hadn't taken a sip yet. Languidly, in slow motion, he put the bottle on the coffee table then slid the package over in front of him. Slowly he slipped the twine over the top edges and carefully unwrapped the package.

It was a painting. A canvas framed in a hand-painted frame. A landscape, colorful in the resonant colors of autumn. A vibrant blue sky with wandering puffy white clouds. Red and yellow and green mountains. A lake as pretty as the sky. A sprawling green lawn sprinkled with little dots of colorful leaves. And in the foreground, a low hedgerow of flowers, and in the middle of those, a tall tuft, a crimson tuft of flowers – chrysanthemums.

In the bottom corner, stuck into the corner of the frame was a tiny white card, blank on the outside, and folded in two, clasping a single red flower. Dodge pulled it out and held it a moment, his hands were quivering. He opened the card. It read simply, *I'm sorry.*

\* \* \*

As soon as Harlow arrived at the office first thing Monday morning, Fletcher Ross was awaiting her. She saw him seated at the chair next to her desk as she walked across the polished wooden floor. She wore a long coat and carried a thin briefcase in one hand, her bag over that shoulder, her other hand occupied a cup of coffee. He heard her heels on the floor and Fletcher jumped up out of the chair and said in a distressed tone, "*What is going on?*"

"Good morning to you too, Fletcher," Harlow returned, sliding her coat off and laying it over the arm of the chair.

"*Really*, Harlow, just tell me *what* is going on."

"I might, if you'd give me a clue as to what you're talking about."

"Dodge!"

"What about Dodge?"

"Didn't he tell you about our meeting this morning? He tells you everything! You must have been aware of it."

"Unfortunately - or maybe fortunately - he *doesn't* tell me everything. So, why don't you sit back down and tell me what's got you in such a tizzy." She took her seat and blew the steam from her coffee lightly across the top.

"I don't believe this!" he was pacing rapidly back and forth with his hands waving in the air. "First he disappears for a fucking month, we hardly hear a word from him, then he comes back showing off his new girlfriend, hardly spends a day, cancels meeting after meeting with the design team, takes off for Milan with you, comes back, raises holy hell with everyone, and then disappears to God only knows where in Europe, and then," he stops in front of Harlow's desk exasperated, "and *then* he calls me Friday from a fucking airplane somewhere and dangles this carrot in front of my nose, and ... and ..." Fletcher fell into the chair and threw his hands up in the air once again and then slapped them loudly onto his legs.

369

"I don't get it," he said, "I just don't get it. I work my ass off all weekend - I mean I think I got maybe twenty minutes sleep – I come up with some phenomenal sketches, drag my ass here at six-thirty this morning, and there's this fucking message from him on my machine, *Fletch it's Dodge,*" he mimicked, "*Gotta reschedule. I'll be in touch.* I mean, what the fuck does that mean?!"

"What carrot?" Harlow asked, her forearms now on her desk, leaning towards him.

Fletcher told her of the conversation he'd had with Dodge. Harlow could tell he was excited by it, and why shouldn't he be. What a great opportunity Dodge was giving him. But now Fletcher was hurt, pissed off, confused, and understandably so. Dodge's movements of late had been the talk of the building. No one seemed to know what was going on in his mind. But she did. She believed she did now, unequivocally. She saw his intentions. She'd glimpsed bits and pieces in their late night conversations, felt the reverberations from his heart, allowed them to mix with hers.

"So ... what? Do you know what's going on with him? Do you know where he is?"

Harlow sat perfectly still, her eyes staring blankly at him.

Fletcher could see her looking at him but her look was somewhere else, far off and somewhere else.

She had lost him before, but she wasn't going to lose him this time. Harlow came around the desk and grabbed her coat. "Not again," she said and stormed out of the studio.

# EPILOGUE

"**B**eeswax?! You cain't use beeswax on these!"

"Sure you can."

"Naw! It'd turn 'em yellow."

"No it wouldn't. Jist seep inta the wood, bring out the natural texture of the grain, give it a nice fresh sheen." Jedediah ran his hands over the tops of the armrests on his rocker. "Too dry, needs some beeswax."

"Turn 'em yellow, I'm tellin' ya,"

"You shoulda never let them jist weather like this. Told you they needed a pro-tectant on 'em. Look. Look at this," Jed pointed to the front edge of his armrest.

"What?" Old Percy stopped his rocker up on its front sway and looked over.

"Right here, see where the woods crackin'?"

"Aw, that's nothin'. You got more cracks on you than that."

"Should fill in all these cracks with putty, then you could put the beeswax on," Jedediah ran his long thin fingers along the other armrest, inspecting for more signs of age. Old Percy didn't pay him any mind. He was long used to Jedediah and his nit-picking. "You worry 'bout the most foolish things, know that?" Percy said. "Always have, always will."

Old Percy sat rocking on his old porch, his feet on the front ends of the rocker bars, his left boot tapping the floor as the chair swung up on its forward movement, keeping the chair in motion, in a slow and steady rhythmic pace. Tap, and then the chair would creak. *Tap ... creak ... tap ... creak ... tap ... creak ...*

The afternoon had turned out better than he'd expected. The morning had been downright cold. Percy was taking his daily walks down to the porch at his old house later and later each morning, giving the shortening sun more time to heat up. She was struggling more and more each day, he thought.

"The old girl's settin' inta her lower arc, takin' the shortcut over the southern horizon. Won't be climbin' back inta the high sky for several months now."

Footsteps came up the stairs and approached him.

"Who you talking to, Percy?" Dodge asked.

Old Percy didn't respond so Dodge took up the vacant rocker next to him.

"Ben said I might find you here," Dodge said. "I'm on my way out of town. Wanted to stop by and say goodbye."

"Where ya headed?"

"Back to New York."

"Oh."

"Little chilly sitting out here isn't it?"

"Aw! That's what Jed says too, but I don't feel it."

They sat awhile rocking together, watching the cars pass by.

"New car?" Percy asked.

"No, a rental. Picked it up at Logan."

"Drivin' it down ta the City?"

"Yeah."

"When you be back?"

"Hoping to be here for Thanksgiving."

"That'd be nice. See you've got the fur sale sign up 'cross the street."

"Yeah. Time to move on, I guess."

"Heard you had big plans for the place."

"Well, things change."

"'Spose so. You close up the lake cottage for the winter?"

"Yeah, Bennie and Brent helped me over the weekend. Took the dock in, put the boat away."

"Winterize those pipes?"

"Yup."

"Put anti-freeze down the drains?"

"Un huh."

"Water cumpnee turn off the spicket?"

"Yes sir."

"Should be fine then. Winter's gonna be a mild one, anyhow."

"That so?"

"Yup, feel it in my bones. Don't ache as much as they usually do first a November. Good sign."

*Tap ... creak ... tap ... creak ...*

Dodge spent awhile with Old Percy. He loved this man, not only because of his friendship with Jedediah, but for his loyalty to that friendship. For what he had done for him. And for all the things Dodge could remember Old Percy doing for him. Some thought him senile and part crazy; that his quips and ramblings were mostly nonsense, but

Dodge didn't. He thought Percy was a remarkable man. Part farmer, part soothsayer. A man with an eye to the sky and an eye on your soul. A man with Merlin's blood in his veins.

He watched the old wizard rocking; staring across the street at Jed and Emma's place. Dodge thought he'd drifted off into one of his spells and figured he'd better get going. He got up and stood before Old Percy, extending his hand, "Well, take care of yourself, old man."

"Heard you fell in love."

The comment came unexpectedly and took Dodge a little by surprise. He leaned against the porch railing; he didn't offer a response.

"That lady you was with. What happened ta her anyhow?"

"Well, I …" he wasn't accustomed to having love talks with Old Percy and was uneasy about how to answer him. Did he even have to? Where did this question come from? "I … to tell you the truth Perce, I really don't know," he suddenly felt okay about it and went with his feelings.

"Cain't tell about women sumtimes."

"Yeah, well, that's an understatement."

"They're like the wind. Blowin' this way and that and every which way. They kin be right in front of you sumtimes and you cain't even see 'em."

"Then sometimes the wind blows them away, I guess."

"She seemed like a nice lady. I liked her."

Dodge got pensive, fiddling his foot on the porch floor, like a pitcher standing on the mound, "Yeah," he said softly, "I kind of liked her too."

"Tweren't lookin' for it were ya?"

"What?"

"Love."

He laughed. "Always and never."

"That's how it operates. Comes at'cha when you least 'xpect it."

"Yeah, well, I sure wasn't expecting that one. Really came out of the blue on me."

"Best kind, sumtimes."

"Well, I gave it a shot anyway, fool that I am. Not sure if I was ever any good at women. My business always got in the way, but I'm working on that now."

"Oh yeah?"

"I think I learned something this fall. I fell in love and got burnt, but I feel better for it all. I guess I'm glad it happened. Made me take a hard look at myself and reevaluate where I'm at and where I'm headed with my life."

"Love can do that to ya."

"It can make you crazy too."

"Ta fall … is ta season."

Dodge didn't know what that meant, and he pondered it awhile.

"Y'know, bein' a fool in love ain't a bad thing," Percy said, "if you know who yur in love with, that is."

"I think I do now. I think love's been staring me in the face for a long time, and I'm finally seeing it."

Percy rocked harder and Dodge had a feeling something was up. "What?" he asked.

"Listen ta yur heart, on these things, not yur mind. Don't give up on love."

"What do you mean?"

"Love's only got one ear, not two."

What did that mean? "You always talk in riddles, Percy," Dodge laughed.

"Plain as day." He resumed his rocking pace.

An easy silence lingered on the porch between the two men. Percy keeping his eye on the farmhouse behind Dodge's back, and Dodge thinking about Percy's words. What was he trying to tell him? Anything? Just the ramblings of an old man on a porch? Dodge knew where he was at, knew what he had to do now. Knew what he wanted, knew what was awaiting him.

"Love is strong and love is frail," Old Percy said.

"And confusing too, don't forget."

"That's part of the mystery. Changes."

"Changes?"

"Sure. Ta you, ta me, ta all of us."

Dodge wondered how Percy knew of such things, how he could speak with such a folklore-like knowledge. He felt mystified listening to him.

"Just like birds in flight, changes happen. Ta the heart, ta the trees … the stars … the seasons … ta even the wind."

And that was it. Neither of them had more to say. Old Percy continued his easy rocking while Dodge mused in the puzzlement of their conversation. Like that cartoon of the bird perched on his birdhouse floating in the water down a flooded landscape, with the caption - *just when you figured you knew where everything was* ... Old Percy had stirred his resolves and once again Dodge could feel them swirling in the uncomforting caldron of uncertainty.

But, not to fret any further. He had made up his mind and couldn't fall victim to the old man's musings. Dodge knew where his future lay and needed to get moving toward it. He pushed himself off the railing and stood before Percy with his hand extended.

"Well," he said, "it's been great talking to you, Perce. Take care of yourself. I gotta go."

"What's yur hurry?"

"Want to get on the road before the traffic."

"Might wanna tend ta yur cumpnee first," he pointed across the road.

The car was parked in the driveway, up near the house. The door opened and she got out. She walked onto the front lawn over to the for sale sign that Jack Cregan had pushed into the ground just the other day. It was the usual realtor's sign, black wrought metal with the pointy ends. She placed her hands on either side of it and pulled upward. The sign came up easily and she set it back down on its pointed ends and let it fall flat onto the ground. She turned and saw him watching her from the porch across the street.

Annison smiled.

# FROM THE AUTHOR:

Hope you enjoyed the story.

Feel free to e-mail a comment and I will add you to my reader's list and keep you posted on upcoming books and events.

And remember, rave reviews on Amazon are always welcome!


Thanks for reading,
Donn


Visit: DonnFleming.com
E-mail: Flemwright@aol.com
Text: 413-204-4477

Also by Donn Fleming:

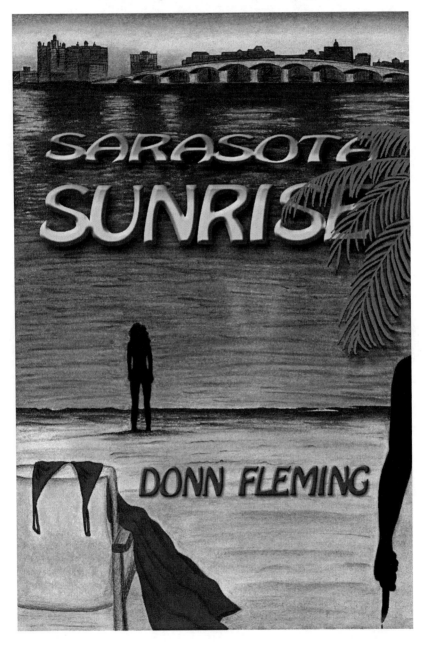

## Also by Donn Fleming: